BLOOD DIVA

VM Gautier

Blood Diva

Notes On This Edition:

Formatting: This book has been professionally edited, proofread, and formatted; however, errors due to format conversion or other causes may exist. Readers are invited to write to the author directly if they spot errors that mar their enjoyment of the text.

Cover Illustration: The cover illustration has been adapted from George Barbier's *La Fontaine de Coquillages* – an image in the public domain. Barbier, a master of Art Deco, often featured work showing women at their most alluring, mysterious, and dangerous. The image has been altered. In the original, the liquid pouring from the fountain is meant to be water, not blood. The author retains rights to the derivative image.

*For C – your unwavering support
and love has made this possible.*

To Deborah —
Happy Reading!
One reviewer dark chocolate
and champagne could be
paired with this book,
which might be best
read in the bath — but
with the lights on.
Best regards
Nom Gautier

Prologue

Simmons was drinking alone and waiting for opportunity, which soon arrived in the form of a slim dark-haired beauty who brushed past him – deliberately he thought – then sat at a stool one over from his.

The first thing that struck him was her scent, probably some fancy perfume – fresh, floral but not heavy. It reminded him of something, but he couldn't place it. *Subtle.* She looked his way. Their eyes met briefly, and she turned her head.

"Could I buy you a drink?" He asked.

"I suppose," she said, in a tone that implied surprise at finding herself in a hotel bar in midtown at two in the morning on a weeknight, as though the whole concept was somehow *amusing*.

He took in more of her as the bartender came over. Her dark hair had a hint of auburn, more visible when the light hit it or when she moved her head. She wore it loose, below her shoulders, slightly unkempt, but in a way that seemed deliberate. *Bedroom hair*, he thought. She was leggy, though not exceptionally tall. He didn't know much about clothes, but sensed her black dress wasn't cheap. Nothing about her seemed cheap, but he knew she was a whore nevertheless.

"The lady'll have …" he looked at her, waiting.

"Whisky," she said, "double, straight up."

"And I'll have another. What you got on tap." He was glad he'd ordered the beer. He wanted her to see him as an ordinary guy, a beer drinker, not one of her fancy johns. "With a whiskey on the side," he added.

"I'm Joe," he said.

"Violetta," she said, opening her mouth to reveal the most perfect set of teeth he'd ever seen, glistening white against the pink tongue and red lips. She couldn't have been much older than twenty-one. Maybe she was even younger than that.

"Violetta," he repeated. He figured it was probably her whore name. Her real one might have been something more prosaic, like Marie.

"Violetta Valéry," she said. Her voice was wispy, soft, girlish. He wondered if she was putting it on.

"What is that? French or something?" He was staring at her eyes. They were so large and dark it was hard to pick out the pupil from the iris, which made her look at once childlike and mysterious.

She laughed. There was nothing cruel in the sound of it, but he felt like she was laughing at him, and that made him want to grab her by the throat.

"I'm sorry," she said.

It took him aback she'd read something in his face. He'd been taking too many risks lately. He knew the ride would be over soon, but he didn't want it to end tonight, not when he had a chance of bagging the prize before him.

"Where are you from, Joe?"

"Here, there, everywhere. And you?"

"Have you ever been to," she hesitated a moment, "Saskatchewan?"

"No."

"That's where I'm from, Saskatchewan."

He smiled. He wanted her to know he was in on the joke. He figured she didn't think he had enough cash for a girl like her. They were only a block from the UN. Maybe she'd just left some visiting diplomat's hotel room after giving him a two-grand blowjob. He had a vision of punching in that lovely mouth and taking out all those pretty teeth, smashing them down like bowling pins.

"Tourist?" He asked.

"No, I live here now."

The bartender put the drinks in front of them. He picked up his glass and nodded towards hers. She caught his cue. The glasses clinked. "To Monday nights," he said.

He watched her gulp down her drink. Saw the movement in her thin neck as the liquid went down her pretty throat.

"What are you? An actress? A model. You look like you could be a model."

She smiled just slightly. She didn't answer the question.

"You're really beautiful," he said.

She looked at him in a way women didn't often look at men,

2

fully appraising his assets. He felt his anger rising, as well as the need to suppress it. There'd be time later.

"You're not so bad yourself," she said in that wispy little girl voice. She reached out a hand, leaned over, touched his arm. "So strong and big. Like a wrestler."

"High school team," he said.

She smiled again showing off those teeth. He imagined she had them bleached regularly.

"I knew it," she squealed. "A girl could feel safe with you." Up close even her breath smelled good.

Joe didn't think she was lying. He couldn't have gotten as far as he had if he didn't look trustworthy, if they didn't find him attractive. But he also knew she was plying her trade. She'd say anything for a buck. Do anything you paid her to. She might not even like men. But still, she was different from the others. No needle marks on those arms. Though she was pale, there was a rosiness to her complexion – the bloom of youth. She took care of herself. She was classy. He could see why men would pay a lot to be with her, but in his eyes that didn't make her any "better" than her sisters.

He grabbed her smooth little hand. It felt cold, a sign of nerves. He wondered if there was a pimp, someone who would beat her if she didn't bring back enough. She might "act" different, but they were all the same. He started to kiss the hand, ran his tongue over the fingertips.

She wriggled slightly, tilted her head back, her mouth half opened as though she were already in ecstasy.

"I got a bottle up in my room," he said. "Imported. The good stuff. We could take the party up there."

"We could," she said uncertainly.

"But?"

"It's late, and uh," she leaned toward him, "I like you. I really, really like you."

"*Voulez-vous couchez avec moi?*" He asked.

She laughed appreciating his cleverness, he thought.

"I'm in kind of a position here," she said.

"Do you have another date tonight?"

She shook her head.

"But you're still on the clock. You need something from me."

She nodded.

He started to kiss each knuckle.

"Two hundred," he said.

She rolled her eyes. "That's not even …"

"Sorry. I'm just a regular Joe. I didn't mean to insult you."

She smiled. She didn't say anything, but he could hear her in his head promising him the best night he'd ever have.

"Five hundred," he whispered.

"Seven-fifty," she said, kissing his neck, "It's still less than I get. Just for you. We could have a really good time, and I'd stay as long as you want."

It seemed like a fair deal to him, especially given she wouldn't actually be leaving with his money.

He told her to wait while he went to the cash machine in the hotel lobby. As he left, he noticed her lean over and say something to the bartender. He wondered if the guy got a cut. When he came back, she grabbed her stuff. They walked out through the exit that went into the hotel. She buried her head in his chest. They were the only ones in the elevator. He pinned her against the wall, raising his hand under her dress, feeling the garter, and to his happy surprise, no panties. She felt so wet and ready.

Once they entered the room, he started to push her down onto the bed, but she pushed him back.

"I could use that drink," she said.

He unwrapped two sanitized hotel glasses, poured from the bottle, and handed her a good-sized shot. Once again their glasses clinked.

"Christ, you're beautiful," he said. It wasn't bullshit. By that point, he was pretty sure she was the most beautiful woman he'd ever seen. He knew how sweet it would feel to fuck her, and how much sweeter it would be after, his hands around her throat, or maybe he would use the knife. No, that would leave a mess. He might *play* with the knife. She wasn't afraid of him yet, but she would be, and there was no better aphrodisiac than fear.

She looked up from her drink. He noticed she was blushing. "Maybe we should get the money out of the way," she said softly.

He counted out the bills. She clenched them in her delicate fist and put them in her bag. Then she walked over, reached up, and kissed him on the lips. The full taste of her mouth was delicious, cool, and sweet. They fell together on the bed.

"You can do what you'd like with me," she said, her soft voice practically a purr.

4

He thought of the others – how fast and tawdry it had been. They had as much disgust for the sexual act as he did, but not this little bitch. She was *unashamed*. For a moment he wondered if he should just go with it, fuck her and let her walk. She wasn't the type. The others had been older, harder, and ordinary. She was anything but ordinary.

But hadn't she just taken his money? Would she be there if she weren't a skank? Walking disease and sin like his grandma used to say?

He unzipped her dress and pulled it over her head. She kicked off her shoes and undid the bra for him. It was the kind that clasped in the front. He rested his head between her legs.

"Oh thank you," she said, "That's so sweet."

The moans seemed real enough. He could feel her throbbing, but he stopped before she was completely there. He pushed her onto her belly. Her ass was the most perfectly matched set of half moons he'd ever seen. A tiny mole on her left cheek. What they'd call a beauty mark. Otherwise, not a blemish. He pushed in from behind as she raised herself up to meet him. Her cunt seemed to welcome him in a way he'd never experienced before, moving him in, deeper and deeper, clasping and releasing. He kept his thoughts clean and focused, lasting until he was sure she had come.

"You want more?" He asked?

She rolled over and they embraced. Then she pulled away gently, got up and poured them each another whisky. She was standing as she handed him the glass. He could see his cum glistening off the front of her twat. He reached up and pushed her hair from her face.

"You look like a kid," he said. "How old are you really?

"I stopped counting after a hundred and fifty," she said.

He laughed, unsure of the joke.

He kissed her. She got on the bed. This time she climbed on top of him. He liked it, more than he should have – just watching her, the look on that beautiful doll face. For a moment he imagined what it would be like to have her again and again, to keep her somewhere, his personal property, but that wasn't something he was set up for. It would have to end that night.

She came again. He was sure it was real, the way her muscles contracted against his dick, like she was squeezing the juice right out of him, like she needed him more than he needed her.

"Don't go anywhere yet," he told her.

"I wasn't planning to. I could do you all night."

"I have an idea."

"I love a man with ideas."

He got his shirt from the floor and tied it around her eyes. "No peeking," he said.

She giggled with delight.

Next he grabbed her arms, pulled them over her head, and placed on the cuffs. There were no posts so he used two pieces of rope to tie them to the lighting fixtures on either side of the bed.

"Wow. A man who brings his own toys," she said.

"Be afraid. Be very afraid."

He held her leg and bit her inner thigh, not hard, just playfully. He caressed her calve and looped some rope around her ankle, tying the other end to the leg of the bed.

It was then she said, "Wait a …"

He slapped the tape over her mouth. He could smell the fear, and it was a sweet thing. She was trying to fight him as he took the other leg and secured it.

He had her spread eagle for easy access. Surveying his handiwork, he adjusted her hair, and pushed a couple of pillows under her butt. He removed the improvised blindfold and held the knife against her throat. Her eyes seemed enormous.

"Scared now, bitch?" He asked, sneering.

She looked uncertain. Not completely sure if it were still a game. Or maybe she thought she could talk or fuck her way out of it. Her mistake.

She nodded.

He slapped her. "You should be." He took out his phone and got a couple of pictures.

"But you love it, right? A girl like you? Now what to do, what to do? Should I stick this knife up into that twat and twist it? It's okay; you can move your head to say yes or no."

She shook her head. Her eyes were pleading.

"Stop looking at me," he demanded.

She did as she was told.

He slapped her harder than before, enough to watch her skin redden.

"You said I could do anything, didn't you?"

She didn't move.

"DIDN'T YOU?"

She nodded, her pupils so wide he thought of squishing them.

For the next few minutes, he told her what a sick disgusting little cunt she was, the lowest of the low – using her body like a parking meter. As he talked, he had his fingers up moving inside her.

"Open your eyes. You're liking this, right? RIGHT? You're going to come. Aren't you? And I'm not even using my dick. So it's not rape. You're having a great time."

He ran the knife lightly along her body.

He put a hand over each of her ears and just began to squeeze. Then he let go and pinched her nose. He could feel her trying to breathe. He'd release. She'd take a few breaths. He'd start again.

It went on for a while more.

"Are we having fun yet?" He asked. When she didn't nod her head like he wanted her to, he punched her – not hard enough to break anything, just to remind her who was in charge.

"I'm getting a woody," he said. "I think it's that time again."

He got on top and pushed at her. It wasn't like before. She was closed up. Fighting him any way she could, but he managed. He pushed himself up and down, in and out, feeling her fear, and his power.

"Cunt, stupid fucking cunt," he muttered over and over.

Still, as he came, he could tell she was wet, and the sound from her throat was a moan of pleasure.

"You still can't get enough. Can you?"

He ran a hand gently through her hair, and started to caress her face. She was trembling.

"I had a really nice time with you tonight. Now, I want you to promise me something. I want you to promise if I take off this tape, you won't scream." His hand was around her throat. "If you scream I'm going to have to hurt you. You understand?"

She nodded.

The tape came off. She started to whimper.

"Please," she said, "Please don't … anything … money …"

He placed his finger on her lips. "Shush," he said. "This is important," he continued, touching her face, "I need you to listen. I want you to beg very softly for your life. Can you do that, *softly*?"

"Please don't hurt me. Please, I'll do anything. Please, I want to live, please."

This is what it comes down to, he thought. Despite the expensive clothes, the good grammar, the *class*, she was no different from any of them. He wasn't hard, but he pushed his groin against her. He wrapped his hand around her throat and started to squeeze. He watched her eyes as they first bulged out, and then the life left them. There was that moment when she knew it was over, when she stopped fighting. He always loved that. Maybe next time he'd set up a camera to capture it. He listened for the final rattle. He closed the eyes. Watched for a minute or two till he was certain he saw no breathing, and could feel no pulse.

He let out a long sigh and got up from the bed. Then he went into the shower.

The water was hot and soothing. He soaped himself off till he couldn't smell her on him anymore. He'd do a little clean up before leaving. He'd put up the do-not-disturb sign, and would have no problem sneaking away without checking out. By the time they found her, he'd be long gone. The clerk might be able to describe him. Maybe they even had him on camera. It didn't matter. He'd be over the border before that bitch-detective even got her warrant. The whore's body would make a nice good-bye. Mexico was a big lawless country. New territory waiting to be explored.

His dick was actually kind of sore. That had been some good night. He dried off, warmed by the steam and bright bathroom light. He opened the door and stepped into the room. He'd barely registered the body wasn't on the bed when he felt something leap onto him, and he hit the floor. He couldn't figure it out, but he didn't scream. She was on top of him. Still naked, saying nothing. It didn't make any sense. He managed to push himself up. He was facing her now, on top. The red marks of his fingers on her neck had completely faded. She quickly slipped from under him, slithering like something boneless, and managed to pin him down again. She couldn't have weighed more than one-ten, but he felt defenseless. He tried to yell, but no sound came out of his mouth. She looked at him, with that doll face, like this was all just a game. She opened her mouth and said, "That was a fun date."

He noticed how sharp and long her cuspids had become. She turned her head slightly, and there it was again – that little half-smile, right before she opened her mouth and bit down. He hardly felt anything. There was a numbness in the area, but he was aware of the sucking. He could feel his own blood moving into her throat, which throbbed as she swallowed in small gulps. Their bodies so close. There was something *pleasant* about it, a feeling of intimacy he had never experienced before, but sought in his own kills. It was peaceful. He knew he should be trying to move, to scream, to fight back – to do *something*. But there was nothing he could do. He could feel the life draining out of him, feel her power – the quick, but fading beating of his heart – the stronger, steadier beating of hers. And then he felt nothing at all.

ACT I – The Present

Meanwhile, from her red mouth the woman, in husky tones,
Twisting her body like a serpent upon hot stones
And straining her white breasts from their imprisonment,
Let fall these words, as potent as a heavy scent:
"My lips are moist and yielding, and I know the way
To keep the antique demon of remorse at bay.
All sorrows die upon my bosom. I can make
Old men laugh happily as children for my sake.
For him who sees me naked in my tresses, I
Replace the sun, the moon, and all the stars of the sky!
Believe me, learned sir, I am so deeply skilled
That when I wind a lover in my soft arms, and yield
My breasts like two ripe fruits for his devouring-both
Shy and voluptuous, insatiable and loath-
Upon his bed that groans and sighs luxuriously
Even the impotent angels would be damned for me!"

– The Metamorphosis of the Vampire, by Charles Baudelaire

Chapter 1

Detective Cara O'Brien and her partner, Jaime Izaguirre were chasing a ghost – searching for their favorite suspect in the murder of Donnalee Miller, a thirty-four year old mother of two, who earned extra cash turning tricks. She'd been found beaten, raped, and strangled in one of the shabbier midtown hotels. Joseph Simmons was a suspect in similar murders in Brooklyn, Queens, Nassau county, and lately New Jersey – that one a double-homicide, but it was in Manhattan they'd gotten the DNA evidence connecting him to the victim. Confronted with what they had, he admitted being a client of Donnalee's, but not her killer, and had his family standing by him with an alibi. Since there were multiple crimes across state lines, the FBI would be moving in soon, which was why Cara and her partner had been pushing it, trying to get everything they could before he killed again, or somebody else got credit for taking him down.

It was his brother-in-law who finally gave him up, admitting Joey hadn't been at the family dinner where his sister and mother placed him, but by the time they got the warrant, the suspect was gone. Cara had a gut feeling he might do something really big and awful before they found him.

He'd been spotted in the area near Grand Central. They'd spent the morning talking to the proprietors of various massage parlors, escort services, and other such establishments, showing his photo, getting a warning out, but also hoping for a solid lead on his whereabouts. Then a call came about a body in a hotel nearby. They assumed it was another female they were too late to save, a sign Simmons was lashing out like a hunted animal. Forensics hadn't been there yet, so there wasn't much they could do, but they wanted to see it. They'd know if it were one of his, and maybe something there would tell them where he was going next.

The Bradley was an institution that had seen better days, but was still a bit upscale for their boy. After they entered the room, it took a few seconds to process that it was not only a *man* lying on the floor, it was *their* man.

"I've seen everything, but not this," said the medical examiner, who'd arrived before them.

Simmons was naked. His eyes closed. There was something about his frozen expression that suggested he was at peace. The body was slightly blue. Around the neck was a large messy wound, more than an inch wide and about four inches across. There was almost no blood near it, indicating it might have been post-mortem. What was even stranger was that there was no blood anywhere else.

"They must have moved him," Cara said. Instinct told her it had to be more than one. If it had been a woman, a potential victim defending herself, she would have called someone to help her clean up. But how could it have been a woman? He was at least six-three, his biceps bigger than some girls' thighs. They didn't know of any near misses, anyone who'd gotten away before.

"Looks like someone cleaned the bathroom," Jaime said, peering in.

Cara asked the ME, "How long?"

"He's still in rigor, but it's receding. Between eight and twelve hours. We'll know more later."

She took a quick look at her watch, a few minutes before three. "So the earliest time of death would have been three and the latest like seven in the morning?"

The ME nodded.

She went on. "They must have killed him in the tub. Blood went down the drain. That's all I got. Otherwise, what?"

Neither her partner nor the examiner said anything.

She continued the monologue silently. "*But why put him back in the main room? Make it easier to clean, but creates a new mess. Doesn't look like anything dragged along the rug. Carried? A big guy like that, maybe two men helping out? There'd be some sign – water under the body if he died in the tub.*"

And then there was that wound.

She wondered why someone would cut into somebody like that after they died. It looked like they could have taken out some skin. Could it be a trophy?

"Bite marks?" her partner asked aloud, anticipating her.

"There aren't any bite marks," the ME said.

"But what if he was getting rough and the girl was fighting back, she bit him, then managed to get a knife and stab him," Jaime said pantomiming. "He goes down and later she or whoever helps her, makes the cut so they can't match her teeth to the bite."

"Problem," said Cara, "That kind of scene is more likely to happen out here, not in the bathroom. And if it happened out here …"

"Then where's the blood?" He asked, finishing her thought. "Still could've happened in the bathroom. They're taking a shower together when he starts to get rough. Or maybe," and here her partner did one of his signature dramatic pauses, as Cara prepared to groan, "maybe she sucked out all his blood."

"You really should be writing movies, Izaguirre."

She wasn't quite sure how she felt about finding Simmons cold and dead. On the one hand, justice served, no more victims, no possibility of his getting away or getting off. On the other, they'd worked hard to get him. She wanted it to be them. She wanted it to be *her*.

Forensics arrived, which meant Cara and Jaime needed to get out of their way. Before they left, Cara politely asked the investigators if they could look around for his wallet, check out the drawers and the pockets of the pants on the floor.

Nothing. The victim's phone seemed to be gone as well. No cash, no watch. They lifted the body a little, just to see if there was dampness indicating he'd been dragged from the tub. *Nope*. No obvious signs he'd been moved. No visible blood in the bathroom. No hairs in the drain, or on the bed for that matter. No prints. The sheets were missing along with whatever DNA evidence they might contain.

"Whoever it was, sure was careful," Jaime said.

Cara had been thinking the same thing. A girl might find herself in a bad situation, get lucky and have a chance to fight back, but the way the room was cleaned, this wasn't anybody's first dance.

After they were politely told to get lost by forensics, they looked for people to interview. The desk clerk and the security guard who'd been on the night before wouldn't be back for their shifts till midnight. The bartender from the bar adjacent to the hotel recognized Simmons from the photo. He remembered serving him, but hadn't spoken to him much. He recalled the lone customer had been "doing stuff" on his phone.

"Like texting?"

"No, more like looking at something. He had his credit card

out," the young man said. He spoke with an Irish accent, one Cara recognized as familiar, Dubliner.

He also remembered his leaving with a woman.

"She come in with him? Or later?"

"Later. She walked in and sat down, here I think," he said indicating with his hand. "He was a seat over and he moved."

"You hear much of the conversation?"

"I was trying to be discreet. Started wiping down the tables. They were just talking. Usual thing."

Jaime thinking out loud said, "Maybe he made a 'date' with her on the phone."

The bartender shrugged. "They started getting chummy. Then he left through the lobby door and came back in, and then they left together."

"He left her alone? Like to use a bathroom? Get a room? What?"

The bartender looked uncertain. "I think I heard the words cash machine."

"Could you describe her?" Cara asked.

He looked like he was about to say something, but then stopped. "I can't remember her face."

"Okay, was she white?"

"I uh … uh sorry, it's just not coming to me."

"Her hair?"

He was blushing.

"You don't remember *anything*?" Cara asked with more than a trace of skepticism.

"I'm drawing a blank. I'm trying to go through it, what's in my mind, and I just can't see her. I know it sounds …"

"Tall? Do you think she was as tall as my partner?" Jaime asked bringing the bartender's attention to Cara.

"Not as tall. I don't think."

"Latina?" Cara asked, "Black? Blonde, like me?"

He shook his head. "Don't see it."

"Pretty? You remember she was pretty?"

"I guess."

"Long hair?"

"If you say so."

"I bet a lot of working girls come in here, late at night," Cara said.

"No, not that many."

"Maybe this one was a personal friend."

"No, I never saw her before."

"So you remember seeing her *last night*, and that you never saw her before, but you can't tell us what she looked like?"

He shook his head.

Jaime took it from there. "Maybe you saw the guy with his credit card out playing with his phone, so you started a conversation, called your friend to see if she was busy?"

"No, I swear, I never ... I don't ..."

"Look," Cara said, leaning into him, "You can understand why we're having some trouble with this. You're telling us a few hours ago an attractive woman walks into the bar. There's only one other customer. She sits down right here. And you can't remember *anything* about her?"

He closed his eyes and squinted in a way that made Cara think of a one-year old about to stink up a diaper.

It didn't make sense to lie that obviously when he could have just bungled the description, but then people weren't always very bright. What else could it be but a lie? And why lie, except to protect someone. He told them he closed the bar at three and walked five blocks to a diner where he had some breakfast before starting his shift as a short-order cook.

They took his information and gave them theirs, "in case" he remembered more. They knew they wouldn't get anything else out of him until they had something on him. Meantime, they went back to the desk clerk on duty, who was actually being useful – getting them a read-out from the door's keycard slot, and downloading the surveillance information onto a flash-drive.

Chapter 2

The horrible buzzing resembled no natural sound. Alphonsine reached out, hitting the alarm clock with enough force to send plastic flying like shrapnel.

"*Merde*," she said, lifting the lilac-scented sleep mask to survey the damage.

The thick black curtains were closed and the room was dark, but she could feel the sun had not quite set. *Next time stick to champagne*, she reminded herself. The copious amount of whiskey had left her head pounding. The fruit of the vine was mother's milk to her, but she'd never had much of a tolerance for grain alcohol, and while the effects were not seen on her face, they might be felt, especially when she awoke before it was time.

But she'd promised Pierre she wouldn't be late. It wasn't that she wished to please him. She simply couldn't stand how smug he'd become about her habits. She hated being predictable.

Her headache would be gone if she waited a few more minutes till sunset, but she didn't have the patience. She reached into her night table, grabbing a small glassine envelope, placed a bit of powder on her finger, and snorted just enough to numb the pain.

She stood up and went to the curtained wall. Despite the stories, her kind did not implode if out before sundown. It was one of many myths designed to keep them safe, not much more truthful than stories about not being able to cross water, needing an invitation to enter a residence, or having an especially strong aversion to garlic.

Daylight, however, was still to be avoided. They were by nature nocturnal, and the longing for sleep might weigh obsessively on the mind. One could use potions to stay awake – drugs in sufficient quantity to kill most mortals, but nothing could overcome the weakness and vulnerability. Worst of all, sunlight caused aging, and at an even more rapid rate than for the day-walkers. The occasional morning stroll, the rare afternoon ride, could over a century add a decade or more, and when one survived on one's looks and charms, any diminishment was perilous. In direct daylight there would be a tingling, a warning mechanism from the body that would become more intense and unpleasant, but when it was essential to be seen, her kind could pass.

She opened the curtain revealing the island across the river, the lights of the city coming on as the orange globe went down. There was something riveting about watching its power wane. Despite her nakedness, she slid open the terrace door and stepped out to take it all in. There it was before her, the shimmering waters of the East River, and beyond it *Manhattan*, lit up in its glory. She felt the wind on her face and stretched out her arms. She made a sound halfway between a scream and a howl, a welcome to the moon. She could feel her energy returning. It was night, and the night was hers.

Lacking was the music of insects, birds, wildcats with their grumbling mating calls, the howls of wolves – what her people called night-song. But then, from the time she first came to Paris at fourteen, she'd always been a city girl, and cities had their own pleasures.

Her bathroom was en-suite, but could be accessed through a second door from the living room. Rosa, who came in the mornings to clean, routinely filled the bath. There was a timed heater that kept the water warm. Alphonsine slipped into the oversized tub.

She dove under the bubbles. While her kind needed to breathe, they could control respiration and stay under for hours. She enjoyed soaking this way in very hot water, allowing herself to think and dream. Her morning kill had been so unusual, so exciting, she wanted to relive every detail.

She hadn't been planning to feed that night, though it had been almost four weeks. She could go five, even six in a pinch, but after that long she felt so fatigued it was hard to distinguish day from night. Pierre and she were planning to get out of town to feast together. He often chided her for her recklessness, pointing out it was not like the old days. Trains, planes, and automobiles made it easy to place distance between oneself and one's prey. No reason to kill where one lived, but sometimes, one couldn't help oneself.

She had left the party feeling a particular restlessness. At first believing sex alone might be enough to stave off the hunger, her plan had been to head downtown or back to Brooklyn to find some pretty thing to hook up with. Then she caught a scent, felt something unique was waiting. Violent images flooded her mind as she entered the bar. It was coming into focus – a mortal who killed, not in war, but for *fun*. While her telepathic powers were weak – she was after all still quite young, she could sense emotions, especially strong ones, and he had been a seething caldron of barely suppressed rage.

Under the warm water, she could still taste it on her tongue, his blood, his essence – all of that delicious hate, and yet in the intimacy of the death-grip, she felt more, his humanity, as though they both were spiraling backwards in time to a moment when even he was innocent.

She'd given him peace. It had been a good death for him. True, she had frightened him when she jumped out. They said in the best hunts the prey never suspected, never felt a moment of unease, but allowances had to be made. After all, he believed he had killed her. She couldn't let him go to his grave thinking that.

Blood was more than nourishment. It was a sacrament. Some said the blood itself contained the very soul. She doubted such a thing existed. She only knew it had something – a power, a magic like nothing else. Strange how easily satisfied beings like her were, hardly the monsters depicted in myth. As pleasurable as it might be to hunt and feast every night, like the noble lion, they only did so when hungry.

No two people tasted the same – not father and son, nor brother and sister, not even twins. This she knew from her own experience. Children's blood had a sweetness like the candied grapes young men once brought her as tokens between acts at the opera. There was a freshness to young blood, like apples picked in the summer at a perfect moment of ripeness. Teenaged girls tasted of secrets, and boys of lust. Women, pretty ones, whose hearts had been broken had a certain tenderness and resignation, especially if you came to them when their looks were fading, and there wasn't much hope. There were men who had an edge like a wine with a bitter after taste, while others were warm and smooth. The old, whom she wasn't fond of, tasted of sadness, disappointment, and defeat, though they would certainly do when convenient. Human blood, like the human voice, had different timbres. Some had the richness and depth of a bass-baritone while others were light but agile like a coloratura soprano.

A killer, however, especially one who dispatched his own so remorselessly, this was a rare treat indeed. The essence would hold within it all whom he had taken. For her to act so boldly, to take so many chances to have him, was a risk, but what would be the point of immortality without gambles? And she had always loved games of chance.

When she walked in and saw him, saw those thick arms, the sandy hair, could already feel what it would be like to fuck him, to take him perhaps when he was inside her, she knew she had to go through with it. The combination of lust and hunger made her almost giddy, barely able to contain herself.

Still immersed, Alphonsine began to touch her thighs, working up to her pussy, replaying the night.

As soon as she sat down at the bar it became clear he had picked her, imagined her as his next victim. It was too delicious! A chance for play-acting. Something different and rough.

Alphonsine lifted her head above the water, feeling the urge to breathe. Her breaths became quick as she felt her release, the first taste of his blood a vivid memory. Her kind not only felt everything more strongly than mortals, but could recall in full sensory detail.

It had been everything she hoped. Feeling him draining, feeling his life force leaving his body, merging into hers. That final beat of his cruel heart. A rush of something – all his anger, perhaps? It overwhelmed her for a second and then was gone. And he had looked so tranquil – transformed by death – beyond the desire to hurt and kill, beyond it all, finally at rest – a gift she had bestowed on him.

She had closed his eyes, and kissed him once softly on the lips before beginning the task of clean up.

The act of remembering left her not hungry for more blood, but still unsatisfied.

She went back to bed, and reaching over to the night table brought out a vibrator, thrusting it in and out until she finally felt normal. It was not unusual after a feeding to be as randy as a teenaged boy. It was always better to hunt with a partner, to wake together in each other's arms, able to satisfy any remaining urges. It didn't matter whether the bedmate was male or female, or what one usually preferred. Often, she and Pierre comforted each other after feeding, though he was naturally drawn to men, and more like an older sibling. That was another thing mortals missed, how gentle and loving they could be with each other. They were, as Pierre had once put it, the bonobos of the supernatural.

When she was ready, she rose from the bed. While her smashed clock was no help, she was sure she was running late as always. There was an important opening at the gallery – a group show of new artists, and she herself had made arrangements for the gala. There

21

would be a poetry slam and a band, and press of course. She pictured the stern look Pierre would give her when she arrived. He kept an apartment above the gallery, and had probably been up since late afternoon, but then a man could afford to look a bit weathered, to pass for forty rather than twenty-five. She could not.

She decided to wear the red dress that night – the one that looked like the one worn by Violetta in that modern dress version of *La Traviata* she'd seen with Pierre. He'd get the reference.

She pulled her long hair back and expertly twisted it into a single high braid. After working on her make-up, she stepped out into the main room. It was about five hundred square feet, large only by New York standards. There was an open space separated from the small kitchen area by a black granite counter. Rosa had left the usual items out – the vase with camellias, only three, cut fresh and sent to her every day, courtesy of an old acquaintance. She grabbed a single one and pinned it in her hair. There were newspapers – *The New York Times* so she could learn what was happening in the world, *Le Monde* because wherever she wandered for however long, Paris would always be her home, and the *New York Post* because she loved reading about the exploits of the fashionable on *Page Six*, where she sometimes got a "shout-out" – or rather her current identity did. To the world she was now Camille St. Valois.

She pressed the button on her espresso machine and waited for the dark liquid to fill the cup, as she checked e-mail on her phone. How wonderful to be living in the twenty-first century, where servants were hardly even necessary, and anyone could have anything in an instant. She had once lived her life at light speed. What else could one do when diagnosed with an inevitably fatal illness while still a teenager? Time had not been an enemy for many years, and yet she still wanted to fill every night with pleasure.

She savored the odor of the Sidamo beans, recalling an Ethiopian prince she'd once known. It had made her sad to kill him, but his suspicions were dangerous and she couldn't resist his sweet royal blood.

Her kind didn't *need* food or drink to survive, but a strong cup of coffee in the dawn of the evening was almost as essential to her as the life giving elixir that flowed from the veins of still-living mortals.

Skimming through the New York papers she saw nothing about her activities the previous evening – neither the gathering she'd attended earlier, nor her feast. Despite having risen early to avoid being late, she decided to enjoy a few more quiet moments before rushing out to work.

Chapter 3

The bartender's story checked out. Receipts put him at the bar, and people put him at the diner with very little time in-between. It was unlikely he could have assisted in a murder or helped clean up a crime scene. They'd still need to see what the lab said, and speak with the desk clerk and guard who were on that night. No reason to *schlep* out to Queens and the Bronx to chat with them. It was a few questions that could be answered by phone if people ever bothered to answer their phones. Otherwise, they could get them at midnight when they came in to work, or catch them early in the morning before they left their shift. Cara knew what Jaime's preference would be. Whether it meant staying late or coming at dawn, he'd tell her to do it herself, or let someone working graveyard do it for them. But then, he had a life and a family to go home to.

As for other hotel guests, so far they hadn't found anyone who'd seen or heard anything. Remaining interviews were going to be basic. They could get help on that.

Back at her desk, laptop in front of her, she watched the surveillance tape. The hotel had just one camera in the lobby by the elevator, nothing up on the fourth floor or inside the car. She found the images quickly – Joe Simmons heading toward the cash machine and then walking back. Joe and mystery chic waiting to go upstairs. The video was unfocused, and not well lit, but clear enough. Simmons was holding what looked like the woman's coat. Her head was on his shoulder. There was no point when she was looking up. When her face wasn't in his chest, it was obscured by her loose dark hair.

Was she purposely avoiding the camera?

That alone would not have made the murder premeditated. It could've been a coincidence, or maybe she was known to the hotel and had been told not to darken their doorstep again.

From what Cara could see, she looked classy. If the face went with the body, she could have been a model. Definitely not coming from a late night in an office, but not dressed like your average hooker either, even the high-class kind. More like she just left some fancy event.

"She looks like somebody," Jaime said.

"Yeah. Question is who?"

"No, I mean like someone famous, on TV. A Kardashian or something."

Hearing Kardashian, a couple of the male detectives gathered round the monitor like hungry dogs. Someone whistled.

"Back it up," one of her colleagues suggested.

Cara clicked until she saw the dark-haired lady turning her head. Her profile could be seen for less than a second. It wasn't clear enough to identify her, but it was a start.

Gladys, the administrative aide, was walking out of the lieutenant's office when she passed by the frozen image on the screen and did her own gawk.

"I know who she looks like," the aide offered.

"You know who it *is*?" Cara asked.

"I didn't say that. You can't really see her. I just know who it *looks* like."

"We already got Kim or Kendell. Who's your pick, Penelope Cruz?"

"No, that one who's always getting on *Page Six*. Saint something."

∾⊛∿

It wasn't even nine o'clock, but the gallery was packed. It didn't hurt that one of the young artists being featured, a sculptor, was also a model and known fashionista, as well as the daughter of a television actress and a rock star. Both her parents were expected to be there with their respective very significant others, but neither had yet arrived. Alphonsine thought the girl's work was silly, but she'd learned enough stock phrases to throw at the press, though for sheer pretentiousness, she'd never match Pierre. She had arranged to have a red carpet and a tie-in to a new Broadway revival. There were a few strikingly tall glammed-out transvestites from the chorus posing for pictures with attendees. The photo sales were going to help an orphanage on Sainte Trinité started by a former intern. The island nation was an especially hot cause following a devastating earthquake, and even more so since a senile American televangelist had publicly blamed the Trinitians for their own troubles, claiming the people had long ago made a deal with the devil.

Alphonsine politely made her way through the crowd of delicious young people. It was like walking through a human garden – the heat radiating off living bodies, the freshly washed smell of them, the various "fashion statements" including everything from standard black jeans, to the latest designers, to designers no one had heard of, to vintage, odd combinations, and the newest fads. While a few of her kind limited contact with humanity to feasts, she was addicted to mortals.

Everywhere smart-phones were in the air. She thought of the myth that images of her kind could not be captured in a portrait, or photo. How impossible that would have made life, but in some ways it might have been better. Many pictures and clips of her in her latest incarnation would live forever on the Internet. Within her community there were concerns about the increased ability of technology to identify faces, the ubiquity of surveillance cameras, and other dangers. Simple hypnosis might work on susceptible individuals, making them forgetful or confused, but cameras forgot nothing. Still, she couldn't stop herself from posing. It was an ingrained habit.

She became aware of Pierre across the large space. Her telepathy was primitive – a not always reliable ability to sense patterns, but Pierre's patterns were so familiar to her, and hers to him, that they could often read each other with amazing clarity. She waved and began to walk toward him. A crowd of some of their more beautiful pets came forward and began walking with her. There were two Russian girls, twin daughters of an oligarch, both dressed identically, in shimmering 1960's style mini-dresses, white lipstick, and even go-go boots. There were a number of handsome young men, a few in evening clothes, but most dressed down in typical artist garb. How she would love to pick one, or maybe share the twins for her next blood meal, but that's not what they were for. The rules were strict when survival was at stake. You could play with them, take them to bed or anywhere you wanted. They might be cultivated – *used* for their connections or financially, but not killed. It would stir up way too much fuss.

For *that*, it was best to take those that would not be missed – to use discretion. She was sure to get an earful later when Pierre realized the extent of her previous evening's transgression.

A boy she'd been to bed with a few times came over to say hello. She hoped he was on to something else and wouldn't make a pest of himself. He gave her a friendly kiss. She playfully grabbed his bicep.

"You've gone back to the gym," she said, "nice!"

He whispered in her ear, asking if she would be interested in meeting him in one of the bathrooms. He had some coke, and a desperate urge to sniff it off her pussy.

"Don't be vulgar, darling," she whispered back, "I'm working."

She wasn't sure exactly why he bored her so. He tried too hard, the hair product, the bleached teeth, the bottled tan. Why didn't they understand that youth was beautiful in and of itself? The physique didn't have to be perfected through endless hours lifting weights, or drinking the right combination of nutrients. The ability to spend the night pleasing a woman did not reside in the hardness of the arms.

By the time she reached Pierre, her entourage had grown. With all the people surrounding him, it was as though two armies were meeting on a battlefield. He kissed her on the cheek, and taking in her distinct afterglow, focused his piercing stare upon her. His thoughts came to her in words, *"You've fed, you naughty girl. I hope you haven't been taking unnecessary risks."*

She looked at him affectionately while answering back with a Mona Lisa smile, *"There is no danger I won't be able to handle."*

He shook his head slightly, and out loud said, "My dear sweet girl."

Human ears were never far away, and this night they were surrounded. They would be careful in all they said, play their roles to perfection.

She greeted many she knew and didn't with kisses and smiles.

"Camille, allow me to present Dashiell Alexander," Pierre said.

Her friend was never without beauty by his side. This one was a bit over six feet, slim but not skinny, with short dirty blond hair, and a bit of stubble. His eyes were an intense shade of turquoise that made her suddenly miss and long for the ocean in sunlight. He was dressed simply, in contrast to most around him, a fashionably faded pair of jeans, a clean white tee, and a dark jacket.

"Mr. Alexander," she said as she put out her hand, which he shook. How she longed then for the old days when her hand would have known his lips. She wondered if Pierre was showing off his latest conquest. The boy looked barely twenty-one. Pierre in contrast could pass for anything between late twenties and late thirties, though these days the official biography listed him as thirty-four. The reality was something over three hundred.

"Dashiell has been dying to meet you," Pierre explained.

"Oh? Are you an artist?" She asked addressing the young man directly. He was a handsome thing whose good looks went even beyond his features. When their hands touched, she felt an instant connection she rarely had these days with the living.

"Artist? No. I write. I act, sing a little, not so much the visual. Lately, I've been trying to pay the rent with journalism. I was telling Mr. ... uh Pierre, how I'm interested in learning more about the whole art scene, maybe for an article? He said you might be a good person to speak to."

She wondered what Pierre's game was. Was he throwing a little diversion her way? He certainly knew her type. In other times, Dashiell Alexander was exactly the sort of young man she might toy with for a few days, maybe weeks. Under the right circumstances, that is if she could get away with it, she'd take him one night for a feast – preferably as near to dawn as possible after an evening of vigorous lovemaking. Even sated, the sweet smell of him was tempting, but she sensed he was not to be physically harmed. He looked like someone who could not disappear without questions being asked. Even if she couldn't kill him, she could still enjoy him.

Pierre shouted above the music, "I told Dashiell we'd be open to him. Maybe the two of you could sit down to talk."

"I'd love to have him over for dinner. Do we charge it to the gallery?"

Pierre gave her a stern big brother look, too subtle for anyone to have caught. "*Bien sûr.*"

She was so used to miming human behavior and emotion – acting it all the time – that it took her a moment to realize how real her attraction to this particular boy was. Her body had gone warm. While she could raise her temperature by concentration, this had happened spontaneously, a rare occurrence except when feeding. Something caught in her throat, and she coughed to clear it.

"Are you all right?" Dashiell asked, yelling to be heard above the music.

She laughed slightly, and said, "Of course."

She sensed judgment from Pierre's look. It was not unlike her to fake fragility to get attention. Old habits died hard.

"You just looked … for a second …"

She took his arm.

The band stopped playing. Voices were lowered. For some reason both she and Dashiell started to laugh.

A champagne bottle was thrust into his hand.

"You're supposed to be some kind of writer. Say something beautiful to give us luck," Pierre said to Dashiell, and then he turned to her, and it took her no time to read her friend's mind. It was the dress – the red dress, her *Traviata* dress, which she'd worn purposely to amuse him. Now he was asking a young man, who was obviously smitten with her, to propose a toast, just as Alfredo was asked to do it in the first act of the opera based on Alphonsine's life.

She nodded slightly and smiled at Pierre – her mentor, her brother, her friend.

Dashiell did not break out in song, or even toast to love, but some sentiment in his words echoed a line from the *Brindisi*. She and Pierre couldn't hold in their laughter, which mystified those around them, Dashiell especially.

The music started again. After they all had champagne, the young man asked her, "What was the joke?"

She pretended not to be able to hear him, and grabbed his arm. "Let's go outside where it's quieter."

They were near the exit when one of the interns ran up, and pulled her away from him, muttering about something "important."

"Camille, I … I … the …"

"What is it, Tracy? Are you having some kind of fit?"

"It's the, the police. They're here. They want to talk to *you*."

৵ ✿ ৵

Once it was established who they were and whom they wanted to see, Cara and Jaime were led through the crowd by an anorexic young woman while another intern ran off to find Ms. St. Valois.

The building, back in the neighborhood's industrial days a factory, had been converted to an atrium, with a large open ground floor. It was several levels high and topped by an elaborate skylight of wrought iron lattice and glass. There was a band playing somewhere, though they couldn't see where through the multitude. Jaime poked Cara and pointed out a shorthaired blonde. They argued over whether she was Carey Mulligan or Michelle Williams or Jennifer Lawrence. They followed their guide to an elevator, and then through a corridor looking down onto the main floor. A burly man working security was already waiting in front of a door, arms folded and an expression so grim, Cara was tempted to give him a hard time for the fun of it.

The skinny girl punched in a security code and explained, "I'm sorry I can't put you somewhere more comfortable, but this is the only room I have a combination for."

"No problem," Jaime said, smiling at her amiably.

The space looked more like a supply closet than a conference room, though it did have a table and a few chairs. The door was left open as there was a slightly dank odor, and while they could still hear the din from the main floor, they could hold a conversation above it without straining their voices too much.

"Can I get you guys something? Champagne, wine?" The intern asked.

"Don't think so," Cara answered.

They sat waiting, fairly certain this whole trip to Brooklyn would turn out to be a waste. They'd spent some time comparing images of Camille St. Valois with the woman on the video. Neither would have placed money on their being the same person. Everything, including Simmons' trip to the cash machine, pointed to her being a pro, and St. Valois had no record of arrests and wasn't "known."

None of that ruled out her turning tricks through one of the city's more discriminating escort services, or on her own. Wouldn't be the first time some college-type needed to make a little extra by selling her body, but from what they could figure it was highly unlikely St. Valois would be selling herself in a mid-town bar. She traveled in higher circles. There was gossip about millionaires she "dated" who'd then made major purchases from the gallery. Who knew what her employment might entail? But that wasn't relevant to their investigation.

The music stopped, and they heard the elevator and the sound of high heels clicking along the corridor. Cara and Jaime both stood up and went over to the door, watching her approach. Cara noticed her partner's expression and whispered, "Down boy."

"Huh," he said, continuing to stare.

She was wearing a red strapless dress and holding an open bottle of champagne in one hand and a small purse in the other. With those items and the five inch heels, she seemed slightly off-balance, but still somehow graceful. Her half-smile seemed to convey, *'Look at me, I can barely hold all these things.'* Her hair was different than on the tape, pulled back exposing her face, but watching the way she moved, Cara was sure they'd found Joey's mystery-date.

"I'm so sorry about the room," she said with a little-girl voice that reminded Cara of a documentary she'd seen about Jacqueline Onassis.

"They told me you wanted to speak with me, but this is impossible. Please, there's a much nicer reception area, conducive to conversation." She didn't have an accent as much as a foreign intonation, an unexpected rhythm to her speech. Cara recalled reading she was half-American, but had been raised in France.

She led them to another door. The bouncer followed silently, staying several paces behind. She started to punch in a code while holding onto the bottle, and keeping her clutch squeezed between her right arm and her side. The purse fell. Cara watched as her partner and Camille both stooped down to retrieve it. Jaime grabbed it first, and kneeling on the ground handed it to her. Their eyes met, their hands touched, and he helped her up. It was so expertly done, Cara thought, as if this woman had gone to some special girl-school where you could major in handkerchief dropping and minor in fainting.

Jaime was now holding the bottle and the clutch. St. Valois pressed the combination. The bouncer pushed open the door.

"It should be quiet in here," St. Valois said, leading them inside.

There was a small white leather couch, a couple of matching chairs, a black coffee table in between, and the expected art on the walls.

Jaime placed the champagne on the table. St. Valois gestured for them to sit. "Let me find some glasses," she said, looking around the room.

"We really can't drink," Cara said.

"Oh," she said, sounding disappointed as she went to a cabinet. Then she smiled, "Well I can, and it would be just rude to drink from the bottle. You must have something. We have some juice here."

She opened a black mini-fridge in a corner. Cara noticed nothing but champagne bottles chilling inside. Camille pulled out a smoothie from the back. "Strawberry, banana, orange," she said, reading the label. "Organic. That can't be against regulations, can it?"

She poured some into two plastic wine glasses and placed them on the table in front of the detectives. She sat down across from them on the couch.

"Are you Camille St. Valois?" Jaime began. He used a playful tone. Everyone knew who she was.

"Of course. How can I help you?" She asked, filling a glass from the bottle for herself. Cara knew nothing of wines, but had seen the vintage mentioned in gossip columns. It was the one that the *classier* celebrities always seemed to be ordering.

Cara was trying to figure out if the woman was doing something to bring attention to her mouth, or if that was just where her eyes wound up. Why was she thinking of vaginas? Most of the time, she was not especially attracted to women. Yet, she couldn't look at her without explicit images flashing through her brain. *Block it*, she told herself.

"Detective?" St. Valois asked. "You were about to say something."

"Right," Cara said. She took out a photo of Simmons and put it down on the table, pushing it toward her. "Do you know this man?"

St. Valois looked at the photo then up at them. Her expression was now serious.

"I'm not a hundred percent. He looks like ... Is this important?"

"Yes, this is part of an investigation," Jaime said evenly.

"I see," she said. Cara watched as she colored slightly, and then took a large gulp of champagne, as though she might need it before she could go on.

"I was at a party last night, a get together really. The Dykemans, over by the UN?" She said *the Dykemans* as though she expected them to be familiar with the name. "They purchased some pieces from us, and were having a dinner. They wanted me there as kind of a docent to explain what they had to the guests."

"Um-hmm," Cara said, nodding her head. She had no idea who the Dykemans were, and doubted Jaime did either, but she had a feeling they were important, and this whole thing might be about to get messy.

"It ran late. Not *late* late, but for a weeknight I suppose. Some people had to be at work in the morning." She emphasized the words "work" and "morning" like both were strange concepts. "Barbara has been a second mother to me, uh Mrs. Dykeman, so we were talking and ..."

"Is that where you met this man?"

"No, no. I meant I should have just left with everyone else. They offered to have their driver take me back to Brooklyn, but I thought I might want to go to the Village or Soho, find out what my friends were doing, and it would be easy to get a cab. I just felt kind of restless. Like you get sometimes."

"What time did you leave the Dykemans?" Cara asked.

"About one-o'clock."

"And then where did you …"

"I started walking west. I wanted to check my messages, send some texts, and there was this bar. There was no point in getting into a taxi if I didn't know where I was going."

"Was it the bar next to the Bradley Hotel?" Jaime asked.

"It was next to a hotel. I wasn't paying attention to the name."

"And that's where you met him?"

"Yes." She looked down for a moment.

"Just tell us what happened," Cara said.

"We had a drink. I guess he was flirting."

"Did you leave the bar with him?" Jaime asked.

She nodded. Cara watched her cheeks redden. *Could they be about to get very lucky?*

"Is this you?" Cara took out a still they'd printed of Simmons and the woman by the elevator.

She moved her head again, and asked, "Is he pressing charges against me or something?"

"What kind of charges would he be pressing against you?"

"Then he's not pressing …"

"Camille, why don't you just tell us your side," Jaime said softly.

"This is kind of embarrassing," she said, that mild blush returning as if on cue.

Neither detective said anything.

She went on. "Okay, I went into the bar because it looked like a quiet place to sit and make some phone calls, and I saw this good-looking guy. He looked like a businessman, but he was kind of nice, and I was sitting near him, and he bought me a drink and we started to talk."

"You went into the hotel with him."

"Yes, but that's not the thing. The thing was he seemed to have the impression I was uh, like an escort or something?"

"Yeah," said Cara.

33

"And I sort of let him think that. I was a little drunk, maybe? I thought it would be kind of fun. I mean, like the stories people post on *Salon*? You know, *The Night I Was Paid for Sex?* Not that I would have gone through with it – the money part I mean. I guess I was bored. It just seemed kind of exciting. Oh God, I feel like such an idiot. Please, don't tell my boss."

"Just tell us what happened after you left the bar," Jaime said. "You're not in any trouble."

Cara noticed how Camille took that in and watched the way she looked at Jaime, and how he looked at her, as though some secret understanding was being developed.

"As long as you tell us everything," Cara added, catching Camille's eyes, and taking them off her partner.

"Well, we left the bar, and then we took the elevator, and then ... uh ... we were in the hallway about to go into the room, and I just got this *feeling*."

"*Feeling?*" Cara repeated.

"You know how sometimes you just get bad vibes about something? Or maybe I was coming to my senses. Like all of the sudden I'm thinking, 'Camille what are you doing about to go into a hotel room at two in the morning with a stranger who thinks you're a hooker?' And I remembered reading about that poor girl in Boston, was it? I just freaked out."

"What happened?"

"I told him I changed my mind. I had to go."

"You didn't go into his room?"

"No. Unless I was more drunk than I thought and I blacked out. I don't think so."

"How did he take this news?" Cara asked trying to keep the skepticism out of her tone.

"He wasn't thrilled. He tried to grab me and I pushed him away," she said putting her hands out in front of her and moving them like the world's worst volleyball player.

"And then I said something like 'please' or something, and I wasn't screaming, but maybe he *thought* I was going to scream, and he put his finger up to his lips and we just looked at each other for a couple of seconds, and I was backing away, and then I turned and kind of ran. What's he saying happened? I didn't take his money or anything."

"Camille, I've looked at the video, the camera is near the

elevator, and we don't have you coming down, and nobody remembers seeing you leave."

"I didn't take the elevator. I was scared to wait, in case he changed his mind and came after me. There were stairs. It said fire exit and something about an alarm, but I pushed the door, and I didn't hear anything."

The detectives looked at each other. They'd already scoped out how someone might have left without being seen. Too many employees and even guests sneaking out the fire doors to catch a smoke, so they didn't have the alarm on.

"So that was about what time?"

"Maybe two."

"And where did you go from there."

"Grabbed a cab, came home.

"And that's over at the Verge, on Kent."

"Yes, that's my building."

"Use a credit card in that cab?"

"I think I had cash."

"So you went straight home and got in sometime between two and three?"

"Before three. That time of night it doesn't take more than ten minutes on the FDR."

"Do you have a roommate? Can anyone verify?"

"There's always someone at the concierge desk. And they must have cameras or something."

"We'll check that out," Jaime said, even though they'd already been told by the night guy she came in "two-fifteen, maybe two-thirty," exactly as she said. There were no lobby-cameras or key-cards that could pin it down further, and they didn't keep logs on residents.

"Look, am I in trouble? What is this about?"

The door opened and a man walked in. Cara couldn't help noticing how handsome he was, the dark curly hair, and the large brown eyes. He looked like he might have been Greek or Italian, full lipped with an olive complexion. Cara hoped she wasn't staring at him as obviously as Jaime had been looking at Camille.

"What is happening here?" He asked, his voice was deep, his accent only slightly more pronounced than St. Valois'.

"These are the police. They're questioning me about something from last night. They think I may have seen something."

"I see," he said. "If the police are questioning you about

anything, perhaps you should get the advice of an attorney. I believe I could find you one downstairs."

"No, no," Camille said, "It's fine."

"I don't think so."

"I can handle it."

"We don't believe Ms. St. Valois is a suspect," Cara said, "We just have some questions."

"Suspect?" Camille asked. "Please, tell me what this is actually about."

Dumont sat down next to Camille on the white leather sofa. Cara took them both in. Two dark-haired beauties in evening clothes. There was something between them, but she couldn't quite read it. They reminded her of a long married couple who'd begun to resemble each other, but they were far too young for that, or maybe a brother and sister whose closeness made others uncomfortable. What they didn't look like were an employer and his assistant.

"Yes," he said, "What *exactly* is going on?"

"You're Mr. Dumont, I take it?" Cara asked.

"I am."

"Mr. Dumont, this is a police investigation. I understand you own this gallery. If it's not possible for us to speak to Ms. St. Valois here, alone, then we can certainly speak with her at headquarters."

Cara watched the look passing between him and Camille. Whatever was going on, and she was certain something was, he knew all about it.

"Would you like me to leave?" He asked his employee.

"I can't imagine this will take much longer. It probably would be better."

"Seriously, Mark Solomon is downstairs, I believe he does criminal law."

She said something to him in French.

"They haven't confiscated your phone, have they?" He asked her, switching back to English.

"Of course not."

"Well call me if you need to."

He left the room.

"He's very protective of you," Cara said.

"He's the world's greatest boss," Camille said. She took a breath, "So please tell me ..."

"The man at the hotel, did you see him go into his room?"

"I looked back before I turned the corner, and he was opening the door. I turned again and he wasn't there. I didn't see him going inside."

"Did you get the impression anyone else was in the room, waiting for him?"

"I didn't hear anything."

Jaime spoke up, "Camille, when you got that bad feeling, was it something he said?"

"I don't know. It was just the whole situation."

"He didn't talk to you about other women. What he liked to do?" Jaime continued.

"No. Nothing like that."

"What did the two of you talk about?" Cara asked. "We heard you weren't in the bar more than half an hour."

"I don't think it was even that long. I mean there was this *attraction*," she said, leaning in toward Cara and looking right at her. "You know how sometimes it just happens, like *that*," she added snapping her dainty fingers.

"Did he even tell you his name?"

She looked like she was thinking. "Joe, maybe?"

"What if I told you Joe was found dead this morning. In that hotel room."

Cara watched the color drain from Camille's face.

"My God," she said, "How?"

"He was killed," Jaime said.

"Killed?"

They were all silent a moment, which struck Cara as weird given that a piece of crap like Simmons didn't merit that much respect.

"Am I, do I need a lawyer?"

"We can't answer that for you," Jaime said. "You're not under arrest. It would help if you tell us everything you know."

"I think I have."

"So you're sure you didn't go into that room?"

"Did you find anything to indicate I did?"

"The crime scene is still being processed. Are we going to find anything?" Cara asked.

"I told you I didn't go in there."

"Not exactly," Cara said. "You told us you didn't *think* you'd gone in. You said you might have blacked out. Is it possible you went into the room?"

Camille put her hand on her forehead. Her eyes went wide. "You think I ... Oh God. Am I ...? Should I even talk to you anymore? I'm sorry. I just ..."

Cara put a hand forward, reaching out to her. "Camille, really, we're on your side. I know what a shock this is. It's just that you were probably the last person to see him alive."

"No I wasn't. You just said he was killed. Whoever killed him was the last person to see him alive. I didn't kill him."

"Of course. I meant the last person other than the killer," Cara said. "We're really stuck here. We need your help. We've already talked to the guests who went up on the elevator after you. It doesn't sound likely it was anyone staying at the hotel."

"I can't help you with this. I don't know anything. You haven't even told me what happened to him."

"He may have tried to hurt someone, a woman," Jaime said. "We think he may have hurt women before, and you were very smart to listen to that feeling."

"Very smart," Cara added.

"We think it's possible he was with someone and things started to get a little crazy, and maybe she hurt him protecting herself."

"She might not have meant to," Cara said.

"Hurt him, how?" Camille asked.

"Or maybe the person he was hurting called someone who came to help her," Jaime suggested.

"It wasn't me. I'm telling you, I went upstairs with him, but then I left. I wish you would tell me what happened. Did he hit his head or something? Could it have been an accident?"

"We don't think so," Cara said.

"But that doesn't mean it was murder," said Jaime. "It could have been self-defense like if he was coming at you."

"I just pushed him a little, but that was in the hall. I swear he didn't even fall. I mean I was back downstairs maybe five minutes after I got up there. And then I went home. Please, check at my building. I think it was Jim on at the desk. He must have seen me. Do you really think I could have gotten into his room and done something to him? He was like twice my size."

"We did check," Cara said. "The concierge says he thinks you got there around two-thirty. But we don't know how long whatever happened would take."

"But I couldn't have done it."

"You sound like you're trying to convince yourself," Cara said.

Camille put her hands up to her head and looked like she was about to cry. "No, you're, you're trying to ... *Merde!* Pierre was right. This is like, like what happened to that girl in Italy. You're telling me things and, and ..." She took her phone from her purse and started to make a call.

Jaime got up. Cara followed her partner's signal. There'd be more time to ask her questions after they got the forensics report. The last thing they wanted was her getting a lawyer.

"Camille," Jaime said, "You've been very helpful. I know it couldn't have been easy for you to tell us all those things. I don't think we have any more questions tonight. Do we, Detective O'Brien?"

Cara shook her head. "I think we're done here."

"This is my card," Jaime said, handing one to her. "If you think of something, anything he might have said or done, call me. And thank you for your cooperation."

He put out his hand to shake hers, but she pulled him in and kissed him on the cheek. Then she turned to Cara, who had never seen a suspect do *that*. Before she had time to react, Camille was leaning in to hug her as well.

"I really do wish you both the best of luck with your investigation," she told her two new friends.

The bouncer-type was still on the other side of the door. Camille asked him to see the two downstairs. "You're welcome to stay around. The evening's barely started," she said.

"You're not coming?" Cara asked.

Camille took a sip of champagne. "That was kind of intense. I think I need to decompress a bit before throwing myself back into the fray."

❧ ✪ ☙

Once she heard the sound of the elevator going down, she texted Pierre. And then she started to laugh. The play-acting had been diverting, not as much as the previous evening, but still fun. They'd never find enough evidence to arrest her. The worst case might involve a little push on the right people. She had been careless about the lobby-camera, but by then what was she to do? She was *so* committed. She had to have him.

The improvised story about saving her own virtue at the last minute might not have been her best work, but it would do. She was glad she'd had the foresight to "remind" the concierge that she came home before two-thirty that morning. Her kind were adept at simple hypnotic suggestion which worked well on the unsuspecting and susceptible, especially when it came to little things like forgetting somebody's features, or what time they arrived.

The police had already told her everything she needed to know. Her alibi would protect her. They were still checking for prints and DNA. None would be found. The only problem would be if the press got too involved and researched her background, but even then, her community had become meticulous over the years, better than any spy network at creating false identities.

Pierre didn't see it that way. She could tell just by the sound of his steps as he approached the room.

"The others will not be so happy about this," he said in her native tongue as he walked in and found her sipping champagne, her bare feet up on the coffee table and a satisfied grin on her face.

"And you're going to run and tell them like a school-boy?"

"Of course not, *ma chère*. In fact, I've already been on the phone making sure this stays quiet. My loyalty is always to you, but you took a stupid chance and this could endanger all of us."

"*I* took a stupid chance? May I remind you of the last time I had an interview with *les gendarmes*? That was on *your* account."

"That was sixty years ago, and one of the reasons we all need to be more cautious."

"There's no danger here, darling. They don't have anything. I grew up in a hovel without servants. I'm very good at cleaning my messes. What do you think is going to happen?"

"They may come back."

"We cover ourselves well. Even during the last world war we never had problems with our papers, and *les boches* could be absolute bastards."

"The world is changing *darling*, as you well know."

She put her hands over her ears and started to hum the first bars of *Sempre Libera* before speaking. "It's tiresome. All this talk about computers, and cameras everywhere and how we're going to need to destroy humanity to protect ourselves. It's ridiculous. They are so many, and we're practically defenseless during the day."

"But that's exactly why …"

"Please don't start. Any attempts we've made to manipulate them, to stave off their development have been disastrous. Wasn't the Great War supposed to set them back centuries? It only encouraged them."

"So you suggest we do nothing until someday our existence becomes impossible?"

"I'm saying we learn to adapt instead of taking actions that will backfire. I'm saying we have no right to ..." She didn't finish the thought. What was the point? Pierre was only goading her. In his heart, he harbored no mad dreams that their kind would someday control the planet or that only humanity's destruction would keep them safe, that the best future for them might be a dystopia where people were few, controlled, and farmed like animals. Who'd want that – outside of a few bitter elders? Where would the music come from? The theater? The art? Her kind was great at destruction, but creativity was not their forte.

"We'll always be smarter than they are. We have that advantage," she continued.

The music was playing again, but their keen ears picked up the sound of the elevator. Although the door was closed, they switched back to English and began to discuss their recent acquisitions. The knock came, and Camille answered.

It was the young man, Dashiell Alexander.

"Hello," Camille said, not even trying to hide her delight.

"I was looking all over for you. You disappeared so suddenly. One of the interns told me you were up here."

"Yes, I had to talk to some people."

"Oh good. I thought maybe you were ... unwell. I think this belongs to you," He brought out a flower he'd been holding behind his back – the white camellia she'd earlier pinned in her hair.

She laughed, feeling the back of her head. "It must have dropped. I didn't even notice. Thank you for returning it." She pulled a bobby pin from her clutch and rearranged it. Turning her head, she caught Pierre's eye. He had a way of looking at her with an equal measure of displeasure, exasperation, and affection.

She stood up and took Dashiell's arm. "I think my employer is getting very cross. I have been neglecting my duties as hostess. We should be getting back downstairs."

The three of them shared the elevator. The earlier band had left, replaced by a quartet – contemporary classical, and while it was still crowded, many of the younger people having had their fill of champagne and snacks had left. She explained to Dashiell that she really would have to spend the rest of the evening guiding the right people to the right artwork and hoping to find buyers. It would be "horribly dull."

Nevertheless, he wanted to accompany her. "If it wouldn't cramp your style," he said.

"It might. I'm kind of a professional flirt."

"How about I keep a discreet distance?"

"If it would amuse you," she said.

For the next few hours, she was sometimes aware of him watching her, close enough at times to hear her insist some unknown's childish pen and ink drawings were the work of "the next Keith Haring." While she explained how a certain collage was a representation of the failed American dream, their eyes met, and she felt self-conscious, afraid he would see her as the phony she knew she was. It was strange his opinion of her would matter. She rarely cared what men "really" thought. She had discovered long ago that most simply wanted to be with a beautiful woman who would flatter them, and even if they recognized her being false with another, she could convince any man she was being sincere to him.

The offers made she would pass along to Pierre. He would handle the actual negotiations. Her job was only to attract the buyers. She resented at times that she had never been completely free. Their community made demands. It was important for some members to work, at least some of the time, contributing to the common treasury. She favored a relatively legitimate business such as this to some of the other activities they'd involved her in, including a couple of *very* short-lived marriages, but she would have preferred even more to wake up each evening beholden to no one.

By two o'clock, most of the artists, buyers, celebrities, and gawkers were gone. She suspected Pierre was up in his loft on the top floor with one or more of the handsomest young men. But not *the* handsomest. That was Dashiell Alexander, and he was for her though she had no plans on making love to him that night. It would be better to have this one wait. Not long, but just a bit. No matter what the mores of the time or of the place, if she had learned anything, it was that men never valued that which came to them too easily.

"Do you want to go to the Beer Garden, and get a bite?" Dashiell asked. "Maybe Brooklyn Bowl? I know someone in the band."

"I know *everyone* in the band," she said. "It's such a nice night. Will you walk with me by the river?"

"In those heels?"

"I'll take them off."

"You might step on glass."

"I'm terribly thick-skinned," she said stepping out of her shoes. Standing next to him barefoot, she felt small and vulnerable. It was a feeling that comforted her somehow, though in reality she could easily overpower him.

They walked outside into the spring air, and down to the East River. There was a breeze.

"Are you cold?" He asked.

"No, not really."

He took off his jacket nevertheless, and wrapped it around her shoulders. He was waiting for some signal from her, and she wasn't going to give it to him, but the next thing she knew they were kissing, and it felt so completely right, as though she had always been kissing him, as though she was truly young again, transformed back to Paris, innocent – or as innocent as she'd ever been.

She pulled away.

He looked hurt.

"I'm sorry," she said.

"No, I'm ... I didn't mean to," he said.

"It's just that ..."

"You don't need to ..."

"I really like you ..."

"But you're seeing someone," he suggested.

"No, it's not that," she said. "It's just been a long evening. I've had a lot of champagne, you know?"

He walked her to her building, and into the lobby. She wouldn't have minded company. It would be another couple of hours till dawn, but even if she could hold out, inviting him up, however innocent her intent, would send the wrong signal.

She kissed him on the cheek.

They agreed to meet for dinner the following evening at a place to be determined.

"Tomorrow," he said.

"Tomorrow," she said. She took the flower from her hair and gave it to him.

He looked at her with curiosity.

"A souvenir," she said. "Do you speak French?"

"I took Spanish."

"The word is French. To remember. You must keep the flower to remind you to call me."

"I can't imagine I'd forget."

She watched him go out the door. As she turned toward the elevator, her sharp ears could hear him humming on the street as he walked away. The sound sent shivers through her.

Chapter 4

"Did they come in with a vacuum cleaner?" Cara asked, letting her eggs get cold. "How could there be *nothing*? Nothing under his fingernails? Nothing on the side of the toilet? Not one single thing?"

Jaime and Cara were sitting at one of New York's last official we-are-pleased-to-serve-you-style Greek diners, having their usual "working" breakfast, discussing the dismal lab results – or lack thereof.

"No blood anywhere. They couldn't find a stray hair – not even in the victim's mouth. No DNA evidence in the room, and the body was clean," she continued.

"You called it that day. You said it looked like a professional job," Jaime said.

"She had help."

"How do you even get *her* in the room?" Her partner asked finishing his BLT, and eyeing the food on her plate. "There's no evidence, and the doorman says she got back by two-thirty, which per the autopsy means it couldn't have been her."

"*Concierge*," Cara reminded him, enunciating. "They don't have a doorman. He's a con-ci-erge. How's this? She gets in the room with him. They start going at it. It gets weird, and she gets lucky with a knife she carries in her purse."

"There'd be blood," Jaime reminded her.

"So it happens in the bathroom. They're in the shower."

"You know they didn't find anything that looked like blood or tissue in the tub or the drain."

"And it's over really quick," Cara continued, "and she calls someone. Maybe even the con-ci-erge. I bet he'd do anything for her." She blinked her eyes in mock-damsel-in-distress mode. She took a sip of coffee and added, "She kind of has that effect on men in case you didn't notice. So he comes up to help her clean. He said he used to be on the job. An ex-cop. He'd know how to do it. He's back

45

at his desk within an hour."

"How come we don't see him get in the hotel?" Jaime asked.

"Same reason we don't see her go out. He uses the fire door. She goes down to let him in."

"Not unless she leaves the door propped open with the body in the room. We don't have a record of anyone putting a key card in the slot till the maid after one the next day."

"You think she's completely innocent?" Cara asked staring him down hard.

"I think we can talk to the concierge again, but even if she got back at five, we still don't have any proof she went into the room," he replied ignoring her provocation, and reaching over to grab a fry off her plate.

"No one saw her leave."

"Which means she could have left at seven in the morning for all we know except for the ..."

They both said, "con-ci-erge" and laughed.

"Let me get this straight," Jaime said, "She overpowers and kills this badass serial killer who as far as we know no one has gotten away from, including when he managed to get two victims at the same time. Then she calls her *doorman?*"

"Maybe they just paid him off to say the time. Maybe she called her boss," Cara suggested.

"He didn't seem like the type to get his hands dirty."

"They have connections. Those bouncers."

"Those weren't even regular guys," he said shaking his head. "They were hired security for the event. You're trying way too hard here."

"You just don't want it to be her because she's your new girlfriend."

Jaime crumbled up a napkin and threw it at her. "Yeah. That's it."

"What's *your* theory?" She asked.

"I didn't buy the pretend-hooker thing. I don't know what happened or what didn't, but let's say the part about not going into the room is true. Maybe somebody else was in the room, waiting."

"A partner?"

"Yeah. I mean that's a possibility we discussed before," Jaime said.

She let him go on.

"Joey comes in without the girl. He and the partner get into a fight. Partner kills him, cleans up, leaves."

"But nobody saw this mystery man," she pointed out.

"They don't stop everyone coming in. He blends. Or maybe leaves the way she did. We got to go back and look. Get the desk clerks to identify everybody on the video. You know what's the best part of my theory?"

"What?"

"It means the serial killer was taken out by a serial killer, in which case we get to make it *los federales'* problem. Which works out great, because we still got the sterile hotel room, a body missing a whole lot of blood, that weird cut on the throat, and all this other spooky shit we are never going to resolve."

"You just don't like a challenge." Cara said allowing her partner to grab the bill.

∾✿∿

Sleep was not always restful. Alphonsine's days were filled with vivid dreams – images, sounds, tastes, and smells from her first life, going back to her childhood, long before she had become a person that anyone would have missed.

She was walking with her father who seemed as tall as a giant. She didn't know she was dreaming, but understood what was happening had happened before. They came to a house. There was something about it that frightened her. Her father said, "The old man will give you all the food you want. He paid good money. It won't hurt much. He just wants to play. This is how men play with pretty girls."

"The way you do Papa, when you come to me at night?"

He glared at her. He didn't like her to talk about that, but then his expression softened. "He'll do something more. It's natural. Don't be scared."

"But Papa, I am not afraid anymore."

His eyes grew big as though he had just seen something horrible, and his mouth opened, but no sound came out. She came toward him. Either he had shrunk or she had grown. She hovered over him. Her fangs descended, and she tore into his neck, but didn't swallow the blood, barely tasted it. It was bitter and as vile as he was. She pushed him down, biting into him like a wolf, fertilizing the earth with his entrails.

She went up to the house, and knocked on the door, but it wasn't the old "uncle" who'd bought her who answered. It was Alexandre – Adet, she called him – AD – his initials. He was the first man she ever really loved – not worshipped or admired, or viewed naively as a savior, but loved as an equal. The house had transformed to the country cottage where they had spent a glorious summer, mostly in bed. It belonged to a man who was paying for her, but he rarely came, and Adet rarely left. They couldn't get enough of each other. It was as though their bodies were only complete when entwined. But in the dream, he was different. She was aware, but not aware, of the difference – the way it happens in dreams. They ate strawberries, sweet fresh strawberries from a nearby farm, and they made love, and he asked, "Do you have to go back to Paris?"

And she told him, "I'm rich now and I don't have to do anything, but we can't stay here."

"Why not?" He asked.

"Because we're both dead."

She woke up startled and unsettled. She reviewed the dream, realizing Adet had been Dashiell, the boy she'd just met.

She grabbed her phone. It was nearly seven. He had left several texts about dinner. She wrote back, "Sorry. Why not here @8? We can order in and I shall teach you everything I know about art."

"U sure? We can go somewhere," he answered.

"Fewer distractions here."

"8 = gr8."

She took a quick dunk in the tub, made up her face, threw on a pair of navy capris and a striped tee-shirt. She decided to let her wet hair dry naturally and went into the living room. She had a cup of espresso and moved the vase with the camellias to the small dining table by the window.

She opened a bottle of champagne just as the concierge called to announce her guest. She greeted him barefoot, kissing him on the cheek and inviting him in.

"Wow. This is something," he said.

"It's just a sublet." The community owned the building through one of its corporate subsidiaries. In addition to wealthy mortal renters, many of the apartments were used as *pieds-a-terre* by her kind, perfect for quick stopovers for hunting, shopping or doing the usual New York things.

"The view is fantastic," he said.

She handed him a glass of champagne. "Shall we look at it from the terrace?"

They stepped out together. It was a clear night. The wind was mild.

"Do you always drink champagne?" He asked.

"It's mostly all I drink," she said.

He was trying to make small talk, asking the usual questions. She'd practiced the answers many times.

He noticed the piano, a white Steinway baby grand. "Do you play?"

"Not well. But the walls are pretty thick, and it relaxes me. Do *you* play?"

His mother was a high school music teacher and had taught him for "about a minute." Later he'd picked up a guitar and learned on his own. He had a band, or rather, was forming one. "It's just for fun. I'm not exactly a prodigy."

"Well, if you guys want to jam here sometime."

"Really?" he said with a smile.

"I like to have people over, people with more talent than I have. I love live music, and having people come play in your home, it's great."

"Speaking of music," he said, "What's that you have on?"

"Liszt," she said. "I love classical."

"What else do you love?" He asked.

He was standing close enough to her that in addition to his smell, she could feel the warmth radiating from his body. She wanted to throw herself against him.

"Dancing, live theater, live everything really."

He was sounding her out, but she felt off her game. Normally, she would be the one managing the man, finding his interests, tuning into him like the instrument she was. But with this one, she felt different. She wanted him to know *her* – know her tastes and desires. She wanted more than to merely reflect his, yet she needed to know more about him as well. Was what she felt merely a physical attraction, or was he someone worthy of her love?

"What about you?" She asked. "You said you were an actor *and* a writer? Which? What have you done?"

"Not much. Double major, writing and drama at Stanford. I had a manuscript that got me an agent, but then we had a meeting with an editor at one of the big houses and I realized it was sophomoric shit. Even if I made the changes and got it accepted, it wasn't what I wanted to be known for. I decided to maybe focus on the acting, playwriting too. Of course, the play I'm writing is about a college romance, not exactly groundbreaking, but I think it's honest."

"I'd love to read it." She took a sip from her glass. "Stanford. That's out west. Isn't it? What brought you to New York?" She was thinking how *young* he seemed. How much younger twenty-two or whatever he was, was now than in her time.

"I needed to be in LA or New York. If I were in LA, it would be too tempting to just do television, so I came here to be a struggling theater actor, learn my craft. Now I'm trying to write some articles because it beats driving a taxi, I guess."

He reminded her of young men she'd known long ago when she'd first arrived in Paris – students of law or philosophy. They hadn't come into their money, lived off of what they considered modest allowances. She was sure he had some supplementary income as well. All the young people around the gallery seemed to, but this one didn't act quite so privileged. She wondered if there had been a time when the money hadn't been so accessible.

Unlike other wannabe actors she'd met, he was comfortable in the role of himself. He had that quality, rare in mortals, of making one feel important in his presence.

They stayed on the terrace talking, until he finally said, "I'm not sure how to bring this up, but weren't we going to have dinner?"

"Oh, I'm sorry. Me too. Starving." She laughed.

They sat at the counter and pouring over take-out menus, settling on a Thai place. He didn't want anything with meat, or even fish. This was not an uncommon affectation among the young people. As her kind could not digest anything with dead blood, it was quite convenient.

When the food came, he took out his wallet, but she told him to put it away. She'd already paid by credit card. He started to say something.

She cut him off. "It's business, remember? I can charge it to the gallery and even deduct it on my taxes," she explained.

She set out the cartons and plates.

"There's enough for an army," he said.

"Is there?"

She enjoyed the tastes and smells, but not needing food, she barely picked.

"So it's true what they say about how the French eat."

She smiled. "A girl has to keep her figure."

After dinner, as he was helping clear the table, she said, "Let's get down to what you really came for."

He stood for a moment, unsure of himself. She felt very satisfied as she got her iPad out and announced, "We can start with a virtual tour of some of the newer local galleries, and I'll be happy to answer your questions."

"Yup, that's what I came for," he said. They were both sitting. He leaned across the table, took her hand, and kissed it.

"You're such a sweetie," she said. "But seriously. Let's work."

She wished it were not necessary to be coy, to continue the charade when she could so easily picture the two of them on her polished wood floor. She'd be on top – careful not to hurt him.

He took out his tablet as well, and they brought up a map of the local art spots. Dashiell was surprisingly well informed, and so she worked to distract him, just enough that her deficits wouldn't seem so obvious.

They had gotten onto a second bottle of champagne, and shared a joint. While a small amount of marijuana would normally have almost no effect on her, she found herself feeling self-conscious, afraid he would sense how much she desired him. She suggested they go out, which was how they found themselves walking once more by the river, on the way to a bar. There was a band playing and Dashiell wanted to check out the drummer. They turned up a street, which unlike the avenue they had come from was dark and deserted. She smelled mortals ahead, their bodies filled with adrenaline, but it would have been awkward to warn him, so she let it play out.

Three emerged from a doorway. They looked young. Boys really. She sensed mostly their anger, and it excited her. It was easy for her to imagine their lives, their poverty in the midst of so much wealth, and the resentment that brings.

The largest was holding a gun and doing the talking. She wondered if any of them were old enough to drink. First, he wanted Dashiell to take out his wallet and phone and give them to her. Then he asked her to go toward one of the others and give it to him, plus her handbag, her earrings, and bracelets.

Dashiell looked calm. He was concentrating, waiting.

After she completed her task, the leader asked her to come over to him. "Show me your tits," he demanded.

Dashiell said, "You don't have time for …"

"Don't fucking tell me what I have time for," he shouted back.

She almost kicked him, and would have if it looked like he was ready to pull the trigger. Getting the gun and killing all of those annoying children would have taken her seconds, but making Dashiell forget any of it happened, would have been trickier.

He told Dashiell to get on the ground.

"Just do what he says," Alphonsine pleaded, trying to sound afraid.

He complied.

"Here's how it's going to go," gun-boy announced looking at her. "I'm giving this to my friend. He's going to keep it pointing at your boyfriend's head, and you're going to do whatever I want."

He gave the gun to the smallest, youngest looking one, who walked over to Dashiell and held it over him. Dashiell reacted so quickly that for a second she forgot he was not of her kind. He grabbed the boy's leg and brought him down. They began to struggle, as Dashiell shouted, "Run, Camille, run."

The big one put her into a headlock, and yelled, "Stop or I break her fucking neck."

She stepped hard on his instep and pushed down on the arm he had in front of her. She heard the pop from his shoulder and then his scream, as she ran toward Dashiell who now held the pistol.

Dashiell told them not to move. He made them put down what they'd taken, and slowly step back away from it.

"Call 911," he said to her.

The idea of being in a police station for hours, possibly till after sunrise, seemed horrific, but she didn't think she'd be able to talk him out of it.

"Hey man, just keep the gun," the older one said. He was radiating pain, but trying not to show it. "You let us go, this ends now. Call the cops, it never ends."

"I'm going to remember you said that," Dashiell said coolly.

"What should I do?" She asked, hoping he'd think about the offer.

"Call the police," he said.

She did.

"You're not really going to shoot us," the leader said. "I bet you never fired a gun before."

Dashiell released the safety, paused, and said softly, "I'd start shooting now if I knew for sure I had at least three bullets."

They heard the sirens. Dashiell handed the weapon over to the cops. They were given a ride to the station where the police took their statements, and then drove them back to her condo.

He walked her into the lobby. "Should I come up?" He asked.

"I'd like that very much," she said.

In her Paris days, she had had no honor to defend. Duels over women like her happened only in stories. Later, in her guises, there had been fighting, but that seemed less about her than about the men acting something out with each other. Dashiell's actions were different. He had protected her life and her virtue, unarmed and with a gun to his head.

"Where did you learn to fight?" She asked him in the elevator. They'd hardly spoken in hours.

"Black belt," he said. "I was a skinny kid. Had to defend myself. You didn't do so bad either."

"Instinct," she said, "but what you did, it was so dangerous."

"I would never let anything happen to you."

"Would you have shot them? Killed them if you had to?"

"That's a tough one," he said, pausing before adding, "I would have done whatever was necessary to keep you safe."

She felt a small shudder. She wanted his protection – even if the concept was absurd. She knew then that she too would do anything to keep *him* safe. She could not remember having so intense a feeling for a mortal, at least not since her elevation. In her first life, she had learned never to give herself fully to love. It always led to disappointment, yet once again she felt its possibilities. She looked into his eyes and could see while he might not have been feeling *exactly* what she was, the depth was equal to her own. There was no question of what would happen once they were inside her apartment though they didn't touch each other till they crossed the threshold and closed the door. Then she jumped onto him, wrapping her arms around his neck and her legs around his waist. He grabbed her ass, and carried her to the bed. They didn't need words to communicate, said almost nothing for the next few hours. He seemed to know her body, know just how to please her instinctively, without even mental projection on her part. His beauty stunned her. He was lean and muscular, his chest and arms almost hairless, yet unlike so many modern men, his beauty seemed natural, his proportions perfect without need of hours spent defining each muscle. His pubic hair was the same shade of gold as the hair on his head. His cock, as she had imagined, was long and thick, and she could see how he was trying (and succeeding) at making his hardness last. He wasn't callous the way some young men could be. He took his time and made sure her pleasure came first. They only stopped when she felt the dawn coming, and she told him she needed to sleep.

"I don't," he said between nibbles on her ear. He was on top of her at that point – their secretions creating a wet glue holding them together. "I could keep going with you forever."

His penis rested against her thigh, semi-erect, hot and throbbing. His neck was by her mouth. She put her lips against his skin, and probed his body with her tongue. The taste of his flesh, the saltiness of his sweat, she wanted more. It would have been so easy to plunge her fangs into him, to take everything at once, to devour.

Of course, then there would be no more. Her kind believed death was a gift. Yet, he was the one who was giving something to her. With Dashiell, she felt not what it was like to be mortal, but what it had been like when she was first reborn. How tempting it was to tell him, to offer him what she had never before bestowed – everlasting life. But that was not how it was done.

"Really, I sleep like the dead, and I'm kind of a bitch if I don't get at least nine hours," she told him.

"Are you asking me to leave?"

She didn't want him to know all she was feeling, but she didn't want him to think this was nothing. "I would love to wake up next to you, but I'm so very tired and if you aren't sleepy, there's no point in your staying."

"I could watch *you* sleep," he said.

"That's so sweet. You have no idea, how sweet that is. Do you? No, it's silly. You should go home. But you must come back tonight."

"Yes, of course."

Her curtains were open. The sky had gone from black to purple, a familiar fatigue was settling in.

He kissed her once more. He asked if he might use the shower. She instructed him to take his things into the bathroom and exit through the door to the living room.

He started to say something, but she put a finger against his lips and smiled as she moved it around. "Tonight. Just buzz me at seven, okay? And you can hang out for a while, but the maid comes at ten, and I wouldn't want to give her a coronary."

"I think I can take a hint," he said.

"It's not a hint. I like you a lot. Please, tonight," she said as she reached down with her hand, putting her own scent on her fingers, then bringing them into his mouth.

When she heard the water running, and was sure he'd left nothing, she got out of bed and bolted the doors leading from the bedroom to the bathroom and living room. Next she pulled closed the two sets of curtains, put on her sleep mask, and got under the dark heavy covers. As she fell into the day-sleep, she thought of the young man with whom she had just shared her bed. Would it be possible for him to love her if he understood what she was? She imagined taking Dashiell's hand and showing him, like the spirits in Dickens' *Christmas Carol*, the key scenes from her past, walking him through the brutality of her childhood, her many transformations. She thought of the saying, "to understand all is to forgive all," but was forgiveness possible when repentance was not?

Act II – The Past

Chapter 1

Paris, 1846-1847

She was too ill to work, and the money would soon be gone.

There were two possible outcomes. She would recover, and there would be more money, or she would die and then it wouldn't matter. Clothilde, her maid, insisted she would get well. The doctors looked away when she asked, and said she must save her strength and not worry about what was in the hands of God.

She spent a good part of most days in her boudoir. It was late fall, but as cold and damp as winter. From her window, it looked as though the city had been drained of color. Sometimes when she was restless, but had a little strength, she would walk through her flat. It felt cavernous without the presence of others. She was haunted, not by ghosts, but by *absence* – the music that wasn't being played, the passionate conversations not taking place, the love not being made.

She was determined to live till the end of January. She reasoned they could hold off the creditors till then. Besides, she wanted to see her twenty-third birthday.

One evening when she was feeling less awful, she had gone to the theater, accompanied by two nephews of Clothilde, who acting as escorts supported her as she walked from her carriage to her box. Early in the second act, she asked one to find her coachman. She'd been coughing, and didn't want to distract the actors.

Traveling the familiar boulevard back to her flat, she spotted a few people she knew emerging from or entering restaurants and cafes. They either didn't notice her carriage or looked away when they recognized it.

She saw the back of a man walking ahead. He was slim and tall. There was something about him that seemed familiar. She looked back as they passed him. She'd seen the face before, but wasn't sure where, which bothered her – as it was a very handsome face, and she should have remembered.

He was well dressed, certainly a gentleman, with a fine hat, a walking stick, and a frock coat. He was not in the first blush of youth, but was far from old. There was a bit of grey in what she could see of his dark hair. She wondered why he wasn't in a carriage, why he was alone, whom he was going to see.

She caught his eye. There was something disconcerting in the way he looked at her. She was used to the gaze of men. This was different. She was sure his mouth hadn't moved, and if it had, she wouldn't have heard him, yet there was a message received as if it had been whispered directly into her ear.

"I will come for you."

The fevers sometimes played with her reason. Nevertheless, when she arrived at her building, she instructed the doorman to allow no visitors that evening.

She felt a bit better once she was settled in at home. She didn't dine, but ate some leftover bread and jam Clothilde had saved for her. She attempted to read, but her attention strayed. She tried to practice the piano but found it frustrating. *Why were her fingers so clumsy?* She moved to her desk and read a letter. She started a reply, but couldn't concentrate, and so retired to her bed though it was still early.

Lying in the darkened room, she remained awake. She *felt* death coming on almost as if it were a season, arriving little by little. *Would it be eternal sleep or would her agitation follow her to the grave?* A coughing fit started, and she reached for the basin. There was a bell she could ring that went to Clothilde's alcove, but she didn't wish to disturb her. After the spasm passed, she found the tin box and lit a match, then a lamp, which she carried into the parlor, planning to pull a book down from the shelf and pass the night reading.

In a corner, sitting on a chair, with her copy of *Don Quixote* opened in his lap, was the man she had seen earlier. Before she could say anything, she heard his voice. Again it was only in her mind, but this time he was saying, *"Don't scream,"* and it became clear to her she would not have been able to.

He stood up, and she swooned. She felt his firm hand on the small of her back breaking her fall. He lifted her, carrying her in his arms. She felt terribly weak, but still aware as he took her back to her boudoir and placed her gently on her bed. He had the most pleasant and unusual scent.

He touched her cheek with refreshingly cool fingers. "You're burning up," he said softly. She was sure this time he'd really spoken. His lips moved. There was kindness in his voice.

She signaled for him to bring her the basin, then pointed to the freshly laundered handkerchiefs on top of her dresser. He brought one to her. She dabbed at her mouth and watched his eyes travel to the bloodstained cloth.

He started to stroke her hand, telling her to relax. The spasm stopped.

"I can end this for you," he said aloud.

She understood immediately he was talking about killing her, and that if she died in his arms it would be without pain.

"I don't want to die," she told him. "I want to be well."

"That too can be arranged."

She looked at him unable to find words.

He continued, "Other lives would need to end for you to live."

"Are you … Death?" She asked, suddenly remembering old tales she'd heard as a girl. "Have you come to bargain with me?"

"No," he said. "I am not Death. I've come to offer you life, but I need you to accept knowing what it would mean."

"Others? What others would die?"

"Innocents and the guilty alike. Many over time, and you would be … directly responsible, but you would never get old, never be sick, and I can promise you, you would most definitely, never be poor."

She couldn't help smiling at that. She decided she was dreaming. It was the only explanation for this absurd conversation.

"Would you be willing to trade the lives of others for immortality, Alphonsine?"

Alphonsine. No one called her that. She had been known as Marie for nearly five years. It was a simple name, but it had belonged to her mother, and therefore it was beautiful to her. Yet, when he called her the old name, it was as though he were speaking to her very soul.

"I suppose not," she said softly. Even in a dream, taking the lives of others was not a choice she could make. "I'd rather die, but not tonight."

She closed her eyes, and when she opened them next, it was mid-day. While she didn't feel *well*, she felt stronger than she had in weeks. She was certain the night visitor had been nothing more or less than the figment of an overactive mind, an effect of her illness.

Yet, this strange vision brought her peace. There were, after all, worse things to fear than death. Certainly, to become a creature that lived through the destruction of others would be one of them. She asked Clothilde to see if she could find the priest, Father Bernays, from the Church of the Magdalene across the street. They had had several talks recently. He had assured her it was not to late for her to confess her sins and repent.

Clothilde sent the porter's son, and Father Bernays soon arrived. Alphonsine dressed and met him in the parlor. Coffee was served along with fresh pastries from the *boulangerie* nearby. The priest, a sandy-haired, freckle-faced man, not much older than she was, spoke with the cadences of her native Normandy. Although she had worked hard to perfect a Parisian accent, five minutes in his presence and she sounded like a farmer's wife.

She wanted his opinion of the strange dream she had had. Had she drawn the correct lesson?

She described her encounter, repeating for him to the best of her memory the odd conversation. She watched him place down his plate, discarding the half-eaten cake as though it had suddenly lost all its flavor. *That was something she hadn't seen before.*

"So Father, please tell me, what am I to make of this?"

"You are correct my dear," he said after a brief hesitation, "There are worse things than death." He looked around at the paintings on the walls, and asked, "Have you no crucifixes?"

She smiled. "Most of what you see were gifts. None of my patrons has ever thought to give me a crucifix."

"So you have none in this house? Not even by your bed?"

Alphonsine laughed, and before she could answer, she noticed the priest was blushing. "I'm sorry, Father. It just struck me as …"

"You might place one there," he suggested quietly. "It doesn't need to be the finest silver. There's a small shop that sells such items on the street behind the church. You could find one for only a few sous."

"But whatever for?"

He hesitated a moment. "It will remind you of your repentance … should you face … temptation." After another sip of coffee, he added, "It will protect your soul."

∾ ✵ ∾

The following week, she accepted a visit from Count Olympe Aguado. He was only eighteen, her youngest suitor, and lately the only one who called though they had no formal arrangement. His features formed themselves in a way that was not quite handsome, but he had dark curly hair and full Spanish lips, and reminded her of a portrait she'd seen of young Lord Byron. She was his first mistress, his first great love. She felt sad for him, knowing the intensity of his feelings and the grief they would bring him.

When she received him, she saw at once a look of horror on his face and understood immediately its cause. The previous afternoon, she had answered his request to call, writing she was feeling stronger. He had only just returned to Paris, had not seen her in more than a fortnight. Her gauntness and pallor must have shocked him.

"You look … beautiful," he said after a moment.

"I am a terrible influence. You are learning to lie almost as well as I do."

Her lover had not yet come into his majority and had little money to help with her debts, but as her illness progressed, he made no demands, and was sincerely concerned for her wellbeing. He provided for her as best he could. The noble thing, the right thing, she was sure, would have been to send him away. There was no point in his ruining himself. He was young and sheltered. Her death would devastate him. She didn't love him. Couldn't bring herself to. It was as though those feelings, those attachments to the world of the living were past her now. Yet, she couldn't bring herself to give him up.

They sat on chairs directly across from each other, their hands touching on the small rosewood table that separated them. She asked him about his visit to his aunt in Provence. He told her about riding, and walks with his cousin. She teased him about this "cousin" who was only sixteen, and reportedly quite pretty. Might he be proposing to her soon?

The poor boy stammered and swore he had been thinking only of *her*.

He wanted to take her out to dine, but she wasn't up for it. They did, however, make it to the opera. From her box, she was sure she spotted the man who had come to her in her dream, but when she tried pointing him out to her companion, he was gone.

Olympe accompanied her home and offered to stay the night, if only to sit by her bed and attend to her needs, but she told him she was tired and preferred to be alone. There was no point in her coughing fits keeping both of them awake. The following afternoon, at Clothilde's insistence, messages were sent to the doctors. There were three of them. She was no longer sure who was paying for which, but hoped Clothilde was not pawning the jewelry, as she wanted to be able to pass something along to her sister's family besides debts and shame.

Dr. Leclair, the Breton, stopped by first. As was his habit, he examined her briefly, and asked if she was taking her enemas. Then he went into the parlor where he stayed – drinking coffee, eating pastries, and chatting with her neighbor, Clarice. Clarice, stout and middle-aged, whose circumstances were reduced after her waistline increased, came often in those days.

Dr. Elgin, the Englishman, arrived later. He also gave her a cursory examination, followed by a short lecture. His accent was so awful she was never sure what he was saying, but she nodded through his admonishments like an obedient child. Then he retreated to the parlor to consult with his colleague and any other vagabonds who had managed to gain admittance. The door of her room was slightly ajar. There was a hallway separating her boudoir from the parlor. She could recognize voices, but could not quite make out what they were saying.

By evening there was the sound of someone else at the door. She was sure from the heavy footsteps it was Dr. Hoffman, the Prussian. He was a large man with a booming voice. He had a kindly smile, and a white beard. She couldn't look at him without remembering a jovial old priest who had once entertained the children of her parish dressed as *Père Noël*.

The other doctors thought he was a fraud. They denigrated his odoriferous elixirs and vibrantly colored tinctures. She was inclined to agree with their assessment of his medical skills, but she didn't believe he *knew* himself to be a fake. He seemed absolutely sincere, and while he couldn't save her, neither could they, so she saw no harm in having him around. He was at least entertaining, with no qualms regarding gossiping about other patients, particularly those of the highest social caste.

Usually, he would come straight in to check on her, but that evening she heard the voices getting louder, arguing. Finally they all came together, pushing each other through the door like something out of a farce. They began speaking at once.

She raised her arm with some effort. "Gentleman, please. I must hear from you one at a time."

There were a couple of false starts. Finally, she had to choose. "Hoffman, why don't you tell me what is so important?"

The Prussian began and was almost immediately interrupted by his colleagues.

"Ssh," she told them, waving a delicate hand. "Allow the man to speak. I'll hear your objections later."

"My dear girl," *Père Noël* began, "I have met the most extraordinary gentleman." He went on to tell her about a young doctor, a Russian, who could be credited with many complete cures throughout the continent – some of his successes had been in even worse condition than she.

"Worse condition? Really, doctor? Does he revive the dead then?" She asked.

The others insisted they'd never heard of the man, and would have, had there been any validity to the claims.

"Will your doctor entertain me?" She asked. "Does he sing? Or play the piano, perhaps? Is he good-looking? Charming? Witty? If he's any of those things, you may tell him to drop by, but also let him know the magistrate has been pounding at the door, and I don't have an extra sou to pay him."

"He is right out front, *mademoiselle la comptesse*," the Prussian said. Though she had been *technically* married to a young man who would one-day inherit a title, and even now was likely standing outside catching his death in the rain, well aware she had no intention of ever seeing him again, very few indulged her by referring to her as a countess, and the Prussian was the only one who managed it with such conviction. It was another reason she was so fond of the sweet charlatan.

"Well, let him in then, before he drowns out there."

Père Noël went to fetch him while his colleagues expressed more skepticism. When the so-called Russian doctor entered the room, there was complete silence.

Perhaps the other physicians were simply in awe of his beauty, because he was indeed one of the most astonishing creatures she had ever seen. Close to two meters tall. His thick dark hair was flecked with gray though his face was barely lined, and there was a boyishness about his features. His hazel eyes had a stare so piercing she could feel it burn. There was something about his mouth as well, a subtle expression, nothing so obvious as a smirk, but she sensed that like herself, he found the absurdities of the world *très amusant.* Alphonsine nearly gasped, as he was none other than the gentleman she had found in her parlor the night she'd gone in to read.

That it was he, and that she had not dreamed his previous appearance, was immediately clear. She instinctively turned to the small silver cross, which now hung on the wall beside the bed. His eyes followed hers to the object, and she saw the slightest smile part his sensuous lips.

"Good evening, mademoiselle. I am Dr. Anton Kerensky, at your service." He clicked his heels, a tad dramatically. She understood he meant the gesture as a joke that only she would understand. She had met Russians before. Those well off enough to visit or stay in Paris usually spoke the language quite well, but he spoke it better than most Frenchmen.

"Good evening, *monsieur le doctor,*" she said putting out her hand. She didn't know how he could have gotten into her flat the night she'd found him there, or what he was after then or in the present, but she didn't believe he meant to harm her.

The doctor took her hand in his, and touched his lips to it. She felt a shiver of pleasure run through her body, to the point that she moaned involuntarily.

"Are you in pain?" The British doctor asked.

"No, no pain," she said, and turning to the Russian added, "You look familiar. Have we met before?"

"Not formally. I did catch a glimpse of you at the opera last night. I came to France, to Paris, specifically to see you, having heard both of your beauty and your plight."

He asked the others to leave the room so he might examine the patient privately.

All of them objected, but she sent them out. England harrumphed, while France spoke of impertinence, and Prussia simply shrugged.

He shut the door and locked it. Then he sat down in the chair by her bedside.

"Who are you?" She asked softly, aware there might be lingering ears nearby.

"I told you. I'm here to help."

"And the other night?"

He took hold of both of her hands. "You aren't shaking," he said. "You aren't afraid?"

"Of you? What's the worst you might do? *End my suffering?*"

His lips didn't move, and not a sound came out of his mouth, but she heard the next question in her mind as clearly as she had ever heard anything. *"Is that what you've decided?"*

She answered him back with words, "I have no wish to hasten my death, nor to live on the terms you've offered."

"I have no desire you make any decision with which you are not comfortable. I only hope to continue our negotiations. You might change your mind," he said quietly.

Impulsively, she reached up, embraced him, and pressed her lips to his. It was not a calculated gesture on her part. The inside of his mouth tasted cool and clean, and as he wrapped his arms around her frail body, she felt both comfort and intense desire.

She reached out to undo his suspenders. Even in her weakened state, she was quite capable of taking down a pair of trousers with one hand. He gently pushed her arm away.

He lifted her peignoir, under which she wore nothing. First he began to massage her décolletage, working down to her breasts. She coughed a bit when he pressed on her chest, but felt the beginning of a release, a lightness. His strong smooth hands continued to travel down her body, reaching her abdomen and finally below. He placed his fingers inside of her, expertly moving them as he looked into her eyes. She started to moan softly and begged him to take her.

"You aren't strong enough," he whispered. "Just allow yourself to be pleased."

He seemed capable of reaching places inside of her that no one had touched. With her eyes closed she imagined herself as a piano being played by a maestro.

"You're quite the virtuoso," she murmured. She thought she would lose her mind with happiness. Young Olympe was eager, but lacked these skills, and most of her lovers had never been particularly concerned with *her* pleasure.

"Some people believe," he said in a voice that managed to be soft, but deep and masculine, "that there are certain … healing humors of the body that may be released by pleasure."

Her sighs she feared might be loud enough for someone listening by the door to overhear. She couldn't help herself. With his free hand, he placed a finger on her mouth, gesturing for her silence, and when she could not control her murmurings, he muffled the sound with his hand.

Her climax was long and intense.

After she had had enough, he lifted the hand that had been working so diligently, and began first to lick his own fingers. Then he offered them to her to suckle, which she did as greedily as a grateful kitten.

She sat up in her bed. Her breath was short, and he brought the basin over to her in case she needed to cough.

"Thank you. It's not so bad now."

He touched her cheek. "There's no need to suffer like this. You should never have to."

"Who *are* you?" She asked him again. "*What* are you?"

"If you accept my offer, there will be time for you to learn everything. If you do not, it's not worth wasting the time you have left to explain."

"How could I see others destroyed so that I might live?"

"I can only tell you, you would feel no pangs of conscience. You would be so above these creatures it would be no different than slaughtering a pig for Christmas."

"Creatures? Am I such a creature? You would take my life so easily?"

He caressed her, beginning at her forehead and lingering over her neck. With his hand hovering by her chest, her breath began to feel freer as though he were somehow lifting the blackness from her lungs.

"There is none like you. That's why your death would be such a pity. Beauty such as yours is a gift to the world. I only wish to preserve it."

"No, no *monsieur*. I cannot accept your terms."

"I should like to visit you again, to attend you as a doctor. May I?"

She took his hand in hers and brought it to her lips, kissing each of his fingers. "I would love for you to *attend* me, though I doubt I'd have the strength to …"

"It doesn't matter," he said. "I can comfort you even if you have little strength left. It would give me pleasure."

"I've had men give me jewels, and great amounts of their fortunes, but I've met no man as *generous* as you."

"Then might I suggest you've been with the wrong men?"

"I shan't change my mind if that's what you are hoping."

"I won't force you to," he assured her.

"Will you stay a bit? I could send for some dinner?"

"Another time. There are matters to which I must attend."

"When will I see you again?"

"Soon. *A la prochaine, madame la comtesse*," he said, taking her hand again, and kissing it gently before taking his leave.

ॐ ✿ ॐ

One afternoon several weeks later, Alphonsine, who had fallen asleep with a book by her side, woke to the sight of her neighbor rummaging through her wardrobe.

She coughed. Not one of her fits, but just to make clear she was awake.

With no sign of embarrassment, Clarice turned to her. "Oh you're up. I just came in to check on you."

"Yes, I'm right here."

"Where else would you be?" Clarice asked. "I thought I might look for … Ah, here it is!" She turned, victoriously waving a green silk scarf. "Remember when you wore this to the ballet?"

"I'd had an awful row with … was it Stackelberg?"

"Exactly! The old goat was threatening to cut you off."

"Now he won't even answer my letters."

"It's so fine," Clarice said, rubbing it against her cheek.

"Would you like to borrow it?" Alphonsine asked, knowing that was precisely what Clarice wanted.

"That would be so kind of you. Yes, maybe for a week or so." She began to wrap it around her wide shoulders.

Alphonsine wondered how long it would take for the old hag to completely empty her wardrobe. She closed her eyes and imagined herself recovered, in a courtroom, wearing rags and trying to explain to the judge that her friend had "borrowed" all of her clothes.

She started to laugh out loud.

"I don't see what's so funny," the older woman said.

"Clarice?"

"Yes?"

"You've been a good friend," Alphonsine replied.

The sudden sincere statement unsettled both women. They had practiced a profession that didn't allow for sentiment. Each of them understood the terms of their relationship, even if they never spoke frankly about its boundaries. Clarice would make herself useful to

Alphonsine. She would introduce her to well-connected men. She would fetch things from shops when Alphonsine wasn't well and Clothilde wasn't available. She would, when necessary, act as a go-between – delivering notes and messages. There were other tasks as well, and in return Alphonsine would loan her a few francs, or more than a few, never to be repaid, or let her borrow a hat (usually last season's) or some other item she likely would never see again.

Clarice was plump and wrinkled, probably near fifty, her true age being a mystery she would likely take to her grave. Long ago she had been the favorite of a certain judge, and for a time the mistress of the famous father of Alphonsine's dear Alexandre. Sometimes, catching a glimpse of her neighbor, listening to her little schemes, Alphonsine wondered whether she was not better off dying while she was still young and beautiful. She thought it unlikely her fame or infamy would last after her death, yet might that be a kinder fate than growing old and being forgotten? Surviving long after her only means of earning an honest living was gone? Hobbling along the boulevard without even being noticed?

"Thank you, darling. You have been almost like a sister," Clarice managed to garble, and then she quickly changed the subject, and asked about the handsome doctor. "That Russian who's been coming so often and sending you flowers. What exactly is he doing for you?"

"It's not *what* he's doing," Alphonsine quipped, "It's *how* he's doing it."

"My dear, if I didn't know you better, I'd say you were falling in love with him."

Was she? Was such a thing still even possible?

After Clarice had gone, she found herself pondering the question of "love."

She certainly looked forward to seeing the mysterious "doctor." She enjoyed his regular "treatments," which he still would not allow her to reciprocate although she longed to. She was amused by the little gifts he would bring her in addition to the three camellias that arrived daily. There might be a dessert from Belmont, a wooden figurine in contrast to all the ivory, silver, and crystal on her shelves. Once he'd brought a book of poetry, in English, untranslated. She told him it was a language she barely spoke, and couldn't read. He explained the gist of what he was going to recite and then read aloud to her in a way that enabled her to catch almost every word. She applauded his performance.

"When one has an endless supply of time, it becomes easy to master languages," he told her.

The day before, he had brought her chocolates.

The Breton and the English doctors had forbidden her from having sweets, but they didn't know. It was one of the secrets they shared.

Was that *love*? The sharing of secrets? No, it couldn't be that. She had *been* many men's secret, and no love had been involved.

She wondered whom among her patrons would attend her funeral. Probably not many would dare. Would respectable women come to throw stones at her casket? Bring their daughters so that her death might serve as a cautionary tale?

Liszt would not be there. Last she heard he was in Egypt, or was it some other exotic locale? What was one woman to him when all the women in the world seemed to suffer for the love of him? The papers had even coined a word for the hysteria he engendered. She loved him as sincerely and strongly as she'd loved any man, and once believed he had loved her as well, at least until his aristocratic mistress called him home. More recently she reached a different conclusion. Making love to the notorious Marie Duplessis had been for him only something to check off on a list of Parisian landmarks and activities. Visit the Louvre, dine at L'Arbre à Cannelle, go to the opera, fuck the queen of the demimonde. She had written him letters, lightly referring to her decrepit state, joking about her imminent death. He hadn't answered, even when she wrote more frankly and directly of her hope to see him just one more time before she died. The thought of it brought bile into her throat. She could imagine him reading of her demise, looking up from his coffee, a forlorn expression on his handsome sensitive face. Then one of his dear children would tug at him, and the reason for his sadness would be forgotten.

She doubted Alexandre, her dear Adet, would watch them put her in the ground. He had been her first deep *amour du coeur*. She was then still a teenager, supported at the time by de Guiche, though the count was losing patience. She told Adet he should feel no guilt if she chose to love him while another was keeping her.

"It's silly. Imagine I was married to him. Would it trouble you then?"

He told her it would have, and that made her see him differently, not as a man with a finer moral sense than herself, but as someone

71

who would never fully understand her or accept her. She could feel her passion for him growing, but he would always think of her only as a possession. He wasn't comfortable using some*thing* that belonged to someone else. Her *feelings* for him didn't enter into it.

It was a horrible realization, almost as bad as drowning in your own blood with every breath – to conclude that what you felt so deeply, what you had been so sure of, was not reciprocated.

She had offered to live off Alexandre's income, though he was struggling to establish himself and had only a small allowance from his wealthy father. He told her such an arrangement would be unfair to *her*. They argued, and it was she who sent him away. Later she realized it was he who wanted the break. She had thought him young and naïve – far less worldly than she was, but he had orchestrated it so smoothly it only *seemed* like it was her choice.

She understood finally, that while she had given all of herself to him, he had always held something back. He could not bring himself to truly love a woman such as she. Others had warned her most men would never forget her past, or forgive her for it. They'd been right. Even as she left life behind, she wondered if she had only been a simple country girl, Rose Alphonsine Plessis, if she had not become Marie Duplessis, would he have loved her then, and for always?

Of course not, she concluded. Alphonsine was vulgar, barely literate, and had never had the opportunity to be either sweet or innocent.

After it was over, she never let anyone see how much Adet had hurt her, never hinted at what he'd meant to her. She always made sure to greet him cordially, but not too warmly when they ran into each other at the opera, or some other public place. She never spoke of him unless his name came up, and then only implied they were acquainted. She had believed that Alexander Dumas *fils* would be a great man someday, perhaps even better known than his father. That she had once dreamed she would be by his side, his mistress, maybe more, seemed so silly now. *Could it really have happened only four years ago?*

Clothilde entered the room with a tray. There was some fresh soup sent to her by the owner of La Grenoble, one of her favorite bistros.

"Take it away. I can hardly taste anything."

"You must try," begged Clothilde. "I'll leave it on the table."

"Did any letters come today? Any notes?"

"No letters," her servant replied. "And a note only from …"

She didn't need to say it. Alphonsine knew from her tone. The note came from her "husband," Count Édouard de Perregaux, Ned, who left one every day, along with freshly cut roses, which only made her sneeze.

"Is he out there now?"

Clothilde looked down, a bit embarrassed. "Yes, mademoiselle. He only wants …"

"Please don't lecture me. What can I do? I've told the little sap I only married him to impress Franz with a title. He thinks I blame him because his family had it annulled. If he wanted to forgive me for being so awful, I would let him up in a minute. But he begs me to forgive *him*, as though the dolt had done me a great wrong. The deluded fool still wants my love, and I cannot give him that. It's so tiring. I won't pretend so he can make a saint out of me and mourn for all the rest of his days."

Clothilde nodded.

Alphonsine looked at the untouched soup in front of her. "Put this in the mug with the broken handle, and bring it out to him with some bread. I won't see him, but I don't wish him to starve out there."

"Yes, mademoiselle," she said, not hiding a smile.

The sun was low in the sky. Anton never came before dark, but he never came very late in the evening. She asked her servant to bring over her hairbrush and the hand mirror, and help her ready herself for the arrival of *monsieur le doctor*.

❦

He brought her nothing that night. Before beginning his usual ministration, he placed a hand on her forehead.

"You're burning up."

"Yes. It's a sign of dying."

"How can you joke when I've offered you a gift men would give up kingdoms to buy?"

"Then go make your offer to the king."

"I don't want the king. I want *you*."

"Then take me," she said lewdly imitating the style, and mocking the accent of one of her professional rivals. "But just my body. Leave my soul alone," she added.

He began this time with his mouth between her legs, every bit as skilled with his tongue as he was with his fingers. He left her writhing on the edge of ecstasy, and then for the first time he allowed her to unbutton his trousers. His cock was impressive – long, hard, and flawlessly straight.

He entered her slowly and moved with expert control.

She was sweating, her fever high, her body burning against his, which was always so cool and dry.

"I haven't bathed in weeks," she said.

"It doesn't matter. I adore the stink of you. You smell like life itself."

She used no special tricks, demonstrated none of her skills, simply allowed herself to be taken, to be loved as though she were any woman. They were in perfect synch, finally reaching the same place at the same time.

After, he gently wiped down her body with a clean wet cloth.

"My sweet one, there is not much time for you to decide," he said.

"Please, let's not talk of this now." She felt faint.

"There may be no other chance."

"Have I given you false hope?" She asked.

"No, you have been very honest. It's only I fear you will change your mind when it is too late."

"You think I'm growing weaker then? That I will die soon?"

"Yes," he said bluntly. "There are arrangements that must be made if we are to leave together."

"Leave *Paris?*"

"If you accept my offer you would need to leave the city."

"Forever?"

"For a good long time."

"Paris has been the best home I've known. Leaving would be a death in itself."

"You would need to start anew in another place. You would not be known as Marie Duplessis. Everyone would believe you had died."

"And telling me this is how you hope to persuade me?"

He was sitting in the chair by her bed now. Holding both of her hands in his. "No, I'm telling you this because our kind never lie to each other, and no matter what you decide I already consider you one of us."

"Will you tell me more then? About *our* kind?"

74

He pulled away. *"Mon Dieu.* You're good. Do you know how long it's been since a mortal woman has twisted me in such knots? No, Alphonsine, while I feel you are like one of us, I still have certain obligations to my community – a community that would love to welcome you as a sister, a daughter, as everything. But you are not that yet, and we do not speak of our existence to mortals. I've already said far more than I should."

"Don't worry. My discretion is legendary."

"You can't lie to me. I can see into your mind, your soul. I know despite the act you put on you are afraid. You poor child."

"The answer is still no, *monsieur.*"

He got up.

"Are you going?"

"Yes. I must."

"Will I see you again?"

"I hope so," he said taking leave of her.

He did not come to her the next day or the day after that.

When the Prussian doctor stopped by a week or so later, she asked, "Is Doctor Kerensky still in Paris?"

"Hasn't he been to see you? I'm sure I don't know his whereabouts. Have you written him?"

"No, I have no idea where he stays," she admitted.

"Well, if I run into him, shall I tell him to call on you?"

"It's not important," she said.

Her fever was constant by then, and her frame so horribly thin she'd asked Clothilde to cover her dressing room mirrors as she had no wish to confront her ever more skeletal visage. It was becoming difficult to distinguish reality from memory and fantasy. She wasn't sure what part, if any, of her time with Anton had been real.

Christmas Eve came and she heard the bells at midnight mass. On Christmas Day, the young priest stopped by, visiting her in her boudoir, as she was too weak to make it into the parlor.

She watched as he entered slowly as though he were about to be struck down by the hand of God – his eyes as wide as a child's as he took in her finely carved bed, its pink canopy, and all her furnishings. She wanted to be good in his presence, to resist the urge to make a quip regarding the wages of sin.

He noticed the cross. "You have it."

"Yes, that. Weeks ago." After a pause she added, "It comforts me." That was not true, but it would please him to hear it.

He offered to hear her confession.

"I've hardly had the opportunity to falter since the last one? Have I?"

"Whether great or small, God is watching."

She wondered what to tell him, debating whether or not to include her recent fornication with Kerensky. If he was in fact a supernatural being would that make the sin worse? Then the urge to cough came on strongly and quickly. To her horror, she had spewed blood onto his cassock.

"I'm going to burn for this. I'm going to burn," she yelled.

He kept telling her it didn't matter, but she screamed for Clothilde and ordered her to find something they could sell to get him a new one.

Her maid and the priest both insisted it could be washed. A note was sent straight away to the laundress.

Alphonsine was certain the stain would never be lifted, but felt too weak to argue. She closed her eyes and became aware the priest was anointing her, giving her the last rites.

"Not yet," she mumbled before losing consciousness.

She did not die that day, or the next. Another week passed. Sometimes she could swear she heard Death himself approaching, stepping down her hallway, using his sickle like a walking stick.

Still, she felt a heat inside of her, and longed for Anton's embrace. If he could read her thoughts, why hadn't he come? But how could he read her thoughts? *How could that be real?* Sometimes, very late at night waking from a dream, she sensed his presence, but when she opened her eyes she could never find him.

As the new year began, she didn't always know where she was or when, but then it would come back to her. She had a small celebration the night of her birthday though few came, and she hardly left the room. Passing that milestone, she felt both a sense of relief and of dread.

One evening, after a particularly intense dream, She opened her eyes. The room was not dark. Clothilde had left a lamp lit and was sitting in an upholstered chair recently moved into the boudoir. She was asleep, her knitting in her lap. Alphonsine desperately wanted a drink of water. There was no cup within her reach and she wasn't sure she had the strength to speak loudly enough to wake her servant.

Then she saw him. When had he even entered the room? He was standing behind Clothilde. She watched him put his hands on the sleeping woman's shoulders. The maid's eyes opened. She looked startled, but only for a second. Before she could turn around, he bent down and seemed to kiss her, very briefly on the neck. Then he whispered into her ear. Her hands slipped from her lap to her sides. The knitting fell to the floor. Her eyes rolled around one time, and then shut. She began to snore.

"She won't wake up until daylight," he said to Alphonsine, as he poured some water from the pitcher on the end table. He held the cup to her lips and tilted it for her.

After draining the glass, she whispered, "But how?"

"It's nothing but a magic trick. I'll teach it to you."

"I am having a lovely dream," she decided. She hoped he would make love to her again. She tried to will herself to feel well, which usually worked when she realized she was sleeping, but she couldn't do it this time. "Please love me," she pleaded with all the strength she had.

"You're so frail. I fear to."

"Please," she said desperately.

He pulled up her peignoir and began to caress her. She burned for his touch. When he ran his fingers lightly over her thighs, her body quaked, and then he placed his head between her legs and began to lick very softly. Awake or asleep, real or fantasy, she hoped she would die like this, in a moment of perfect pleasure. Just before she would have reached that point, he stopped, raised his head and asked, "Will you accept my ..."

"Yes," she shouted, "Yes, I want to live forever."

"You understand the ..."

"Yes, yes. Do it." She pushed his head back down, and gave herself over to him in a way she could not have imagined.

Chapter 2

She felt a cold compress against her forehead, and heard a soft voice call her name.

When she opened her eyes, Alphonsine saw a beautiful woman with long lustrous dark hair. She thought she was in heaven, gazing on the countenance of the mother who had left her so long ago. She felt great joy that God had accepted her repentance.

"Mama, I'm here," she said already drifting back into unconsciousness. She felt a light tap against each cheek.

"Try to stay awake, dear. You must eat."

Eat. As her disease had progressed, food had lost its flavor. She hadn't felt hunger for months, but now she was famished. She knew then she wasn't dead.

The dark-haired Madonna turned to a servant standing by the door and said, "Bring her something."

Alphonsine noticed a window and through the glass the glow of a not quite full moon. The scene became clearer as she blinked. Her vision, which had never been especially sharp at distances, was suddenly quite acute.

She became aware of her surroundings. She was lying in a bed with freshly laundered linens and soft pillows filled with fluffy down. The blanket was warm and free from moth holes. The room was not large, and the furnishings plain. There was a bookcase in a corner. Although there was only a single lamp lit, she could make out the titles – *A Tale of Two Cities, Candide.* She owned copies, but these were not the same editions, and she was not at home. This was not the infamous bed with the pink satin canopy. There was no wallpaper, and very little decoration of any kind.

She had a strange feeling as though she had woken up after a night of too much champagne. Only she was certain it was not one evening she had forgotten, but a much longer period of time. She was startled by the size of the breaths she could take. Her lungs felt clear. There was no dizziness although when she tried to get out of bed, the beautiful lady warned her, "You're not as strong as you think. Not just yet."

The servant, an older peasant woman, returned carrying a ceramic bowl on a silver tray. She put it down on a table near the bed. The lady dismissed her with a wave of her hand, and brought the bowl to Alphonsine.

"Take it," she said.

Alphonsine took the bowl in both hands. There was no spoon.

"Drink."

She did as she was told. The tepid liquid had a metallic taste, which was somehow familiar. Alphonsine could not judge the flavor as good or bad. She only knew she needed to get it into her system and felt a sense of warmth spread throughout her body once she had drunk it down.

When she finished, she made the most unladylike belch.

The lady laughed, but beyond the laughter there was something kind in her face. It seemed to glow, to radiate love. "We were all concerned about you," she said. "We almost never take one so ill. Minutes from death, I've been told although *he* has been known to exaggerate. And you were out for so long. The journey could not have been easy."

"I don't remember it."

"You barely stirred. He said he had to feed you every night, like an injured bird that fell from a nest. You didn't even open your eyes, but he told us you drank greedily." She clapped her hands loudly, and the servant appeared again. "Get more," she commanded.

"Is *he* here?" Alphonsine asked.

"No. He had matters to attend to. I'm sure you'll see him soon. He comes when he can."

"Then this is *his* house?"

The woman smiled. "You are in the *L'Abbaye des Âmes Perdues*. This belongs to us, all of our kind. It's your patrimony, Alphonsine. You are home with your true family."

"Our kind," she repeated softly. She understood she had been transformed. But to what? Had she accepted Anton's offer? She had been on the edge of delirium those last weeks, and might have said yes to anything. *But to survive on the death of others?* Had she agreed to *that?*

The servant appeared with more of the liquid, which she

downed quickly.

"It feels so good to be able to breathe again," she said.

"It's better when you don't have to," her new friend replied.

Alphonsine reached out and touched the woman's face. Her skin was soft and cool. "You're real," she said.

"Very. My name is Ana." She took Alphonsine's hand from her cheek, and began to kiss it, her eyes locked on Alphonsine's.

Alphonsine knew women in her profession who secretly preferred the company of other women to any of their patrons. While she had had lovers who enjoyed watching women together, the desire to be with one of her sex was not strong in her, yet there was something about Ana that made her very much want to kiss her, to lay with her in her arms.

Ana seemed to sense this and leaned in, "You may kiss me if you'd like. Nothing is forbidden here."

Alphonsine reached up, and with her tongue, explored the inside of Ana's cool mouth. Something in the taste of her reminded her of Anton, and she imagined he was watching them. When Alphonsine tried to grab onto Ana, to bring her down onto the bed, Ana pressed her away gently.

The servant returned, shuttered the window, and moved a thick black curtain to cover it.

"You're going to have feelings, desires, stranger and stronger than any you've known," Ana said. "There's no shame for us, but it's almost daylight, and you must rest. Tomorrow our lessons will begin."

"Lessons?"

"There's much for you to learn about our kind."

"Anton wouldn't tell me anything."

"He was not at liberty. Our secrets keep us safe. The less mortals understand of our true nature, the better."

"But what are we?"

"The enlightened say we are superstition. The imbeciles believe we are devils, dirty creatures, revenants, dead flesh that walks among the living, frightened away by a crucifix or a string of garlic, burned by their so-called holy water. They say we sleep in coffins and will turn to ash in the sun. They call us many names – *nosferatu, estrie, mullo, succubus, strigoi, vampyre.*"

"But this is not what we are," Alphonsine said feeling the words had been put into her mouth, though she wasn't sure by whom, or where, or when.

"Of course not. Those are tales to frighten children."

"Then what …?"

"We call ourselves *divos*. We are gods."

∾✦∿

When next she woke, she was in a different, larger room though she had no memory of how she had come to be there. Either someone had moved her as she slept, or she had become a somnambulist. The new quarters were closer to what she was accustomed to. The bed had a proper canopy – a bit faded perhaps, but it would afford her a little privacy. There was a marble fireplace with fine inlay and a full warm flame. An open door led to a private bath. The walls were stylishly papered. A few small paintings had been hung, which included a watercolor. She rose to examine it, confirming it was indeed the same portrait of her that had adorned her foyer until a few months earlier when she had asked Clothilde to sell it before the creditors put it in their catalogue.

She not only felt stronger than she could remember ever feeling, but it was as though her body were somehow lighter as well. She began to spin around like a ballerina and kicked up her leg effortlessly, stretching it higher than she'd ever gotten it before. She walked out to a small verandah. Snow and icicles hung off trees. The forest before her glittered like crystal. She could feel the blustery wind whip through her light peignoir, but it didn't bother her. She had an urge to leap, to run into the woods.

"I can show you around the grounds if you'd like," said a gentle voice behind her.

It was Ana. She'd entered the room as quietly as a nun, and handed Alphonsine a cup with more of the warm liquid.

Alphonsine drank it greedily, not realizing how thirsty she had been.

Ana reached out and touched her cheek. "You look well."

"I feel so strong," Alphonsine replied. The touch of Ana's hand against her skin ignited feelings within her. She had taken pride in always being able to read situations, but felt unsure of herself in this place.

Ana clapped for a servant. The girl was younger than the one Alphonsine had seen the previous evening, but looked like she might

VM Gautier

have been her sister or perhaps her daughter. In addition to coloring and features, both shared a blankness to their countenance.

"This is Sara. She is to be yours. Later, I will show you how you must … *care* for her." Ana turned to the girl. "Draw mademoiselle's bath. Make sure the water is hot."

As the tub started to run, Ana explained, "We're quite up to date here. We have running water, and as you'll see a heater.

The girl continued to watch the tub. It was Ana who helped Alphonsine undress. Alphonsine noticed a full-length mirror and caught a glimpse of her body. She let out a gasp of surprise.

"What's wrong?" Ana asked, looking at the reflection as well.

"I lost some weight when I was ill. It seems to have come back. My breasts were as flat as crepes."

"Does it please you?"

She turned around twisting her head to see her backside. "Yes. But it seems odd."

Ana smiled and flushed slightly. Alphonsine noticed the way her eyes lingered on her body.

"We have a way of filling out … in the right places." She paused before adding, "You'll see that in the gentleman as well."

Alphonsine felt herself color, or rather she felt modesty meant she should color at such a remark, and once the thought came to her she blushed. She "unthought" it and felt the color drain. She looked into the mirror and began practicing – flush, not-flush, flush, not-flush.

She could not remember ever being able to do *that* before.

Ana said, "There's a lot we can control – respiration, the speed at which our hearts beat. Much more. If you think of heat, your body will warm. We can even fool their doctors with practice."

Alphonsine climbed into the tub. The water was quite hot, but felt incredibly comforting.

"I shall leave you to enjoy your bath," Ana said. "Sara will remain outside this door to help you. You need only clap when you are ready."

"But …"

"There are dresses and things in the wardrobe. We aren't very formal here. You may wear what you like, and Sara can lead you to the drawing room. I'll meet you there. Perhaps we can enjoy a walk through the gardens."

Alphonsine ducked her head under the water, something she

had liked to do even as a child. She was anxious to see how long she'd be able to hold her breath. After what felt like several minutes, she stopped, not because she felt the need to come up for air, but because she had become bored.

When she clapped her hands, Sara came in and took a large towel that was hanging, wrapping it expertly around Alphonsine's body.

"Thank you," Alphonsine said as the girl helped her put on a robe. They walked to the dressing area. Alphonsine sat down. There was a face mirror in front of her and several beauty implements. Sara brushed out Alphonsine's hair, and began to gently wrap strands in soft paper for ringlets, as expertly as if she'd been doing such work for years.

"You know I was terribly poor when I was a girl," Alphonsine said, watching Sara through her mirror, "and people tell me I am entirely too intimate with my servants. So you mustn't mind too much if I babble."

The girl said nothing. Nor did her expression change.

"How long have you been in this house, Sara?"

"I don't know, mademoiselle."

"How far away is your home?"

"I'm not certain."

"Do you have family? Do you miss them?"

"I can't recall, mademoiselle."

"You can't? How unusual. Tell me Sara, do they treat you well here?"

"They treat me well."

"And Mademoiselle Ana, what she said about caring for you. It sounded so odd. Do you have any idea what she meant?"

"No."

There seemed little point in continuing the conversation. The girl did not smell of drink and completed her tasks competently, but seemed to be suffering from some defect.

Sara continued to be useless when it came to assisting in picking a dress. Unlike Clothilde, who was quite a skilled seamstress, the girl appeared to have no sense of color or knowledge of style.

"Are there men staying in this house?" Alphonsine asked, as she would have dressed more casually if it were only women.

"Yes."

But why should that matter? Anton had told her she would be rich, but hadn't exactly said how. Was she expected to be his mistress? Did he have a wife? Or was he planning to pass her off to some other gentleman, and would that gentleman be staying downstairs?

She chose something simple in design though the color was a rich burgundy.

"You may show me to the drawing room."

Stepping into the hallway, Alphonsine was aware she was in a great house. She had read of castles like this, but had only been inside one once when she was with Ned. They'd run off and had a civil marriage in England where they were received by some lesser lord and his family who had no idea who she was. Even that house was less grand than this. As they descended the stairs, she noticed the portraits. All the faces were of people who looked young and very beautiful. Two seemed to be of Ana, and one resembled Anton.

Sara led her to the drawing room where Ana was chatting with a blonde-haired woman, who had a delightfully full figure, and a pouty mouth that made her look at once innocent and depraved.

"You look lovely," Ana said standing up to greet her.

"This is ..." Ana turned to the other woman, "What are you calling yourself these days?"

"You may call me Jane. A simple name for a simple lass." She spoke decent French, but with a pronounced English accent.

"Jane has only just arrived after a stay in America."

"Twelve years," Jane said. "It was easy. Out in the towns you can blame the Indians, not that you need to. It's a lawless place, and the cities are full of treasure. You should see the hall ..."

Ana interrupted, telling Jane, "She's still quite new to us. She may find your stories confusing."

"I see." Jane looked at her as one might look at a slow child. Then she took both her hands in her own and kissed her on each cheek. "Welcome sister." She turned to Ana. "One of Anton's?"

Ana nodded.

"Nice pick."

"And that studious, charming fellow in the corner," Ana said lightly, "is Pierre."

Alphonsine hadn't even noticed the man who had been stooped down, looking at books on a low shelf. He rose and came toward her, taking her hand and kissing it.

"Good evening, mademoiselle."

"Marie," she said, keeping in mind their penchant for using

given names.

"I thought you'd gone back to Alphonsine," Ana said.

Jane said, "It doesn't matter. We're always changing our names. But to my true friends, I'm always Jane."

"I guess I shall be Alphonsine while I'm here."

Pierre was slim and tall. He looked a little older than she was, but younger than Anton. His dark hair was naturally curly, as was her own. While he was undeniably handsome, she did not feel an immediate spark, but something more familial.

A servant came to refill their glasses. Everyone was drinking champagne. It was night, but because she hadn't been up long, it felt earlier. Though she hadn't eaten, not even the strange broth Ana had been giving her, she felt no desire for food. She drank the champagne, enjoying the feeling of each bubble popping on her tongue.

"Shall I show you the gardens?" Ana asked.

As they made their way towards the front door, Alphonsine inquired, "Isn't it rather chilly?"

"We shan't need cloaks. All you must do to stay warm is to think of warmth."

They stepped outside and she saw a wide path had been cleared. The moon was not full, and the stars were obscured by clouds, yet she could see as well as if it had been daylight. There were mountains in the distance and many tall pine trees.

"Where is this place?"

"Just east of the border a bit. In Switzerland," Ana said.

Alphonsine breathed deeply taking in a mélange of scents – snow, leaves, dirt, living creatures borrowing nearby, and larger ones hovering further. They didn't drown out another odor, quite distinct – death, perhaps a freshly dug grave.

"You'll find your senses becoming sharper," her guide told her. "It may be overwhelming. But you'll adjust."

They walked to an enclosed glass greenhouse and entered. There were several lit stoves venting heat. Although there were no lamps, Alphonsine could see the colors of the flowers, some of which were familiar to her, though many were not.

The scents came at her all at once, almost assaultive, but she found with concentration she could make out each one distinctly – rose, begonia, dandelion, and something beautifully sweet she didn't know.

"Hibiscus," Ana told her without her needing to ask. "It grows in the West Indies. Someone brought us back seeds."

"It's lovely."

They continued their tour. There were some enclosures with small creatures – lizards and snakes of types she hadn't seen before. Ana told her the names and from where they were brought.

"You must have questions," her guide said.

Alphonsine felt both relief and anxiety at the invitation to discuss them.

"I can't remember the last time I woke before noon, but here I've slept entire days," she began.

"We wake when the sun sets and are active through the night. As dawn approaches you'll experience an overwhelming desire to rest. If there's even a crack of light through a curtain, you'll feel it, and will be miserable through the day."

"What if I want to be awake during the day?"

"There's almost nothing that cannot be done after dark. You won't *want* to walk in daylight. If it's necessary, there are means."

"Means?"

"Precautions. Daylight will weaken and age you quickly. The senses will be dulled. It's not pleasant. But if you can avoid the direct light of the sun, there are things you can take that will help combat the fatigue."

"What things?"

Ana pointed at the various plants. "Herbs. Concoctions. Poisons that would kill mortals, cause their hearts to explode. For us, they will only act as mild stimulants. Before you leave this place, you will learn what to use."

"You describe *this place* as though it were a school."

"It's more I would hope. A retreat, a refuge you may return to when you are weary from the world. A true home."

"You stay here?"

"For some time, yes."

"How long?"

Ana didn't answer, at least not with words, but Alphonsine understood that it was many years, lifetimes of years.

"Why don't I feel a desire for food?"

"We don't need to feed often. You've been given small amounts, even before you were conscious. Usually, we take a lot at once and may not need more for weeks. But ones so new to us are like baby birds with insatiable appetites."

"More what?" Alphonsine asked, afraid she already knew the answer.

"Come," Ana said as they exited the greenhouse. "Let me show you our woods."

They took a narrow path. She found she could keep her footing easily, and while she could hear the howl of the wind through the trees, and understood it was bitterly cold, neither the wind nor the temperature bothered her so long as she willed them not to. She saw the eyes of a creature peering out beside some bushes, and was startled to realize it was a wolf. Aware of her gaze, it ran away.

"We do not require food or even water for our survival," Ana continued. "There is only one nutrient we must have, though we need little."

Alphonsine and Ana were holding each other's arms as they wandered further. Ana went on, "We must have blood, human blood."

"And that was what you've been feeding me?" Alphonsine asked calmly.

"Yes," Ana answered.

"You killed someone, so that I might live?"

"No, my dear girl. We don't kill when it isn't necessary. The blood needs to come from a living creature. If removed from the body it must be taken within moments or it is no good. Because you are so *young*, you must drink often but can only handle small amounts. That should change now that you are fully awake, but it would have been wasteful to kill your prey when we needed to keep feeding you."

"But how …?"

"Perhaps we should save those details for another time."

"Anton told me we needed to take life to survive. But you're saying we can take blood without killing."

"Anton is correct. We could live, I suppose, by keeping human captives and treating them like milk cows, but that would be infinitely more cruel than a quick and merciful death, wouldn't you agree?"

"I'm not sure. This seems so …"

"We have ways to keep them sedated, but it isn't natural, and it would be wrong to have them in such a state *indefinitely*, sapping their will and taking their very essence little by little, night by night."

"I suppose."

"And besides, we have an instinct to hunt. A desire as strong, stronger at times than the desire to feed. That too must be satisfied."

"But you said, the one I'm feeding from is kept alive."

"Yes. There are actually a few we are using. But it's only until you can feed yourself and handle larger portions, and that will be soon."

"And then they'll be free?"

Ana looked at her for a moment. She sighed slightly before saying, "Of course, *ma chère*. We shall free them."

Neither said anything. They were walking toward the house when Alphonsine next found her voice. "When you say free them, do you mean …?"

"My dear, we will speak of these things again, but not at the moment, please. I understand you play the piano. Pierre is a decent fiddler, and Jane has a beautiful voice. Let's go in, shall we? We have hours ahead of us and should have lovely music tonight."

Chapter 3

Over the next week, new guests arrived. All were beautiful. Most appeared young, while a few had a slightly hardened countenance, and like Anton seemed more mature. They came from countries she knew, and some she'd barely heard of. There was a woman from Japan. Years earlier, a gentleman had shown Alphonsine wood cuts of Japanese women in various positions, and told her that her almond shaped eyes reminded him of the Orient, but never before had she seen anyone so dainty and refined as their visitor. There was a young man the color of *cafe au lait* they said came from Morocco in Africa. While all were friendly, they seemed cautious around her, as though they had been told she was to be given information little by little.

This much she had gathered – while her kind appeared intelligent, educated, witty and genteel, they survived on thievery and deception. Jane had brought with her an actual chest full of jewels. Pierre would be leaving soon for a short visit to Paris to sell some of the goods. The bulk of the money would go into a community treasury, which would help with the upkeep of the abbey. A portion too would go to "the elders." There was some joking about this, with bitterness behind it.

Her senses, as Ana promised, had gained acuity. In particular she noticed the smell of the servants, especially of the one she'd seen the first night, who seemed an older plumper version of her assigned maid, Sara. There was something familiar about her. Alphonsine understood without being told that at least some of the blood she had tasted had come from her. She rarely saw the woman, who was called Jeanne when they called her anything. Passing her in the hallway or on the stairs, she had a great desire to touch her, to lick her, to in some way, *have* her.

From dusk until just before dawn, there was much activity. Moonlight strolls and children's games played by adults in the woods

– hide and seek was a favorite. Indoors they might play chess or charades. Pierre and Jane would read scenes from plays, acting them out expertly. Alphonsine had at times joined in. Among the guests, most played at least one instrument or sang, so the house was often filled with music. As for her own attempts at the piano, she noticed her ability to hear individual notes had improved, and her fingers were more nimble. Sometimes when there weren't too many others around, she practiced.

Just a few hours before dawn one night, Ana invited Alphonsine to see her chamber. Alphonsine was surprised as they walked to another wing of the house, and up a stairwell. When she entered the small room she saw it was simple and much like the one in which she had first woken.

"You live here?" She asked.

"I prefer it," Ana said.

Alphonsine was surprised by the lack of decoration.

"I'm not very complex," Ana added, reading her thoughts. "Have you been hungry?"

"Since you stopped bringing me the blood?"

"Yes, my dear fledgling. I wanted to see if your appetite would develop. Has it?"

"I suppose it has."

"Good." She clapped her hands and both Jeanne and Sara walked in.

There were two wooden chairs in the room. Ana commanded them to sit. They did as they were told. Alphonsine noticed their expressions, or lack of them. There was neither fear nor joy nor sadness, only a far away look in their eyes, completely unreadable.

"Do you sense anything from them?"

"What do you mean?"

"Their thoughts, their emotions. Yes, you will be able to read mortals as well as our kind. It takes both skill and talent, and especially practice and patience – like the piano. Some of us are more adept than others, but all of us have some ability."

"They are … blank."

"That's what comes from keeping them too long sedated. They lose more and more of themselves. In time, it dulls them permanently. Let me show you something," she said moving behind Jeanne's chair.

Ana began to sniff around the woman's face and neck. "See

what I do here," she said as she opened her mouth. Alphonsine could see two of her teeth had grown longer and sharper.

"The smell of them and the taste will lead you where you need to go," Ana explained, licking the woman's neck until she seemed to have found something. She plunged her fangs, but only for a moment and pulled away. Her victim barely stirred.

"Sleep Jeanne," Ana commanded.

Alphonsine watched the victim's eyes flutter as her head fell and her chin met her neck.

"We have a substance. A kind of venom," Ana continued, pointing to her teeth which had already receded and looked normal. As soon as we bite down, it's released into the prey. If we're feeding, it acts as a kind of medicine that kills the pain and relaxes them. But if we pull away without beginning to feed, it allows us to control them."

"I saw Anton do this to my maid, Clothilde. He kept her asleep."

"Yes. Sometimes we can do as much just by speaking to them. Our voices have a mesmerizing effect, but it doesn't work on all of them, and not if they don't trust us. The venom *always* works, and you can ask them to do anything. Why don't you try it now on the younger one?"

Alphonsine looked at Sara who was still impassively staring ahead. She walked behind her and sniffed at the girl's neck. She licked her flesh, and finally began to feel a sensation in her mouth. She realized she'd felt this before, when she was drinking the blood that had been prepared for her. Her canine teeth had grown.

"Just bite, but be very careful. If you taste her blood, it's going to be difficult to stop."

Her mouth found the spot. As she pressed in, a bit of blood squirted onto her tongue, the taste of it a hundred times stronger than the stale brew they'd been feeding her.

"Spit it out. Don't swallow," Ana warned firmly. "Pull away."

It felt like disengaging a strong magnet, but she managed.

"Now tell her to do something."

"Sara, clap your hands."

The girl did so.

"We can do better than that," Ana said. "Sara, would you go to my dresser and take the letter-opener."

She rose and did as she was told.

"Go to your mother and plunge it into her stomach."

The girl started walking toward Jeanne. Alphonsine shouted, "No, Sara. Drop the letter opener now." She turned to Ana and asked, "How could you?"

"She wouldn't have felt it. Besides I knew you would stop her. Sara, sit down."

"They're mother and daughter," Alphonsine said, acknowledging what she had heard.

"Yes. Shall I tell you about them?" Ana asked as she stood beside the chair on which Jeanne was sitting. "She was a country girl, a peasant in Burgundy. She was always, as you see, a juicy thing," Ana said leaning down, and touching the woman's thigh and then her breast for emphasis. "When she was thirteen the landlord took her, whether by brute force or coercion, it was not with her consent, and her daughter was the result. Because he was known to take away his bastard children, and no one was certain what he did with them, she kept the baby hidden, but word spread, so she took the child and ran away.

"As you know, there wouldn't have been many options, and unlike your own mama, she was illiterate and while desirable in a course way, lacked the natural gentility of your line. Eventually, she found herself in a brothel, and when her daughter was ripe, it was her turn to join the trade. The whoremaster beat them both, and enjoyed the idea of mother and daughter sharing their degradation. Anton paid a good deal to procure the pair, offering them a choice of simple freedom or the opportunity to work here as servants. They chose us, so you see this was their destiny.

"I greeted them myself, the evening they arrived. They were so excited, and could hardly believe the feast we had laid out for them in the kitchen. We gave them oranges. From the West Indies. Neither one had ever seen an orange before, much less tasted one.

"They went to their room that night. The fire was warm and there were plenty of blankets. But of course, soon they would have begun to wonder about the strange habits of the household, and so we treated them with the venom.

"The effects are temporary. When they wear off, the memories come back, even if only as strange dreams at first. But if we continue, over time it dulls the mind and the spirit."

Ana was running her hand through Jeanne's hair. She began to stroke her arm, as she continued. "The world did not treat her well.

They might have been dead by now if we hadn't taken them in, but even that would have been better than continuing their wretched existence. Their blood carries the harlot's curse. You'll soon enough be able to distinguish its taste though you needn't worry. It's quite harmless to us. So which would have been worse? Leaving them, or bringing them here, where they've never known fear, or hunger or pain?"

"But ..." Alphonsine began, trying to gather her thoughts.

"It's cruel to leave them like this, isn't it? In a sense they died that first night, after they settled down to sleep and we came to them. They died contented. She was happy she saved her daughter and herself. And little Sara? She might have been imagining *a future* as she slept with a full belly."

Alphonsine recalled a scene from her own adolescence, shortly after she'd arrived in Paris. A man had seen her looking at a street vendor selling fried potatoes and bought some for her. They were by far the best thing she had ever tasted. If she had died when the taste of them was still on her tongue, she would have died in ecstasy.

"To imprison sentient creatures, to take away their will, is not just," Ana continued. "Yet, we must have servants. The abbey does not run itself. But to keep them in perpetuity would be a greater wrong. Wouldn't it?"

"I suppose." Alphonsine said.

"And so we have been brought new servants, and it's time to end their suffering – even though they are already in a state beyond it. If the soul resides in the body, it must be released. Which would you like?"

"Which would ...?"

"For your first feast. I'm here to show you exactly how."

"I don't want ... I don't need ..."

"Of course you do, and what's more we must not keep them like this any longer. It's this one, isn't it?" She asked gently rubbing Jeanne's cheek. "I have no special claim on her. She smells delicious doesn't she? Like the countryside, or an earthy wine. Perhaps not wine, but the grapes themselves, and women with bare feat smashing them. Come ... you must."

Alphonsine went to the woman's side. Ana instructed her to kneel in front of her. Then Ana lifted the servant's dress, revealing two thick muscular legs. There were no undergarments, and the curly hair covering her vulva was the same shade of copper as that on her head.

Ana pressed Alphonsine's face onto Jeanne's thighs. "Smell her leg. Lick it if you'd like. Your mouth will find the best place for the blood. The leg is almost as good as the neck for us and sometimes more convenient."

Alphonsine lacked the will to stop. The scent was overwhelming, course soap and sweat, garlic emanating from the pores – but something more – a sweetness, motherhood, sacrifice, work, and suffering. With her hands she embraced the outside of the flanks below the hips. Her tongue was startled by the salty-sweet taste of the flesh, and then she felt her fangs descending and finding their way to a particular spot on the inner thigh. She bit in and couldn't let go. She felt attached to this woman, as if they were one. The warm liquid flowed into her mouth. She was swallowing quickly, almost desperately, as though she would die if she stopped. She could hear Ana telling her to slow down, to savor.

There was a sensation of heat. She'd felt satisfaction when they had fed her, but this was so much more. She could feel the blood pulsing inside of Jeanne, and through her into her own body, reaching every part of her, flowing and mixing with her own blood to create something new. She could sense bits and pieces of Jeanne's life, maybe from the story Ana told her, or perhaps from the recesses of the woman's mind. There was a sense of intimacy far more intense than any she had ever felt in her life. As Jeanne's pulse weakened, Alphonsine began to feel stronger than she ever had. Her only anxiety came from knowing this experience would end soon, and she instinctively began kneading the woman's thigh – like a kitten pawing at its mother's breast, trying to squeeze out every last drop of milk.

"She's done, child," Ana said. "Enough."

She placed a hand on Alphonsine's shoulder. Alphonsine lifted her head. She looked at the body slumped in the chair and screamed. She began to sob and cried, "*Mon Dieu! Mon Dieu!* What have I done?"

Ana wrapped her arms around her, and touched her face, turning it toward the lifeless woman. "Look at her. You should have seen the moment of her death. You released her. See how beautiful she is. How serene. Look at her eyes. She's finally at peace. You understand now, don't you?"

They both noticed Sara, still standing, staring out blankly, awaiting new orders.

"Sara, go to Mademoiselle Jane. She's waiting for you."

Sara rose, and without even turning to look at her mother's corpse, she left the room.

Alphonsine asked, "Is Jane going to … ?"

"Jane's had a long journey. She needs nourishment."

Ana took a blanket from on top of her wardrobe and wrapped it over Jeanne's body. "Stay here. I'll just be a moment." She lifted her burden as though it were no heavier than an infant, and cradling it in her arms, carried it out of the room.

Alphonsine was aware that despite her initial horror, there was excitement too – a feeling of well-being, *happiness*. She sensed she had pleased her teacher with her accomplishment.

Ana returned. Alphonsine was by now leaning against Ana's bed. Ana knelt beside her, and kissed her on the mouth, her tongue probing for remnants of Jeanne's blood.

"Hmm. Just as I thought. You're lucky to have had her, *ma chère*. We never forget our first." She stroked Alphonsine's hair. "How do you feel now?"

Alphonsine started to speak, but found she couldn't. She wasn't sure she could put her feelings into words. She had just killed, yet she felt no remorse. The act seemed completely natural, and she realized she would do it again and again. She understood this was part of her new life. There could be no going back. Marie Duplessis was truly dead, but who was she then?

Ana hugged her tightly, and having read her thoughts, whispered an answer. "You are Alphonsine. You are *our* Alphonsine."

She helped her remove her dress, then untied her boots, gently pulling each one off, loosened the corset, and finally relieved her of her undergarments. Then she lifted her as though she, like Jeanne, were weightless. She placed her on the bed, covering her with the sheet, but not before commenting, "You have a magnificent body."

Alphonsine sat up and began to wordlessly help Ana disrobe. She was aware Ana was a beautiful woman, but was surprised by the perfection of her figure – her breasts almost but not quite too large for her narrow frame, the nipples a deep rose-brown, the fleshy firm buttocks, which Alphonsine grasped onto, pulling Ana into the bed. First they lay facing each other, and then they began to slowly explore, touching each other's arms, legs, and bodies. They moved closer and embraced, rolling until Ana was on top, the heat building up as they rubbed their montes as though such friction could start a fire. Ana expertly plunged two fingers inside of Alphonsine's vagina, while a third reached into that smaller hole. Alphonsine was grasping Ana's backside with one hand, with the other, she tried to mirror her mentor's movements. Fingers and torsos moved up and down, side to side, sometimes traveling in small circles. When they both reached the summit, when any more pleasure would have been too much, it felt as though they understood each other's thoughts and feelings. It was another blending, a oneness, as it was with the blood.

Afterward, resting in each other's arms, Ana asked, "Do you see it now?"

"I think so," Alphonsine said, rubbing her head against Ana's chest.

"You should stay here tonight. We're always *emotional* afterwards, usually into the next evening."

"I'd like that. Ana, how many have you ..."

"I don't know. I remembered each one at first quite distinctly, but after so many years. The feeling of it doesn't change so much. Occasionally you question. Might there have been a reason *not* to take this one?"

"What kind of reason?"

"Perhaps he or she would have done something worthwhile later, for the world. We try not to take lives that have that kind of potential although not all of us share that view. Some can be very cynical about humanity. Cruel at times, but there's no reason to be. You won't be that way, will you?"

"I'll try not to be."

"We can relieve them of their suffering. We need not contribute to it."

"Ana, do you still think about, remember ... *before?*"

"I have been who I am for so long. The other, those few short years, they seem more and more like a dream."

"It's funny, but I'm already beginning to feel that way."

Ana laughed, "Already? *Meu Deus*, you? The infamous Marie Duplessis?"

"In a year, no one will remember me. They'll be a new girl."

"It won't matter to you."

It was rare, not only for Alphonsine to be so physically intimate with another woman, but to even speak to one who did not share her profession. Respectable ladies would not acknowledge her. Perhaps

96

that was why she was so curious about Ana's past.

"Ana, tell me please what, who were you? What was your life like?"

"Compared to yours, I'm sure it was … uneventful."

Alphonsine kissed her friend's bare shoulder. "Please. I'd like to know."

"None of us are high-born. We seek others who have a kind of natural nobility, but not aristocrats. They are not suited to live in a community where all are equal, and they've given us trouble in the past."

"I don't want more lessons. Just talk to me."

"My father was a painter with some wealthy patrons," Ana began, "This was in Portugal. My mother was an illiterate peasant girl, his model. He acknowledged and supported me, saw to it I learned to read and write, even set aside a small dowry, so that I might be properly married in the church."

"When?"

"A long time ago. From childhood I had a dread of men. There was an uncle who had tried to … It's not important, but it was clear to me as I grew that my feelings for women were much stronger. I also loved to read and to study, and so when the time came, the dowry was given to the church and I joined an order."

"*Sacre bleu!* You were a nun."

Ana turned her head, and seeing the shocked expression on Alphonsine's face, she laughed. "I was a nun. And I was chaste, though I can't speak for every woman in my order. That's not to say I didn't love. There was a novice. She had green eyes and lovely auburn hair. Of course, we covered our hair, but you could see the color in her brows. We never did anything improper. Never even spoke, and certainly didn't touch, but sometimes we'd catch each other's eye. I knew she loved me too. It was enough.

"I was quite content with my life. Jesus Christ was the ideal husband, a man who never actually touched me, and allowed me to work. I loved that even with all of the structure, I had time to myself, to read, to translate texts, to learn about herbs and their healing properties. It was a wonderful existence."

"Then why …?"

"There was a war. The Spanish war. It went on for a very long time. They came. A regiment took the convent. Obviously, we were no threat to them. They wanted our food, they wanted our gold, and they wanted *us*. The mother superior was as shrewd as she was cold, and when threatening their leader with hellfire didn't move him, she *negotiated*."

"How?"

"She offered to give him four young, healthy, free from pox virgins to do with as he pleased if he promised to leave the rest of the sisters in peace. She brought together those of us in their novitiate and also sisters like me who had completed that period, but had not yet taken final vows. We were to draw straws. I was not selected. But my beloved was. When I saw the look of fear in her face, imagined the suffering she would endure, I spoke up and offered to go in her place.

"Our leader was livid, *'You'll go all right. But you don't get to choose a favorite.'* They drew once more to see who would be saved as a result of my gesture. The one who was chosen to stay *happened* to be the niece of our dear reverend mother. It was then I first started to seriously doubt the existence of a merciful God."

Ana stopped there.

"Tell me the rest," Alphonsine said. "How you came to be ..."

"It'll be dawn soon."

"There's time."

"There was an old crone they put in charge of us. She followed the soldiers, selling and trading. They paid her to keep us fed and moving, to ration us, so they wouldn't fuck us to death too quickly. She had a son, stupid but strong as an ox, who would guard us, usually taking a turn with one or all when the soldiers were through. He'd fall asleep on top, and it was a miracle we didn't suffocate. It was made clear if one ran, we would all be killed, and if all ran we wouldn't get far. Two died within the month, leaving myself and the sweet sister I'd tried to save."

Alphonsine was stroking Ana's hair, wondering if she should have let her stop, but she wanted to hear the rest.

"Our insides would hurt so much. It was difficult to walk let alone march to follow the regiment. The old woman had no kindness in her. I tried to protect the girl, to help as much as I could. One night, after they were done, and the idiot son had passed out drunk, I begged her to run away with me. But she said I should go on my own, she was too weak, too sick. That was the only time I ever touched her. To feel her head. She was burning with fever. I couldn't leave her. The next day, when the soldiers broke camp, I begged the old one to let us stay and rest. We could catch up in a few days.

That's not what they're paying us for,' she told me. *Us,* as though she gave us more than crumbs.

'She won't be worth anything when she's dead,' I told her.

'It's in God's hands,' she said. I thought of strangling her then. The oaf would have stopped me of course, and she was strong, but it might have been worth it.

"There was no moon that night. Nothing to break the darkness. We were near each other in a field. I could hear her cries as they were on her, one after the other. They were on me too, but I didn't feel them anymore. And then her yelling stopped, and a few moments later I heard one of them shout, *'I think mine's dead.'* And then they laughed and kept going.

"When our keeper realized they were fucking a corpse, she told them we were done for the night, and she'd speak to the captain in the morning about the need for more girls.

"I asked if she were planning to leave her out there. She told me the oaf would bury her in the morning. I took my blanket and made sure she was covered, and then I started to walk away, back in the direction we'd come from.

'Where are you going? I'll wake my son. He'll kill you,' the crone was shouting at me.

'I don't care,' I shouted back.

"The soldiers burned as they marched. Most of the farms were gone. Still I knew what was safe to eat in the woods. I had a vague plan to go back to the convent and kill the reverend mother. I was half mad at least. Whatever I had been before, I was no longer. I walked for days and nights, mostly in the woods to avoid others – charting by the sun and the stars. Finally, I stumbled upon an abandoned cottage. It was near a pond, and I managed to clean myself. I gathered some wild berries and brought them to a village where I sold them. A tavern owner took me on. I looked too rough for a serving wench, but I'd do to scrub the floors, clean the chamber pots and other such tasks in return for food.

"One night a man arrived at the inn. I noticed him watching me. I had come to almost believe I was invisible, but I could feel his eyes burning into me. I wasn't sure if he was someone I had known. For all I knew, he could have been one of the soldiers who'd had me. It was dark when they came, and I tried not to look at their faces.

"Although I worked from dawn till late into the night, I always walked back to my cottage to sleep. I had no lamp, but I knew the way, even in the dark. I had a feeling I was being followed, and got the knife I always carried ready. I made it to my haven, and walked inside. Someone grabbed me from behind. A hand was over my mouth to muffle my screams – not that a soul would have heard them. He took the knife from me. As soon as he spoke, I lost my fear. There was something about him. He said he could end my miserable existence if that's what I wished."

Alphonsine did not need to ask the identity of the stranger. She was certain it had been Anton.

"I wasn't afraid," Ana continued. "Relieved perhaps. I sensed what he was. I had grown up on stories of creatures who walked by night. I was prepared to be taken, and almost limp in his arms. He asked, *'Are you going to make it that easy for me, Ana Vargas?'*

'If you wanted a challenge you shouldn't have taken my knife.'

'You would have only hurt yourself with that toy,' he replied.

"My eyes were beginning to adjust. I turned my head and saw his face, recognized him as the stranger from the tavern. *'You don't look much like a succubus,'* I said. *'Please get this over with.'*

'Is there nothing you'd like to do before you die? Something you think about all the time? A wish to be fulfilled?'

"As a child, my father encouraged me to read everything. I had even snuck a look at the tales of Scheherazade. So I asked him, *'A wish? Are you a bruxso or a jinn?'*

'I've been watching you, Ana Vargas. I know your hunger for vengeance is stronger even than my thirst for blood. You're smart, and strong, and beautiful. You have no idea of your potential.'

"No one had ever said words like that to me. I felt strangely excited."

"You loved him?" Alphonsine asked.

"You surprise me. Such a romantic! No, I don't think it was love. But I was intrigued. He told me he could make me as he was, and I would be able to hunt down and kill all who had hurt me. He would teach me, help me, fight with me and for me.

"I told him there were too many I longed to see dead.

'It doesn't matter,' he said. *'We have time.'*

'And will killing them be worth spending eternity in hell?' I asked.

'You no longer believe in those fairytales,' he said. *'Besides you won't ever need to die.'* And then he offered me more. I would be able to love whom I wished with no shame. I would have a community – stronger

and more loyal than the one I had left.

'Your kind thrives on death,' I told him.

'But there are so many who deserve to die or for whom death would be a blessing,' he reminded me.

'I do not wish to live as a monster, feeding off others.'

'Very well then. I cannot resist the smell of your sweet blood and all that's within you. It will be painless although I wish to savor every minute and can't guarantee it will be quick. If you'd like you may pray first to that God who's been so protective of you and those you loved. I suppose I'll have to drain you dry and release you from your earthly shell, since you do not wish me to give you the opportunity to feed off of your tormentors.'

'Get on with it,' I said.

'Of course if you joined us, after you have sought your vengeance, I could kill you if you wish. We can be killed. It's just difficult.'

"I managed to wriggle an arm free and raised my hair, exposing my neck for him.

'I am ready to die,' I told him.

"He looked genuinely disappointed. He started to lick the area, perhaps longer than he needed, maybe hoping I would change my mind. And finally he said, *'Ana Vargas, you are too precious to destroy. I'll find another tonight.'*

"He let me go abruptly. I staggered almost falling. He started to leave. I felt I had made a mistake, and was about to tell him, but he heard my thought before it was uttered.

'Say it,' he said taking me in his arms. This time we were facing each other.

'Yes,' I said. *'Yes. Do with me what you will.'*

"And he did."

"Did you seek your revenge?" Alphonsine asked.

"I took the officer who had taken us, and found the man who had laughed at my dead sister. I was going to kill the old lady, but her heart failed when she saw me and realized who and what I was. Even without feeding on her blood I could taste her fear, and it was delicious. As for her son, I snapped his neck as easily as a twig, but didn't even bother with his blood. There were some others too. Anton and I made it to the convent. The mother superior damned me to hell and cried for mercy in the same breath. Then she begged, reminding me in condemning four, she saved many. She asked what I would have done in her place.

"I told her I would let her live, but hell awaited her.

'It awaits you too,' she said.

'Perhaps,' I answered. *'But you'll be there much sooner than I will.'*

Alphonsine was feeling the fatigue that came with the rising sun. "Will you tell more, please? Tomorrow?" She asked.

"Of course, my darling. We don't keep secrets here."

❮⊛❯

It was decided Alphonsine should have fencing lessons. As Ana explained, she needed to learn to control her new strength, coordinate her body. Pierre would be her teacher. They met in the ballroom, which was usually empty early in the evening. It was lined with windows, and on clear nights one could see the mountains by starlight. Alphonsine was given men's clothing to wear, garments she could move about in easily. Despite seeing Ana lift a hefty corpse as though it were a baby, she was surprised by how light the foils felt in her hands. She had never fenced before, never even heard of a woman trying it. The idea seemed absurd, but not uninteresting. She saw how the sport could be like dancing. Pierre was certainly graceful. She kept trying to engage him in conversation, and while he admonished her at first, telling her to focus, he soon gave in.

"Why did you choose this?" She asked, the point of her foil under his chin.

He parried expertly, then thrust. She barely avoided feeling the tip of the blade at her throat. "Why did I choose to be rich and immortal when I could have been struggling for bread with a price on my head?"

"Why did you choose this knowing you would need to kill to survive?" She asked as he forced her to step backwards.

"Killing wasn't new to me."

He had forced to the ground, and hovered over her. There was a moment when she thought of pulling him down to her, into an embrace. Their eyes met and she realized he understood, and might have accepted an invitation to make love. Her kind seemed always ready for that. Instead, she managed to slide her body away from him.

He smiled, and though it was still difficult for her to read his mind, she understood he was amused, proud of her even, and she took the opportunity of his distraction to thrust her foil, touching his chest.

"Tomorrow we try it with real swords," he told her.

Alphonsine looked at him.

"It won't hurt … much," he added, and then he took a small sharp knife and plunged it into his heart.

She screamed.

He laughed and pulled it out. There was a rip in his shirt, but only a few drops of blood. The smell of it was like perfume, and she wanted to lick the wound.

"Hurry," he said. "It'll heal in a moment."

She came over and tore into his shirt. She lapped his blood, watching as the wound closed. He grabbed her by the buttocks as she wrapped her legs around him. He backed into a wall and they struggled with each other's clothes until they both were naked and entwined. Their mouths were locked together, and she felt him inside of her, the movement – *thrust and parry, thrust and parry.*

She hadn't said the words out loud, but he heard them, and taking his mouth off hers, he laughed.

Somehow they made it to the floor with her on top. She used her inner muscles to relax and then tighten, always in control. They kept it going for hours, each somehow holding off climax, turning it into a kind of competition until he whispered, "The day comes."

Alphonsine was amazed by the intensity of her release although it had been equally as strong with Ana. She wondered if it would be like this with mortals as well.

"Sometimes," came the answer.

"Do you know *everything* I'm thinking?" She asked aloud. They were laying side by side.

"Mostly. Even when we met. With you it was easy. Sometimes we find another of our kind with whom we have *simpatico.*"

"And *love?*"

"We all love each other. Not in the way of mortals, the sickness of it, the neediness and jealousy. We share. We separate. We have *time.*"

☙ ✴ ❧

She shared Ana's bed a few times after the night of her first kill, but her mentor could be distant, and was often difficult to find. One evening, Alphonsine set out to look for her. Instead, she ran into Pierre and Jane in the drawing room.

"She's not here." Jane replied in answer to her inquiry.

"Has she left the abbey?"

"I'm sure she hasn't."

"Do you know where she is?"

Pierre suggested they find a fourth and play tennis, and so they walked over to the court.

While it was obvious something was being kept from her, she sensed it would be both impolite and ineffective to press the matter. Despite what Pierre had told her regarding her kind's lack of jealousy, she wondered if Ana had found a new favorite, or whether she had in some way offended her.

They played casually, lobbing the balls back and forth. It was cloudy and the moon not full, but there was plenty of light for her kind. They took breaks and talked while playing. She was teamed with Jane while Pierre played with Jamal – a new arrival, from Morocco. It was clear they shared an intimacy far more meaningful than her occasional trysts with her fencing master.

Jane noticed something too, and shouted, "I know you two haven't seen each other in forty years. It would be perfectly reasonable if you wanted to be alone."

"We can wait till the end of the game," Jamal said. "For that matter, we can wait until the Grand Feast."

Pierre looked at Jane with mock annoyance. "Waiting can sometimes be very sweet, dear sister. But you wouldn't know that."

"Feast?" Alphonsine asked. She had noticed her hunger growing, which was one reason she was so eager to find Ana. She wasn't sure how her need would be provided for.

Jane smiled and said, "Don't worry, fledgling. They'll be plenty for you."

She soon grew tired of the game, and started to wonder how long she would be cooped up in the abbey. Despite her affection for Ana, and enjoyment of her new vitality, she longed to visit the places so many spoke of. Then she heard a familiar voice in her head saying, *"You are not a prisoner, ma chère."*

"Anton," she said, realizing he was near.

Despite herself she raced toward the house, still unsure what she was feeling or how she would greet him. He was the only one who had known her before – her only link with her old life. It was as though seeing him would prove her previous existence had not been a fantasy, but there were other feelings as well. She was sure she was

104

damned. While her time might now be long, an even longer punishment awaited her, and she blamed him for that.

She entered the drawing room, which had the air of a party. There was a quartet she recognized as being part of the new coterie of servants. They were skilled, but it didn't sound like they had played together before. She could smell the venom emanating from their bodies, but even without the scent, their blank expressions and lack of passion would have told her they were enslaved.

She looked around, but didn't see Anton. Jane, now by her side, whispered, "He's probably bathing after his journey. I'm sure he'll be down soon."

There were four strange women in the room, mortals. They were dressed in bright colors and their faces were heavy with cheap paint. There was no doubt in her mind they were common prostitutes, the lowest sort – from a brothel, the type of women one would never see in a house like this. She could not decipher their thoughts, but was aware they *were* thinking and realized they were free of the venom.

Men of her kind were conversing with them. Listening, she gathered that Anton had brought them. They seemed to be trying, rather comically, to pass themselves off as something other than what they were. The gentleman kept referring to them as mademoiselle this or mademoiselle that, fussing over each with exaggerated courtesy. The creatures were idiotic enough to believe they were indeed fooling them. She thought back to highborn men who had treated her as though she were a duchess, complimented her manners, her delicacy. *Had it been a joke to them as well?* A servant came and announced dinner. The men offered their arms to the girls, escorting them to the dining room.

Given how easily they all gave love to one another, she wondered what their purpose might be.

Pierre, like Jane, had followed her into the house and was standing behind her. She heard his words, "Guests of honor," as images of carnage flooded her mind. She understood they were meant to be prey.

"Why is it always whores?" She asked wearily.

"They're easy to procure," said Jane.

"And won't be missed," added Pierre.

"So what do they think they're here for?"

"To entertain the decadent nobility of the household. A wealthy man's folly, and their great good luck," Jane explained. "They're being treated quite well."

Alphonsine was used to discretion, to keeping her true opinions to herself, to going along with the desires of others, but she couldn't stay silent. "Do we *only* feed on women?"

"They are more pliable," said Pierre.

"If it makes you feel better, I can tell you in our entire time in the Americas, we hardly ever touched the whores," Jane said. "At least not the professionals, and of course men can be taken as well."

"It hardly seems fair," Alphonsine said. "They have no chance."

"They're all so short-lived to begin with. What difference does it make?" Jane asked.

Alphonsine said nothing more, afraid she'd already said too much, but her thoughts must have betrayed her.

"And you would starve then?" It was Anton. She hadn't seen him enter the room. Despite herself, when her eyes met his, she felt a longing, an attraction as strong as she could ever remember feeling.

"Or perhaps you'd prefer to dine on kings?" He asked. "If you don't wish to join us for the feast, other arrangements can be made. It's of no importance. From Ana's report I thought you were overcoming your sensitivities."

"Anton, may we speak, privately?"

"Of course, my child. Shall we walk? I'm eager to see what's blooming in the night gardens."

As he offered his arm, she thought of the girls being led out of the room.

"What's bothering you? Aren't they treating you well?"

"Very well. Everyone's been so kind."

"But ... "

"You told me you wouldn't take me without my consent."

"And I had it."

"No, Anton. That's impossible. I would never have ..."

"Marie Duplessis," he said, "Are you now playing the innocent? Like some young lady who finds herself with child, and suddenly claims rape? I am shocked by the pretense."

"But I said no to you a dozen times."

He took her hand and kissed it. "You only needed to say yes once."

"I must have been delirious."

"You aren't the first woman to develop a convenient memory."

They had entered the greenhouse and were sitting on a bench.

"It would have been better to have let me die a natural death."

"Oh please, Alphonsine. I've never seen anyone more resistant to death than you. You wished to live with every fiber of your being. Whether you are willing to admit this to yourself or not, it was *you* who summoned me."

She sat silently, unable to answer his arguments, but convinced he was wrong. She had not wished for this. She had been many things, but a murderer was not one of them, and while she lost no sleep after taking the servant, it was the very lack of remorse, and the knowledge it would become even easier, which troubled her.

"I went to a great deal of difficulty," he continued. "I had to find someone to fill the coffin, a slim dark-haired girl like yourself, and she had to be placed there after the viewing, but before the burial. Later, that boy you used to go around with insisted on digging you up and moving the body. Fortunately, I'd taken the girl's eyes out as they were lighter than yours and might have given away the game. She was quite putrid and he didn't notice the difference. Mortals see what they wish to."

"That poor thing."

"I doubt he'll be joining a monastery."

"I meant the unfortunate girl you killed."

"She wasn't wasted."

Alphonsine stared at the ground.

"My sweet thing, nobody is born a killer – except possibly your fencing master. But you'll learn. You have a quality, an innocence that keeps the worst sins from ever being seen on that lovely face. It's what men paid for." He paused, and then added with the slightest hint of pride in his voice, "And now that quality will be eternal."

"What they paid for was …"

"You have no idea how extraordinary you are, do you?"

He touched her face, stroking her cheek lightly. Despite everything, she wanted to kiss his hand, but held herself back.

"The papers were full of stories," he continued. "The auction for your belongings brought the finest ladies in Paris to your apartment."

"They never would have come when I was alive."

"Alive? Stop talking as though you are some sort of animated corpse. Charles Dickens was there."

"From England?"

"He said it was as though Joan of Arc herself had died. Even though I'm not French, how could I have allowed Joan of Arc to die?"

"It's horrid what we do."

"You know it is not. You're just afraid of what you're feeling."

She said nothing.

"If you really wish to we *can* die. It's just not easily done. Beheading works, so does burning if the fire goes on until nothing is left. It would have to happen during the day, and I'm sure it would be quite painful. Is that what you'd like?"

"You know I'm a coward. Besides, I'm already damned."

"There's no need to pretend to believe in …"

"I'm not sure what I believe, but I assure you I am not pretending."

He withdrew his hand. "I expected to find you happy. You look well. You're free."

"Am I?"

"What an ungrateful child you are."

"Stop calling me that. I'm not a child."

"Then don't act like one," Anton said impatiently. He walked away leaving her to sit among the orchids and other hothouse flowers.

She could see inside the house, the rooms bright with the light of many lamps. In the drawing room, the musicians continued to play, and there was dancing. Meanwhile, the girls were eating heartily in the dining room. Several of her kind had joined them, looking on with hunger and lust.

She sat awhile, and then went to look for Ana whose comfort she sought, but she couldn't find her in her room or anywhere in the house. She asked a servant if she had seen her. The dull-eyed dolt seemed confused by the question. After injecting some venom, she asked again.

"Mademoiselle Ana is in the nursery."

"The nursery? I don't know it. Take me there."

The servant led her outside and took her to a cottage on the grounds. She'd noticed it before, but had not thought about its use. An unlocked door led to a cozy room with several upholstered chairs and a couch. There she found Ana combing the tangled hair of a little girl of about eight, as another even smaller child played with a doll near the fire.

"Good evening, Alphonsine."

"Who are …?"

"Anton had them sent to me. Has he arrived yet?"

"Yes."

"I'll have to thank him. Children, this is Mademoiselle Alphonsine."

"Good evening, mademoiselle. My name is Isabelle," said the child Ana was handling. She curtsied.

"That was very good, Isabelle," said Ana. She gave the girl a chocolate as a reward, which she ate greedily.

The other one barely looked up.

Ana addressed her, "Christine, won't you say hello to mademoiselle?"

The child stared at Alphonsine, then dropped the doll, walked over and hugged her. Instinctively, Alphonsine hugged her back. She had been recently bathed, but Alphonsine could smell her blood, could see it circulating underneath the thin skin, *hear* it, feel how fragile the little thing was, how delightfully easy it would be to crush her in her arms.

"Christine doesn't speak," Ana said. "Anton found them both on the street. That one is a singer. Isabelle won't you sing something for us?"

The child began to warble. Her voice was loud but off key.

"And the other?"

"She'd pass around the cup. They've been here a week and have already fattened up quite nicely."

"How long will they … stay?"

Ana looked at Isabelle, and then at her. Alphonsine understood these things couldn't be spoken of in front of the children.

"Mademoiselle Ana says she is my new mother," Isabelle told her. "And I may stay here with her forever," she added hugging Ana.

Ana hugged her in return and kissed her forehead. Alphonsine noticed Ana's eyes lingering at the child's neck.

"What a good little girl you are," Ana said. "Children, you may continue to play. Mademoiselle and I are going to the kitchen to have some coffee."

"May I go with you?" Isabelle asked.

"No my darling, but I shall bring you back something sweet. Would you like that?"

"Yes, please."

The kitchen had a plain wooden table as might be used for simple dining or food preparation. There was a servant sitting by the stove. After she had poured their coffees, Ana sent her to the main room with two cups of sweet cocoa for the children.

Ana asked, "Aren't they lovely?"

"What will you do with them?"

"Play with them. Enjoy them. Did you ever have children, Alphonsine?"

"I had a boy when I was seventeen. They took him from me, but his father told me they gave him a good home. Later, he told me he died, but I think he only said that to stop me asking to see him."

"The quiet one likes you. She's yours if you wish. Perhaps you can get her to speak?"

"Are you going to drain them?"

"I can't keep them with me forever. But they've never been happier, and now they have hope. You'll see what it's like. One night I will tell them a story and they'll fall asleep in my arms. Sometimes you see a little smile and you know they're dreaming. I'll release them without even a moment of fear or pain. Isabelle was born with tainted blood. Her mother went mad from it. Neither of the children has great beauty, nor intelligence nor any useful talent. What would become of them?"

"But don't you have feelings for them? Don't you become attached?"

"I do, but if I imagine what's ahead, it's easier. Death is hardly the worst thing that can happen. I no longer have faith, but I can't help imagining that peace, if not heaven, awaits them. It's good to have children with you sometimes – to remind you of the cycle of mortality, even if you are no longer a part of it. They have been through so much, yet they retain some innocence. Like you." She reached across the table and put her hand on Alphonsine's. "I can come to your room if you'd like, after they're asleep. I've missed you."

"I would like that."

"Something is troubling you," Ana said, trying to probe Alphonsine's thoughts. "To do with Anton?"

"He thinks I'm an ungrateful child."

"You're still too close to your old life. It will pass. You'll see how it is after you've had more experience. Come. Let's return to the children. They smell so wonderful don't they? Would you like to read to them? I have a copy of Grimm's. They've never had adults read them stories before."

∂◉∽

There was increasing frivolity and debauchery as the feast grew closer. More whores arrived, and it was becoming common to see them fornicating with the males even in the most public places.

Although she had been to her share of orgies, the cheapness of the women, and perhaps knowing their imminent fates, made her uncomfortable. She was spending more time with Ana and the children.

She noticed Isabelle was curious about letters, and had begun to learn them.

"Couldn't we do something for her?" Alphonsine asked Ana. "She seems to have some potential."

"What are you suggesting?"

"I don't know. She could be sent to the nuns. They could teach her and raise her."

"As though *they* could protect her," Ana said bitterly. "Are you forgetting what's already in her blood? She'll be mad before she's grown, and no doubt her bastards will be as well someday. You see her now at her most perfect, but what is to come?"

It was useless to argue.

As for Anton, she tried to avoid him. While she was aware the women he brought were prey, it stung her to see him enjoying their flirtations. Life had taught her to keep her truest feelings private, but now it was difficult to master her emotions, which were not only strong, but impulsive. She had made up her mind to despise Anton for denying her a natural death, for turning her into an insatiable blood-lusting creature. Yet, she reacted to the sight of his making love with other women as though she was his sweetheart, or his wife. She wondered sometimes if she was going mad, if insanity was another part of the price to be paid.

One night, after her fencing lesson with Pierre had again ended with the two of them rolling on the floor enjoying the power of their bodies, she asked him, "Is it expected that I feel so much? Such a storm within me?"

"We're passionate. We feel things more deeply. You'll gain control of it in time. Physical discipline helps."

"Hmm," she said. "I hope so. Most of our kind seem so childish. The men are going after those prostitutes like they'd just been released from a vow."

He laughed. "Mademoiselle, this is what men are like. I thought you of all ..."

"But you haven't been spending too much time with our mortal guests."

"I'm not so interested in women."

"You seem to enjoy *me*."

"You're not mortal. And you are very much like a man."

"Am I growing a penis?" She asked, looking at her genitals, separating the lips of her vulva as though searching.

"If you were it would be huge," he said demonstrating by placing his hands far apart as if he were holding a baguette. "Forgive me if I'm wrong, but from my understanding, you took what you wanted, more in the way of a man than a woman."

"You're saying I was hard. I couldn't afford not to be."

"No. Something other than that or more than that, perhaps. It's easy to see why Anton wanted you to join us."

"Do *we* take on many new recruits?"

"Very few. There were more of us once, long before I came into this world. There was a count and countess, someplace in the east. They offered us great wealth in exchange for immortality, but they were crude, cruel, and obvious. Villagers sacked their castle, and then there was a purge. We became the hunted – burnt or beheaded – sometimes both by people who mistook us for witches or heretics, and took many innocents as well. Anton is among the youngest who survived those times. We call them the elders, and you won't see them here, except for him. Then Anton found Ana. It was her idea we must learn to live so quietly they would forget our existence, and that we must explore our nature to understand our limits and strengths, develop our own laws, work together for the common good."

"The common good?"

"They say there's safety in numbers. But there's also safety in stealth. Ana decided we must not create new *divos* merely because we had become attached to a particular mortal. We must not give in when wealthy or powerful beings discover us and come to us with bribes. Those who get too close need to be destroyed. As for aristocracy, they are useless. Here we believe in liberty, equality, and fraternity. We share our wealth and ..."

"Were all of *us* whores and murderers then? Cutpurses? Swindlers?"

"We all showed certain abilities in our previous lives that would predict success in this one. The ability to be discreet is important, to walk amongst the wealthy or the poor. A certain level of charm is required."

"And beauty," Alphonsine added.

"Would you wish to spend eternity with someone ugly? Besides, beauty is a kind of currency, isn't it?"

"It can certainly help you get currency," Alphonsine sighed. "Will they be sending me out to practice my previous occupation for the next thousand years? Is that to be my fate?"

"Hardly. You shall be free to live as you wish, but with certain obligations perhaps, to your family. Treasures can be lost or may have to be abandoned. There's always a need to accumulate more however we can. Jane and I became good at playing cards. It was easy to read the marks and know who was bluffing, but slow work to do it well enough not to arouse suspicion. Do you enjoy gambling?"

"Very much."

"Knowing you will win takes away some of the excitement, but greed can be dangerous. We also have holdings in many parts of the world. At times, it's a question of looking in to see how they are being managed. It might be necessary to seduce a mortal occasionally, but usually it will be one who will give you pleasure, and you'll always have the power."

Their conversation was interrupted by noise from inside the house – laughter, shrieks, and sounds particular to certain physical acts.

"It's begun," said Pierre.

She understood he was referring to the feast.

"I don't want to …"

"Then you must leave. Spend the night with Ana at the nursery."

"And you?" She asked.

"I need to feed. I'll find one and take her quickly. Perhaps I'll join the two of you later. We could all play a game of cards."

"Weren't you going to spend some time with Jamal?"

"Oh that. We're already bored with each other."

They dressed. Pierre headed down a hallway while Alphonsine walked toward the kitchen, which would lead her to the exit closest to the cottage. Turning a corner, she noticed a young woman clad only in a worn pair of knickers and a corset. She was kneeling while Anton stood against the wall, enjoying her services.

Anton patted the woman's unkempt auburn hair while looking straight at Alphonsine. He opened his mouth slightly, baring his fangs and licking his lips. The woman, busy at her task, did not look up, but then having sensed another's presence, she released his cock and turned her head. She must have caught the expression of pity on Alphonsine's face, and met her gaze with a look of defiance before returning to her labors. She could hear the girl's thought, *"Who are you to judge me?"* But behind that, she also sensed shame.

Alphonsine turned and took another route. Two naked women ran past her laughing as they were chased by two men of her kind. The girls were not afraid. While she still had no wish to participate in this particular form of merriment, she was relieved they didn't seem to be suffering.

It was a clear night with a full moon. She decided to sit for a bit and gaze up at the stars. There were smells in the woods that interested her, thoughts in the air, the sounds of insects, predators, and prey.

She might have been there a few minutes, or more than an hour, feeling very much one with the night. There was a short scream, and then she saw a figure running toward her. She recognized the outline and knickers, almost translucent from wear. It was the young woman she had seen with Anton. The poor thing's fear smelled as heavy and as sweet as ripe fruit. Alphonsine began to salivate and felt a tingling in her teeth.

"They're killing us," the girl shouted, running up to her. "They've all gone mad. We must hide. We must run from them."

Alphonsine grabbed her by the shoulders and whispered, "What are you talking about?"

"The men in the house, mademoiselle. They invited us to a ball but they are maniacs. I thought it was a game. But it is no game."

"You're shaking. Are you sure?"

"We must go. Do you think they can help us, in that house?" She was looking toward the cottage.

Alphonsine thought of Isabelle and Christine. They'd been trained to sleep during the day, and might still be awake. It would be upsetting to them if they saw this half-naked hysterical stranger. "There are only my aunt and her children."

"But we must tell them. They aren't safe," the young woman

insisted.

Standing so close, Alphonsine could see now the poor thing was barely grown. "My aunt's been here for years. We are laundresses. We've never had a problem," she said calmly, without releasing her grip.

"We must get help. You can come with me or not," said the other, pulling away.

There was a delicate vein on the side of the girl's face that seemed to glow. The skin itself appeared almost translucent. Colors bounced off and surrounded her, moving as she did, yet she seemed unaware of her display, oblivious to how enticing, how *tasty* she appeared. They had told Alphonsine her vision would "improve." Could this have been what they meant? There was a faint but distinctive sound, the blood as it circulated through the nubile body, and above that the drumming of the heart. It was slowing down, but just slightly.

It was all Alphonsine could do not to take her right then. It had been weeks since she'd had Jeanne. Yet, she pitied this lost creature, and wondered if there might be some way to save her, even if it meant another life would need to be substituted.

She sensed an additional presence nearby.

"Did you hear something?" The girl asked, watching Alphonsine's eyes as they scanned.

"No, nothing."

It was Anton. He was trying to communicate with her mentally. *"You've found our stray. I'll leave her to you."*

"There's a village a few kilometers away. I know a path through the woods. We'll both go," Alphonsine said.

"Won't there be wolves or, or ..."

"You're telling me they've all gone mad at the house, and you're afraid now of wolves?"

She grabbed the girl's hand and they began to run.

The mortal soon tired. They arrived in a small clearing by a pond. Alphonsine had come upon it before. She had no idea if the path they were on would lead to a village or simply circle back.

"We must stop and rest," she said. "I don't think they'll find us here. We'll be safe."

They sat. Alphonsine watched as the girl caught her breath. She was becoming less frightened, more trusting. Alphonsine wanted so badly to touch her, lick her, taste her salty flesh, and drink her sweet life-giving blood. But could she do it? It would be hours till dawn, hours to decide.

It was exciting being in the middle of the forest with this creature whose life she could so easily end, but it had been easier with the other one. Ana had been there, and besides Jeanne had been enslaved, no longer fully sentient, but this girl was vibrant and alive with every fiber of her being. She had no wish to die.

"Did you have any champagne?" Alphonsine asked. "Maybe you didn't see what you thought you did."

"It does seem so crazy now."

Alphonsine nodded her head.

"But I know what I saw."

She patted the girl's hand.

"What's your name?" Alphonsine asked.

"I am Marie."

"Marie," she repeated. "That was my mother's name. I'm Alphonsine."

"Mademoiselle, what you saw in the house …"

"You hardly need to …"

"No, I want to explain. I feel I must. It's true I came because a gentleman offered me money for him to do with me as he pleased."

"You don't owe me an explanation."

"It is for my daughter. I sinned with my cousins. When they started I didn't understand what they were doing. When my parents saw my belly they threw me out, and this was the only way I could put food into our mouths."

"Where is your daughter now?"

"She lives with a miller and his wife. I pay for her board and visit her sometimes. They think I work at a …"

"How old are you?"

"I believe I am seventeen, mademoiselle."

"Seventeen?"

The girl nodded.

"And the child?"

"Almost three years old."

The child wouldn't remember her mother if she died tonight, would believe herself to have been abandoned. Would the miller keep her? Would she have to make her way in the world alone?

"I am sorry for you."

The girl began to sob, and despite her desire, Alphonsine still wondered if it would be possible to save the creature, or at least find out where she came from, make some arrangement for the welfare of her daughter. Or might it not be better to take the child to Ana? For it to enjoy a few blessed weeks of love and pampering?

They heard a wolf's howl, not so distant.

The girl gasped, and then threw her arms around Alphonsine.

"They're very far away," Alphonsine said. "You don't need to be afraid." The predators of the forest would not approach any of her kind. They were waiting to take what she left. She patted the girl's back.

"But I am so frightened," Marie said still holding her tightly.

"When we get to the village, what will you tell them? The family at the estate are well-respected and wealthy."

"I will tell them what I saw. They are monsters."

"Mightn't it be better to forget what you imagined you saw?"

"The ones they killed were my friends. They must be stopped."

"I see," Alphonsine said. Everyone in the abbey including herself would be in danger if Marie got away. Her mouth was so close to the girl's neck. She felt hard nipples through the threadbare corset rubbing against her chest.

It was the girl who kissed her first.

Alphonsine was startled and pulled away.

Marie looked shocked as well. "I'm sorry Mademoiselle Alphonsine. I don't know what …"

"There's no need to feel shame," she said looking at the poor thing, projecting thoughts of the two of them. They came toward each other. Alphonsine kissed her long and passionately, then loosened her corset, removing it entirely. "I don't know how you could breathe in that."

"But the howling?" Marie asked.

"We're safe here," Alphonsine said slowly, trying to mimic the tone Ana took with the servants. She could see the girl was calming down, and remembered what she'd been told about how her voice alone could have this effect on mortals. She continued, "We must have a little time to rest. They won't find us. I promise you. Just a little time. Besides, look at the pond. Doesn't the water seem inviting? Wouldn't you like to bathe before we get to the village?"

Marie nodded.

Alphonsine's eyes took in the younger woman's breasts. They were full and despite the child who'd fed from them, firm and youthful. She buried her head in Marie's chest and began to warm the nipples with her tongue.

Marie groaned, but it was with pleasure. She pulled down her knickers, and helped Alphonsine undress.

The moon was full above them. The grass smelled almost as delicious and sweet as the girl. Soon they were rolling on top of each other, fucking each other with their fingers, rolling down the grass slope into the cool pond.

"I don't understand how …" the girl said sounding bewildered.

"Let's just enjoy the moment." Alphonsine told her.

The girl emerged from the water wet and shivering.

"You feel so warm," she said hugging Alphonsine.

"I feel hot in your arms," Alphonsine answered. "I've never felt this way before. Have you?"

"No," the girl said grasping onto her. "I'm not so afraid anymore."

They sank to the wet ground. Alphonsine kissed her on her throat and worked her way down tenderly. Marie's juices flowed into her mouth, and while they were delicious, it was another liquid she sought. Alphonsine heard her moan, and with her tongue felt the vibrations inside her. She pulled herself up and faced her once more.

"That was …"

"It was," Alphonsine replied.

"Let me …"

"Later."

There were more kisses. Alphonsine rolled over and they were both side by side. "We should get going. It'll be dawn soon," she said, resting her head on her elbow and looking at Marie.

The girl said nothing. She wore an expression of complete trust.

"Tell me more about your little girl. What is her name?"

"Marie Louise. But she is called Louise."

"That's a pretty name. And the village where she stays?" Alphonsine's free hand was making small circles on the girl's stomach.

"Mortrée. It's near …"

"I know it," she said. It chilled her that the child was so close to the town she had come from.

Alphonsine leaned over and kissed the girl as though she were ready for more.

Marie pulled away slightly.

"Don't you want to?" Alphonsine asked.

"Yes," she said.

Alphonsine pulled her and rolled her on top. She felt the girl's fingers working in her vagina and clasped them into her.

"I'll see Louise is cared for. I promise," she said before plunging her fangs into the young woman's neck.

There was a sound, resigned more than frightened, as though a weight had been lifted. Strangely, the girl grasped her more tightly rather than trying to pull away. Alphonsine tilted her head to see the face. The expression grew in innocence as the blood drained. She tightened her inner grip on the girl's fingers, could feel those muscles pulse, and as she kept sucking, she plunged her own fingers inside of Marie and felt the young whore's *chatte* tighten around them, could feel her pleasure even now that she understood, despite the venom, that death was coming. She was welcoming it. Alphonsine was sure of that. She was giving herself over to a goddess. Dying in the arms of a goddess. What greater gift was there? She caressed the girl as she drained her.

"You sweet thing. You sweet, sweet thing." She said the words only mentally as she continued, but was sure they'd been understood. She could feel her prey's body relax as it weakened, while her own grew stronger. Once the heart stopped, she released her grip, allowing the warm body to cover her for a few moments like a blanket.

Then she turned it onto its back. The girl looked as untouched and pure as the Madonna herself. She caressed her a final time, shut the eyes, and gave her a chaste peck on the cheek. Alphonsine felt no guilt or shame for what she had done. She was proud to have pulled it off with so little fuss, and it had ended with the girl at rest. Ana had been right. There was nothing more beautiful than a body at peace.

"Good-bye, my sweet Marie."

The wolves were back. She couldn't see them, and they weren't howling, but she sensed them waiting like lap dogs looking forward to table scraps. She was already feeling sleepy, could see the sky beginning to lighten in the east. She did not bother to dress, but ran through the woods naked and unafraid, barely making it to bed by sunrise.

☙ ✾ ❧

The evening following the feast, there was a gathering in the drawing room, the first of many small parties given for departing guests. The blank expressions of the musicians no longer bothered her. Every note sounded rich, enhanced, individual. She danced with Pierre feeling more in tune with the music than ever before. Her energy was limitless.

Then Anton cut in.

"Good evening," he said.

"Hello." She was determined to be civil though she was still angry with him for calling her a child, and for not admitting he had brought her into this world against her wishes.

"Did you enjoy the little present I left you last night?"

"Present?" It took her a moment to understand, and then she felt very stupid.

"*Ma chère*, surely, you didn't think the tart escaped us without help?"

"No, of course not," she said, as though it was no surprise. She could tell Anton knew she was lying. He could, after all, read her mind. But she was doing her best to block her thoughts.

"It pleased you then?"

"She was terrified when she came to me. I thought we weren't supposed to do that."

"No doubt you calmed her down," he whispered into her ear.

"But Ana said we ought not frighten them."

"We can't all be like our sainted Ana. Fear is a fine old wine. An expensive treat. One not to be indulged in too often. You made it up to her, I'm certain."

"May I talk to you about something?"

He nodded. She pulled him away from the music, and started to tell him about Marie's now orphaned child.

"Who is Marie?"

"The girl from last night."

"Oh, I see. You'd like the child then. For yourself, or as a gift to Ana?"

"No, no. Before I ... I told her I would see her daughter was taken care of."

"You did what? Are you mad?"

"I promised."

"That was *nice* of you. You realize she's beyond caring about that?"

"But we could spare a few francs."

"It's not a question of what we can spare. We don't interfere with them, with their lives."

"But we have already. The child depended on her."

"It becomes complicated. A web of deception that can ensnare us."

"Please. I won't ask more of you."

He laughed. "I'm sure you're lying now. You are known for *always* asking for more."

Despite his skepticism, he agreed without any conditions save that she would put aside her rancor, "for the sake of this house."

"I'll be more polite," she said. "I'm afraid I could never hide my true feelings from you."

"No, you cannot," he said, "though you are very skilled *mademoiselle la comtesse*, at hiding them from yourself."

She left him to look for Ana, whom she found in the cottage. There was a chill in the air and though the cold didn't bother their kind, Ana was sitting by the fire in the main room, weaving a tapestry. The children were asleep. Alphonsine could hear their snoring, along with the other noises of the night, the crickets, the howls, the rustling of small creatures.

"Alphonsine, I thought you'd be at the dance until dawn. You look lovely. That dress suits you."

She sat down on the bare floor, like a child at Ana's feet. "Thank you. Why did you not come?"

"I'd just rather be here with them. Christine spoke a complete sentence today. It's your influence. She's yours if you'd like."

"When are you planning to …?"

"Not till next month, I think. They're having so much fun. But what's on your mind? You look pensive, and your thoughts are so tangled. I can't pick them out."

Alphonsine told her about the previous evening, and what the girl had seen in the house.

"Poor soul. I agree there was no reason for her to witness that. It's difficult sometimes not to feed on their fear when it's our nature to hunt. Perhaps more difficult for the men to control their baser desires. But you didn't do anything wrong *ma chère*. You handled her well. Did you enjoy yourself?

Alphonsine looked down at the floor, and then back up. "It was the most exhilarating experience I've ever had. It was … "

"It's magical, isn't it?" Ana said leaning down and taking her hand. "When you connect with mortality like that, take in all of their suffering and their joy. There's that feeling of finality, when they know it's hopeless and ending. You understand the whole universe, don't you? And your place in it. Blood may feed our hunger, but we have an appetite for death. It's our ambrosia. We are gods, Alphonsine. You see that now?"

"I'm beginning to," she replied. "It was so clear last night. So natural. But what if the power is too much for me? What if I couldn't face … Ana, is there no way back?"

"There's always death, but I would so hate to lose you to it."

"I meant to become mortal again, to not have to hunt."

"I see," Ana said.

"I didn't mean to offend. You have been a most wonderful teacher and friend."

"What you are going through, becoming, you fear it, the desires, the … thirst."

"Yes."

"We all go through that," Ana said reaching out to her.

"But is there a way?"

"Would you really wish to walk that path again? The solitude they live with, the knowledge that life will be short and brutal, that every day will bring some new diminishment of their bodies and minds?"

"But when I think of the eternity of the night, of never … "

"Aren't you being a bit theatrical? The night always ends in a restful day," Ana said, smiling slightly as though she was indulging one of the children. "And besides, you've long been a creature of the night."

They were both silent for a moment and then Ana said softly, "There is a way. I'm the only one who knows it. I should tell someone, Jane perhaps – in case something were to happen. But then maybe it would be better if it died with me."

"Why? Why would it be better?"

"There was an elder. The one who brought Anton into this life. After almost a thousand years, she was tired, and she was in love."

"She was willing to give up immortality for love?"

"We tried to talk her out of it. But she wouldn't see reason. She couldn't give him up, and knew if presented with a choice – to join us or to die, her lover would choose death. Anton and I tried to convince her that that kind of attachment never lasts. But she didn't care. She said if she only had five years with him, one year with him, it would be enough. Such a thing had never been done. She was clear if there was no way, she would destroy herself. We wanted her happiness, and I'll admit I was interested in the challenge."

"The challenge?"

"The oldest left amongst us had little more knowledge than you. What if this would give us answers? What if it could change our natures? There were a couple of experiments that failed, and then I had a vision, of how it might be done.

"It was not an easy path, and I wasn't sure it would work. But in less than a month, her desire for blood had stopped. Of course, she lost much else. Her strength was reduced to that of a mortal. She needed food and drink to survive. She was no longer one of us. She would age and die."

"And did she live with the man?"

"She married him, and within a year he buried her. She died in childbirth. The son was born healthy. But then he took sick and died as well."

"Still, she had a child. Were there others who returned to mortality?"

"The second had been in the religious life and wished to go back to it. To repent. We were afraid he might betray us, but he convinced us he wouldn't. He considered us God's creatures as well. Within two years he went insane. We tried to get to him, but they – the church – had put him somewhere out of our reach. We believe he may have told them things. It was after that more tales of our existence emerged, and we were not so safe."

"And if I wanted this thing? If I promised to keep my silence, if I could live with …"

Ana shook her head. "You wouldn't live. The disease within you hasn't been cured, only suppressed. We brought you from the brink. I would never send you back to that precipice."

"So you're telling me there is a way, but it's not for me."

"I'm afraid so, *ma chère*. There was one who like you was sick. We didn't know. He didn't. But after he changed, tumors began to appear on his body and he was dead within weeks. We offered him a chance to come back to us, but he insisted on dying what he called a natural death. He said he saw things differently and could never return to his old way of being. So, I'm afraid you are trapped." Ana said those last words lightly, as she ran her fingers through Alphonsine's hair. "But you will see this life is not so bad. You have a family now, a family that will love you for eternity." She took Alphonsine's wrist and brought her hand to her mouth, kissing it softly. "Come, I can feel the morning near. Let's go back to my room. We'll spend the day sleeping in each other's arms."

There was more to learn over the next months, and though she sometimes grew restless at the slow pace of country life, she was beginning to find a sense of peace. Ana had been both right and wrong about her outgrowing her misgivings. She came to accept her life depended on taking the lives of others, and this could be done with minimal cruelty and great satisfaction, but she also held onto the idea that she had not chosen freely.

She developed the ability to block her thoughts from Anton and the rest, but still could not read them easily when they weren't purposely projecting. The hungrier she was, the more she could read mortals, but mostly she only gained a sense of them. Their minds seemed blurry and primitive. She had progressed in other ways, including the ability to climb walls, to move as quietly as a panther and leap even further, to snap a man's neck with one hand – though that was considered a waste of blood, and only to be done in emergencies.

After the Great Feast, there were few visitors. Anton came and went frequently. Jane had decided to stay on, to learn from Ana about plants, and rest from the world. The closeness between Ana and Jane made Alphonsine feel she was interrupting them with her presence, despite their protests that this was never the case. She was always welcome, even when they were sharing a bed.

Alphonsine understood she was free to leave whenever she wished, but she must go some place where no one had ever heard of Marie Duplessis, and she'd need to stay away for many years.

One evening, when Anton was visiting, she brought up the subject of her departure.

"I've been thinking about where you might go and with whom," he said. "We won't send you out alone. You still have much to learn. Pierre will be leaving soon to attend to some business. It might be good for you to travel with him."

"Do all of us engage in business?" Alphonsine asked.

"We all do something to support the community," Anton explained. "It isn't exactly hard labor."

"But it often involves swindling of some kind."

"And this offends the delicate sensibilities of *mademoiselle la comtesse*?" He asked pointedly.

"I may have earned my living on my back, *monsieur*, but I was no outlaw. I was honest about what I did."

"Our very existence must involve deception. As for our alleged thievery, all wealth is theft. I said as much, or something like it in a tavern one night, and some idiot put it in a book."

"I don't think that gives us a license to …"

"My dear girl, do you need a license to shear a lamb? To take an excess feather from a peacock and place it in a lovely bonnet? We are superior to them in every possible way. We have domain. They have no more inherent right to their property than cows have to their fields. Besides, how do you think most of them obtained what they had? How many of your patrons could you name who built their own fortunes?"

She could think of none. "Why must you bring up my former life? Are you expecting me to work as I did before? Is that why you revived me?"

"I *revived* you, as you put it, so that you might be a queen. Beautiful forever. So that you might make eternity more delightful for all of us. Did I think you'd be able to contribute financially to our community? It was a consideration. If I expected you to be a useless drain on our resources I would have been outvoted."

"Outvoted?"

"You still have much to learn. We try to get the approval of at least two others before we take anyone on. Sometimes one loses objectivity. In your case, it was thought …"

"I would happily prostitute myself for eternity?"

"You misunderstand. There are many ways to earn money. You'll see how it is. Selling your favors will hardly enter into it, though your beauty and charm, no doubt, will be useful."

❧ ✦ ❧

"Of course it's never easy for us to travel by ship," Ana explained, as they went through some clothes trying to decide which dresses Alphonsine might take with her.

Questions would be asked about passengers who rarely ventured from their cabins in daylight, who never touched meat or fish, and had, perhaps, other unusual habits. It was fortunate that with the new steamships, the crossing could be accomplished between feedings, and they would leave with a supply of herbs that would enable them to remain awake when necessary during daylight, though such exposure should always be kept at a minimum, as it might "destroy one's face."

It was in the spring of 1848, more than a year after the alleged demise of Marie Duplessis that Alphonsine set forth to discover the New World.

Act III – The Present

Chapter 1

Cara's eyes kept drifting to the wedding photo on Lt. Santini's desk. The groom's resemblance to the young John Travolta as Tony Manero was uncanny, right down to the white polyester suit. Present day, he looked more like what she imagined the real Tony would look like thirty years later – fat and alcoholic, puffy-faced with a turned down mouth that told a sad story even when shut.

He had called her and Jaime into the office and told them to close the door. She could read his expression well enough to sense two things – he was not happy, but he did not directly blame them.

"How's Simmons going?" He asked.

Jaime explained there had been no usable physical evidence left on the body or in the room.

"Then you don't actually have anything on the society girl?"

Society girl? Cara stifled a laugh. *Was that even still a thing? Like calling a female college student a coed. Did the man have an AOL account?*

She hoped she hadn't been smirking, and answered, "We know St. Valois got in the elevator with him, and no one saw her leave the hotel."

"But her ex-cop doorman puts her home before Simmons could have died based on what the ME says. Correct?" The boss answered and asked.

"Concierge," Jaime said.

"What?"

"He's not the doorman. He's the concierge."

Santini put his hand up in a gesture Cara interpreted as, *"Please stop wasting my fucking time."*

"She was cooperative when we talked to her," Jaime continued. "She stuck to her story. Said she never went into that room. There's no evidence she did."

Cara thought of contradicting this, but understood the difference between gut and evidence.

Santini pulled a pack of cigarettes out of his top desk draw, placing it in front of him. "And you only talked to her because of a hunch it was her on the video?"

"Yes."

"But she admitted it was? Didn't deny it?"

"She absolutely admitted it was her," Jaime answered.

"She knew we had something," Cara added.

Santini nodded, but his attention was focused on the cigarettes. He stared at the pack with an expression that conveyed both love and frustration, like a parent looking at a child who has always managed to disappoint him. He took one out, slowly bringing it between his lips. From the desk, he pulled a lighter and a small ash-stained plate.

"I could get in big trouble for this," he said.

Cara and Jaime watched silently.

"Politicians," he added contemptuously as he lit up.

They'd heard his rants before, but this time Cara caught different emotions in his voice – resignation, resentment, defeat. "Seems like his honor, the mayor, was at a dinner party for the filthy rich interested in the money side of art, and your girl was there to talk about some paintings."

He leaned back and let out three smoke rings, which they watched dissipate.

"His majesty thought she was charming. He thinks the idea she could have stabbed an alleged serial killer later that very evening is highly unlikely, and he'd like us to leave her the fuck alone unless we have actual proof." He paused taking the type of deep drag usually reserved for marijuana, and then exhaled more rings, each one smaller than the one before. "Do we have that?"

Jaime and Cara answered in unison, "No."

She almost added something, but stopped herself. *What was the point?* A decision had been made many levels up.

"Anything get in the papers?" Santini asked.

"We were pretty tight-lipped about Donnalee," Jaime said. "We said we had a person of interest, but they never had Simmons' name. He's just some guy from Staten Island got robbed in a hotel room – it looks like. A few lines in the *Post* and the *News*."

"Good. Let's keep it quiet. We'll all be happier."

Cara and Jaime waited to be dismissed. Santini continued blowing smoke. After a silence that was becoming awkward, the lieutenant exhaled, stamped the butt, and asked, "Leaving the girl out of it, what's the theory?"

Jaime took over. "We think he called someone – probably an escort, who got in and out without being seen. She could have been working with staff inside the hotel. We can continue to lean, see if anyone saw anything or got paid not to. We've already ruled out the registered guests."

"We can agree whomever did whatever did us a favor. Can't we?"

Jaime nodded. Cara did not like where this was going.

"You want to keep working on it, but you got more on your plates. Maybe this one you let go. Not every case needs to be closed."

He gestured with his hand. The meeting was over.

When they left the office, Cara turned to her partner. "We know it had to be *her*, yes?"

Jaime shook his head. "You aren't talking about facts."

"Bullshit," Cara replied. "You're the one who's got feelings mixed up into this. She's not *right*. She's off."

"She's *French*."

"That's not it."

"Off doesn't make her a murderer."

Chapter 2

That night's work consisted of showing Chinese visitors around, balancing being polite to the women while acknowledging the crude flirtations of the men. Later, Alphonsine joined Pierre in the apartment he kept above the gallery – a large high-ceilinged loft space.

They changed into suitable attire. She wore black exercise tights with a hot pink sports bra. He was bare-chested, in white men's yoga pants, which somehow looked not ridiculous on him though a bit obscene as he wore nothing underneath, and even flaccid there was a good-sized bulge. Neither wore shoes. Pierre put on Shostakovich's *Jazz Suite*, and threw her a foil.

"How are things going with the boy?" he asked, posing like a B-movie pirate. Then he leaped fifteen feet or so to where she was standing and said, "*En garde.*"

"I am very much enjoying him," she answered as she lunged.

They were soon fully engaged in *phrases de armes*.

"Then why aren't you with him tonight?"

"He's rehearsing. I told you he formed a band. I wasn't going to make a nuisance of myself. Do I look like Yoko Ono?"

"A rock and roll baaaand," Pierre said, managing to stretch out the syllable. "That sounds a bit juvenile." He was blocking her.

"Really? I find it charming. He also acts. He's written a play. They're interested in it. In Hollywood."

"Any good?" Pierre asked as they parried.

"It has great potential," she answered.

"Does it?" He managed to hit her arm with his tip. "You're never as good when you're preoccupied."

In the next round, she surprised him with a quick thrust he barely escaped. She kept going, not giving him time to prepare and managed to bring him to the ground.

"So how does this romance end?" Pierre asked, slipping from

her grip and coming back with a new attack.

"I hadn't thought about its ending."

"He's too high profile for a feast, I think."

"I have no intention of hurting him," she said, "And would be very upset if anyone else did."

"Have you considered …?"

"He lacks the killer instinct."

They were standing close. Both foils almost vertical and locked together. His eyes moved off of hers, to her hard nipples, as her gaze drifted to his thighs. They dropped their weapons and embraced, tearing at each other's clothes. She jumped onto him, grabbing his neck as he squeezed her buttocks till she was tight against him. He staggered backward to the wall and began moving her around expertly. After so long, they knew each other's bodies as well as they knew their own.

They moved from standing to lying down. First with her on top, then with her on all fours. They could have played together till dawn, but there was no need to. An hour or so later they were both side by side on the floor, looking up at the skylight.

"That was sweet," she purred.

"I've missed you."

"It's only been …"

"Almost three weeks. Since you started seeing the boy."

"Don't blame me. You're with someone different every night."

"Does he know we sometimes …"

"Hunt down mortals together and drink them dry?" She asked with mock-innocence. "Oh, you meant this! God no. He's so *American*. It's not like we've discussed exclusivity. I'm sure he understands the concept of what do they call it these days?"

"Friends with benefits."

"But I don't think he'd approve."

"My sweet girl. I haven't seen you like this in decades. It worries me. I remember when you had to take that unfortunate …"

"Must you always bring that up? It was ages ago," she said distantly. "I had no choice. He had worked out too much about us. Damn, he was sweet."

"And then there was the one you …"

She punched him playfully on the arm. "That was 1849. I was barely trained. I blame you."

"You were so upset at the time."

"I got carried away."

"So what happens with this one? You just break it off at some point, or arrange that he will? Have him discover your infidelity. Am I to play a role in the drama?"

"Let's not talk about it. I only know when I'm with him I feel …"

"What?"

She smiled, "Almost human again." She wrapped her hands around her bare chest, hugging herself. "Sometimes, laying in his arms after we make love, I imagine dying there, content."

"That is not good,"

They showered and put on clothes. Pierre was going dancing with some of the more attractive hangers-on. There would be ecstasy, a drug her kind avoided taking as it led them to express their affection for humans in rather unfortunate ways. Still it was fun to watch mortals under its influence at play. They could be so energetic and puppy-like. He asked if she was interested in joining the fun.

"I don't think so. I imagine I'll hook up with Dashiell later."

"Are you sure *he* wouldn't be interested?"

"I'm sure *I* wouldn't be interested in sharing him."

"You are becoming a bit possessive. I've invited that Italian boy, and the twins. I know you like them, and that very submissive girl with the hairy twat. She's not my type, but I bet you'd love to corrupt her, reminds me of that blushing virgin back in Buenos Aires you …"

"It sounds like fun, but see, he's texted." She read his message out loud, "See you at Harry's Bar, Java Street, Greenpoint. Boys in band plus sig others invited."

"How cute," Pierre teased. "You're his *sig*."

"Fuck you, Pierre," she said lightly.

"I hate it when you curse," he said. "It sounds so twentieth century. I was hoping this new millennium would be more refined, but so far it's disappointing. Would you like some coffee before you go? Or a bit of blow?"

"I'm always up for either or both," she said. They each did a few lines though the effect of cocaine on their kind was mild.

He poured her a cup of Sumatra made with his French press. She noticed how deliberate he was being, and that he was blocking her from his mind.

"Uh-oh," Alphonsine said, certain he was about to tell her

something that would not please her. "Just say it."

"Mayor Piccolini has taken quite a liking to you."

"I'm rather fond of the hobbit myself," she replied.

"He's interested in investing in some paintings."

"Tell me what I don't already know."

"I met with him a few evenings ago. He's looking to buy those impressionists we got back …"

"I know the ones. I helped you get them."

"He made me an offer."

Even without telepathy she could see where this was going.

"It's considerably more than we would get at auction," Pierre continued.

"Surprising for a businessman."

"He doesn't want to take a chance on being outbid. The Russians are buying up everything. He says the price will rise no matter what he pays, so he's willing to pay a premium, but there's something he wants in return."

"I got that part."

"Just three dates."

"Oh? Is that what they call them these days?"

"Alphonsine, it's a lot of money, for all of us. When was the last time I asked you?"

"Two years ago, when I first came to New York," she answered quickly. " It really started things for the gallery, but the stench is still on me."

"We were discreet. Besides you're talking as though I had you on the street. It was five …"

"Six. Plus one of them always wanted his wife *and* the girlfriend there."

"It wasn't that bad. To the public those looked like *romances*."

She rolled her eyes. "Romances with older filthy-rich patrons of the arts."

"Just chatter. It's not like in your day. Now a little notoriety is *de rigueur*. Does your scandalous past upset the boyfriend?"

"I'm sure he's dismissed whatever he's heard. I'm not as blunt as I used to be with my suitors. But managing this, something ongoing," she paused a moment to think. "It's going to be tricky."

"But you have a lot of experience with such … tricks."

She felt a genuine flash of anger, also disappointment that Pierre, after all this time, still thought of her that way.

"Why can't I just give his honor a little nip and order him to meet our price? I could make him think something already happened."

"There's always the risk he'd figure out it didn't. It would be an unnecessary complication. This needs to be clean. We can't just kill him, and we can't afford for him to suspect later that we drugged him or used some other means. With his resources, that could be very dangerous."

"So you consider my fucking him *clean*?"

She felt him cringe at her word choice.

"He doesn't want anything to interfere with his ambitions. He and his wife both benefit from the fiction of his marriage. As you pointed out, Americans like to pretend that monogamy is normal. He's known to be generous, and he's careful about what gets out to the public. The young man who thinks so highly of your virtue, need not know. After it happens, it'll be exactly like it didn't. This is the simplest and safest means of securing our deal."

"How overvalued are those paintings?"

"I'd say several million above what we might get, even from those stupid oligarchs."

"How nice for the community."

"Isn't it?"

"And me?"

"You're part of *us*. What needs do you have we aren't meeting? You have an apartment. Clothing. Access to the plane. Would you like me to reduce your *work* hours?"

"Cash. I'd like some, and I don't mean the pitiful allowance I get twice a month. "

"You're an employee. It's called a paycheck."

"My favors are quite expensive, *monsieur*. I think a million dollars would be a bargain."

Pierre shook his head. "Paid to you as an individual? They'll never agree to that."

She didn't say anything.

"What about five hundred thousand? I could ask Anton," Pierre offered.

"One million," she said slowly. "It's a fraction of what he's going to pay for the paintings, which were procured with my help. You can tell Anton or whomever talks directly with the elders that I know my rights and I won't cheapen myself."

She could tell he was trying to read her, and she was doing her best to remain opaque.

"What on earth has gotten into you?" Her friend asked. "You know our survival is based on cooperation. Are you trying to prove some point?"

"Maybe," she said. "Maybe I'm simply tired of always being given these particular duties. I'd like at least to get paid for them."

Pierre looked at her a moment before saying, "I'll talk to Anton. I'm sorry if I offended you when I said …"

"No, it's to be expected. Men have amazingly long memories when it comes to a woman's past – especially, when she repeats those behaviors again and again." Changing the subject, she asked, "Have you an idea of his tastes?"

"The usual as far as I know. I believe he likes shoes."

"They *all* like shoes."

"My understanding is he wants …"

"I know what he wants. That I should have the manners of a duchess and the skills of … well, *me*. He wants to be my debaser and my savior. He would like to be convinced my need for him is greater than his for me, that I'm enjoying every moment, and it's never about the money until it's time for me to leave. Or were you referring to something else?"

"I know you aren't happy about this, but it's important he think …"

"Please, I'm not exactly an amateur."

"Besides, haven't you always been *attracted* to older men with money?"

"I was never attracted to the *men*. Oh *merde*, Pierre, it's much worse now. They were grateful for so little in the old days. Now with their blue pills they think they're doing me some great favor. But I suppose the money will buy a little freedom, won't it?"

☙ ✤ ❧

It wasn't a date.

Cara had known Justin since high school, when they were both in the criminal justice club at Brooklyn Tech. They'd been classmates at John Jay College, where he was pre-law, and she studied enforcement. She couldn't pin down when exactly it was she realized she harbored feelings beyond friendship for him. He was more cute than handsome, but even in high school he always had a girlfriend, or she was dating someone, and so they had early on settled into friendship. For a while, she was with his brother which killed the idea of anything happening between them, but sometimes Cara wondered whether or not, at a time like this, when neither was seeing anyone else, the subject could or should be broached.

"Greenpoint's looking more and more like Williamsburg," Justin noted as they walked along Kent Avenue passing a bookstore, a consignment shop for maternity and kids' clothes, a bubble tea house, and something with plants in the window that neither of them could figure out.

"You're not kidding. If my aunt hadn't left me the house, I'd never be able to afford to live here. Maybe I'll cash-in in a couple of years and retire to the country."

Justin shook his head. "Not you. You've worked much too hard for that, *detective*."

"Yeah, well, you graduated law school when you were twenty-four, so don't act like I'm the over achiever."

Cara led him over to her new local. They passed the crowd of smokers outside and somehow made their way to a tiny table in the back. Justin offered to get their drinks.

"Maybe you'll get lucky while I'm up there."

"Maybe you'll meet someone at the bar," she said, knowing if she were ever going to bring up her lingering attraction to him, much liquor would be required.

Her vantage point allowed her a partial view of a booth. There was a group of young men, a couple with hipster scruffiness, one with short blond hair, light eyes, and a mouth that screamed kiss me. He had just the right amount of stubble and a kind of celebrity glow. For all she knew, this being New York, he might have been famous. Justin had been right, exactly the type you'd expect to see a mile to the south in Williamsburg. She had a feeling she'd seen him before, but couldn't place him. She fantasized going over to his table all swagger and asking, "Are you *somebody*?" She wasn't close enough to hear them, but saw the others get up, heading for the pool table while Handsome checked his texts.

Justin came back carrying two beers. He spotted the direction of her eyes before she had a chance to divert them.

"Go for it," he said without bothering to turn around. "You know you want to."

"Don't play match … holy fuck damn …"

He looked over his shoulder to see what had brought that on.

"Ah," Justin said, taking in the brunette, "She's uh …"

"Camille St. Valois," Cara answered.

"Since when are you following art gossip? I wouldn't have thought you'd even know the name."

"She was a person of interest," Cara whispered, watching Camille greet young-Fabio with a lot of tongue.

"Really?" he said. "Let's go and say hello."

"I don't think …"

But he had already started walking over. She followed him. He spoke first, addressing the golden couple.

"Hi, I don't know if you remember me," he said looking at the man.

Handsome shook his hand. "Wein, right? The prosecutor?"

"Justin, please."

Dashiell gestured for them to sit. Camille was doing an excellent job of looking like she didn't recognize Cara, whom Justin introduced to the couple. Then he turned to her and explained, "Mr. Alexander and Ms. St. Valois were victims of a crime in our fair city. It would have been much worse if Mr. Alexander …"

"Dashiell, please," the blond said.

"Dashiell hadn't acted so heroically."

"Or recklessly," Dashiell said flashing the straightest, whitest, most perfect smile at Cara. "And Camille was pretty awesome. She managed to dislocate a guy's shoulder."

Cara listened with great interest.

Camille blushed slightly, and said in that baby voice, "It was just instinct."

Justin started telling Cara how they had the perps who had been facing a list of charges, but then the "weirdest thing" happened.

"What weirdest thing was that?" Cara asked.

"Cesar Mendez, he's got a long record with a lot of gang shit." Justin stopped at the word "shit" and looked at Camille, like he thought he might have offended her delicate sensibilities. "He was the one with the gun. The other two were younger – his brother and a cousin. None of them made bail. Cesar hangs himself a day after he was arraigned. Then the brother slips on a soapy bathroom floor, hits his head and dies. I think the family's looking to sue the city. And the cousin whose upstate in juvey winds up getting stabbed over some teenage drama."

"And dies too?" Cara asked.

There was a moment before anyone spoke and then it was Camille's turn. "The one who threatened us, I can't say I'm not sorry he's dead. But the other two were just … boys. I mean they deserved to be in jail, but this was so …"

Justin and Dashiell were both actively sympathizing with the poor thing. Cara was fascinated by their reactions. *Were men really that stupid?* It occurred to her she must have seen Dashiell at the gallery. She wondered how long he'd been serving as Camille's knight-in-shining-armor, and asked, "That's something to go through together. Were you two dating long when …"

"It was a *first* date," he said. "In fact, I don't even think it was a real date."

"Oh, but he was so brave," Camille said, her eyes two searchlights beaming on Prince Charming. She turned toward Cara and asked, "How could you not fall in love with him?" Cara heard the subtext, *"I own this man. Stay the fuck away."*

"How long ago did this happen?" Cara asked.

Dashiell told her the day. She realized it was the night after her conversation with Camille about Simmons. At the least, the girl had a way of attracting mayhem.

"I know Detective O'Brien, too," Camille announced.

"You do?" Dashiell asked.

"Yes, she came to the gallery, with her partner. It was at that opening where we met. They wanted to talk to me because I might have been the last person to talk to this man besides whoever killed him."

"What man?"

"I didn't know him," she told her beau. "There was a business dinner, and I left and went into a bar on my way home to check some texts. He bought me a drink and we talked."

"Maybe you shouldn't talk to strangers in bars," he said with a slight edge.

"Maybe I shouldn't," she said looking at him with a grin that Cara read as both lewd and lascivious, yet somehow at the same time demure and innocent. Adorable was the word that popped into her mind. Somehow this woman managed not only to be outrageously attractive, but *adorable* – as in men, all men, seemed to adore her.

Cara now feared an imminent PDA was coming, and there it

was, just a quick smooch on the lips, fortunately no exchange of bodily fluids.

"Did you ever find the murderer?" The *femme fatale* asked, directing her attention to Cara.

"The case is still open," Cara replied. She sensed Camille was aware of her suspicions and mentally volleying back, *"You'll never know. And if you keep trying to find out you'll wind up dead like those boys."*

A couple of the men Cara had noticed earlier came back from the poolroom. It turned out they were all in a band with Dashiell, who of course was the lead singer. Introductions were made and the two couples joined the others for some games. Watching Camille set up her shots, it looked to Cara almost as though she was underplaying. *What could that be about? Sparing their egos, or something else?*

One of Dashiell's band mates whom she had just beaten in pool, asked Cara whether or not she was with Justin.

"In the sense of came here with, but we're not dating," she told him, thinking at first he was gay and interested in her friend. In Camille's presence, she felt almost invisible to men.

It surprised her when he asked for her number, but it was Justin who accompanied her home. Given the late hour and long walk to the train, he stayed over, but slept chastely on the living room couch.

Chapter 3

Dashiell would be going to California for almost a week. An independent movie producer, the father of a college friend, was interested in his as yet unproduced play – a romantic dramedy set in a university much like the one he'd attended. His agent had arranged a couple of long-shot auditions for movie roles. He asked her to go with him, but Alphonsine came up with a "work related" excuse. Travel always complicated things. Sooner or later he'd note her reluctance to go out into the sun. He'd never suspect the truth, but he'd suspect something that might muck things up. She could mesmerize him or use a more powerful tool like dream-walking, which entailed injecting a small amount of venom into a sleeping subject. It worked well for planting memories or feelings, and while the effects might wear off, he'd have no memory of her actually nipping him. But she hated the idea of playing with his mind. She was proud he loved her for herself, and while she might not have been completely honest with him about every aspect of her life, what woman was?

His flight was scheduled for that evening. She'd lent (not given) him a key, and left the bedroom door unbolted, so that he could let himself in, and they could have more time together before together before he left for the airport. It took him a while to rouse her.

"Bathroom," she mumbled, staggering out of bed. She took out the small zippered case she kept hidden under the sink, and injected a combination of coke and amphetamine strong enough to get her through till dusk.

"Feel better?" He asked. He was naked, waiting for her on the bed. Hard and ready.

"Splashed some cold water on my face," she said, coughing slightly as she sometimes did when she woke too early. She swigged the espresso he'd brought for her, but ignored the croissant. The idea of food at that hour repelled her. He started to nibble on her toes

142

and was working his way up. While her desire for him was strong, she wondered whether it might be a good time to spice things up.

"I have an idea," she said.

"I love your ideas," he said, having worked his way up to her knees.

She reached over and took the handcuffs from her drawer. They'd played with some of her other toys, but she hadn't introduced him to these. The idea of his having control over her – especially during daylight when she'd be physically vulnerable, appealed to her.

"I could be your slave," she said. "You could make me do anything you want."

"You already do everything I want," he said.

"You're not into it?"

"Is it something you need?"

"I need whatever you need."

"Are you bored with what we have?"

"Never," she answered, "I was worried you might be. Men so love variety."

"Why would I want anything else? You're fantastic. Sometimes when you're sucking me off I get the feeling you could swallow my entire dick."

"What a romantic thing to say," she replied throwing a pillow at him.

"Word fail," he said. "I meant well."

"A girl's got to earn a living," she said lightly, but then she saw a look of horror in his eyes. "I'm kidding. It was a joke."

"I know. I'm sorry," he said running his long fingers through her hair. "It's just sometimes I can't believe my luck. That you love me."

"I do."

"And I love you," he continued, " and we've created this, this *paradise* here in this room, which for some reason you keep so dark, but my point is you used to party every night, and now you're spending all your time with me. And I know you don't need anyone to take care of you, but I feel like I am somehow."

She kissed him, and then they rolled over till she was on top. She grabbed his arms playfully. Then quickly, and with his cooperation, cuffed his wrists to the bedpost.

She could feel his enjoyment, tinged with the slightest bit of anxiety.

"Maybe you don't want me as your slave. But I'd love to have you as mine," she said.

"What are you going to do to me?"

"I don't know. I haven't decided. Maybe fuck you to death."

"I'd like to see you try."

"Shut up, I'm serious," she said. "I could bite right into your neck while you're inside me and drain all of your blood." It felt so good to say it. She stroked his cock lightly with one hand as the other caressed his thighs and she began to lick. "Would you like to die in my embrace?"

"Christ," he said. "Please, inside you – not the mouth."

She slapped him. "You don't give me orders." But then she climbed on top as he wished, slipping him in. She moved just slightly at first, gripping with her muscles.

"We're going to take this nice and slow," she said.

The curtains were closed tight, but she could feel the night coming, and her strength returning. She began to ride him more and more violently commanding him not to come until she ordered it. Her pace increased. He had no idea she was still holding back. It was barely sundown, but her desire to feast on him was strong. Had she not stolen away on a hunt a few evenings before, it might have overwhelmed her. Finally, he let out a groan, and with it an apology because he knew she wasn't yet sated.

"Let me rest a minute," he said.

She looked at him harshly.

"Please, mistress. Let me rest. I beg you."

She climbed off and began to lick him. She knew it would take very little to get him aroused again.

"Could you let me out of these?" He asked.

She shook her head. "I say when."

"I'm thirsty," he said. "Please could you bring me some water?"

She rose and went into the bathroom where she used a douche bottle to fill her pussy. She came out a minute later.

He looked at her uncertainly.

"You'll get your water, you lazy slave, but first you must satisfy your mistress."

She climbed onto the bed placing her cunt in his face. He started to do his duty.

"Here's your water," she said relaxing her muscles and quiffing out the liquid she'd stored for him.

She could feel him choking and then beginning to swallow. He kept sucking, even after the water was gone. She loved the feel of her wet twat against his stubble, the liquid from her pussy mixing with his saliva. She continued to ride his lips and mouth, reaching back with one arm to stroke his reanimated member, but she had to let go as she came. Her body was on fire, and while her kind rarely ran out of breath, she had begun to hyperventilate.

After, she moved off and rested by his side.

"Christ," he said. "That was …"

"Shut up," she told him working her way down and sucking him for all of three seconds before a rush of cum hit her throat.

"Wow," he said as she unlocked the cuffs. "Where did you learn that?"

"You haven't been with many French girls, have you?"

They showered together as there wasn't much time till the car would come to take him to Kennedy. Drinking their final espressos, he began to talk about his upcoming trip.

"I may meet my dad, for lunch, in LA."

"Your dad?"

"You sound surprised."

"It's just you hardly mention him. I know he paid for your college. But I didn't think you were close."

"We're not. He wasn't all that nice to my mother. She was number three by the way."

"Three?"

"Out of the five wives of. I don't think he ever thought my mom was woman-of-great-man material."

"Great man?" Alphonsine felt a strange queasiness, a sense of *déjà vu*.

"You really don't know, do you? I never said anything, but I assumed …"

She stared at him blankly.

"My father is David Alexander."

"Who is?"

"The novelist," he said, and then he went on to name a few titles, which sounded familiar as spy and action movies she had never seen.

She began laughing. "*Your* father is a famous writer."

It was a mere coincidence, she thought, that this handsome young man with whom she had felt an immediate connection, was so like another similarly inclined youth whom she had once loved. How

145

strange to find out both had famous fathers who were writers. *One lives long enough and runs into oddities.*

"What's so funny?"

"Nothing," she said quickly. "So that's your darkest secret."

"No, I just don't talk about him a lot." He bit into a croissant and added, "It was my grandfather who kept the big family secret."

"Do tell," she said, sipping her espresso, and wondering if the similarities to her long lost love made her feelings for him even deeper – if that were even possible. With Alexandre *fils* she never stood a chance. The conventions of the day were against them, but Dashiell thought of her as a social equal. Of course now, there was that matter of the other impediment – her immortality and need to kill.

"Actually, my father wrote about it a few years ago. You may have read something."

"Darling, until a minute ago I hadn't even heard of him."

"He was doing research into his ancestry, and found out his dad was Creole from New Orleans. His grandparents were very light-skinned, moved north, and identified as white people. It's possible my grandfather didn't know. My grandmother certainly didn't."

"Your part …?"

"Black. I mean probably one sixteenth or something."

"How interesting." She was trying not to babble, but how strange that in addition to his own literary aspirations and having a famous writer father, his family, like that of her Adet, had some African roots. She reached out and touched his head. "Probably explains your curly locks. Well, say hello to your father for me."

"I doubt it's going to happen. He'll probably be out of town. I don't even have his phone number," he said shaking his head. "I have his assistant's cell."

The buzzer rang. The car had arrived. She took the ride with him. After she got back from the airport, Pierre stopped by with some attractive new young people. They all had a blast until dawn.

Chapter 4

Cara and Justin had a lunch date at an old staple, a Polish joint on the north side of Williamsburg, just across McCarren Park from Greenpoint. She brought up the jailhouse deaths of Dashiell and Camille's attackers.

"Violent people meet violent ends," Justin told her. "A suicide, a fight, an accident. It's not so mysterious."

"And what did you think of her?"

"In addition to being gorgeous and charming?"

"That's it," Cara said. "The *charming* thing. She's not the most beautiful woman in the world, is she? I mean feature by feature?"

"She may be close," Justin said, a dreamy look in his eyes. "But yeah, it's not *just* her looks. There's like a light within her, or maybe the way the light reflects on her. You want to … save her, but at the same time there's something a little dangerous about her. She's sexy, but also innocent like she's not trying to be sexy or trying not to be sexy or … I'm babbling aren't I?"

"Little bit."

"You see it too, don't you? Even though you're a woman?"

"I do see it. But I wanted to hear your take. You don't think it's *weird*?"

He looked at her a long while.

"What? *What?*" Cara asked.

"I was just thinking, you seem …" he trailed off.

"Seem what?"

"It's none of my business."

She gave him a look.

"Is it possible you could be maybe a little *attracted* to her yourself?" He asked.

Cara shook her head. "What is it with men? You're all obsessed with women being together, aren't you?"

"I'm just saying you talk about her a lot."

"I used to date your brother."

"That was a long time ago. Women have a lot more," he paused looking for the word while chewing a pierogi, "flexibility. Or so I've heard."

"Fuck you, Justin. Even if I were hot for women, which I'm not by the way, not that, you know, I wouldn't be ..."

"Why not? She's amazing. And if I were into dudes, I would totally do her boyfriend. I mean they're like gods."

The restaurant, which Cara remembered as once being a hangout for groups of immigrant working men looking for inexpensive home cooking, was now filled, as was the entire community, with the young and hip. There was a line forming out front, and once they finished their food, the waitress started eyeing them impatiently as they continued to sip their coffee.

"I really can't stand this neighborhood anymore," Cara said sadly.

"Well today we have a mission," Justin replied.

They walked down Bedford Avenue browsing boutiques and bookstores. Justin was looking for a birthday present for his sister-in-law, whom Cara might have been, if she hadn't dumped his brother.

The right thing, whatever it was, eluded them. When they reached North 2nd, she couldn't help herself. "Dumont Gallery is down the block," she said.

Justin didn't say anything, but gave her a look that did.

"I only bring it up," she continued, "Because they have some cheap stuff there – for the tourists and day-trippers, like us."

The gallery sold prints of well-known photos, a few from their own recent exhibitions, along with some locally made jewelry, coffee mugs featuring the logo, fine art magnets, phone cases, and other such items as might be found in a museum shop.

It was Justin who scanned the room, and then spoke to the young woman behind the display case, as Cara read information about how a percentage of sales on selected items went to support an orphanage in Sainte Trinité managed by a former gallery intern.

"Is Camille here? We're friends of hers," Justin asked the attractive cashier.

Cara wondered if he was trying to impress the girl, who looked maybe nineteen and way too arty to date a prosecutor.

"I've never seen her."

Cara was interested. "You work here, and you've never seen

her?"

"I only work during the day."

"Yeah, so?"

"You said you were her friend." The girl shrugged like that explained it.

He bought a print. The next stop would be a framer nearby. As they were walking, Justin asked, "What's up now? You look a million miles away."

"I'm just thinking. The other night, you'd met him before, right? It didn't seem like you met *her*."

"Yeah. I asked them both to come in for a victim interview. She couldn't make it."

"You didn't conference her in or anything?"

"No. We were playing telephone tag, and she finally left a message saying Dashiell could speak for her. Why?"

"It's going to sound whacky, but I don't think anyone ever sees her while the sun's up."

"Yeah, that's it," Justin said. "You're not obsessed or anything. You just think she survives on the blood of virgins."

"Who said they had to be virgins?" Cara replied. "I mean around here that would be pretty unlikely."

≈⊛≪

Alphonsine's first date with the mayor was scheduled while Dashiell was still in Los Angeles.

Dashiell skyped her at dusk. "I was going to leave you a video. I didn't expect you to be up. Isn't it still daylight?"

It took her a second to get this was not an accusation.

"Sundown on the East Coast," she reminded him.

"What are you doing?"

"Deciding what to wear. Client dinner."

"Where?"

"I don't know. Pierre's hosting."

"I like what you got on. You look amazing."

"This?" She asked, stepping back so he could get a full view. "It's just a little black dress."

"It shimmers," he replied.

"But the beading makes me look fat," she said, turning around so he could see from all angles."

"Not fat," he said.

With her back to him, she reached around to hug herself, and then pulled down the zipper allowing the sleeves to fall from her slim shoulders. She wriggled a bit until the dress slipped to the floor, and then she quickly bent down with her legs straight to pick it up. She turned around to face him, holding it in front of her body. Then she let it drop, exposing her bra, panties, and garters. She walked closer to the screen until Dashiell had a close up of her breasts.

"I hope you're alone," she said.

"If I weren't, it would be too late."

He had taken off his shirt, but not his jeans. He opened the fly and she could see his erection.

"What's that music you have on?" He asked.

"Opera." She was now straddling a wheeled office chair.

"I get that," he said. "It's familiar. What is it?"

She still had almost an hour before the car would come for her – time enough to play.

"*Dona e mobile*. From *Rigoletto*," she said stepping out of her shoes. She turned around, and reached her arm back to unhook her bra, then threw it onto the floor. She placed one foot on the coffee table and began slowly rolling a stocking down a long shapely leg.

"Really," he replied slightly breathless. His hand moved slowly. She could see he was trying to make it last. "What's it about?"

"There's this innocent girl named Gilda. She's a teenager. A virgin," she said, tossing the stocking toward the screen and beginning to roll down the other one. "Her father, Rigoletto, is very protective and doesn't let her out of his sight. She meets a young man in church and falls in love. She *thinks* he's a poor student who loves her too."

"But he's not?" Dashiell asked, continuing to lightly stroke his shaft.

She shook her head as she began to play with her nipples. "He's really the duke. And the duke is an evil rat-bastard seducer."

"Tell me more."

She moved her body into various positions. The music, her own opera mix, was now playing the *Seguidilla* from *Carmen*.

"Rigoletto works for the duke, so do a bunch of other guys, but they don't like how Rigoletto always makes jokes at their expense, so they decide to kidnap Gilda. And they take her to the duke and …"

"Oh yeah. I like that," Dashiell said as she wriggled out of her black panties, and spread her legs. Realizing the office chair would not work for what she had in mind, she blew him a kiss and went off screen for a moment, coming back pushing the ottoman, all while continuing the narrative.

" … and the duke *takes* her," she told him laying down with her legs out wide, stroking her pussy, which was exposed to the screen. She continued to move her legs in the air – up and down, side to side, circles, striking various poses, like a Bob Fosse dancer.

"Takes her," Dashiell repeated. "I like that."

"He takes her every way he can. He takes her tied up and tied down. He takes her up the ass and in the mouth. He sucks on that virgin twat until she's dying of pleasure, than slowly he sticks his big hard dick inside her and she feels like he's cutting right through her, but she loves it."

She sat up and shook her hair out like Rita Hayworth. "And then her daddy comes to rescue her, but she's still crazy in love with that bad boy duke."

She stood up, then for variety turned her back again, bent down, and with her face between her legs pulled her butt cheeks apart, giving him a dual entry view. An idea came to her. "Be right back," she said before running to the bedroom.

"Crap, not now," Dashiell said.

Maria Callas, *Sempre Libera* was blasting from the speakers.

She returned with a vibrating dildo.

"You got skills," Dashiell shouted at the screen laughing. His cock looked like it was about to explode.

She licked her lips and continued the story, talking faster and faster while stroking and occasionally licking the phallus. "Rigoletto hires an assassin to take out the duke, and the duke goes out to the assassin's sleazy inn, and the killer's sister, Magdalena, is getting the duke drunk, so her brother can strike when he's asleep. Meantime Gilda and her father are listening outside and watching through a window as the duke is making love to the killer's sister.

"Tell me what Magdalena looks like," Dashiell demanded.

"She's a complete slut," Alphonsine told him, arching her back with her legs up in the air. "She has long wild hair," she said playing with her own. "And firm hard titties. And her pussy is always open for business," she said as she spread her lips and plunged the toy inside of her.

"Oh God. Don't stop," Dashiell cried.

151

"But wait, there's more," she told him laughing. "Seriously, hold back for two more minutes."

"I'll do my best."

"Hands free," she commanded.

"All right you tease," he said putting his hands behind his head.

She was thrusting the dildo in and out, hugging herself and writhing.

"Rigoletto tells Gilda he's sending her out of town and the duke is already a dead man. She begs him not to go through with the murder, but he grabs her and they leave. Then while daddy's out making some arrangement, she sneaks back to warn her lover." Alphonsine sat up, playing with her tits. "She's wearing men's clothes."

"Why?"

"Because the night is dangerous. She's outside the window at the inn. The duke's sleeping, and Magdalena is begging her brother not to kill him because even though she's a hardened whore who's fucked hundreds of men, she can't resist him."

Alphonsine paused for a moment and looked at Dashiell's face and said, "She loves him."

"I can't wait much ..."

She continued on her back again, sliding the toy in and out of her hot, wet vagina, as Dashiell returned to stroking his cock. She was breathing heavily, pausing between words, "So, the killer, agrees to murder, the next person who, walks in, and let the duke live, and Gilda, goes into the inn, knowing she'll be killed to save ..."

"Oh God," they both yelled at the same time.

"... save the duke," she continued after a breath.

They were looking at each other's image on the screen. She was naked. He was bare-chested, and she could see the sweat glistening on him, and the glob of cum, shiny on his pants.

"You've stained yourself," she said. "I wish I was there to lick it off."

"Camille, I know one thing's for sure," Dashiell said.

"Huh?"

"When I get back to the city, we're going to the opera."

She had barely gotten her dress back on when the concierge

announced that Pierre's driver was waiting. He took her through the back roads of Queens, avoiding the commuter traffic on the major thoroughfares. As they passed neighborhood after neighborhood she wondered who lived in these villages, and how big a deal the occasional missing person might be. Certainly, they weren't like the *favelas*, where bodies could be left on the street question free, but they might do when other arrangements couldn't be made.

They were going to a place out on Long Island used by the mayor for his assignations. It was an old mansion, on the North Shore, an area Alphonsine had visited decades ago, before it had turned into subdivisions filled with middle management.

As instructed, the driver let her out and drove away. She walked up to the door and rang the bell. The blonde who answered was obviously not a servant. She looked to be close to thirty, taller than Alphonsine, more buxom, and dressed in a not inexpensive off-white business suit. It was cut short enough to show off her legs, but not short to the point of vulgarity, though the heels were a bit too high and pointy for the office. The feet themselves did not look dainty.

"You must be Camille," the woman said, shaking her hand as though they were about to enter a boardroom.

"Yes," she answered, wondering how many the little man had invited to the party.

"I'm Natalie," the woman said. "It's a pleasure to meet you." It didn't take telepathic power to hear the disconnect in the words and the tone.

There were nuts in a glass bowl on a glass table. Natalie sat down on a beige couch just a shade darker than her clothes, and Alphonsine joined her. The room was not very large. The floors were bare wood. There was little furniture. The ceilings were high. There were glass doors leading to a deck and a view of the bay.

"He'll be down in a few minutes," Natalie said. "We only just arrived ourselves. He's showering."

"How considerate of him." There was an open bottle of champagne in an ice-bucket on the table along with three clean glasses. Alphonsine poured one for herself and one for Natalie.

She raised her glass, as did the other woman.

"To good times," Alphonsine said. "Have you known his honor long?"

"I work for him. For the city," Natalie said.

The implication that a woman, even in the twenty-first century, would still need to sleep with a powerful man to get ahead was not a surprise to Alphonsine, but it saddened her to think there had been so little progress.

"So it's kind of an office romance," Alphonsine said.

Natalie looked at her. Alphonsine could tell she was trying to work out whether or not she was being ironic. Of course she was, but her simulation of innocence had been her trademark for so long, she had quite perfected it.

"You could say that. I guess," Natalie said. "We're very close."

It didn't take telepathy for Alphonsine to understand the sentiment. *"He is mine, sister. No matter what he does with you tonight, don't forget it."*

"And I'm sure this invitation must be from both of you then."

"Naturally," Natalie answered too quickly, gulping down her champagne. "We thought it would …"

Piccolini was coming down the stairs, dressed in a silk men's robe. It didn't look like there was anything underneath.

"Good evening, Camille," he said smiling. "I see you've met Natalie."

"Yes," she said, "only just." Looking over the blonde, it finally came to her who it was she reminded her of – a young Jerry Hall. *Now, that had been a threesome!*

"Natalie is a lawyer. From Harvard," he said.

She smiled politely at both of them. "Harvard. Your parents must be so proud." She could smell the emotions she was revving up in Natalie. They'd make for fireworks later. His honor too was picking up on the tension.

He turned towards his paramour. "And you're familiar with Ms. St. Valois' work."

"I'm a big fan of Dumont's," she said.

Alphonsine wondered whether Natalie was merely trying to keep her job, or perhaps the poor girl had delusions of being the next Mrs. Mayor Piccolini. She'd met the missus and was certain she would not go quietly. Nor could she imagine the ambitious politician taking on a trophy wife and losing the vote of most women over forty.

She wondered whether her presence that evening was meant to provoke Natalie, degrade her, and push her away. She'd seen that trick used before.

They made the smallest of small talk. The mayor took out a

cigar. Alphonsine instinctively reached for it, bit off the end, and lit it before handing it back to him.

While the mayor thanked her and smiled, both he and Natalie were surprised by the gesture, and Alphonsine found herself explaining, "My father smoked cigars."

Given the rules he so diligently enforced regarding the use of tobacco, Alphonsine thought it ironic to see him light up, but not surprising. *How often did public rhetoric match private behavior?*

Natalie announced she was going to change into something less formal. The mayor made a throat clearing noise and asked her to bring in the something. He mumbled the last word, but she seemed to understand.

When they were alone he said, "I hope you don't mind I asked her to come to our little party."

She wasn't quite sure how he wanted her to play it. She tried to look slightly uncomfortable but accepting. "She seems very nice, and she's so pretty."

He moved in close. He had placed a hand on her thigh. "I think she might be nervous. I don't think she's done this kind of thing a lot."

"I'll let you in on a little secret," she whispered, "I haven't much either. I know people have ideas about me, but ..."

"I know," he said, beginning to move the hand up under her dress. "You're really just a sweet girl. Otherwise, I never would have invited you."

As his stubby fingers reached under her panties, she was tempted to snap his neck. There didn't seem to be any security around or servants. She could drain Natalie after, and be on a plane and into a new identity before anyone would even know. But of course, that was ridiculous. The community would be angry. She'd be broke, and it would mean giving up Dashiell, which was unimaginable.

He pulled his hand away when he heard Natalie on the stairs. The blonde was now wearing her own version of the little black cocktail dress. She was holding a small silver tray on which there was a small silver box that she placed on the table. The box was filled with cocaine.

"Oh my," Alphonsine said.

The rest of the evening passed unremarkably, and involved the usual display of girl on girl for the entertainment of the master, some unpleasant attempts at butt-sex, awkward business with shoes, and spanking. Plus more ego massage than Alphonsine had attempted in years.

Between the cocaine and the Viagra, the little man managed to stay up and *up* till almost four in the morning when he more or less collapsed with the women on either side of him. Natalie, who'd imbibed almost a fifth of vodka, was passed out as well. Alphonsine changed into a pair of capris and a tee-shirt she'd rolled into her bag, and walked onto the porch, listening to the sounds of the night. She felt uncomfortably restless, and the desire to hunt was strong.

The sound of the car, and two brief honks got her to her feet. The first thing she did when she'd settled into the backseat was check her messages. She decided not to respond to Dashiell's. She could make up an excuse later. She sent a text to Pierre, *"Merde. The things I do for money."*

Pierre texted her back, inviting her to his place. There was still time enough before dawn for them to take the day sleep together, something they hadn't done much lately. While she resented his role in setting up her "dates," he was still her best friend, and one of the few beings with whom she could discuss almost anything.

She entered the loft using the lock combination. Pierre was sitting on his couch in the midst of getting sucked off by Mika, a handsome but bland young actor with whom he was lately spending time.

Mika took his mouth off Pierre's cock, turning to look at her. Pierre moved his head back where it belonged, telling him to go on.

Alphonsine poured herself some champagne from an open bottle and sat down as Pierre let out a loud sigh.

"Now go to sleep," he said. Mika, still kneeling, leaned his head against the couch, closed his eyes, and began snoring softly.

"You've been giving him venom?" She asked with exaggerated shock, "Tsk-tsk."

"That sounds so old-fashioned. I've been calling it *l'elisir d'amore* since Rossini."

"Seriously, *mon cher*, what will you do with him?"

"Enjoy him."

"And do you also sip him then? Little by little?"

Pierre smiled. "Some of us have enough self-control to stop before they get too greedy."

"One time," Alphonsine replied, annoyed he was always going

to remind her of that unfortunate young man she'd meant only to share a bed with but had wound up feasting on in the throes of passion.

"I find regular infusions help me get through those afternoon meetings without too much damage to the skin. You might try it sometime. He's very pretty, isn't he?" Pierre asked touching the boy's golden locks. "Maybe I shall make him a god."

Alphonsine spit out champagne, laughing.

"You're right. He's not too bright," Pierre said caressing Mika's shoulders. "I suppose I'll have to end him eventually. Can't have him begin to put it together, and he's already so addled. But it's tricky these days taking someone you've been associated with. The police investigate everything. I hate the complexities of modern life."

"Let's get out the violins and talk about how our time has passed," she said raising her eyebrows.

"It has, *ma chère*. With all the cameras and *le* CSI, the sophistication of their medical tests. How much time do you think we have?"

She leaned her head back, "Pierre, after my evening, I really don't …"

"Sixty years? Eighty? I think I'd like to be here, in America, when it happens. Indians, gunslingers, even dinosaurs. It's the home of obsolescence and extinction."

"You can't say we didn't have a good run," she said.

"Look at you. Being all philosophical about death. I recall hearing you begged Anton for your life."

"I didn't beg. He badgered. You've never been through dying. You can't understand."

"We're all dying. Some of us just much more slowly." He leaned down, put his mouth on Mika's neck, and began to feed, just for a few seconds. Then he pulled away. "Have some. Don't worry, I'll push you off if it gets too much. You could use it, waking up early to see the billionaire."

Alphonsine walked over and leaned down by the boy. He smelled of youth and ambition. She picked up Pierre's cum on his breath – close enough to the mortal kind to fool them, but distinct with a certain smoky flavor. Her mouth salivated as her fangs came out and she bit in.

The next thing she was aware of was Pierre calling out her name while pushing her hard. She disengaged, licking off a few drops of blood from his skin, and then licking her own lips. "God, that was good. But you didn't need to do that. I would have stopped."

They both laughed, knowing she wouldn't have. The boy's blood was a sweet dessert, and the kind of control her friend had was beyond her.

Pierre reminded him to stay asleep until daylight. "The last thing you'll remember is having too much wine at dinner. You'll dress and leave quietly." The marks would be long gone by sunrise. They disappeared quickly from living tissue.

Alphonsine and Pierre climbed into his sleeping loft, took off their clothes, and shut the blackout curtain. They spooned with each other, but didn't make love. As they waited for dawn, she asked, "Pierre, have you ever thought of going back?"

He answered with silence.

"It's only," she continued, "If you believe it's the end of our time and …"

"You're asking if I would go through some mysterious, but reportedly horrible process in order to again become mortal so I could monitor my own decay?"

"Yes, but only if we were being hunted or exposed."

"If the choice was to die as a day-walker or as a divinity? My sweet, it was for just such a circumstance that I bought that antique guillotine."

Chapter 5

Atlantic City was Pierre's idea. Close to New York, but far enough. A place where there were many whose disappearance would hardly be noticed. They brought their mortals with them, along with a few of the hangers-on, ostensibly for a concert and a night of dancing and gambling. Pierre had arranged for two limos and booked several rooms, all with ocean view, at the Avalon – a hotel that featured thick curtains to block out the day sun. They'd reserved two nights so they wouldn't need to leave before dark.

Alphonsine hoped seeing Pierre with his alleged boyfriend would cure Dashiell of any lingering jealousy or suspicion – not that he ever said anything, but she knew he wondered. After the concert, there was dancing, then gambling. In her first life, she'd been fascinated with casinos, but now it was less exciting. Once, a lucky spin had meant debts paid and months of freedom. What could it buy her now?

She and Dashiell retreated to their room relatively early. They made love as usual. She suggested a nightcap. His was spiked. She was afraid if she nipped him he might remember later, but even more frightened she wouldn't be able to resist going further. Once he was out of it, she dressed quickly. Pierre was waiting on her balcony. The two jumped onto the sand. Walking to the street, they came upon four frat-boy types, very drunk, heading for a car. They took them from behind, leaving them unconscious but unharmed. They would wake with little memory of the previous evening.

Pierre drove the boys' car to another part of town, away from the tourists. He pulled over, and left her alone while he went to make arrangements. She waited for his text, which was almost unnecessary given the strength of their mental connection. She drove to a motel a block from where he'd left her, and knocked on a door. He let her in.

"My wife will be joining the party," he said to the two women already with him.

She was dressed simply, had tied her hair back, and wore a pair of glasses to make herself less recognizable. The women looked at her blankly. While he'd used no venom on them, he might as well have. They both seemed so beaten down.

He took out a small bag of cocaine and poured some of the contents on the laminated card featuring the available cable channels.

"Money first, hon," the older of them said.

Both women had light reddish hair and pale skin with freckles. The younger of the two was almost pretty or might have been if it weren't for a pallor and hardness. The older was a bit overweight, her belly protruding from her stretchy shirt. The first impression was they might have been sisters, but then Alphonsine felt it. They were mother and daughter. The knowledge at once sickened her and was also familiar, bringing her back to Ana's lessons at the abbey.

She wished they could hurry, do what they needed to and leave.

Pierre was in her head, reminding her everything was for *their* sake, to make it all seem normal, to not provoke fear. They were not sadists. The thing couldn't be hurried.

Pierre took out two hundred dollars handing it to the mother. "Like I said. There's another two coming."

"What do you want?" The younger one asked with a bit of suspicion. Alphonsine sensed they'd made it too easy. Two attractive people, coke and more cash than they'd normally see. They'd have to be stupid not to suspect there was a catch.

Alphonsine took out a twenty and rolled it into a straw, used it to snort a few lines and handed it to the younger woman. "We want you to get naked and show us how it's done."

"With each other?"

"For a start. A little, you know, preview."

While Alphonsine and Pierre remained clothed, standing and watching, the women stripped without finesse and got onto the bed. Both had stretch marks and needle marks. The blood would quench her hunger, but leave her with a hangover of the misery of their lives. Ana would argue they were giving them peace, releasing them. But even after all this time, she wondered, "*Why is it always whores?*"

Pierre answered her thought, *"Because they are so rarely missed."*

She tried to shut him out, as she watched the two of them on the bed, doing something more akin to wrestling than screwing.

Pierre was throwing bills at them, cheering them on – faking both enthusiasm and an American accent.

Keeping it all normal.

She thought of her last hotel room kill. It had gotten her off taking another predator. She'd thought herself superior to him, not just because of her strength, but *morally*. He tortured his victims, and killed for pleasure. Her kind also got pleasure from the kill, but they restrained themselves, strived to make it painless, and they hunted for survival. *But was she really any better than he was?*

The women seemed to have run out of moves, were waiting for the next command. She watched the look they gave each other. They were somehow untouched, laughing at their customers. It was, after all, always a trick. They'd even used the word in her day.

"What else, handsome?" the older one asked. She got up from the bed and took a few lines of cocaine. Alphonsine watched her pendulous breasts, her complete ease and lack of shame. She might not even be forty, but she was ancient for what she was – battered, addicted, abused – a victim of what one of Alphonsine's long dead patrons termed "the vicissitudes of life." Yet, there was something proud, *defiant* about her. Her daughter looked more defeated.

Pierre had unzipped his pants and signaled for the younger of the two. She was about to go down on her knees, but he held her up. "I want to kiss you," he said.

Alphonsine knew he just wanted to get closer to her neck. He'd take his prey as soon as she was ready with hers.

"Stay where you are pretty momma," she called to the older one. "Spread your legs, I really want to taste you."

Seconds later they both began to feed, he from the young one's neck, she from the older's femoral artery.

Alphonsine heard the body drop from Pierre's grip to the floor at the same time as the pulse stopped on hers. She turned to look at him, licking her lips. He came over to the bed. She pushed the mother's corpse onto the floor and mounted him. They licked the remaining blood out of each other's mouths. Both women had bitter lives, and tasted of it, but also there was the love they had for each other, the mother's protectiveness of her daughter, the daughter's connection to her own children. It was so very sad that their lives had been so empty, yet their sacrifice would sustain her and Pierre. The blood had after all been sweet enough, full enough of life to warm every part of her.

She was riding Pierre hard, a fury of emotions she couldn't begin to name flowing through her. He was holding her ass tightly, and she was glad her kind didn't retain marks or bruises.

She came first, screaming aloud, which made him laugh.

They dressed, then placed the bodies on the bed, and did a bit of clean up. She took a bottle from her bag, poured the contents on the women and around the bed, threw the match as they left. They drove to where they'd found the car. The boys were still asleep on the sidewalk, but a compact was now partially in the space. They parked in front of it, blocking a hydrant.

They walked back to the beach, shed their clothes, and ran into the icy waters of the Atlantic. She felt cleaner coming out. There was a faint glow over the water far into the east, but dawn wasn't imminent.

As they dressed, Pierre suggested they sit at one of the outdoor tables by the bar and have a drink before heading for their rooms. "Fast food always makes me thirsty."

"Have you ever thought that human souls might be immortal?" She asked Pierre after downing a glass of champagne. "That our immortality of the body is a kind of illusion, that maybe they are reborn again and again?"

He looked at her like she might have been crazy, "What brought this on?"

"The women I suppose. They were so like others I've had. What if they're the same souls acting out the same lives with the same fate over time only in different bodies."

"That sounds hellish," he said lighting a Gauloise.

"It would be, I suppose. Unless there's the possibility of something else, of different outcomes."

"Did the blood make you *high?*"

"Don't be cynical. Dashiell talks about it all the time, *karma*. The cycle of birth and death. The possibility of perfecting ourselves over time."

"You don't need to *perfect* yourself. You're perfect as you are. If he doesn't appreciate that, he's an idiot."

"But what if we're missing something by *not* dying. We don't … *evolve.*"

"Have you lost your senses?" He stomped out his cigarette. "The sun'll be up in a minute. We should get to our rooms."

Chapter 6

Dashiell was surprised to find she was such a fan of films from the 1920's and 30's. They were in bed, watching DVDs and eating popcorn seasoned with vegan "butter" and various spices. The first on the bill that evening was a silent, Louise Brook's in *Pandora's Box*. He remarked on her resemblance to Lulu.

"Louise Brooks? She came up to here on me," Alphonsine told him, placing a hand out by her chest. "And she was a little more ... meaty," she added creating an hourglass with her hands.

"You say that like you knew her."

She smiled, remembering that crazy night in Berlin. Lou had wanted her to play the lesbian lover in Pabst's masterpiece. Alphonsine claimed camera shyness, knowing she'd never get through the daylight filming.

"I guess it's something about her spirit that reminds me of you," Dashiell said. "Her openness. But what attracts you to the time period?"

"Young century. Everything felt new and alive. Even World War I and later the Great Depression couldn't kill the optimism."

"You're doing it again."

"Doing what?"

"Talking about history like you lived it."

"You're the one that thinks that's possible, right? That we've been here before. What do you want to watch next?

"Pick your favorite," he told her.

She chose *The Lady Eve*, a screwball comedy in which a naïve young man falls for a congenital cardsharp, then dumps her when he finds out what she is, only to be fooled when she comes back pretending to be someone else.

"It's a silly movie, but it's so true," she said when it was over.

"True? How?"

"Men. What she says about how they imagine women and how

wrong they are." She quoted a line, "The good ones aren't half as good as you think, and the bad ones are never so bad."

His eyes went wide watching her stretching herself out on the bed.

"Why are you looking at me like that?"

"You're so not what I'd thought you'd be."

"How so?"

"I mean stuff about you on line. Out with celebrities, partying."

"The Lindsey Lohan of the art world," she said with laugh.

"Something like that. But you couldn't look the way you do and have a drug problem, and it's not like there's a sex tape out there."

"No, Pierre and I always collect all the electronic devices before our orgies," she said deadpan.

"I saw you a couple of times on the street, before we met. I never expected we'd …"

She kissed him hard before he could complete the thought.

"And you," she said touching his face. "Do you know how special you are? How far you'll go? With your acting, your music, your writing? I don't think people even see me when I'm with you."

"I doubt that."

There was a lull that involved the two of them looking at each other, not touching, but together on the bed, a bowl of popcorn between them.

"You have some oil on your chin," she said, touching near his mouth.

He smiled.

And that was enough for her to start licking his body. She wished she could feel complete abandon, but it took control to keep her fangs down, not to nip. Still the buttery skin itself was so delicious. Ana had told her that epochs ago her kind ate the live flesh of their prey, and though that practice had been forbidden for millennia, sometimes the urge might be felt.

He was licking her too, and it didn't take long till they were perfectly aligned, mouth to cock, mouth to pussy. The popcorn spilled, but it didn't stop them. They were rolling in it. Afterward, Dashiell spooned her while picking tiny yellow bits out of her hair.

"What are you doing with the rest of your life?" He asked.

"Staying in this bed with you."

"Actually, I meant, what do you want to do? We spend so much time talking about my ambitions, but not yours. Do you want to own a gallery? Or are you a secret artist?"

"I've never been ambitious, and I'm no artist.

"I've heard you play the piano. You're ..."

"I have supple hands," she said extending them. "And a good ear. But no genius. Any of the pieces you've heard, I've practiced *forever*. I have no talent."

"I wouldn't say that," he said. He kissed the back of her head. "You can dance. You have great taste in everything."

"Especially men," she purred. "Could I confess something? It's going to sound very old fashioned."

"Sure."

"I see myself as kind of a muse. The one behind the great man who creates. His inspiration."

"I think you'd get bored."

"Not if I loved the man. Not if I believed in him." She turned toward him, and they kissed. Their bodies were slick from sweat and grease. It was hours before they finally made it to the shower and bothered to change the salty, seasoned sheets.

��⊛��

The following night was their opera date, a first for Dashiell.

She'd told him not to wear a tux. "It's not opening night. The only men in evening clothes are pretenders."

When she saw him in his linen suit, his beauty took her by surprise and made her ache. She wondered if that might have been the climax of his perfection, and it saddened her there was only one way to make it last forever.

"Is this good?" He asked.

Not wanting to feed his ego too much, she noted the small but elegant leather pouch he wore over his shoulder and said, "You may be the only American I know who can actually pull off the man purse."

Dashiell had asked her specifically to wear the beaded dress she'd had on that time they'd discussed *Rigoletto* over Skype. She had already donated it to charity, as the odor of the mayor's cigar could not be lifted. She'd found another, similar, but a dark violet color that set off her hair and eyes.

"A lot of gray heads," he whispered to her as they moved into the lobby of the opera house.

"Gray heads, pretty boys and music students," she whispered back.

She'd called in the dinner reservation at the restaurant inside the complex. The host greeted her by name and with a kiss. He kept turning his head to them as he led them to their table, appraising Dashiell, unable to take his eyes off him. They sat by the enormous glass wall overlooking the famous fountain. The waiter, with whom she was also acquainted, asked about Pierre. The chef himself told them about the off-menu appetizers – grilled organic vegetables, and a mushroom risotto – vegan "experiments" he'd planned especially for them.

"It pays to have connections," Dashiell said as they began to dig in.

"Pierre buys up a lot of tickets. Mostly he gives them away to clients. Sometimes we go together to be seen. I'm a bigger fan than he is. I think he was relieved when I asked if I could take you. Did you have time to look this one up?

"Just to get an overview. I got busy with my writing."

"Don't tell me! Your novel? Your play? Your screenplay?"

"A television pilot. Paranormal thing. It's on spec, but you never know. Mine's original, *really*.

"Do they sparkle or explode?" She asked rolling her eyes.

"They're sex vampires."

"That would be nice. Living off love."

"They emotionally drain their victims and leave them hollow shells, but there's no blood."

"No blood. Where's the fun in that?"

The warning sounded just as their empty plates were being taken away. The bottle of wine they started would remain on the table. The main course would be ready for them at the first intermission.

"Explain to me again why this is better than sitting below," Dashiell asked as they made their way to the front row of the section just above the orchestra.

"The overhang puts us as close as some of the floor seats, but with a more panoramic view, and you can take in everything from here – the musicians, the audience. Also the higher you are, the clearer the sound."

She watched as he took a quick look at his program before the chandeliers were raised and the lights dimmed. It was a score she knew almost by heart, and a production she'd seen more than once, but one of her favorite baritones would be in it, a tall, dashing Russian who reminded her a little of Anton. This was the soprano's first attempt at the role. She was young and beautiful, though a bit full figured for the part that Maria Callas had once starved herself to fit, and then owned. Of course, this one didn't have the advantage she'd given Callas – a woman whose dreams she had literally haunted.

As for the tenor, there was a sweetness in his voice that made her very much want to taste him.

When intermission came it was Dashiell who spoke first, "Wow."

"You liked it?"

"I didn't expect it to be so emotionally riveting. The stark set made it even clearer – love and death."

"That's not typical – the set I mean. Nor the modern dress. But I think it's truer to the spirit. Verdi wanted realism, *verisimo*. It was supposed to be set in the nineteenth century when it was written, but …"

"He had to set it earlier because it was so scandalous. I got that."

As they made their way back to the restaurant, several people stopped her to say hello. Air kisses were exchanged, and she apologized more than once for needing to get to her waiting dinner.

Dashiell poured the wine himself. They clinked glasses. "To my fate, which is to love you," he said referencing a line from the famous act one aria.

"*Prends garde à toi.*" she said. "That's from *Carmen*."

"Everyone knows *Carmen*," he said, and then he began to hum the toreador song.

The waiter came with their entrees – seitan scaloppini in a faux-cream sauce with a side of udon noodles and organic asparagus.

Dashiell said, "So tell me about Marie Duplessis."

"What?" she asked calmly.

"When I was looking up *La Traviata* on Wikipedia, there was a link to her."

"Oh yes, the *real* Violetta. Well, then you know Verdi saw the play *La Dame Aux Camellias*, which was based on the novel."

"About her affair with Alexandre Dumas."

"*Fils,*" Alphonsine added automatically. "Of course, everything about the bourgeois father and her agreeing to break up with her lover so that his sister can have a good marriage, that's pure fiction."

"I couldn't find a lot about her. I thought growing up in France you'd ..."

"I don't know how much she's remembered, even there. They say people still come to her grave. I doubt too many. Opera lovers, maybe. Tourists. I'm sure if it weren't for ... *this*, no living soul would have heard of her. It's ironic."

"How so?"

"There's a watercolor of her at the opera, and mention of her going in the novel. Imagine what her first visit would have been like. It must have been something for a simple country girl who'd never before been inside any type of theater, never expected to be. Could you with your actor's mind even conceive how fantastical it must have been, especially to a girl so *hungry* for everything?

"Later the director of the company, one of her platonic friends, would ask her advice, trust her taste – which was completely instinctive. It's doubtful she really *appreciated* the opera. She went to be seen, to meet people, to make *arrangements*. It was like part of her job, you know?"

"There was a portrait I saw online. You look so much like her," he said adjusting his hands to create a frame.

"Last night you said I looked like Louise Brooks. Do you think I look like everyone?"

"Maybe I see your face in every beautiful woman."

"Nice try."

"No, but you *do* look like her, your features. Or maybe it's just something about you that's timeless. Were you named for her?"

"You mean Camille, for her flowers? It's not so uncommon, my name."

"But you always have fresh cut camellias."

"A friend started sending them. It was a joke."

"A friend?"

"He's out of my life. I don't know why he hasn't stopped the order."

"Is he hoping to win you back?"

"More likely he wants to bring on asthma. He's ... eccentric. I think he does it to annoy me."

"So you'd never go back to him."

"Not in a thousand years."

"Whatever he did, I wouldn't."

"No, you wouldn't," she said.

"Is it your favorite, *La Traviata?*"

"It has a place in my heart. I love *Turandot*. It's less realistic."

"A woman dying of tuberculosis singing arias is realistic?"

"I suppose not."

"What would I recognize from *Turandot?*"

She hummed a little of *Nessun Dorma*.

He listened closely, focusing on the tune and joining her. Then he sang out uncertainly, "*Vencere, vencere.*"

"That's it. Pavarotti sang it at the World Cup once."

"What's the story?" He asked.

"Beautiful princess with intimacy problems puts exiled prince through a test."

The waiter cleared the plates, and announced they still had time for dessert. "We have dairy free dark chocolate chip cookies."

"We'll have coffee as well," Dashiell said.

He reached over to his bag, and pulled out two gift-wrapped boxes. The first was tiny, earrings she thought, or maybe a ring. The second not much bigger.

"I wanted to give you something. It doesn't have to mean more than you want it to. Or less. I don't know where we're going, Camille. I just wanted …"

"You really didn't have to," she said already unwrapping the box. "Oh, this is exquisite."

The smaller box was indeed earrings – hanging gold ones with rubies, a modern design with old tones. The larger box contained a matching necklace. She took off what she had and put them on.

"They must have cost …"

"It's not important."

"Jewelry. It's so deliciously retro, isn't it? I mean men don't do this anymore, do they? I could eat you up. You're so sweet."

She was putting on the necklace as the waiter returned. "Whoa," he said looking at them both.

The warning chimed as they were finishing dessert. Dashiell walked her back to her seat with his arm around her waist. The lights dimmed and Act II began. There were the lovers enjoying each other in the country. Dashiell was right, she thought. It was "emotionally real." And while very little could drive her to tears, she was close. The story was not *exactly* her story. Marie Duplessis had never met the Italian composer or the librettist, yet they had caught something she recognized and remembered. The core of Alexandre's fairytale was still there. It had been an almost perfect idyll, a true *affair du coeur*. But unlike his fictional counterpart, Alexandre's heart had cooled soon after the reality of who and what she was set in.

She looked at Dashiell's profile for a moment. He was transfixed by the spectacle. Listening with his entire soul. Their love was just as hopeless as that between Violetta and Alfredo, or Armand and Marguerite as they'd been named in the novel, but her poor boy didn't know it.

When it was over they went out for drinks and then dancing at a club in Chelsea. She ran into Marcela, an Argentinean model who reminded her a little of Ana. At one point the three of them were dancing together. Marcella came close enough to kiss her, but only whispered in her ear, "I've got an eight-ball in my purse. I'd love to party with the two of you, maybe back at your place?"

She shook her head with a smile, then signaled to Dashiell it was time to move on.

Marcella caught her while his back was turned. "What's wrong? He's very pretty, and you're usually so generous with your toys."

Alphonsine laughed recalling their last encounter. "He doesn't even do coke, and I don't think he'd be into a threesome."

"That would be a first."

"He's just very *American* that way," she added.

But the truth was, it was she who wasn't ready to share *him*. She didn't want him to see her with anyone else, and more than that, she didn't want to see him enjoying himself with another woman, even if it were only sex. It might be something they'd do later, to add some spice, but not now. It was still a beginning and she wanted to savor it.

They cabbed it back to Williamsburg.

As they walked toward the elevator, Dashiell said, "Maybe we should stay up together and watch the sunrise. We could get breakfast and then keep going till we crash."

"You've got more energy than I do," she replied in the elevator, hugging him. "Let's make love now, before I *crash*."

Her opera-mix was their mood music. Afterwards, as she felt herself drifting off in his arms, she thought of her own contentment. She felt so in tune with him, so intimate. It was as though she had already tasted his blood. She hadn't felt that way about anyone in so long.

"Thank you for tonight, for introducing me to opera," he said.

"Thank you for the earrings and the necklace."

"So what are we going to see next?"

"*Carmen*, maybe. Or *Turandot*."

"The one with the victory song," he said and began to softly hum the tune.

She smiled.

"What's the story?" He asked. "You started to tell me, but I can't remember. Is it another fallen woman, or a seduced virgin?"

"Neither. She's a beautiful princess in China."

"China?"

"Not real China, fairytale China. She has trust issues."

"They always do, those princesses." He sidled up even closer.

"She thinks she's an incarnation of an ancestor who was betrayed and killed by a lover, so she makes all her suitors answer riddles. When they can't, and none of them can, she has them beheaded."

"Yikes," he said.

"The people are growing restless. Her father, the emperor, is afraid her behavior will bring on a war. An exiled prince, whose identity is unknown, falls in love with her and he successfully answers the riddles."

"And they live happily ever after?"

"She's so upset he makes another deal with her. He'll forfeit his life if she can guess his name by dawn. That's where that *'vencere'* song comes in. It's a long night and her guards are out killing people, trying to find someone who knows who he is."

"And does she find out?"

"Not exactly, but she falls in love with him."

"Why him?"

"Maybe because he was willing to die twice," she said, trying for herself to come up with a logical answer. "Maybe because the one woman who knew his secret martyred herself rather than betray him. Or because he just wouldn't give up. He knew he could change her. He had faith."

"I'd die for you. I have faith," he said lightly, running his fingers through her thick dark hair. Then he asked, "So do they wind up together or does it end in tragedy?"

"Someone dies, but Turandot and the prince live happily ever after."

Despite what he'd said earlier about staying awake, she could feel his deep even breaths, signaling sleep was coming.

"Dashiell?"

"Hmm."

"Do you think if you were the prince, you would have forgiven Turandot?

"Mass murder. That's a tough one."

"But if you loved her?" She asked turning to face him although his eyes were already closed.

"I don't know. Maybe. It's only a story. Why not?"

She kissed him softly on the lips, unsure if he was still fully conscious, and she whispered. "*A la prochaine, mon amour.* Always know I love you."

Chapter 7

She had to walk some rich Italians through MOMA during their evening hours. This was followed by wining and dining them with Pierre at a new place in Williamsburg. Though the brilliant young chef had labored in some of the world's finest kitchens, their guests acted like they were slumming. They were dreadful people, the kind who thought their titles still meant something, but they were collectors and she and Pierre were trying to cultivate them.

"How is it possible to have old money and still be *nouveau riche?*" She asked him, once they'd parted from their company and were back at his place.

"Aren't you glad we have a ban on bringing royalty into our family?" He asked offering her a cup of freshly pressed organic Kona blend. "Could you imagine going through eternity with them?"

He sat down, casually looking at some gallery paperwork. "Of course, we were chosen for our *natural* aristocracy." He noticed she didn't answer, and looked at her. "*Mon Dieu.* You're thinking of that boy. What a mopey teenager, you've become."

"He's special," she said.

"I have eyes."

"It's more than that. I feel like I've always known him. I told you how his father is also a writer, and he's part Creole and ..."

"You think he's the reincarnation of your beloved Alexandre."

"Maybe he is."

"Tell me how that ended again. The real life version. Don't forget, I was with you when you saw the silly play."

"I haven't forgotten. Sarah Bernhardt had to be sixty. Marguerite Gautier, my ass. It was absurd."

"You thought it sentimental rubbish and came up with a dozen reasons why Marguerite would never have given him up – at least not without enough in cash or jewels to get through a cold winter."

"I said a season at a spa, for her consumption. She should have held out for that."

"If I recall you were also very angry with Adet, as you called him, for in your words 'exploiting' the relationship before you were even cold in the ground."

"It's stood the test of time, so I forgive him."

"I was also by your side at the Teatro Colon, for the Latin America premiere of that opera. He hummed a few bars of a second act aria while gathering his thoughts. "The audience was in tears when Germont is begging Violetta to break with Alfredo so that his pure as an angel daughter can get married, and you were laughing. Quite loudly. I had to poke you to stop the spectacle. You told me later the only request Dumas *père* ever made was for a blowjob."

"He was drunk at the time," she said.

"You never told me your reply."

"Tra la la la la la la la la," she sang in her best *Carmen*.

Pierre clapped his hands. "Brilliant evasion. You should have gone into politics. *Ma chère*, almost two centuries ago you created a character. You played the part with genius, but now you've come to believe your own myth. What did you ever give up for love?"

"I would have given anything for ..."

"Liszt? Or Alexandre?"

"Either, if they'd given me a chance. Nobody understood that I *loved*, that I *could* love. Dashiell doesn't think of me as a trophy or an object that can be bought, but as a healthy, vibrant woman who loves him."

"Good thing he doesn't realize you're an *undead* woman."

"What a word, taken from third-rate penny dreadfuls."

"In any case, you are going to have to give him up."

"Years from now."

"How long do you think it will be safe for us here? We make our money. We have some fun. We move on before they notice our peculiarities, which are a lot easier to spot these days than ever before."

"But we're established. We're careful where we hunt. No one gets old. They Botox and have their skin tightened," she said, demonstrating by pulling on her face. "It'll be years before anyone even suspects."

"We're already too high profile. And by we, I mean you. The elders tolerate it because we bring in a lot of money, but if you're right about him, he'll be famous soon. And we don't need that kind of attention."

"Of course you're making sense. I just can't think about…"

Pierre began playing an imaginary violin. "Life without him?"

"Something like that."

"You could …"

"No, I couldn't. He doesn't eat meat because he doesn't believe we should kill farm animals. He'd never accept the taking of human life to survive."

"It might be less painful to kill him then to go on knowing he's somewhere in the world. Being reminded of him when you see movie posters, reading about his exploits – his marriages, his triumphs. Watching from afar as he grows old. You've been through that before. Think of it. You could get married, go off on a honeymoon, spend the perfect night together, even a day or two with some chemical helpers, take him quickly at the peak of his happiness, and lose the body at sea. What man wouldn't want to die in your arms? And he'd make such a beautiful corpse."

"I won't hurt him. Maybe that's the grand sacrifice I was meant to make."

"In the opera doesn't Violetta's sacrifice bring on her death?"

"But I can't die. At least, not so easily, from a broken heart."

"*Ma chère*, we must take a trip, a vacation when this business is done. You shouldn't have to work again for decades."

Her phone buzzed. It was the subject of their conversation. She and Dashiell made plans for him to drop by later. Neither was in the mood to go out, but they talked about possibly catching a movie on Sunday. She watched Pierre gesture, trying to tell her something, but she couldn't get it, even mentally.

"Love you too." She ended the call and looked at her friend. "*What?*"

"I'm sorry, my love, but tomorrow night there is a certain vertically challenged billionaire requesting your presence."

"Oh Pierre, I can't."

"Of course you can. You agreed to three dates."

"What will I tell Dashiell?"

"That's a tough one given you've never before lied to a man."

She took a sip of coffee, which left a bitter aftertaste. "What is the point to life if we aren't free to love?" She asked.

"You really do spend too much time at the opera."

❧ ✾ ☙

Cara was convinced she did her best work while riding her bicycle, especially on empty streets or through quiet neighborhoods. Must have been the blood pumping. New perspectives and patterns would pop into her mind as though placed there by an outside force.

She crossed through Greenpoint into the Hassidic part of Williamsburg, then passed a no-man's land of factories and the occasional outpost of early-onset gentrification, eventually reaching newly renovated brownstones in once iffy neighborhoods, as she headed towards Prospect Park. It was a sunny day, and the oasis was filled with the perfect Brooklyn combo of Park Slope gentry pushing designer baby strollers, West Indian immigrants blasting old school reggae from vintage boom boxes, and too many other groups and ethnicities to count. She was on her second lap around, passing the lake, planning on coming out along Ocean Parkway and taking its wide, car-free bike lane over to the boardwalk for a quick peek at the Atlantic.

Riding heightened her senses. She could be in a zone where she was aware of the cars and the pedestrians, and at the same time she could be somewhere else, seeing everything from a different angle.

There was a tall male in front of her on a vintage Nasbar touring bike. A savvy choice if he wasn't interested in speed and got it cheap on Craigslist. His helmet covered his hair. His legs were strong, long and lean, and the ass truly a thing of beauty. She could maintain her pace and watch his glutes, or she could push ahead and grab a look at his face. Turning around, even for a moment might be tricky with so many other bikers, plus joggers, skaters and walkers doing the loop, but it was tempting.

She easily caught up, managed to get alongside of him, and blurted out, "Nice bike."

He turned his head, and she almost lost her balance when she realized who it was.

Dashiell smiled and called out, "Hello, Detective Cara."

Better to pretend she recognized him all along, rather than let him think she was trying to pick him up.

They made bike talk while riding. He suggested taking a break by the lake, said he needed to stretch his legs.

"Great. I could use a bathroom," she told him.

"That works. I'll watch your bike while you're in. Then you can watch mine."

"Deal," she said.

And that was how she found herself with Dashiell Alexander, possibly the handsomest man she'd ever seen in real life, and the lover of a woman she still suspected of, at least, something.

He was surprisingly easy to talk to. She couldn't forget how attractive he was, but felt she was managing not to sound like a complete idiot. He complained about tightness in his tendon. She showed him some of her favorite stretches, aware of his eyes on her body. He asked about her routes. She was surprised he hadn't ridden to the beaches of New York, or even seen them yet.

"I was just going out to Coney Island. We're only a few miles from the ocean," she told him.

"Do you mind if we ride together?"

"Not at all. I love showing off the wonders of my hometown."

There wasn't much talking on the ride itself. They needed to stay single file on the road. She led, as she was the one who knew the way. This left her at the disadvantage of not being able to enjoy the view of Dashiell, but it was probably better that way she reasoned. She wasn't going to try to compete with Camille, and still hadn't ruled out the possibility he was covering for her.

Was she imagining she could feel his eyes on her back? Probably her fantasy, she decided, or meaningless in any case. There was just a little too much respect in the way he spoke to her, an awareness she was a few years older than he. It was clear he'd already put her in the friend box. Just what she needed, another male buddy for whom she secretly harbored an attraction.

They stopped for a few minutes to walk their bikes along the boardwalk and check out the damage from the previous fall's storm.

Cara started telling him about the clean-up. She'd helped out a couple of weekends.

"It's amazing with your work and everything you found time." he said admiringly.

They made it back to Williamsburg taking a route that ranged from renovated Victorians with small but carefully tended gardens, to scruffier pockets. She gave him a short bike tour of Greenpoint, showing him where new buildings were going up, as well as a small park, the Catholic church she'd attended as a child, and the adjacent parochial school. Afterwards, he wanted to buy her a beer to thank her, and so they headed to the bar where they'd run into each other before.

"Do you want to text Justin to join us?" Dashiell asked.

She thought of trying to explain they weren't a couple, but why bother? It was clear Dashiell was not in any way flirting with her. Besides, he was in love with Camille St. Valois.

Before she could answer, he was focusing on his phone, checking for messages from his beautiful girlfriend, and composing a text.

"I don't know why I bother," he said. "It's only five. She's probably still sleeping."

"She have a late night?"

"She has a late night every night. Her sleep wake cycle is completely reversed."

"That's a little weird, isn't it?"

"She has to put in appearances to promote the gallery – parties, clubs."

"I wouldn't have thought of working at a gallery as a night job," she said sipping her Brooklyn Lager. "Does she *ever* come out during the day?"

"Not much."

"Hmm. Have you ever *seen* her during the day."

"Of course I've seen her. She doesn't sleep in a coffin if that's what …"

"I'm sorry. It's the cop thing. I can't always turn it off."

"I bet you're pretty good at it."

"I work hard."

They talked a little about *his* work, the writing, as well as the acting. She didn't find him as insufferable as other artist types she'd met. He seemed genuinely interested in who she was and what she did. She wondered how she might act if he came onto her. Usually, she stayed away from men in relationships, and especially men in relationships with potential suspects, but what if her instincts about Camille were valid? Could she rescue him by taking him away from her? And what were the odds of her being able to pull *that* off?

As he went on talking, she tried to listen, but couldn't help her mental travels. She understood she was attracted to him because who wouldn't be? But why would someone with Camille be attracted to anyone else, unless he was aware there was something about her just a little or maybe a lot off.

She casually steered the conversation toward the subject of his girlfriend.

"You know, she really admires you. She told me what you did

was *real*," Dashiell said.

"She said that after we met at the bar?"

"Yeah, we were talking about it."

"But when she talked about how we met, she hadn't told you that before, about being questioned."

"I think you're being a cop again."

"Sorry. Tell me more about what happened when you guys got mugged."

She listened, asking questions about exactly what Camille did and when she did it.

"She sounds surprisingly strong."

"She said it must have been an adrenaline thing, but she was pretty amazing. It was like she knew exactly what I was going to do before I did it. Almost like ... this is going to sound ..."

"What?"

"Like she was with me in my head."

"Isn't that what love's supposed to be like?"

"I guess it is. But we hardly knew each other at the time. It was really this awesome connection."

Cara had the impression he was on the verge of continuing, about to tell her how the night ended with their having the best sex of his life, but he managed to stop himself.

"Do you mind if I ask you something?" She asked.

"What?"

"Okay. I am not obsessed with your girlfriend. But when I was involved in that investigation, I did a little checking around. I mean, she's shown up at some benefits, and all the Sainte Trinité stuff, but there's a lot of gossip out there about her and her boss and ..."

"That's all it is, gossip," Dashiell said, coolly.

"Sorry. I didn't mean ..."

"I guess when you're dating a beautiful woman, there's going to be talk. But it's all bull. You've met her. You know how unpretentious she is, how honest, and *nice*. She doesn't have a mean side. You heard the way she talked about the robbery and those men who ..."

"Yeah, she did say she felt sorry for them. That's so strange, right? That all the guys who tried to hurt her are dead within two weeks."

"You probably know more about that than I do."

"I never heard anything like it before."

He changed the subject rather deliberately to suppositions about what the couple at the table in the corner might be saying to each other. It looked to him like a break-up, while Cara suspected another kind of bombshell, maybe a pregnancy, or a confession. He told her he liked mixing her police perspective with his actor/writer take, and asked about hanging out with homicide for research. He was trying to write a television pilot, on "spec" – a concept he explained to her.

She realized any attraction was in her head. He was being friendly, chatting her up for the possibility of a ride along.

They ran into the band mate, John, the one who'd asked for her number but never called. She felt embarrassed, wondering if he thought she'd come into the bar hoping to run into him. He offered a rematch at the pool table.

"I've actually got to get going. Maybe another time."

John went to order a drink. Dashiell walked her to the door.

"Look, I hope I didn't offend you if I said anything about Camille that …"

"Forgiven."

"Dashiell, I don't want to act all big sister and stuff, but …"

"You don't like my girlfriend."

"I don't *know* her. I just think maybe you don't know her as much as you think either. And I'm not saying this from a bad place. I don't know *you* either."

"That's right," he said, "You don't. I had a great time biking with you. Maybe we could even do that again. Or the four of us could hang. But the ground rule is, I don't want to listen to any shit about Camille."

"I get it." She put out her hand and he took it. Then he brought her into a "we're good" hug. She said good-bye and left, not sure if she should have said more, or less.

Chapter 8

The second date was at the same North Shore location, but this time his honor himself answered the door, dressed in slacks and wearing the kind of sports jacket a man might wear on his yacht.

"Good evening," he said.

"Hi," she cooed. She looked around the room. "Are we alone?"

"Yes."

"Good," she said, and then she got close. He reached up to kiss her.

"Sit down," he said. "I'll get you a drink."

"Champagne, if you have it."

"Of course."

"I'm sorry if you were uncomfortable last time," he said.

She wasn't sure what he was apologizing for.

He caught something in her expression, and continued, "Natalie and I, bringing you into our insanity. We're not seeing each other anymore."

"I'm sorry to hear that. She seemed nice."

"She's very *ambitious*."

"I would think you'd like that in a woman."

"You'd be wrong."

"What do you like?" She asked, casually rubbing his shoulders. She could see the straggly grey hairs arranged to cover his bald spot. She wondered why a man in his position even bothered.

"Beauty. I like beauty. It's too bad you haven't seen my home. I'll have to arrange a dinner or some excuse to get you there. Maybe you could do that thing where you talk about the paintings. It's not like this place. There's stuff there – sculpture, antiques, art. Everything is meant to please. Like you."

She smiled slightly.

He took her hand and kissed it. "You look absolutely stunning. Turn around for a second, I want to get it from all the angles."

She stood up with her back to him. "Like it?" She asked, throwing her hair back and turning her head toward her shoulder to catch a glimpse of him."

"Very much," he said.

"It's not Channel," she said of her dress, "But it reminds me of the old Channel."

She moved to face him, her belly at the same level as his head. He took her hand and rubbed his lips across it managing in the process to slather her fingers with his saliva.

She smiled at him in a way that was meant to be adoring, mysterious, and demure, as she reached down to stroke his thigh.

Conversation faded as she bent down to undo his slacks. Then she sunk to her knees. It seemed like he hadn't taken his pill yet, but she worked with what she had, and got him off quickly.

Afterwards, he announced they should have some dinner. Everything was warming in the oven. He asked her if she'd mind bringing it in and serving. It seemed an odd request, but it had to be one of them. They ate sitting side by side on the couch.

Despite her efforts to change the topic, he kept asking her questions about her background, her education, her past.

"I'm not that interesting," she told him.

"Let me be frank. A man in my position needs to be selective. It's not just about looks. There's got to be class. When I saw you at the Dykemans, I knew I had to see you again. I'm sorry if you felt pressure from your employer."

"He doesn't own me. He just told me you wanted to meet privately."

"I'm no idiot, Camille. I know he told you a bit more than that."

"Don't you realize how attractive power is to a woman?" She asked, leaning back on the couch. "You're one of the most important men in the world. Do you have any idea how thrilled I was to hear you wanted to spend time with *me*?"

"And last time. How was that for you?"

"I only wish I didn't have to share you. But I'm happy to do whatever you'd like."

"I know you agreed to meet me three times. After our third date, my business with Dumont's will be concluded. I hope you would consider our continuing to see each other."

She took a sip of champagne, allowing him to continue.

"I like having companionship. Unfortunately, we'd need to keep things very low key."

"What did you have in mind?" She asked.

"Well, I would hope you would *want* to be exclusive with me. Obviously, it's different for men. We need variety ..."

"Especially a man as vital and virile as you," she said leaning over to run her fingers through his comb-over.

"Besides all that, I'm married and I love my wife very much."

"That's *nice*," she said. "So many men in your position would simply marry someone younger, but you're too kind to ..."

"I won't lie to you. I'm not going to leave her, but women change. I'm really not interested in making love to a sixty-five year old woman. You can understand that."

"Of course," she said, thinking of the irony of his enjoying making love to one far older than that. "Women must throw themselves at you. You're faced with temptation all the time. I certainly wouldn't expect you to be exclusive to anyone."

"So you would consider being my ..."

"Girlfriend?"

"Yes."

"I love being with you. All of this is so romantic and exciting. But the terms you set, I might need some time."

"I understand. There would be rewards but also sacrifices. I don't want you under any illusions."

"I don't think I have any."

"I'm just asking you to consider it. I can be very ... generous. But I'm a busy man. There are times I might need you to be available on short notice."

She knew what Pierre would want her to say, what Anton and all of them would want. Take the sucker for all you can get. Bleed him dry figuratively if not literally, all for "the good" of the community. But there wasn't enough blood in him to fill a thimble, and no amount of money would change this frog into a prince. Even back in Paris, there had been plenty of men who could not buy her favors at any price.

She hoped he wouldn't mention this offer to Pierre. They couldn't force her to do anything, but they might find other means to pressure her. Meantime, she had to walk a line and not offend him, at least not until all the contracts with the gallery were signed.

He picked up on her silence. "Is there anyone special in your life now?"

"You mean aside from you?"

"Yes."

"Not really."

He looked relieved. She wondered if she should have hinted at something. It had been an automatic response.

"But I haven't exactly been a nun either," she added.

The rest of the evening was routine. He asked her to dance for him, by which he meant shed her clothes and masturbate to music while allowing him a full gynecological view. He seemed delighted when she offered him something more, an actual dance performance ending in a classic slow strip. He took his pills, allowing him to perform, unfortunately for far longer than she would have liked.

It was hard for her to concentrate on her work as he rutted away. She felt both there and not there, visualizing various old men, trying to remember them in order, beginning with the old reprobate her father had sold her to. Then there was Stackelberg, who could at least be funny and kind. He'd tried to "educate" her, paid for her to be tutored in practically everything. He'd actually *cared* about her, and for a man his age, he could even be *interesting* in bed, bringing a lifetime of experience, including some rather exotic practices he'd picked up in his travels.

The mayor was wheezing a bit.

The thought came into her brain like a motto – *Alphonsine Plessis, servicing the infirm for one hundred seventy-four years*. She tried to keep her eyes closed, think of something, anything that would get her off or at least help pass the time, but there was no fantasy she could build around the soft belly slapping against her, or the tiny penis that kept slipping out no matter how hard she tried to control her muscles to keep it in.

Dashiell would simply be appalled. And if she tried to explain it to him? To tell him it had nothing to do with how she felt in her heart? The idea that she would choose to be with this toad for any reason would have degraded her in his eyes. It had been exactly the same with Alexandre. Why did they think it *meant* anything?

As for the mayor's desire she not share her body with others, that was easier for her to fathom. It was his need to believe she was with him for any reason other than material gain. It would be a terrible affront for a man in his position to know there were others she might love freely, to be reminded of his own shortcomings. How absurd. It was as though she visited her cleaning woman's home and finding it neater than her own, murdered the poor thing in a rage.

Piccolini was no closer to coming, but now he was beginning to perspire. She could feel his accelerated heartbeat. Perhaps the sight of her fangs alone would be enough to frighten him into a natural death. She could tell Pierre it just happened. But that was not an option. Even if her community forgave her, even if she was willing to forfeit the money, it would create dangerous publicity. At the least, she would need to disappear, which would mean giving up Dashiell.

Finally the old thing was getting close to a climax. She began to expertly fake one.

There was no fun in this game. At least in the old days she might have seen how many wealthy men she could keep on a string. But now she was in love, and there was only one man she was interested in holding on to. The knowledge she wouldn't be able to hold him forever was depressing.

As they disengaged, she decided the only noble option would be to break it off with Dashiell, perhaps arrange for him to find out about her little liaison. Free him so he might find someone he deserved, someone who could walk with him in daylight, bear his children, age with him.

But Pierre had been right when they'd spoken the day before. She had never acted against her own interest when it came to love. That was only in the stories made up by men. Marguerite Gautier and Violetta Valéry were fictional. Of course she wasn't going to give up Dashiell.

His honor left the bed to urinate.

She closed her eyes and imagined herself in a black and white 1950's television show, wearing an apron and a dress with tasteful pearls. Dashiell would be her husband coming home from work, and there would be tow-headed children she'd be cooking for. But even in her fantasy, the back of the dress was cut away and her behind exposed for easy access, as it had been at one or two of the rougher parties her early patrons had made her attend.

Chapter 9

"She's very attractive," Alphonsine said, after Dashiell mentioned running into Cara while out biking the day before. "You're lucky I'm not the jealous type."

"So are you. Blowing me off last night."

"I told you, Pierre needed a date for that stupid *thing*."

They were making cookies together, vegan oatmeal, with small pieces of dark organic chocolate. They had just put a batch in the oven and were working on a second tray.

She was stirring the batter. He came up behind her, placing his left arm around her waist. With his right hand, he dipped a finger into the bowl, then placed the finger in her mouth.

"You're *my* type," he said as she sucked on his thumb.

He moved his hand from her mouth down over her neck, cupped a breast, traveled down into her pants, massaging her vulva, becoming rougher and rougher, as she leaned against him. Then he stopped, leaving her wanting more. She grabbed his hand kissing each of his fingers. She took a spoonful of batter into her mouth, and standing on her toes, turned to kiss him – the cookie dough going from her mouth to his.

He lifted her on to the counter. She grabbed more batter. The metal bowl crashed to the floor momentarily breaking their concentration. He pulled off her jeans as she worked on her top. He was about to climb up when she gestured toward the freezer. He brought out a carton of coconut-vanilla vegan ice cream.

He spooned it out with his hands, feeding her with his fingers and plastering her body with a mixture of ice cream and dough.

"Taste the sweetness," she said helping him smear her face, her breasts, her pussy. "Eat me."

She imagined being consumed by him, that he was licking her away like hard candy.

Much later, after they'd showered off the stickiness, and made love again, it was time to rest. They lay together spooning, talking about nothing. She steered the subject back to his encounter with *mademoiselle la détective*. She wondered whether Cara had somehow arranged to run into him though she didn't share that suspicion. It wasn't likely, but she sensed Dashiell was holding something back. She doubted Cara would have given him details about her interview. Still, she seemed like the type who was never off-duty. *But what did it matter?* Cara could suspect whatever she wanted. There was no evidence, and Dashiell would never believe anything bad about her.

❧ ❀ ❧

Pierre wasn't so dismissive when she mentioned that Cara had run into Dashiell.

"Your stalker? She's been to the gallery. I think she's obsessed with you."

"She wouldn't be the first. But I doubt she's much of a threat."

"Maybe getting her off the case so quickly was a mistake. It might have wetted her appetite," Pierre suggested.

"There are plenty of people – gossip columnists, paparazzi, who are far more troublesome," she replied.

"But not so smart."

"What do you have in mind?" She asked.

"It would solve problems if she were to meet with an accident."

"That seems extreme. It would raise questions."

"It's a job that could be outsourced. It wouldn't get back to us."

"I like her. I don't want her killed."

"You *like* her?" Pierre asked, skepticism in his voice and thoughts.

"I don't *like* her like her. I guess I admire her. She's strong. She's smart, and she doesn't seem to give a shit what men think of her. It's refreshing."

"It's surprising you'd feel that way."

"I'm a bit surprised by it myself," Alphonsine said lightly, "but she's the 'new woman' they used to talk about in books. Independent, *useful*. Besides, she'd be missed."

"By whom? Her cats?"

"I'm sure she does some good for humanity, locking away murderers and all."

"We can't just let her go on with this campaign against you."

"I don't know that it's as bad as all that. Leave her to me."

"What's your plan?"

"I'll think of something. I'm sure I'll find a way to divert her attention.

❧ ✤ ☙

Alphonsine purposely made it an "early night." After making love, Dashiell fell asleep in her arms before three a.m. She'd again managed to sneak a sedative into his drink, still afraid even to nip him.

She took the stairs down and left via the garage exit. Because her building had been developed through a corporation owned by her kind, there were no cameras to avoid. It was only a question of getting past the concierge. Her destination was less than two miles away. She could run there in minutes, but even keeping alongside buildings, a woman moving so quickly might be noticed. Slower, but safer to take the rarely used Vespa she kept in the underground parking garage.

The address was a modest house with pale yellow vinyl siding on a side street in Greenpoint – too long a walk from the river, the shops and the subway station to ever become fashionable. Alphonsine did a quick drive by. There was a vacant lot with overgrown weeds protected by a chain link fence to the left of the property, and a small auto supply store to the right. Across the street was the entrance to some kind of factory where she could hear the faint hum of machinery.

She parked the bike a couple of blocks away, near a bar, where it was less likely to get stolen, and walked back. She went around and saw the small untended backyard. There were better kept ones on the other side of the fence and a neat line of attached row houses. None had on any lights.

The first floor windows of the little yellow house all had metal gates, but there was a partially open second floor window. Alphonsine thought this was likely where she would find Cara asleep. There was a small window with frosted glass to the left of it – probably a bathroom. It was narrow, but so was Alphonsine, and her kind had an ability like rats, to squeeze through impossibly small spaces.

The bedroom would be easier, she thought, but there was a

chance of waking Cara, no matter how quiet she was, and that would complicate things. While there were no lights on in the houses across the way, there were streetlights, so she'd need to be quick and careful. She took a running start and leapt up, grabbing the second floor bathroom sill. Holding on securely with one hand, she used the other to push up the frosted glass. Then she heard the creaking sound of a bedspring and nearby footsteps. She quickly pushed the glass back down and held tight. A light came on in the bathroom. She peeked up and could make out the silhouette of a woman on the toilet. She was relieved to hear her flush, and see the figure rise.

Alphonsine raised the window again and maneuvered herself through the narrow space. Concentrating, she could picture the bedroom, feel the vibration of Cara's heartbeat. She waited for the rhythm to slow. It took a couple of minutes before she was sure the detective was again asleep.

She felt amazingly alive. This was the easiest kind of hunting, slipping into the prey's home and taking them while they slept, but it was rarely done these days, now that one could no longer leave a body out in the woods for wolves and vultures.

She reminded herself that however tempting it might be to give in to her instincts and drain the detective, it was not what she'd come to do. She had fed recently enough, and her aim was to *save* Cara, to protect her from her own curiosity. In a perverse way, she felt like she was doing it for Dashiell, who seemed chastely fond of the cop.

Her kind were experts at moving soundlessly even on old wooden floors. She made her way down the hall. Cara had left her bedroom door slightly ajar. Alphonsine pushed it further with her breath. It moved without a squeak. She entered and planted herself beside Cara's bed.

She placed a hand over the blonde's eyes without touching the skin. She bit quickly, but not deeply into Cara's neck, releasing the venom, but not taking any blood. Her victim did not stir. Alphonsine let out a sigh of relief. She would sleep through all of it, so there was little chance of her remembering the encounter as anything other than a dream.

"Cara, you are going to keep your eyes closed. You are still sleeping. But you will be able to answer my questions. Do you understand?"

"Yes."

It was freakishly rare that mortals were immune to the venom.

In this case, Alphonsine could tell based on the slow respiration and heartbeat that Cara was not faking being under its influence.

"Do you have any kind of camera or recording device active in this room?"

"No."

"Do you recognize my voice?"

"Yes."

"Who am I?"

"Camille St. Valois."

"In the morning, when you wake, you will not remember I was here or that I spoke with you. If any memories come to you, the voice you remember will be your own. You are listening to your own voice in a dream." She paused. "Whose voice do you hear?"

"My own."

Alphonsine placed herself on the bed behind Cara. Her back rested against the headboard, her legs spread out on either side of the woman's head. She pulled the cop from under her shoulders until the back of Cara's head was leaning against her tits.

"You are dreaming. What are you doing?"

"I am dreaming."

Alphonsine began to stroke Cara's hair. "You are having a wonderful dream. You are on a beach. The sun is strong and bright. It feels hot on your skin, but you love this heat. There's heat within you too. You can feel your hot blood flowing. You're lying on damp cool sand. The water comes in and out touching your toes. How do you feel?"

"Feels good."

"The tide is coming in," Alphonsine continued, casually moving her hands down, rubbing Cara's tits until she felt the nipples harden, and the rate of respiration increase. "Now the water is lapping up to your pussy. Now it's over your stomach. Reaching your face. You get up and go for a swim. You're naked and it feels wonderful. The cool ocean water is coming up inside you. You find you can put your head underwater and see and breathe. There are dolphins and tropical fish, colorful schools of fish. You think you see a mermaid swim by. She has a green tail, and long dark hair. You almost recognize her, but she goes by fast. Then you see it. There's a shark and it's coming up on you."

Alphonsine could hear the rapidity of Cara's heartbeat.

"You don't know you're dreaming, and you can't wake up. You

swim quickly, but suddenly there's sea-grass and it's slowing you down. Then you feel it. Someone has grabbed your shoulders. You're gasping for breath now and you're coming up to the surface. You've broken through to the air. You're in Camille's arms. She's the swimmer rescuing you. You're very weak, and she gets you to shore.

"She places you on the warm dry sand. There's no one else around.

"You're so grateful to her for saving your life.

"Have you ever been with a woman, Cara?"

"No," the officer answered in a monotone.

"Not even in college?" Alphonsine asked, as she moved her hands down and began to explore Cara's vulva.

"No."

"No lonely nights with your roommate? You'd both had too much to drink?"

"I commuted."

"But you've been curious?"

"Yes."

"You've been curious, about Camille St. Valois." This she stated rather than asked.

"Yes."

"Yes? Good. She stirs up everything, doesn't she? You want to taste her. You want to press your tongue into her mouth, into all of her places. Don't you?" Alphonsine asked, before licking the side of the officers face. "And now she's pulled you up onto the sand. You are so grateful to her for saving your life, and so very hot for her. It's like a fever. Your pussy is so wet. Isn't it? You'd put anything inside you just for relief.

"You get on top of her. She wraps her long legs around you and brings you in tight. You thrust and land moving your pussy onto hers, rubbing it against hers. You're unsure of yourself. She rolls on top of you, reaches into you with expert fingers. Fucks you with her fingers. You are paralyzed with pleasure.

"Now she's moving down, sucking on those big titties of yours, kissing you on the belly and finally her tongue is darting in and out of you, while her hands continue to do something, you aren't even sure what. It's all so new to you. She reaches a finger into your asshole and moves it somehow toward your belly," Alphonsine said as she actually completed that act, "and it seems to hit something that opens you up and releases a great amount of pleasure."

Cara's breaths became quick but heavy.

"You can hardly contain yourself. The ecstasy you're feeling. You might explode. You might die from the pleasure. But this is a dream. It won't wake you.

"Let it go, NOW," Alphonsine said matching her breaths to Cara's. "Feel everything."

Cara shouted, "Oh mother of God."

Alphonsine wiped her fingers against the sheet.

"Do you use an alarm clock?"

"Yes."

"When it goes off in the morning, you will wake up and vividly remember the dream you just had. You will not remember the conversation we are now having. The dream is going to bother you. At some point during the morning you will conclude you have sexual feelings toward Camille St. Valois. You will realize trying to suppress these feelings has led to your being overly suspicious of her. There's nothing linking her to any crime. There's nothing *wrong* with her. It's all been in your head because of your feelings. You haven't been objective.

"Are you going to want to talk to anyone about this?"

"No," Cara answered.

"Of course not. You're going to acknowledge it to yourself and move on, as you always do. The feelings will dissipate, and within a few days they'll be barely a memory. If you see Camille, you'll still retain the sense you were unfair to her – judgmental, and you'll have insight into why. You'll feel a need to give her a chance. So tell me, do you still believe Camille may have been involved in a murder?"

"No."

"Why not?"

"I'm not objective. It's all in my head because of my feelings."

"What did you dream about her?"

"I dreamed we had sex."

"How did it make you feel?"

"It was wonderful."

"Are you going to continue to investigate her?"

"No."

"Good. By the time you get to work, you will have decided Camille St. Valois is just a young woman who works for an art gallery and goes to a lot of parties. She is not guilty of any crime. There is nothing 'mysterious' about her. She invokes a lot of feelings –

jealousy, desire. But that's all based on her looks. Tell me, who is Camille St. Valois?"

"She works in an art gallery and goes to parties. She hasn't committed any crimes."

It was almost five in the morning. Alphonsine decided not to bother going through the house although she was a bit curious. She left the way she came.

Chapter 10

She could barely remember a time she'd felt such contentment. She hadn't had as much as a friendly fuck with Pierre in weeks, though they often saw each other at the gallery. Besides Dashiell, the only person she'd been with was his honor, and that was business.

She and her consort went out almost every night, sometimes just for dinner, often to a bar, a club or a show. They always returned to her apartment. She only wished they could wake together, but even when she kept him up till dawn, he usually rose before noon and then would be off – writing, rehearsing, always something. It had been years since she'd met a mortal that energetic, or good at so many different things.

He had developed a friendship with Cara. It was based on drinking beer, talking about sports teams and riding a bicycle. She knew he wanted to "experience" police life and use it for his art. In her first life she'd often had platonic male friends. They'd been useful. What right did she have to deny him? On the other hand, she thought it might be a good idea to monitor things. That was why she'd maneuvered a night out – she and Dashiell and Cara and Cara's friend Justin.

The plan had been to listen to music, maybe dance, which was what she was dressed for, but the others decided bowling would be fun. It was a first for Alphonsine. When she easily knocked down all the pins twice in a row and they began to make a fuss, she realized her superior hand to eye coordination would seem odd.

"Beginner's luck," she said, shrugging her shoulders. The next turn she carefully made sure to bowl a difficult split.

Afterwards, the four of them went to a bar. Dashiell started extolling the virtues of opera, which he now enjoyed. She noticed Cara looking at her admiringly, but not obsessively. She was glad she hadn't agreed to have her killed.

The topic turned, she wasn't sure how, to past lives. Cara

pointed out the idiocy of people always believing they were the reincarnation of the rich and powerful.

"So you don't believe in an afterlife?" Alphonsine asked.

"Jury's out. I guess I believe in what Dashiell calls karma. Somehow we reap what we sow."

"But karma may work itself out over several lifetimes," Dashiell said.

"Karma, maybe. But as an officer of the law, I hope justice is swift," Cara answered.

Justin looked at Alphonsine and asked, "What about you, Camille? Who were you before?"

"Now *she* really could have been a princess," Cara said.

"Me? No. I imagine I was a poor peasant girl who died young. Someone who didn't get a chance to have a good time, which is why I never want to stop having one in this life."

"Sounds right," Dashiell said.

"What about you?" Cara asked looking at Dashiell. "Were you a prince or a pauper?"

"Sometimes when I'm writing or acting, or playing music, and I don't know where it comes from, I think, yeah, I must have done this before, been doing it for a long time. But I have no idea if I was successful or even good at it."

"I bet you were," Alphonsine said seriously. "I bet *you* were famous."

The couples split up. Two in the morning was a late night for the prosecutor and the detective. Alphonsine and Dashiell went walking by the river. She mentioned some places they might go – performance venues, clubs.

He ran his fingers over her lips. "You're all the entertainment I need."

They found a spot by the side of a building. No one was around. Standing against a wall he lifted her skirt. She wrapped her legs around him. She loved the feel of the hard brick against her back, and the hardness of her lover in front of her. She enjoyed the excitement of knowing that strangers might glimpse something. It reminded her of her early days in Paris, the boys she'd meet at cafes, so eager. Dashiell would not have taken a chance like that weeks ago. It excited her she was destroying his inhibitions. She wondered what else she might make him do.

He was holding himself inside of her when she whispered in his ear, "I love you so desperately. I suppose I shouldn't admit that."

"Why not? I love you ... desperately."

"Men don't like ... clingy ... women," she said between deep breaths.

He stopped moving for a moment and shook his head, then continued his thrusts. There were footsteps, but they didn't stop. It didn't take long for either of them.

When they were finished, she smoothed down her skirt. He zippered his fly. They walked arm and arm. It was Dashiell who spoke first. "He must have done a number on you."

"Who?"

"Whomever it is you never talk about," he answered. "It amazes me how scared you seem to be of rejection. Who could ever say no to that face? To anything about you?"

"Is my face all that interests you?"

"No. Everything about you fascinates me."

"Not all men are like you."

"Sometimes I get the feeling you're holding back. That there's something you think would make me feel differently."

She looked at him afraid for a moment he was capable of guessing all her secrets.

"There's nothing that could make me love you any less," he said holding her. "Not anything in your past, nothing you could have done."

"Nothing?" she asked playfully.

"Try me."

"Shoplifting."

"I think it's considered an illness these days.. We'll get you medication."

"Burglary."

"Reckless youth. Don't do it again."

"Murder."

"Nobody's perfect."

She laughed. It was a line from a Marilyn Monroe film they'd watched together. Monroe was one of her favorites. Maybe it was the Dickensian childhood they both shared, or a certain self-awareness peeking through the dumb blonde facade, or perhaps Marilyn's ability to eradicate her past and live as the persona she created – though it may have killed her.

She was aware that Marilyn had once been "scouted" for a much different role. After the Second World War, Anton had made his home and hunting ground in Hollywood. Before she was famous, he had managed, in the guise of a foreign movie producer, to get close to her. He had the idea of preserving her beauty for the ages, but found her ambition and need to be loved made her unsuitable for the life of a *diva*.

When Alphonsine heard the story, after Monroe's death, she wondered whether Anton had underestimated *her* need for love. Had he thought of the infamous Marie Duplessis, as hard and heartless? What if he had met her a few years earlier when her career had barely begun? Might he have considered her nothing more than a tasty morsel?

Dashiell didn't think of her that way. She felt he knew her as she *might have been* in her first life, if only she had been truly loved.

They stayed out, went to a club in the city, a small venue someone told them about where there was a performance of "traditional" Persian dance. They watched as a long-legged woman with a magnificently fit body, writhed on the stage.

If she had been out with Pierre, they both would have talked to the dancer, gotten her interested in a threesome, possibly even nipped her if she wasn't game, but she would've been. They would have charmed her and she would have gone willingly, and they would have plied her cocaine or ecstasy or whatever she wished, and the three of them would have had a great night, or at least a good couple of hours. In another time, or another place, where life was considerably cheaper, the chances of the dancer surviving till morning would have been slim.

After the show, Alphonsine gave Dashiell a long kiss, which seemed to continue even as they got into a taxi and headed back to Brooklyn.

The thought that it would be dawn in a couple of hours was the only thing putting a damper on her mood. She wished she could spend a solid week in bed with him uninterrupted by the need to sleep.

So deeply was she immersed in her desires that she felt nothing, no mental alarm bells as she entered her apartment, and out of consideration to her mortal, turned on a light.

It was then they both noticed the open terrace doors and the two men standing outside.

"Good-evening," Anton said, pausing before he added,

"Camille."

"Sorry if we gave you a start. Monsieur Vorostovsky arrived this evening, and we thought we would surprise you," explained Pierre.

"You certainly did," she said.

She turned to Dashiell, introducing Anton as a partner in Dumont's.

"A silent partner," Anton said, placing a finger to his lips.

"I don't know if Camille has told you," Pierre went on for Dashiell's benefit, "We are on the verge of a major sale of a private collection. She's been helping us to secure our business with a wealthy client."

"She may have mentioned something," Dashiell said.

"Mentioned something?" Anton asked. "Our girl has always been so ... modest. She was essential."

On the counter there was a bottle of champagne with a white bow and a bouquet of red camellias.

She wondered if there was any special meaning to the color he'd chosen, but Anton was keeping his mind opaque. In her first life, if she wore a red camellia it would signal unavailability either due to her period or a previous engagement. *Could Anton mean that he didn't want her to be available to Dashiell during his visit?* She would not permit that.

"I'll go get water for these," she said. "Dashiell, would you mind opening up the champagne? We must get our guests a drink."

"Oh no, we didn't mean to impose," Anton said.

"It's no trouble," she said aloud, while mentally she was shouting something else.

She was hoping if she feigned nonchalance, pretended her employers letting themselves in at four in the morning was a perfectly ordinary occurrence, then Dashiell would accept it as such.

The conversation was polite. Anton was staying at "a friend's" apartment in her building, two floors above hers.

"We'll be neighbors," he said. "Just like old times."

"We used to live on the same street in Paris," she explained to Dashiell.

"Camille, did you recently get your teeth bleached? They're looking very white," Pierre said.

"Thank you, Pierre. It must be my toothpaste," she answered sweetly. '*I lie to keep my teeth white*' was a line attributed to her in her courtesan days. She'd taken credit for it, but it had been fabricated by a journalist friend.

Anton was looking at Dashiell the way a man might size up a romantic rival. She knew Dashiell would likely spot that as well. Of course he wouldn't ask, and while she didn't usually feel a need to explain herself, she wanted him to know there was nothing, absolutely nothing between her and this man.

It didn't take long for the four of them to polish off the bottle. Anton had brought some Cuban cigars, which he suggested smoking on the terrace.

"I'm sorry," she said. "Not even out there. You know how allergic I am to tobacco."

"I apologize *ma chère*. I'd forgotten about your lung troubles." He invited Dashiell to come up to his place for a few minutes with Pierre to enjoy them.

"*You wouldn't dare harm him*," she mentally projected.

"*I wouldn't even think of it*," Anton telepathically shot back.

They might not lie to each other, but they sure knew how to use sarcasm.

"I'll pass," Dashiell said. "I don't smoke."

"It's late," Pierre said. "Come Anton. We must leave these two alone."

After they were gone, Alphonsine made a point of using the bolt lock, which couldn't be opened from the outside.

Dashiell looked at her and asked, "Lung troubles?"

"I was allergic to a dog he once had."

"Were you two close?"

She thought for a moment of nipping his neck, making him forget the whole thing, but he was wide awake, and it might come back to him.

"It was long ago. I was a teenager."

"He's an attractive man. Was he like a professor or something?"

She laughed. "No, just someone. I was sixteen and he was so much older. It seemed very daring at the time."

"Was he your ..."

"Darling, I'm half-French."

"He's the one, isn't he? The flowers?"

"So what if he is?"

"Nothing. I just sensed some unfinished business."

"I assure you, my only business with him is business, and even that, rarely. He's never been involved in the gallery except as an investor." She paused before adding, "And I was never in love with him. Besides, you are the only man in my life."

"When I gave you that necklace ... "

"At the opera." she said, suddenly feeling fearful. "Do you want it back?"

"No, not that. I gave you the necklace and the earrings, but there was something else. I didn't want to give it to you then because I thought it might be ..." His voice trailed off as he reached into his bag and brought out a small box.

"This isn't a proposal," he said. "I mean, I know it's much too soon for that. But I want there to be something between us, some kind of ..."

"Symbol?"

"Yes."

"*Mon Dieu*. It's lovely," she said slipping the delicate gold and ruby ring onto her finger.

"It's a pre-engagement ring," he said as though he had just thought of it.

"*Merde*, I already put it on. Were you supposed to do it? Do you need to ask me?"

"Don't take it off. Ever. That might be bad luck." He got down on his knees, and asked, "Camille St. Valois will you someday perhaps consider becoming engaged to marry me?"

"I just might," she said sinking down to meet him.

She snuck off into the bathroom at dawn, for a quick shot of speed. It was worth a little aging to spend the morning with him.

"I don't think I've ever seen you go outside during the day," he said as they headed to a cafe for a champagne brunch.

"Well, you see the rumors aren't true then."

"Which ones?"

"That I would burst into flames," she said, though her skin felt prickly in the light, and it was harder to catch her breath.

It was almost noon when they made it back and again made love. Exhausted, they fell asleep in each other's arms, and when dusk came, she got her wish and woke up with him sleeping by her side. Just watching him breathe gave her a sense of joy almost beyond any she had known. She knew then that if her choice was a short life filled with this, or a long one alone, she would take this.

But of course, she reminded herself, that was a *feeling*. Feelings were temporary, and while it was one thing to live purely for pleasure, it was another to risk everything for sentiment.

Chapter 11

Police had never been a problem for her, but then traditionally police had been men. She could convince a man of anything. Women were tougher. They were not questioning her about Simmons' death, but Alphonsine had new concerns about Cara. Dashiell had gone out with her and her partner on investigations. They'd met for lunch twice while Alphonsine was asleep, and had been bicycle riding a few times, including early mornings. Alphonsine understood some of this was research. She was a character Dashiell was exploring – the brave, perhaps flawed, female detective. He wanted authenticity for his work. It was not unlike dating a painter who needed to use the lowest women for models. He was really still a sheltered boy, and Cara could show him the mean streets and underside, or at least tell him stories. That was probably all there was to it. On the other hand, that might be exciting for him, and Cara was very attractive in a one-of-the boys way that contemporary men seemed to like.

Jealousy. The most human of emotions. She hadn't felt it in a very long time. What did it matter? Even if he made love to Cara, it would mean nothing. But then Cara could offer him so much she couldn't.

"I hope you aren't doing anything dangerous," Alphonsine said when Dashiell came to her one evening and told her about his day spent with the detective and her partner at work.

"It's okay," he said, "She can protect me."

"Not even in jest. I'd die if anything happened to you."

There wasn't much she could do to thwart the friendship. Another night visit seemed too risky, and she doubted Cara would do anything to harm "Camille" having so unfairly judged her. But Dashiell was a man, and men were fickle.

Both Dashiell and Cara would see through her if she tried to undermine their relationship through ordinary means, and she hated the idea of manipulating Dashiell through extraordinary ones, so she decided the best thing she could do was join in. She still had Cara's card, and called her up at work to discuss "the four of them" going out again.

Cara admitted Justin was only a friend who might be pursuing other interests, and she didn't wish to be a third wheel. Alphonsine, then suggested the two of them meet somewhere for dinner. Cara was squirming to come up with an excuse, still self-conscious. The effects of the dream-walk hadn't completely worn off.

"If you keep saying no to me, maybe I will start to think you're after Dashiell," Alphonsine teased.

Cara finally agreed to meet her after work, which is how Alphonsine found herself at one of the new places in Greenpoint. Though she had never been there, the waiter recognized her and the cook came out to meet her, assuring her anything she wanted could be made to her specifications.

"It's like you're famous," Cara said.

Yes, she thought. *It's exactly like that.* "Famous in Brooklyn, maybe," she answered dismissively. "Isn't everyone famous in Brooklyn these days?"

"Not me," Cara replied, "but I'm a native."

The conversation had some awkward starts and stops. After they had ordered, a process that involved Alphonsine asking the server several questions regarding the ingredients and preparation of the food, Cara asked whether she had been a vegan before she met Dashiell.

"Oh for years, but honestly," she whispered, "it started because I had digestive issues." Alphonsine also admitted to not having many close female friends.

"Well obviously, a lot of women would find you threatening," Cara said, as the waiter came by with a bottle of wine courtesy of a couple of financial services types at a nearby table.

"Tell them thank you," Alphonsine told him, "but please make it clear we prefer not to be disturbed."

"That happen to you a lot?" Cara asked.

"What happen to me?"

"Strangers send over an eighty dollar bottle of wine?"

"Constantly," Alphonsine said. "They're probably writing it off. Did you want to meet them? The one with the lighter hair looks like that actor."

"I don't even think they see me."

"I doubt that's true. They probably think we're out on a date and it's getting them even hotter."

Alphonsine noticed Cara's face redden.

The conversation stopped as they drank and nibbled on their appetizers. Alphonsine tried to focus on the cop's mind, but she was difficult to read even after the dream-walk, and Alphonsine had the feeling that on some level Cara could read *her* far better than she could read Cara.

"Look," Cara said breaking a silence. "Can I ask you something?"

"Anything. As long as it's not part of a criminal investigation."

Cara flushed again. "I am over that. Really. No, I just wanted to ask whether you're okay with Dashiell doing the drive along and ..."

"I'm not crazy about the idea. He could get hurt. But he's a big boy."

"And with him and me sometimes hanging out together?"

"He can have friends. And I don't think you want anything else."

"I wouldn't step between the two of you. It's not how I operate, besides he's absolutely in love with you, and you're ... *you.*"

"I also love him very much," she said. "You haven't told him, have you, about those things I told you?"

"No. I haven't said anything. But I'm glad you brought it up. I've been feeling like I really needed to apologize to you. The concierge backed up the time you said you got home. We knew that before we even questioned you. I know you had nothing to do with Simmons' death."

"You don't need to be sorry for doing your job." Alphonsine took a sip of her wine. "Can I ask *you* something?"

"Why did I become a cop?"

That had, in fact, been the question. Having a mortal guess her thought was more than a little disconcerting. She nodded.

"My dad was a detective, undercover," Cara told her. "He was killed on the job, and my mom died, cancer."

"I'm so sorry."

"I was raised by my aunt and my gram. They used to talk about him all the time. I grew up wanting to be like him."

Unusual as it was for mortals to evoke her sympathy, Cara's losing her parents touched her. She felt suddenly aware of how removed she was from all that – the cycles of life and death, and family. For so many years her family had been the other *divos*. She rarely ever thought of her sister, her nieces, or for that matter of the son she was sure had lived to adulthood despite what she'd been told. Even if he'd died a very old man, he'd have been dead nearly a century.

"That's some story," she said, in response to Cara.

"But it's not what I thought it would be like. It's not chasing bad guys or being a hero. It's building cases, and maybe if you're lucky getting at the truth, giving somebody closure."

"That sounds important," Alphonsine said. "You speak for the dead. You bring them justice." Her aim had been to disarm an opponent, but as she said the words, she felt something more though she couldn't have named what.

"Yeah. I suppose. I guess it's why I like it."

"It must give your life so much ..." Alphonsine paused and then they both said the word at the same time, "*meaning*."

Chapter 12

Alphonsine greeted Dashiell, kissing him with a mouth full of fresh organic strawberries.

"Delicious," he said.

"There's lots more."

She led him to the bedroom where they both undressed as eagerly as they had their first night together. She had set out strawberries on the bed in the shape of a giant heart.

He lay down first in the center of it. She got on top and squeezed a fistful of the berries in her hand, dripping red juice onto his stomach and balls, then licking it off.

"The sheets," he said turning his head noticing the stains.

She looked up at him without removing his cock from her mouth. "*I don't care,*" she projected. He seemed to get it.

After he came, she playfully demanded he go down on her. She laughed when she felt his tongue reach the berries she had hidden inside. She squeezed them out and he caught them in his mouth. He brought them up to her lips and offered them back to her. Their lips and tongues locked as they shared them.

"What else is in there?" He asked.

"Why don't you go back and keep looking?" She suggested, pushing his head down.

The sun had not yet set. He would be leaving once more for the West Coast. Pierre and Anton had warned her she was risking her face with these early hours, but she just couldn't bear being apart from him, even in sleep. His journey to stardom was happening quickly. He was too special, too charismatic, to remain unknown. Even the bar band he'd started "for fun" was now getting gigs at the trendiest venues. She feared his fame would be the end for them, yet she was happy for him.

He described the upcoming meeting as "a very long" audition. While the producers loved the story of his play, they felt they needed to match him with a more experienced screenwriter, and still hadn't decided if they could afford to gamble on using him in the lead role, or whether they needed someone better known.

In the shower, she leaned her stomach against the tiled wall as he took her from behind.

He'd be gone a week and she didn't know how she'd be able to stand it.

They dressed in their robes. Hers satin, his soft terry-cloth. She'd bought it for him at Barney's, which like every store in the city had late evening hours that suited her kind. The robe had never left her apartment. As he slept there most nights, what would've been the point?

Drinking coffee at her kitchen counter, she reached over to his still damp hair. "We got the stickiness out." She licked his head. "But I can still taste the sweetness."

"You're the sweetness," he said, pulling off the belt of her robe. She wriggled her narrow shoulders and it fell to the ground while she managed to land naked on his lap.

They talked about his trip.

"So it could still fall apart? This deal?" She asked nibbling on his neck.

"Not if they like me."

"They'd be idiots not to."

He grabbed another strawberry – that time from a bowl on the counter.

"I thought you'd had enough," she said.

"There's a story about strawberries." He began to tell her a Buddhist folktale of a monk chased by a tiger. "So he runs until he's at the edge. It's the tiger or the cliff. Fall to a certain quick death or be torn apart, so he jumps, but then he's able to grab onto a branch growing off the side. And he's thinking maybe he can hold on till the tiger leaves, but it's too weak. It's going to break. He knows he's going to die, so he picks a strawberry as he lets go."

"And?" she asked.

"It was delicious."

He saw her bewilderment. "The moment," he said. "It's all we have."

"I see," she replied. She did and she didn't. It suddenly frightened her to think of his fragile mortal body. She followed him back to the bedroom and watched as he began to dress.

"It was funny," he said.

"What was?" She asked, buttoning his shirt, smelling his chest.

"There was a very passionate moment when we were making love, and I had the feeling you were going to bite me, like really hard."

"Well I do love strawberries," she said sinking to her knees.

"I really have to go," he said, as she hugged his ass and began to burrow her head in his crotch. "You're insatiable. How are you going to survive without me for a week?"

"Skype," she suggested undoing his zipper.

"Christ," he said grabbing her. "I don't care if I smell like pussy on that plane as long as it's yours." Then he got down with her on the floor.

They had to dress again quickly when the car arrived. Pierre had once more offered the use of his limo and driver. She would go out to the airport with him. The car had dark windows and a divider that when closed kept the chauffeur from seeing them. They began to mess around in the back seat, which proved to be awkward. She wound up with the soles of her feet thumping against the back window.

"It's a good thing they're tinted," Dashiell joked.

"Do you think I care about that?" She asked, holding his cock inside of her. She sat still, allowing him to move her as he pleased. "I'd make love to you in Yankee Stadium if you wanted me to."

"You would, wouldn't you?" He asked as though he had just realized something essential. They stared into each other's eyes.

"Traffic's light," she said, "We better cut to the chase."

As they approached the airport, he gave her a final kiss. "At least we got in enough to last a while."

"Not even a day," she said, watching him leave.

As the car pulled away, she started checking her messages. There were several texts from Pierre. She called him.

"What is it?"

"Our mutual friend wants that third date tonight."

"Fuck him."

"Exactly. He said something got cancelled, so it's easy for him to get away, and he wants to have the deal tomorrow. Listen, I don't like that he treats me like your pimp."

"You don't? Under the circumstances …"

"I've spoken to the driver and told him to take you straight

207

there."

"That's ridiculous. I'm wearing jeans and a tee-shirt. I need a shower."

"You can take one when you get there. I'll tell him you're coming from the gym. He wants to sign the contract tomorrow, and he wants this to happen tonight."

"Pierre, I'm never doing anything like this again. And I will be very upset with you if you even ask me."

"Never is a very long time," he reminded her. "Especially for us."

She thought about that as the car headed out to Long Island. It was tempting to say screw the whole thing, even if she got nothing and the deal fell apart. She reminded herself she had wanted enough money to say no next time, to have something that was hers alone. She'd never equated selling her body with selling her soul. Having started so young, there had always been a clear dichotomy between what she did for love, what she did for pleasure, and what she did for cash. There was a part of her very few men could touch, and Piccolini would never have access to that. Yet, she could imagine everything as it would look through Dashiell's eyes. Maybe he'd be able to forgive her the occasional friendly fuck with Pierre, but even that she doubted. How would he react if he knew her ability to fake not only orgasm, but enjoyment and love? If he saw the mayor doing things to her that he would never suggest, he'd despise her. She was certain of it although there was no rational reason for him to feel that way.

It had been the same with Adet. He had the advantage of knowing exactly what she was, but once he'd begun to have feelings for her, the idea of loving a woman whose favors could be bought disgusted him. No mortal man could get past it. Adet had pushed her away, denied it was anything more than a fling. Later, after her "death," he'd created an idealized version of her, a woman more worthy than she had been. She had no wish to be remembered fondly by Dashiell, to be romanticized by him after they were no longer together. How he remembered her was of little interest. She wanted him to love her.

After this she would try to be good in a way she never had before, she told herself. She would take no other lovers as long as she was with him. She began to imagine what it might be like if he agreed to become her eternal companion. *How long would the intensity last? Fifty years? A hundred? A thousand?*

Of course if he were her kind, he'd understand the ridiculousness of physical monogamy. They'd make love to other members of the community, and mortals as well. With the exception of Ana, she didn't know any of her kind who didn't occasionally enjoy their prey sexually before or during feasting.

Alphonsine looked out the window. She was only a few minutes away. She tried to banish thoughts of a future with Dashiell from her brain. There was no possibility he'd agree to join them, nor would she ever risk making him the offer. She wouldn't have loved him if he was like her – able to kill so easily, and all of her kind could, no matter who they'd been before.

Besides, it would be horribly cruel to change someone with so much left to do, so much potential. He was going to have a brilliant career. He wouldn't be notorious as she had been, or merely a footnote – famous as the paramour of someone important. *His* immortality would be the work he left behind.

How much more time might they have together? After him, would there ever be another she loved so well?

The car pulled into the familiar driveway. Piccolini opened the front door for her while speaking to someone over the phone. Some kind of business deal. As she went toward the bathroom, she wondered how many millions of dollars he had just made.

She'd been hoping to sleep with Dashiell's scent on her – to wallow in it, but she stepped into the shower and hot water rushed against her skin, rinsing him away. There were several spa-style nozzles, including one that was movable and offered enough water pressure and a narrow enough stream for her to freshen up the inside of her pussy.

Her panties reeked of Dashiell's cum. She threw them into a zippered compartment in her handbag. She had no clean ones, but going without would work. She quickly fixed her make up. There was a blow dryer, but she left her hair loose and damp. It wasn't that she was badly dressed. She was never *badly* dressed. She just wasn't in what she thought of as appropriate attire for an assignation with a billionaire.

His honor didn't seem to mind. "You look like a kid," he said. "One of those anarchists. Occupy me, baby."

He poured some champagne for her. She noticed the bottle, Veuve Clicquot 2004, her new favorite, though no wine was as good

209

as they made them when she was younger. The soil had been cleaner then. The air purer. Everything, no matter how high the price tag was dirty now, corrupt in this new world.

"Thank you," she said. She didn't think the brand a coincidence. He'd done some homework. It was clear from his vibe he *liked* her. "Nice champagne."

"I made some inquiries," he said.

There was a light supper already spread out on the dining table.

"Have you thought about what we discussed last time?" He asked. "I don't want you to feel any pressure. The business with the paintings will be settled by noon no matter what. This would just be between us."

"I like you a lot, Sam. "

"It's your young man. Dashiell Alexander."

He did keep up.

"You've been doing your research."

"Due diligence. As I told you I can't afford any indiscretions. I was hoping it wasn't serious."

"You're a very charming man."

"I know exactly what I am," he said.

"We have tonight. Let me prove to you the extent of my regard," she told him.

"Oh, I'm perfectly willing to do that."

By now they were next to each other on the couch. She had her champagne glass in hand. He had put his down to take off her shoes and nibble on her toes.

"Let me slip out of these clothes," she said standing. "They're so restrictive." She began to slowly strip for him, and then sat back down, posing naked on the couch while casually sipping champagne.

"Vixen," he said.

"That sounds so old-fashioned."

He was looking at her hungrily but not reaching for her just yet. She was hoping to get him aroused and get out quickly, but in addition to the blue pills, she was sure he'd be using coke or something else, so it was probably going to be a long night.

"Did I mention I know his father, David Alexander?" Piccolini asked.

She didn't say anything.

"Don't worry. I've never had to resort to blackmail to get a woman to have sex with me."

210

"I'm relieved to hear that."

"Although David and I have occasionally discussed our conquests," the mayor added.

"That's interesting," she said feigning indifference.

"I have no plans on mentioning that we're any more than friends."

"I appreciate that."

"So you wouldn't reconsider even if you could keep your boyfriend, and have me as your filthy little secret."

"No. I *love* him." The response was so quick she hadn't even thought before she spoke, which was rare for her. She almost never admitted loving a man to his rival. When she had, it was usually to either drive someone away or because she knew nothing could.

"I love my wife. It doesn't mean I don't hunger for something different, and I do mean hunger. I could devour you. Would you like to know what else I found out, besides your preferred vintage?"

"Only if you'd like to tell me," she said adjusting herself slightly to improve his view.

"Very little. And I'm left wondering whether your background is one-hundred percent bullshit or only ninety-nine."

"What do you mean?"

"You are a sweet girl. But *nobody* fucks the way you do. It's like Serena Williams showing up at a tennis club pretending to be a Sunday player. Besides there's *something* about you."

"Are you saying I'm a fake? That I didn't fit in with the Dykemans?"

"You're superior to the Dykemans. You have the manners of a duchess. And I've actually met one – the ugly hag Prince Charles was boning when he was with Diana. That was nuts, right? What an asshole!" He shook his head. "I mean if you're going for the strange, at least it should be comparable. Anyway, I noticed something the first time I saw you at some event."

"Noticed something?"

"A look maybe, when you thought no one saw you. I've seen it before. It always belongs to people who know what it's like to have nothing and find themselves in the middle of a crowd with no idea. People who built themselves up. Everything about you is studied. Purposeful. A perfect simulation. Like an old time painting that looks so real you could mistake it for a photograph, but nothing in nature is that perfect. Or maybe it takes a bullshitter to know one."

"You're very insightful. I didn't exactly come from a privileged background."

"What were you then? High class escort or did Dumont find you on a street corner?"

Her instinct was to kill him, but she held off. If he wasn't around to sign those papers in the morning, Pierre would be very cross with her. Besides, she didn't sense he'd meant it as an insult, or was even aware she would take it that way. To a man like him, the ability to pass oneself off as something one was not, was an admirable quality.

"I think that's a movie plot," she said calmly, "a rather cliché one. I've never worked as an escort, much less walked the streets. But if it would turn you on to think I had, I don't have a problem with that."

"Your official biography per Dumont's website is *dreck*."

"You're a smart man. I guess you wouldn't be where you are if you couldn't read people."

"So tell me about it."

She understood that to be an order, not a request.

"Ever since I was a teenager, there have always been men, older wealthy men who wanted to take care of me. One of them even paid for my education."

"How very French."

"But I've been trying to get away from all that."

"Good luck."

"You don't think I can change?"

"I don't think you'd be here if you meant to."

"Not even for you?"

"You're good," he said. "And I don't just mean in bed. A very unusual girl. If it was some other time, men would be fighting duels over you."

"You're imagining too much. My job for Dumont is a job. I don't do things like this a lot."

"A lot?" He laughed. "Only when your boss asks you to." He lit a cigar. "How much are they taking me for on the paintings?"

"What do you mean?"

"How much am I overpaying?"

"You're not. You've had the collection appraised. You're probably paying more than we'd get at auction, but you never know how an auction is going to go, so I'd say you're getting a deal."

"Well done. And what's your cut? For our *dates*?"

"A million dollars."

He whistled. "That's not bad for a few hours' work, but it's less than you deserve."

"Are you going to make it up to me?"

"Not without something more in return."

"I can't."

"Why not? We could cut out the middleman and I could make you very rich. Why stop at three if one would upset your boyfriend?"

"Because I have enough. It can buy me a little *freedom*."

"Would you mind if I give you some advice?"

"*Business* advice? Coming from you? I'd love it."

"You should leave the gallery. A girl like you. No matter what they're giving you, they're taking advantage. If you don't like my terms, it's understandable, but give up the boy. I'm sure there's a rich old goat out there who'd be proud to take you out in public, take very good care of you. Maybe even marry you."

"But didn't you just say you'd never leave your wife?"

"Me? No. I actually didn't mean … Oh, you're playing with me now." He chuckled. "I'll never be rich enough, and if I did divorce her, I'd have to find someone a bit more age appropriate. Public image. But lots of men don't feel that way."

She shook her head, "I love my independence. Besides as I told you, I love *him*."

"I get it. Transformed by love. I respect that. I hope he treats you like a goddess. He doesn't know you're doing this?"

"No. I don't think he'd understand."

"Or about your past?"

"It hasn't come up. But we're not living in the nineteenth century," she said. "Men don't expect …"

He shook his head. "I should shut my trap. I'm boring you, aren't I?" He asked casually squeezing her breast and looking her over as though she were Galatea come to life.

"No, Sam, honestly, I'm interested in what you have to say."

"Maybe less has changed than we like to think. When it comes to the women we imagine as the mothers of our children, there's still a double standard. Don't tell him your business."

"You know something?"

"What?"

"You're really not as bad as I thought," she said reaching to hug him. " I don't even want to snap your neck anymore."

"The night is still young," he quipped. "Now, how about licking my balls?"

❧ ⊛ ☙

She met with Anton the next evening to discuss her "commission."

She wanted it in cash, and not from any account traceable to Dumont.

"I don't want it to go to the United States government," she pointed out.

"That goes without saying," Anton replied, "but there are other ways to handle it."

"Like what?"

"We can have our lawyers look into it. We did give you an American mother. Inheritance under a million isn't taxed here. We can probably figure something out."

"I appreciate your concern. That would be most generous."

"So what are you going to do now? Quit your *job*?"

"I love my job. It's just certain aspects of it, I despise."

"Aspects you are perfectly free to say no to."

"It doesn't always feel that way. And you? With this business over, will you be moving on?"

"Not immediately. I haven't been in this city for a very long time. I'm curious to know it again. I have no intention of making a nuisance of myself or interfering in your little romance."

"Glad to hear it."

"You still hate me, don't you?"

"I don't really think of you much. If you're asking if I forgive you for ..."

"Saving your life?"

"Damning me for eternity," she said so lightly they both smiled. "You can read my mind, Anton. You know I forgave you long ago, but I still believe you took advantage of my illness. I'll always believe that, but we don't need to continue to feud over it."

"We'll agree to disagree then."

"Yes."

"Would you like to join me on a hunt? A few days in a place ... Atlantic City."

"Pierre and I were just there. And there's a trip to Sainte Trinité planned for me."

"Oh yes. The charity."

"Good works are good for business."

"And life is cheap on that island." He added wistfully, "It has such an exotic flavor."

"Hmm," she said, recalling a previous trip.

"Could we at least go out tonight? Listen to music? Dance? We've never done that."

"Then why start now?"

She tried to block her mind from all the emotions he provoked. She was not unaware that despite her resentment, a physical attraction lingered, and if she let down her guard, he might be difficult to resist. But becoming closer to him would mean giving ground, allowing that his transforming her had been justified, that she had wanted it. Besides she didn't wish to cheat on Dashiell, and being with Anton, for reasons she wasn't quite certain of, felt more like what mortals considered infidelity than being with Pierre, or Piccolini, or any random prey.

He read her thoughts and answered in words, "That boy? Really? You wouldn't sleep the day by my side after a hunt, or enjoy a bit of physical pleasure, because of *him*?"

"It's a question of loyalty."

He laughed. She knew he was thinking of her liaison with the mayor.

"That was for money. And it's over."

"I see," he said. "Your moral reasoning is perhaps too subtle for an uneducated idiot such as myself." She was about to leave the office when he added, "Of course, having made this rather lucrative deal, it might be time to put Dumont's under new management or close up shop. It's all gotten a bit too … public."

"Should I pack a suitcase?" She asked coolly.

"Not just yet. But keep a passport handy. Have you thought about your next life?"

"Would it matter if I had? My impression was the elders want me to have a much lower profile."

"It wouldn't be a bad idea. Though I doubt you could manage it. The problem now is if you're known one place, you're known every place."

"Yes, not with stakes through the heart, nor crosses and holy

215

water. Who could have foreseen these *devices* as the ultimate threat to our way of life?"

"It's a problem. We could alter your appearance I suppose. Hair dye is much better than it used to be."

"I make a very conspicuous blonde."

"You make a conspicuous everything. We'll figure out something, for as long as we may have."

"So you also don't believe we are long for this world?"

"We have longer than any of *them*, I hope," Anton replied. "But the world has become so much smaller, and their means of discovering us much sharper. I wouldn't bet we have even a century."

Less than a century? And she hadn't even reached two. There was so much left to do.

"That would mean I'd have barely lived longer than a few of their lifetimes," she said.

"Don't you sometimes feel two centuries of debauchery, mayhem, and murder is enough?" Anton asked.

She wasn't sure if there was some agenda behind the question, whether she was being tested.

"Do you?" She asked.

He smiled. "Certainly not."

Chapter 13

Le Jardin Des Infants was an orphanage started by one of Dumont's former interns, Melanie Beck, of the Wall Street Becks. Located on the island nation of Sainte-Trinité, medical supplies, clothing, toys, and packaged foods were needed. It was the "pet project" of the gallery. Occasionally, Pierre Dumont, accompanied by Camille St. Valois, would deliver supplies personally. Visits were documented with clips and photos placed on the websites of both the orphanage and the gallery. Alphonsine would be making this run alone, as Pierre had other matters to attend to.

The island was a backwater of corruption and desolation where life was short, brutal, and owing to a plethora of natural disasters including volcanoes, earthquakes, tidal waves, and epidemics – chaotic. It was an ideal stop over for the *divos*. Well before the islanders rose up against their French oppressors, Alphonsine's kind had had a presence there, and still maintained a house a few blocks from the main square in the capital city, Sainte Lucie. The title had transferred through many different entities. It was rarely used, but remained guarded, and despite the economic desperation of the people, was generally left alone. The reasons for this were the subject of some speculation within the *divos* community. The islanders practiced a unique combination of voodoo and Catholicism, one that acknowledged the existence of creatures who walked the night. Perhaps they simply took a *laissez-faire* attitude towards them. As long as they were discreet, and did no more than cull the herd, as long as they didn't interfere in politics, or take out anyone important, or overstay their welcome, they would be left alone.

Given the short distance, it was a rough trip. She had to travel during daylight as the airport was closed at night due to looters. The plane, which was owned by one of their shells, had special "relaxation" compartments as dark as tombs, but her sleep was not restful. She dreamed of her mother, who had morphed into Ana.

217

They had just fed and were talking softly to each other in bed, as though the discarded bodies surrounding them were alive and might overhear. She was telling Ana about Dashiell, how much she loved him and wanted to be with him forever. Ana's advice to her, unfortunately, was no different from Pierre's or Anton's.

"You must give him a very peaceful death," she said.

Alphonsine was crying, trying to explain she didn't wish for Dashiell to die.

"Everyone dies," Ana replied.

Turbulence woke her. Through the intercom built into her compartment, she learned it would be another hour before they landed.

While the dream version of Ana had let her down, she found herself missing her friend intensely. She thought of how gentle and loving Ana was with the children, taking them in their sleep so they would not feel even a second of pain or fear. Alphonsine had had only a couple of little ones since she left the abbey, and none within a century, but her memories of them were vivid, what it was like to gain their trust, the unconditional love they were so ready to give. She'd kept them only a few nights. She was certain she'd grow too attached if she had them longer, and wasn't sure how Ana managed it. Thinking about their smiles, bathing them, brushing out their hair, gave her a peculiar feeling in her womb.

Dashiell would sometimes talk about children, and she'd go along, meaning every word when she told him she'd like nothing better than to have his someday. It wasn't a lie. She only wished it were possible.

"I hope she has your eyes," he'd said referring to their future daughter, and she could almost see the child in her arms. She thought then of her son. She'd only held him that once before they took him away. The father wouldn't let her nurse, told her it would ruin her breasts. He had a woman for that. That was the way the rich operated then – a woman to scrub the pots, another to draw the bath, someone to fuck in addition to a wife and/or a more high-born mistress, a woman to breast-feed one's legitimate heirs, and a separate one for the bastards born to the teenage whore.

Did the wealthy still employ wet-nurses? She didn't think so. Everything was do-it-yourself. Cook your own meals, drive your own car. Given all the acts respectable wives now performed regularly with their husbands, and all the unattached women willing to happily

218

debase themselves, it was surprising even that her old profession was still thriving.

The pilot announced they were about to land. Still on her back in her compartment, she gulped down a few amphetamines. It wasn't until the plane stopped moving that she put on her sunglasses, and pressed the button to open the enclosure.

It was late afternoon. Even with a large floppy hat and her vintage Jackie O shades, she could feel the horrid power of the sun on her face and neck. She hurried to the waiting car, and sat behind tinted windows. The air was running full blast and there was a large black blanket for her in the back seat. Most of the supplies were left on the plane, which would remain under guard through the night.

The capital looked little improved since she'd last seen it, despite the international aide that had poured in. Good old Sainte Trinité, as corrupt and inefficient as ever. *Plus ça change, plus c'est la même chose*

With nothing to see, she lay down on the seat with the blanket protecting her. She sat up when the car slowed down. They'd reached the small gatehouse. The guard opened the gate, and they pulled up a short driveway to the entrance. Her key creaked, but worked. The driver helped her with her luggage and left.

The housekeeper was always warned when guests were coming. She kept the place clean and well-stocked, but stayed far away from the visitors and did not live in. There was no sign of others of her kind. Alphonsine would have the place to herself. There were still a couple of hours till dusk. She found her way to the darkest bedroom and lay down, feeling the wideness of the bed and an acute sense of loneliness.

The simplicity of her surroundings reminded her of the abbey, and her thoughts turned again to Ana. There was a Portuguese word her friend had taught her, *saudade*. It was a feeling, a longing for someone or something that is absent. She hadn't seen Ana since shortly before the Great War when she'd made her first trip back to the continent. The plan had been for her to visit points north of France, though some did not approve of her visiting Europe at all while any mortal who might have seen Marie Duplessis was yet alive. Ana hadn't judged her decision to return, but accepted her once more with great warmth and tact. It was Ana more than anyone who taught her death could be a gift, every feast a sacrament, that the hunt could be even more exciting when the prey lacked awareness of its aim, and that she must always strive to overcome her desire to inflict pain.

As she fell back into the day sleep, she decided with certainty she would look for a child – a hopeless hungry one unlikely to survive to adulthood. It would not only pay homage to her teacher, but serve as a symbol to bridge the distance of time and space between them.

When she rose that evening, she thought of how best to dress. Her white skin would stand out, and very few people dared walk in the capital after dark. She put on jeans and a blouse. She tied back her hair, wore no make-up, and threw on a pair of clear glasses she kept to tone down her appearance. She thought she might pass herself off as an aide worker or a missionary, and just to add to that illusion, she put on a large gold cross, though she knew it might attract thieves.

She found what she sought on the street behind the central square, or rather the girl found her, came right up and tapped her on the leg, then took her hand to her mouth in the universal gesture of hunger. Ana would have taken this as a sign. *She came to you of her own free will. It was her destiny.*

"What is your name, my sweet?"

The child seemed shocked then delighted to hear the question in the island's Creole. She was not an especially pretty girl, her unkempt hair an uneven mess of kink, her clothes filthy, her dark skin sallow. There were marks on her arms that might have been some sort of rash, but she had a beautiful smile and large dark amber eyes.

"I am Marie-Thérèse. Please mademoiselle, I am very hungry."

"Of course," Alphonsine replied. She took out a bag of chips she had brought for just such an occasion, and handed it to the girl who eagerly opened it with her teeth.

Watching her tear into them, Alphonsine recalled a time she'd been hungry and a stranger bought her a similar treat – fresh *pomme frites* from a street vendor. Strange, he hadn't wanted anything in return though he told her she was beautiful. Years later, he became a great friend though never anything more.

The chips disappeared in seconds, and the girl was eager to tell the stranger her story. Her mother was dead. She had last been in the care of a woman she referred to as her "Auntie" but was more likely someone who had bought her for a servant from her father. It was a common arrangement on the island. Auntie had two children of her own, who unlike Marie-Thérèse, went to school, ate until their bellies

220

were full, and slept on beds with pillows made of feathers. They bullied her mercilessly. She was on her way home from the market when the quake hit. The house was flattened, and she took it as her opportunity to run.

"But I have been hiding from the demons," she said, her eyes wide with fear.

"The demons?"

"Yes. They steal the kidneys and the heart and sell them to the Americans," the child told her. The way she said "Americans" she made them sound worse than the demons themselves.

Alphonsine smiled. "But I'm an American, and I would never harm you."

The girl laughed. She didn't believe Alphonsine could possibly be an American.

"I have an idea," Alphonsine said, "Why don't you come with me to my house? It's right around the corner. I can make you a nice supper, and give you a bath, and you can even sleep on a bed."

The girl looked at her uncertainly, as though she couldn't decide whether or not the proposal had been a joke. When she realized she was serious, she hugged her. Alphonsine scooped her prize in her arms and carried her back to the house.

There was a wall surrounding the residence, and a guard booth, but the guard was asleep, drunk on the rum Alphonsine had brought him. She had also "suggested" he drink it till he passed out.

Instructions had been left with the housekeeper for several contingencies. In the refrigerator, they found the requested chicken, plucked and quartered, ready for the frying pan.

Marie-Thérèse's eyes went wide. "This is for me?"

"Of course it is. But would you like a mango shake first?"

The child could not remember how long it had been since she'd even had a mango, much less a shake, and was thrilled to watch the ice-cubes whirr in the blender with the fresh milk and mango slices. She gulped the liquid down quickly, as Alphonsine set the chicken and plantains over a low flame.

"There is one thing we must do before we eat," Alphonsine announced.

"Thank the Lord Jesus?" The girl asked.

Alphonsine laughed. "Well, yes, I suppose you should say grace, but I meant you must have a bath." She showed the girl to the bathroom, and started the tub.

There was so much dirt on the poor thing's skin it turned the water dark. As Alphonsine ran her fingers through the unkempt hair, she was surprised *not* to find lice, just grime and dust.

Marie-Thérèse had been made to clean herself by her "auntie," but could recall no one helping her before.

"I'm sure you just don't remember. I'm sure your sweet mama, before she died, bathed you every night."

She was worried Alphonsine would get wet.

"It's okay. Water won't kill me."

Once Marie-Thérèse was convinced there was no problem, she started splashing on purpose, and soon the two of them were engaged in a water fight.

After some time Alphonsine said, "The water is getting cold. And look! Your fingers are like raisins."

The girl looked at the back of her hands with astonishment. "This happens sometimes when I scrub Auntie's floor," she said.

"Aren't you glad you'll never have to scrub anyone's floor again?"

"What do you mean, mademoiselle?"

"I told you to call me Camille."

"Yes, Mademoiselle Camille. Why won't I ever have to scrub a floor?"

"Because I'm going to take you to America. And you're going to be my daughter, and I promise you there won't be demons."

The naked little thing hugged her, and Alphonsine lifted her from the tub. Smelling her clean neck, she was tempted to take her blood right then, but resisted. *It must be done right*, she reminded herself, and they had hours to play.

"You're soaked, Mademoiselle Camille."

"So I am," she said, as she helped dry the girl off. "We'll both need to change. Shall we both be princesses?"

Marie-Thérèse smiled, but clearly had no idea what Alphonsine was talking about. Alphonsine had a suitcase full of children's clothes and toys she was going to hand out personally and on video at the orphanage. From this, she took out a princess costume, complete with tiara.

She had only a simple black dress for herself, but it would do for the evening. The child asked to wear a pair of her heels. Despite the toilet paper they stuffed into the toes, Marie-Thérèse couldn't walk in the things. This sent both of them into peals of laughter. Alphonsine looked through the donations in her case and found a pair of glittery slippers that fit her better.

She wasn't sure what to do about the girl's hair, but managed to form some tight braids, approximating cornrows. When all was done, Marie-Thérèse was quite transformed. Looking into a mirror she said, "*Mon Deus*, I *am* a Princess."

"Of course you are *ma chère*."

The girl hugged her again and said, "I love you."

And though she knew, from her own bitter experience, how easy it was to obtain the love of a child who had no one to give it to, it made her whole being quake with happiness to hear the words.

"Darling, if you can't call me Camille, you must call me *manman*."

"*Manman*," the child cried out the Creole word for mother. She repeated it dancing and spinning till she finally dropped to the ground.

They set out the plates. The little one greedily ate the chicken, while Alphonsine nibbled on some plantains.

Afterward there was more play and more laughter. Alphonsine took out a couple of dolls.

"May I keep this one? After tonight?" Marie-Thérèse asked shyly.

"Of course. Always and forever," Alphonsine told her.

Finally, the child was winding down, and the adult's hunger was becoming stronger. While part of her wished this could go on, she was growing impatient. She could hear the child's beating heart, the very high-pitched sound of blood flowing through the girl's veins. She imagined how that blood would taste, its unmatched sweetness and purity, the way the first sip would warm her throat and the heat would spread throughout her body, and finally there'd be an all-encompassing silence once the tiny heart had stopped.

She'd want to stay with her the rest of the night, snuggle next to the body as it cooled. But it would hardly be enough to satisfy. She'd need to find more. This morsel was only an appetizer, but a prized one.

She helped the girl change into a pair of pajamas with feet. This too was new to her and made her laugh.

Marie-Thérèse was allowed to choose from among the children's books, which were in French and English. "But I can't read," she said.

223

"It's not important. I shall read to you. Just choose the one with the prettiest pictures."

She settled on some awful American book, part of a series. Alphonsine improvised, creating an entirely new scenario as she translated it into broken Creole. The girl fell asleep almost too quickly, which made Alphonsine sad. As much as she had longed for this moment, now she was dreading it. She wished it could have gone on longer, wished she'd had weeks to enjoy Marie-Thérèse, to savor her.

"You are sleeping very soundly," she said, not bothering to nick her. Marie-Thérèse trusted her completely. Her voice alone would work. She began to describe a simple dream. The poor orphan had a mama and papa who loved her and always took care of her. She had a white pony and a room full of dolls and storybooks.

Alphonsine was lying down, by the little girl's side. Smelling her hair. Whispering in her ear as her senses searched the spot into which she would release her venom and begin to drink. Then something salty reached her tongue. It took her a moment to recognize her own tears. She'd never reacted that way before to prey. It startled her.

She turned away, feeling her fangs recede. She could almost see Dashiell standing by the bed – watching them. Would she ever have been able to do this to *him*? And if not, why not? How was he different from Marie-Thérèse?

"How stupid I'm being," she told herself.

Dashiell was special. He had an important destiny. This girl had nothing but an enchanting laugh.

And then it came to her, the thought that had been on the edge of her consciousness since that flash of memory when the Marie-Thérèse grabbed at the potato chips. When she came to Paris, before that even, she would have been ideal prey. There would have been no one to miss or mourn her. Her beauty was not unique. A thousand girls had that. None could have predicted that in just a few years she would become Marie Duplessis, the queen of the *demimonde*.

Who knew what *this* child might become if she lived through the night?

But if it had been her destiny to live, she never would have found her way here. The thought came to her in Ana's voice.

Yet, what if this child had a fate they could not see or know?

What was the point of this internal argument? Why could she not shut off her mind? *Blood was life.* She needed blood to survive. It might as well be that child's, but the idea nagged at her – *she could have been that child.*

She had to get out. Needed to think. She changed into street clothes and left the house, left the little girl snoring softly, with all her blood pumping peacefully.

She'd seen an old woman earlier, blind, toothless, crippled, begging on a street near the main square. It would be a kindness to take her. As she turned a corner, she sensed others coming. There were three young men with shining knives.

"I speak English," one of them said.

"You give money no hurt," said another.

The third said something in Creole. She might not have gotten all the words, but the sentiment was clear.

Within seconds, two lay on the ground, their heads almost backwards, their open eyes seeing nothing. The third was running. She leapt onto his back. He grunted as his knees hit the pavement. It was the last sound he'd make. As she drank from his neck, as his blood fell freely down her throat, satisfying for a time her constant thirst, she imagined it was the father of Marie-Thérèse she was drinking, the animal who had sold his daughter.

She didn't drain him completely, but left him to bleed the final drops onto the cracked pavement. She used his own knife to cut into his neck, creating a wound that would appear to have been the fatal strike.

"Take me demon," a feeble voice called out. The old woman she had seen earlier was lying with her back against a long-shuttered storefront nearby. Though her milky eyes registered nothing, she was aware of the carnage.

Alphonsine came close, hissing and bearing her fangs instinctively.

"Kill me," the woman pleaded without fear. "Give me peace."

Alphonsine got down on the ground. The beggar was easy to read. Not nearly as ancient as she appeared. Everyone she'd ever loved had died. Alphonsine began to tenderly stroke her hair. She started to sing her a lullaby, remembered from her own childhood. Her willing prey began to hum the tune. Alphonsine bit down. The woman sighed as her body went limp from the venom. It was difficult to draw out the blood as sometimes happened with the old and infirm. She drank slowly, tasting the sadness.

When she returned to the house, the child was still sleeping. It was nearly dawn. She took some pills to get her through the morning. She woke Marie-Thérèse and helped her dress in donated but almost new designer jeans, a striped tee-shirt, and a brand new pair of kid's Nikes, which had come to them in bulk. She cooked a simple breakfast, oatmeal and fruit.

"Will I eat like this every day when we live in America, *manman?*" Marie-Thérèse asked.

Alphonsine answered only with a hug. It was daylight now, and she had no special powers. She couldn't mesmerize the child and ask her to forget their conversation.

"Hurry up, my sweet," she told the girl. "The car will be here soon. We're going to the country."

Marie-Thérèse had never been in a private car and was quite amazed by it.

"Where are we going?" The child asked when they were beyond the slum and sprawl of the city.

"We're going to a wonderful place. It's filled with children, and a very kind lady, a friend of mine, runs it. The children don't work. They play, and go to school, and there's always plenty to eat."

"We're going to America?" the girl asked.

"No, my dear one. Just a nice place in the country."

The girl laughed as she had the night before with the same uncertainty. It was just too hard to believe such a place existed.

Melanie came to greet them when the car pulled up. The truck with the supplies had already arrived and was being unpacked. As Marie-Thérèse ran off to play with the other children, Alphonsine quickly explained she'd found her on the street, and thought there might be room for her at the orphanage. Maybe there was a miscommunication due to her limited Creole, but somehow the poor thing thought she was going to adopt her and take her to America.

"That's unfortunate," Melanie said. She warned Alphonsine if it turned out the girl had family or legal guardians, especially ones who were looking for her, her presence could cause problems. Besides they were not allowing any children to be taken out of the country.

"Adoptions are frozen at the moment. Even people who don't think we're selling organs, believe we're kidnappers."

"I'm sorry, Mellie. She has no one. I didn't know what to do. I can write you a check, personally, for her board."

"I'd appreciate that. I suppose we can get her information and make sure no one has a claim on her. They get under your skin, these kids. They attach too easily, need so desperately to love and be loved."

"Don't we all?" Alphonsine asked.

One of the volunteers was acting as videographer, filming the children unwrapping packages, playing with toys, trying on clothes. The normally glamorous Camille St. Valois looked very much at home as she handed out gifts and sang with the orphans.

She followed Melanie around, allowing her to show off all the wonders made possible by the generosity of the gallery and its patrons.

They came to the infirmary.

"These are going to be life savers," Melanie announced pointing to some medications. Alphonsine picked up a bottle and held it as the camera looked on.

Melanie explained there were enough pills to treat a child with tuberculosis and save its life.

"It's completely curable?" Alphonsine asked.

"If there are no other underlying conditions like HIV, it usually responds well to treatment. It's a bacterial infection."

"Yes, but I mean they don't stay sickly? They have normal lives?"

"If we can treat them. Kids here die from diarrhea, all kinds of things that wouldn't kill them in the developed world."

She became fatigued. She'd been in daylight much longer than usual. The air felt heavy, and she was relieved when the driver reminded her they needed to go back to the airport.

Melanie offered to help explain things to Marie-Thérèse.

"I'd be grateful for that," Alphonsine said.

She watched as the Wall Street heiress knelt down to look the girl in the eye, and told her, "Mademoiselle Camille has to go back to America. She can't take you. The authorities won't let us take children out of the country. We'd love to have you here. You could play with the others, and eat three meals every day, and we'll keep you safe."

"But I want to go with Mademoiselle Camille," the child cried grabbing Alphonsine's leg."

"You can go back to the city, where she found you, or you can stay here. We have lots of toys and books. Wouldn't you like to go to school?"

Marie-Thérèse looked imploringly at Alphonsine, whose head was pounding from the sun. She could feel the light pricking her skin, aging her every second. She was already beginning to regret her mercy. The girl had become a complication. The creed of her kind was to avoid such entanglements.

"It's best for you to stay here, my sweet," Alphonsine told her. "I'll send you presents, and I'll come to visit."

"Promise?"

"Promise," she said, making the sign of the cross on her chest.

The child went back to Melanie's arms, as though *she* were now "*manman*." It struck Alphonsine again, how much like her she had once been, willing to go with whatever stranger could offer her something, anything.

Safely in the car, she lay down in the backseat placing the black blanket over her, but still she could feel daylight seeping through the tinted windows. If they were stopped and robbed, if she were shot or stabbed, she could possibly die before nightfall. It wasn't likely to happen, but the thought weighed on her. They'd hired the best driver and he carried weapons, as did the two armed guards in the car in front of them. Besides, even the gangs had principles, and were unlikely to harm a woman on a charity mission. Still, she felt vulnerable.

Once, decades before, she had been sleeping, squeezed into a steamer trunk on a train that derailed. The trunk bounced along rocks, finally opening and throwing her. She landed on her chest, and found herself gasping for air. It was worse even than consumption. She had a vision of her own sweet mother welcoming her to the afterlife. She prayed for forgiveness. She felt herself about to lose consciousness, but then she could see the sun beginning to set, and the night brought her strength and healed her. There were stories of others, not so lucky. Daylight killed, and once dead you couldn't rise.

Underneath her blanket, her body was quiet, but her thoughts raced. She was certain she would die someday, though the day might not come for a thousand years. She could not imagine ever being able to accept her own demise with grace. She sometimes envied her prey. They either never saw it coming, or seemed to experience a profound release. Of course, the venom sapped them of the will to fight, but wasn't that a blessing?

In her last days as Marie Duplessis she made jokes about her expected expiration, gave away possessions, talked about her burial plot, but part of her always hoped. And while she believed Anton had exploited that hope, coming to her at her weakest, she could understand he was not completely wrong when he told her she had willed it though she would never have admitted as much to him.

She thought of the priest who had come to her home. What must it have been like for him to cross her sinful threshold? She had been generous to the church, to orphans and other unfortunates, yet it was rare that a clergyman would even acknowledge her existence. That young one, whose name she couldn't remember was an exception. He'd seemed like a cousin, a brother even, with his familiar Norman accent.

"God will forgive you. You have nothing to fear," he'd told her. She could almost hear his words.

Would she be in heaven if she had died? Would she be at peace or was it, as Dashiell believed, an endless cycle of rebirth? Or was it nothingness? Or worse?

She was aware she was crying, but for whom or why was a mystery. That girl – Marie-Thérèse? Or herself? Certainly for herself. The girl was better off than she had ever been. Her life would still be short and hard, but probably less short and less hard than if they had not met.

Alphonsine wondered what would have happened if she had only been born later, in the late twentieth century, in a place where education was mandatory, and children would be taken out of bad situations. No doubt she would still have used her beauty, but she might not have needed to sell herself in the same way. And if she had become consumptive, she would have taken some pills and been cured. *How unbelievable that was.* Even Anton would agree humanity was clever.

She'd known they'd made progress, remembered reading about the actress, Vivien Leigh, who had lived with the disease into her fifties. It came out later she was quite eccentric, and some attributed it to the "tubercular temperament," but Alphonsine believed it was not the bacteria itself which made one mad, but being young and living with the knowledge that life would be short.

The car stopped. The driver helped her onto the plane. She closed herself into the custom built sleeper, and was out almost immediately, waking as they landed at dusk in Miami. The plan had been for her to spend a night in South Beach, just in case she hadn't been able to feed in Sainte Trinité. Since she was quite sated, she thought she might simply call Dashiell. They could make remote love. She missed him terribly and needed to work off the energy of the previous evening's hunt.

A hired car was waiting to take her to an Art Deco mansion off Ocean Drive. At the door, she pressed in the combination she'd been given. Once inside, she could feel and smell the presence of another of her kind.

A familiar buxom blonde descended a staircase wearing a red beaded dress, low cut and very short. It seemed a bit vulgar to Alphonsine, too obvious, but perhaps practical if the aim was to attract prey.

"What do you think?" Jane asked, turning around to show herself. She was smiling at Alphonsine in a knowing way, obviously having read her thoughts.

"*Tres jolie*. I think I must be jealous of your figure. I could never fill it so well."

Jane laughed and embraced her, pulling her close. Each of her kind had a distinctive scent, which was strongest when they were most hungry. Jane was full scented. There were hints of vanilla, cinnamon, something harder to name – sweet but not cloying.

Alphonsine was enjoying being held, the feel of Jane's soft flesh. If only she'd had a companion the previous evening to help her work off her excess energy. Her kind could always comfort each other, and do so with a minimum of words or fuss. Jane stuck her tongue deep into Alphonsine's mouth. Alphonsine could taste Jane's hunger. She exposed her neck in a gesture of submission, allowing Jane to nip into her, and gain a bit of sustenance.

She felt Jane's gratitude mentally, and then physically as Jane pushed her against the wall, loosened Alphonsine's jeans and thrust two fingers inside of her. Alphonsine leaned toward her, and somehow the two of them lost their normally remarkable balance and fell. They broke out laughing, and lay together by each other's side.

"My sweet sister, how long has it been?" Jane asked.

"The Côte d'Azur, I think. '52?" Alphonsine suggested.

"I know you've never loved me," Jane said.

Alphonsine might have blushed then if she'd been mortal. "No, it's only that ..."

"We don't lie to each other," Jane continued. "I've never been one of your favorites. I don't blame you. You loved Ana and Pierre and were so new to us, still tied to human foibles. I must have seemed like a rival."

230

"That was so long ago," Alphonsine said, "Lifetimes. And if you were offended, I was completely to blame."

Jane ran her fingers through Alphonsine's hair, as Alphonsine looked into Jane's huge green eyes. She felt at once a sense of love, lust, and compassion. She reached over and kissed the blonde. Clothes flew off and soon they were furious in their lovemaking, Alphonsine on top, sinking her head into Jane's pendulous breasts, sucking on her sweetly scented nipples. This was a first; they'd been together before but always with either Ana or Pierre beside them.

"I'm *starving*," Jane said when they were through.

"Do you need more?" Alphonsine asked, ready to offer again.

"No, you sweet thing, I need to hunt. But what I had from you was scrumptious. You had more than one? They blended, but I got a distinct sense of someone old, in need of release. A woman?"

Alphonsine nodded.

"And the other, young and dangerous. Without mercy, but finally also at peace. I think you gave them good ends. Ana taught you well."

"I hope so."

"I know you're not in need, but you'll come with me tonight, won't you?"

"Of course." It was their custom not to refuse such an invitation, even if it was only to act as a look out and assist. "I'd like that."

"And after …?" Jane asked trailing off before she finished her question.

"Yes," Alphonsine said, "after."

The women showered together, continuing their exploration, their "catching up." Alphonsine had brought hardly any clothes, so they looked through the closets in the house, and found a glittery tube of a dress. Subtlety was not what they needed this night. Jane had a definite idea of what she was in the mood for.

"I want a man I can take while he's inside me. Hard and handsome. I want to drain him dry, and maybe have a second if it doesn't seem too greedy."

"I'm sure we'll find something nice. *Merde*, do you mind if I make a quick call before we go?"

Jane looked at her curiously.

While no explanation was necessary, Alphonsine offered one. "A mortal. An *affaire de coeur.*"

"A what?"

Alphonsine realized while Jane might understand the French, she was not familiar with the reference. "Back when I was in Paris, it's what we girls called it when you were with someone only for love."

"You're in love?"

"As much as I am capable."

"In love like a teenager?"

"In love like in an opera."

"With a mortal?"

She nodded and knew there was an unasked question left hanging in the air. *What will you do with him?* She didn't really have an answer, and Jane seemed to understand.

"There's no rush. Give him a call."

She stepped onto a small patio in back of the house.

"I'm with people, having dinner. Can I call you in an hour?" Dashiell asked.

"Maybe not, darling. I'm staying in South Beach with an old friend."

"A friend?"

"Don't worry. A woman. But we haven't eaten yet. We're about to go out to get a bite."

"Out? You in South Beach? I don't think I want to know."

"There's only you, *mon cher*. You own my heart."

He needed to go back. She told him she'd call him the following evening, and promised to send him the video from the orphanage.

She was certain Jane heard the conversation. She wondered if they might have a chance to talk to each other later, if Jane, as a woman, would have more insight, more sympathy for her than Pierre or Anton. She was tired of their condescension.

Jane drove the rental car to a bar she had scoped out near a university. They were soon surrounded by and talking to a small group of young men who all lived together.

"Like a fraternity house?" Alphonsine asked.

"Sort of. Not officially. Just some guys with a lease who like to have fun."

"I like to have fun."

Jane playfully grabbed her hand. A boy asked them to kiss. But everyone had a phone, meaning everyone had a camera.

"I have a better idea," Jane said. "Why don't we go back to your house and have a real party?"

"Do you have any more friends?" One of them asked. He seemed to be their leader.

Jane whispered in his ear, "You don't need more girls. Believe me, we're all the girls you can handle."

They gave them the address. Driving over, Jane and Alphonsine discussed a plan. Besides the five at the bar, there were two more roommates – one of whom was at his girlfriend's and not expected home. The other was Jane's potential prey – a studious, moody type who didn't socialize much, and would likely be home.

The place was a typical testosterone filled lair. It smelled so strongly of cum that Alphonsine thought even a mortal would be able to pick up the scent.

They were offered drinks. A roofy wouldn't have had much effect on either of them, but they hadn't bothered to spike hers. Jane pretended to be drunk and sick. She ran to the upstairs bathroom.

"Don't worry about her. She'll be fine in a few minutes," Alphonsine assured the boys. "Forget she's even here."

One of them was already kissing her neck and fondling her breasts. He had blond hair and light eyes like Dashiell, but he wasn't as pretty – more rugged, rougher around the edges, the kind who would lose his looks to drink and drugs within a few years. His thoughts, which were easy to read, were primitive. She wanted to get him alone, but needed to keep the others close by and away from Jane while she was busy.

"Let's go to my room," he said. He was looking over at a door next to the kitchen.

"Your room is down here?"

"Yup. Right there. You ready?"

"What about your friends?" She asked.

They were staring at her, following the conversation.

"You want them to watch?" He asked nibbling her neck.

"No, I mean, I just thought we'd all hang out and party together."

"Hey, you want to *party* with all of us, that's chill," another said.

"I don't know," she said looking down for a second, "It sounds so dirty."

"You can trust us …"

"It's just I never," she made herself blush a little and sputtered, "I've never done anything like this before. It's just been a, a fantasy."

They were watching her intensely.

"How about you and me go into the room, and I'll give you a massage?" The blond asked. She could feel his hard prick against her back. "I'll get you warmed up and relaxed, and then we can see what happens."

The skinny one with the soul patch who looked like he wouldn't have been out of place in Brooklyn, spoke up. "Hey, we could come in one at a time. We're not like animals."

"Do you want me to?" She asked the blond.

"Totally," he said. "I'd really respect you for that. For trusting us all."

"And you all will be waiting. Till I'm ready?"

Brooklyn said, "We're not going anywhere. Right guys? We're gonna nuke some za or something."

"Okay," she said. "You're so nice," she added, remembering to slur her words.

She took Blondie's hand and stepped into his room. There wasn't much inside. Clothes on the floor. A double bed that didn't look clean, but that was good too. She wanted it dirty.

She took off her clothes quickly, as though she couldn't wait. She matched the desire she saw in his eyes. Already naked, she placed a hand on the bulge in his jeans. She pulled off his tee-shirt. It wasn't that his body was better than Dashiell's, but it was at least as good, rock hard abs, well defined, and the Florida sun had roasted his skin a nice golden brown. It would be fun to fuck him, she thought, but if she hadn't fed off two mortals the night before, it would have been great to drain him dry.

When the pants came off, she looked at his large hard dick with admiration.

"What do you think?" he asked posing like he was in a contest. His narcissism was so amusing.

"I think we're going to have a very nice time."

She pushed him onto the bed. He seemed a little taken aback by her newfound assertiveness.

"I thought you needed a little relaxing."

"But I do," she said.

He pulled out some cuffs from a side table.

She told him, "I want my hands free. How about you?"

He declined.

"Oh come on. Are you afraid of *me*?" She asked coyly.

She grabbed his wrists and cuffed him before he had a chance to realize her strength. He accepted his condition. She knew he would. He wouldn't admit even to himself he'd been powerless to get out of her grip. It solved a number of problems including the ever present issue of photos or videos going out on the net. There was a knock on the door.

"Not yet," he said. "Give us ten minutes."

"Fifteen," she called out.

Of course he wouldn't want his friends to see him like that.

"But I thought …" a voice said.

"Later, dude." He looked at her, "You're still going to give him some, right?"

"Maybe," she said. "If you're a good boy."

She sat on his face. He had skills. When she was satisfied, she slithered down his body dripping a mix of cunt juice and saliva onto his chin, his neck and chest. She started to lick his toes, and worked her way up to his thighs, gently massaging them, and avoiding the temptation of his femoral artery.

"Do it, fucking do it," he said. "I can't take anymore."

She slapped him. "Don't you ever tell me what to do," she said.

He looked confused for a second, but then she saw the slight smile. He was enjoying this. It was fun and games, and not just another girl too drunk to say no. He was getting off on her desire. He might have been the type to use force, and then convince himself the next day he hadn't crossed a line. With her, he wouldn't have to. She briefly sucked on his cock, but just to tease. Then she slipped into him, her torso vertical, closing her eyes, grinding in small circles. She was thinking of Dashiell. This one was a poor approximation – technically proficient, but not even close. Still he would suffice. With each thrust, she was aware of the feast-blood pumping through her, the aggression of the young thug, the sadness of the old lady. It was as though they were there with her, also feeling the build up of heat, the friction preceding the fiery explosion.

They came at the same time.

"Fucking A," the blond yelled. He tried to move his arms, only to realize he was still in restraints. "Let me out of these."

She looked at him sternly.

"Please let me out of these," he said in a less demanding tone.

"Why should I?"

"Because I'd like to stick my cock up your fine ass, and I'd like my hands free."

"Okay," she said.

He immediately rolled her onto her stomach. "On your knees, bitch," he said now showing her who was in charge.

"Ask me again, nicely," she commanded.

"Would you mind, please?"

She did as he asked. He slathered on some KY conveniently left out on top of an adjacent table. Just as he'd managed to slide in, the knock came again, and this time her stud said, "Come in."

Merde, she thought, worried they might have phones. She *hated* an uncontrolled environment.

She turned her head and saw one of them fiddling with a device. Fortunately, she saw something else. Jane was behind them. She came up so fast they never saw her coming. They went down one by one as Jane gave each a nip of venom. Facing the bedpost, the boy still up her ass had no idea Jane was approaching.

He started groaning, and Alphonsine could feel the release of his cum inside her. "What the hell ..." he said before he collapsed, his chest landing on her back as she pulled herself away.

Both women began to laugh as they surveyed the scene. After running to the downstairs bathroom to clean off, she returned and dressed quickly. As she went around to check for devices and their contents, Jane was telling the boys to stay asleep until someone woke them.

"You've all had a lot to drink and smoke. You're going to have terrible hangovers and everything that happened tonight will be fuzzy. You won't remember what we looked like, or how long we stayed, and you won't be able to describe us."

When Jane was done, Alphonsine spoke. "You look flush."

"Oh I am," Jane said. "He said he was studying, but he had porn going." She made a gesture with her hand, and shook her head. "I don't think he'd ever been with a live girl. Not my dream date, but nice, especially once he took off the specs. I acted like I was scared of his friends. He got to be my white knight, and I rewarded him accordingly."

"Where'd you leave him?"

"In the tub, upstairs. Wrists slashed. Looks like the blood went down the drain. I stopped when there was still a faint beat, so the bite mark closed. Well, it does sort of look like a hickey or a bruise, but I don't think it'll be noticed. It's on his thigh."

"I bet he enjoyed that."

"You wouldn't be wrong. Best night of the poor sod's life."

"Yes, but was it good for you?"

Alphonsine noticed a little blood on the outside of Jane's mouth. She licked it off. "Sweet." Then she looked around at the boys, and got an idea.

What are you doing?" Jane asked.

Alphonsine began undressing the Brooklyn hipster.

"Just having a little fun," she said as she tossed him onto the bed next to the blond and posed them together. Not quite satisfied with the display, she handcuffed the blond's right wrist to the hipster's left. "That's better."

Jane giggled. "You naughty, naughty girl."

Before they left, they turned off the music, and did a walk through. Their kind could usually hear the high-pitched hum of electronics, and pick out any hidden cams or audio equipment. While they carried mini-jammers, the range was very limited, and they could be unreliable or at times dangerously obvious.

"Anything?" Jane asked.

"No. You?"

"No."

They turned the music back on before they left, setting the stage for the other roommate to come back from his girlfriend's and discover his friends sleeping off a typical night of debauchery, except for the suicide in the upstairs bathroom.

When they got back to the house, they both had some espresso, and Jane ate a few cookies, explaining how lately she'd developed a sugar craving after feasting.

"Must be from all that high fructose corn syrup in their blood," Alphonsine suggested.

Spooning Jane, running her fingers through her hair as they lay together waiting for the day sleep, Alphonsine felt almost guilty for the resentment she sometimes felt towards her community. She was so lucky, she thought, not only for her longevity, but to have a family, who in the end were always loyal and loving. Jane's body vibrated a contagious joy. The blood had warmed her, and to Alphonsine she'd never looked lovelier. She kissed the back of Jane's neck, while tenderly touching her breasts. Yet, as close as she felt to her, she couldn't help wanting more, imagining what it would be like if only she could share this joy with Dashiell. If only he were her kind, and the two of them could be together for eternity.

Jane was rattling on about the feast, not picking up on Alphonsine's thoughts. They both became drowsy, and although the room was completely dark, they knew the sun would soon rise. There'd be time enough once it set again to work off more of their energy before parting.

Chapter 14

Dying was still etched in her memory. In this she was unique among her kind, most of whom had been taken in the peak of youth and health. Often she dreamed of her final days and nights – being carried to her box at the theatre – determined to go, to show herself, almost as an affront to all who had abandoned her, a way of reminding them she wasn't dead yet. There were those last weeks when her boudoir became her world, and finally her world was limited to her bed.

So many years later, the memories might come to her at any time in flashes. Diversion helped. She rarely spent nights alone. She enjoyed some solitary activities – reading, playing the piano, but then she would begin to feel restless, compelled to find a party or throw one, and if there wasn't a crowd, or a public entertainment, or an open shop, she could at least find someone with whom to share some time.

It changed when Dashiell entered her life. His return from California was only two days away, and while she felt his absence as tangibly as she might feel the lack of a limb, there was also a newfound ease that came from knowing he would be back. As she awoke, she found herself looking forward for the first time in decades to spending an entire evening alone. There were some tasks she had to do for the gallery, egos that needed her attention, but this she could accomplish remotely via a few short texts, so like the little notes she would send out in the old days.

Shortly after dusk, she took a walk along the East River green path. It wasn't crowded, but neither was it deserted, a few joggers and skaters, some couples. Her kind didn't need exercise to stay fit, but she wanted to enjoy the lights of the city, the reflection on the water, and the modern convenience of personal music on her iPhone. Miles Davis' *Bitches Brew* was the soundtrack when she recognized a man coming toward her. He was about average height, but had a strong build, and a full head of wavy black hair, along with a well-groomed goatee. They'd had a delightful encounter over a year earlier, meeting by chance along this same road. She'd caught his thought in a visual flash and projected her own. She'd followed him into a very tight alley between two nearby buildings. It had been wordless and quick, but not too quick. She felt a tingle remembering the feeling of him thrusting from behind, his hands covering her breasts, holding them like handles, her face sometimes brushing against rough brick. He had almost become her prey, but she noticed his wedding band, sensed children, and thought his death or disappearance might bring too many questions.

He was now only a few yards from her. He winked, and moved his head in the direction of the alley. She smiled slightly, shook her head, and kept going. She wondered why she had turned him down when being with him would have been so easy. She was looking forward to some planned face time with Dashiell later, but so what? One couldn't get off too many times in a night, especially one of her kind.

In her mortal days she had been choosy about those who could buy her favors, and those to whom they might be freely given, but as a *diva* there was no reason to turn down pleasure. None of the human concerns – physical danger, disease, or pregnancy – were even possible. There could be no emotional attachment with the stranger. She wouldn't have denied Dashiell an opportunity like that. Why did she feel she should deny herself for him? In what way did her denial benefit him? How was this different from her encounter at the frat the week before?

That last question was the only one she could answer to her own satisfaction. It had been her duty to help Jane, and an easy way to keep the boys distracted, to prevent an even messier bloodbath. Having sex with the stranger on the path however, would have been purely recreational.

But why did that make it "wrong"? She tried to think it through using whatever was left of what she thought of as her "human brain," but even when she'd been mortal, monogamy had not been her usual practice. She understood if Dashiell found out, he would be disappointed in her, and she didn't wish to do anything behind his back she wouldn't do in front of him, even though she understood that was impossible.

Walking home, she took a call from Cara, an invitation to go bowling the following night. Alphonsine wondered if Dashiell put her up to it. It would have been easy to give a gallery related excuse, but she said yes. It would be a mildly amusing way to pass some time and would keep her from temptation. When she returned to her apartment, she spent a few hours listening to Marian McPartland and Mary Lou Williams, resigning herself to the realization that even with more than a century of practice, superior agility, and hearing, she would never master improvisation – at least not musically.

The bowling party consisted of Cara, her prosecutor friend Justin, and two others, both policemen. While Alphonsine was always aware of how men watched her, she noticed how oblivious the otherwise observant Cara was to her own allure – the way the men's eyes admired her round behind as she strolled up to the line and released the ball, the stolen glances at her ample chest.

Alphonsine was certain that Justin, in particular, was not immune to the detective's charms, and that Cara was attracted to him as well. She considered suggesting another outing with Cara for some "girl talk." She had never before played matchmaker. What a very *human* thing to do. Of course, any advice would go one way. She would never talk to her about Dashiell. Aside from Cara's own friendship with him, there was simply too much she couldn't say.

They went out for pizza after the game, and from there to a bar with a band that no one paid attention to. It surprised her how much she was enjoying the evening – despite the absence of her lover. She supposed there was some novelty in spending time with ordinary people. It reminded her a bit of her youth, meeting students in Parisian cafes – talking through the night. In those days they might discuss profound subjects like philosophy, but they'd also joke about current matters, politics and gossip. It had been her first glimpse of higher learning. "Hanging out" with Cara's friends, the level of discourse was less heady, but it evoked something. She felt again that longing – *saudade*, though she couldn't have said exactly what it was she was longing for.

While the Parisian students may have professed their love for her, it had been business. The light dinner, the glass or two of wine, would be paid for by some boy, whom she might reward with her favors, which in those early days, could be had in back alleys at discount rates, especially if as part of the exchange she learned something about the world, which she hadn't known before, and might use later.

It was not yet two o'clock when the party ran out of steam. She went home alone. She'd been texting Dashiell, knew he'd already gone to bed even though it was hours earlier where he was. Bored, she spread out some sex toys. In the quiet of the night, she thought for a moment she heard Anton's voice in her head, chiding her that masturbation was so beneath her kind. She wondered if it actually was him, still able to peek inside her mind despite her best efforts to keep him out. He hadn't left New York yet. More likely, she decided, it was her imagination.

She rubbed some massage oil on her vulva. It had a slight mint kick, which worked its way in and made her incredibly hot. She took one of her vibrators, slowly drawing circles around her slit, barely touching her skin because it was already so sensitive. The toy had a beaded texture, the beads moving, going over her like the rough tongue of a large cat. Then she pushed it in, just an inch or so. She wanted to think of Dashiell, imagine it was his tongue inside of her, but somehow she kept picturing Anton, remembering pieces of that night when she had been changed, though the details had always eluded her.

She came, but felt almost violated, still unsure if she truly owned her thoughts, or if the Russian, who would always be far more powerful than she, was somehow in control. It would be madness to dwell on it. He never stayed any place long. Even if he was in her head, so what? He couldn't force her to do anything. It was only that she saw him so rarely, and was out of practice at blocking him.

When dawn arrived, she went to sleep clutching a pillow, fantasizing it was Dashiell by her side, reminding herself he'd be home the next evening. She awoke feeling a warm strong arm around her naked body. There he was beside her. His eyes were open. He was wearing jeans, but no shirt.

They kissed. "Good morning," he said.

"But how?"

He kissed her again. "I got an earlier flight."

Between smooches she asked, "How did you get in?"

"Rosa."

"She leaves at noon. It must be ..."

"Seven. I spent the day reading. I had to order take out. You have nothing but champagne in your fridge. What do you live on?"

"Love?" She asked, beginning to come around. "But the bedroom door, I always leave it bolted."

"I thought I'd just wait for you to wake up, but I tried the door from the bathroom, and it was open."

"I'm getting careless," she said, "but I'm glad."

She pulled down his pants and rubbed her head in his crotch, licking his balls, nearly swooning from the scent of him, the very slight hint of ammonia, the sweet freshness that his vegetable diet brought. There was nothing rotting within him. He was one hundred percent organic and plant based. She started sucking, admiring the smooth beauty of his uncut penis, rubbing her twat against his leg. She knew if she took even a little sip of his blood, despite her feelings for him, it would be almost impossible to stop.

Someday, she imagined, if her kind ruled humanity – not that she had any ambition in that regard, they might clone Dashiell Alexanders, keep them on a farm, to be used as studs and superfine prey, saved for special feast days. How wonderful that would be, a chance to feed on him again and again and again.

Despite, Ana's precepts, her kind desired the hunt, loved the smell of fear. In her fantasies, she might give her Dashiell-clone a head start, allow him to hide, to think he'd outsmarted her, but then she would pounce ready for the kill. Of course he'd submit to her first. How could he not?

The real Dashiell, the one in her bed whose hard throbbing shaft was in her mouth, began moaning softly as his pre-cum went down her throat. She drew out his semen enjoying every drop, but wishing so much she could drink all of him, and then bring him to immortality.

He flipped her onto her back and moved his head between her legs. She was tempted to pull him up by grabbing his hair. It would be so easy to bite his neck, drain him while their bodies were interlocked.

"*Mon Dieu, mon Dieu, mon Dieu,*" she shouted as he brought her to climax.

He looked up at her. She could feel her canine teeth extended, and was careful to keep her mouth closed. She tried to conjure the smell of rotting meat, of anything that would shrink her fangs.

He brought his body up to kiss her face. She loved that she could taste herself on him. It bothered her that in the midst of passion she often imagined killing him, but that was natural for her kind. Afterwards, she only had the tenderest of feelings towards him, and would have harmed anyone who threatened his safety.

They were next to each other, staring at the ceiling. "Wouldn't it be wonderful if we could live forever?" She asked. "Always be young. Spend centuries making love."

"But what's the meaning of life if there's no death?" He asked. "What's the point of it? No one would ever create anything, or bring children into the world. It would always be the same."

"Don't you think it would be fun? To be free of fear, of disease? To never grow old and infirm? To live for pleasure?"

"I suppose," he said, not sounding convinced. "But we'd still be corporeal. Stuck inside a body with its own demands."

"Is that how you think of love? As a demand of the body?"

"I love you," he said, "but what just happened was lust. Desire."

"How romantic," she said, sarcastically. "You don't think of it as an expression of our feelings?"

"Anything we do together could be an expression of our feelings – dancing, singing a duet, preparing a meal. Love would be doing *it* with each other when I'm so old I can't even get it up, and your beautiful breasts aren't so firm."

"My breasts will always be firm."

"My point is I'll love you when they aren't."

She kissed him again for that, but knew it was foolish drivel. Dashiell could conceive of a soul, that there was more to them than flesh. While Alphonsine sometimes imagined she might burn in hell, or that her mother was safe in heaven, most of the time she was certain nothing beyond the body existed, and if it did, none of the men who had ever professed to love her, had done so for that part of her. Even the ones who'd been obsessed would never have been so blind as to think they'd have any use for her once her beauty faded.

Yet, she was sure she'd love *him* when he was ancient and withered – if she didn't kill him first. She would still see him as he was at that moment. She knew she'd have to leave him long before that, but wondered if it might be their destiny, that she would return one day, when he was decrepit. She would come to him as though in a dream, looking exactly as he'd last seen her – if she were careful about staying out of the sun – and then she'd feed on him, satisfying an eternal hunger, and relieving him of the misery of old age.

"Crap," he said, "We have dinner reservations at nine-thirty."

She looked at the clock.

"Cancel," she said.

"Can't. Kind of a surprise. Let's go."

He wouldn't tell her what he had in mind. She couldn't read him precisely, only got a sense he was excited and nervous, and whatever it was involved another person.

They showered together and quickly dressed. They grabbed a cab into Manhattan to Suzanne's Place, a new upscale vegan bistro in Soho. George Clooney and Alec Baldwin had been recently spotted, and there were often more fashion models than one might see at a billionaire's soiree in the Hamptons.

The hostess told them the other party had already been seated and walked them toward the back section. Heads turned as they passed. Alphonsine recognized the man sitting alone at the corner booth although she'd never seen him in person. It was David Alexander, her lover's father. He kissed her hand as she arrived at the table, "*Enchanté, mademoiselle*," he said.

She looked at both men, and couldn't help noting how strange it was that Dashiell and David bore the same resemblance to each other as her Adet had to his father, Alexandre Dumas, *père*. In both cases, the father was a shorter, broader, courser, less handsome older version of the son. In this case, add to a poorer diet, and probable alcoholism.

They had run into each other on the plane.

"What brings you to New York?" Alphonsine asked. She noticed the intensity of the old man's gaze. She caught something from him – the smell of fear. Not what she would have expected. It excited her.

"He came to see a cardiologist," Dashiell answered for him.

Alphonsine looked alarmed. "You have a problem with your heart?"

"Not really. Just the usual complaints of all American males my age. The problem is they have me on a medicine that prevents my being able to take a medicine also popular with American males my age."

She laughed. He took a sip of the scotch in front of him. The waitress came by and they did the best they could with the limited vegan wine menu – vintners she hadn't heard of who used no bone or other animal products in their filtration process. As it didn't affect her kind's prohibition against dead blood, she didn't usually worry about how her wine was made.

They ordered appetizers. David made remarks about this being his first vegan dining experience, something he might need to get used to, as it was working out so well for Clinton and others. She noticed him staring at her mouth as she popped in a piece of fried artichoke. Then he caught her watching him and looked away.

"How long have you been a vegan, Camille?" He asked.

"Awhile," she said. "Unlike Dashiell, for me it wasn't so much a moral issue. It's a good way to stay slim."

"That doesn't look like it would be a problem for you," he said, and then after a moment continued, "So it doesn't bother you, killing for food?"

"I probably differ here from your son," she said, looking over at Dashiell. "I don't think it's necessarily wrong, but the conditions on factory farms are cruel. There's no reason for that."

"And you'd have no trouble with hunting then, if you ate your prey?"

"I suppose not," she said, trying to sound thoughtful. "I've never been. Have you?"

"A few times," he answered, "a few."

She hoped the subject would change, though she didn't want to initiate it. The old man continued, "In fact, I was hunting once with your mayor."

"Piccolini?" Dashiell asked.

"The same. But that was back before he got really rich when he was a mere-multi-millionaire.

"Camille's met him," Dashiell said.

"Oh yes," David said, "I seem to recall something on the Internet."

"Just at some events for the gallery," Alphonsine said as lightly as she could. "Are you close friends?" She asked as their entrees arrived.

"I haven't seen him in a few years. Meeting him for lunch tomorrow. Shall I tell him you say hello?"

"If you'd like. I doubt he'd even remember me."

"I'd think you'd be very difficult to forget," David said.

They talked throughout the meal, never touching on anything personal. If not for the resemblance, she noted to herself, no one would have known the men were related. By the time they were waiting for dessert, the subject had turned to the west versus east coasts.

"Liz Taylor used to say that New York had the shopping, but Los Angeles had the weather.

"You knew her?" Alphonsine asked, sure he would claim he had. He'd been dropping famous names casually into the conversation all evening. Still, there was something about the old hack she found charming.

"I'm sure less intimately than you know the mayor," he teased.

"I think Camille looks like a young Elizabeth Taylor," Dashiell blurted.

"Liz was a little more ..." David moved his hands to indicate large breasts, "And she had those light eyes. Camille's an Audrey Hepburn type, a bit Holly Golightly."

She wondered exactly how he'd meant that, but Dashiell, who'd probably never seen the movie, didn't catch it.

"Oh, Dashiell thinks I look like everybody," she said. "Who did you say the other day? Louise Brooks? And then we were watching some old movie with Jennifer Jones."

"You sound a bit like Jennifer Jones, that wispiness, but I'll go with," David paused a moment, "Maria Callas. The dark hair and eyes, that slightly exotic look. Of course, your nose isn't so ethnic."

There was something in his tone that sounded rehearsed.

"It's funny tha ... " Dashiell began.

"Maybe we should take this conversation elsewhere? An after dinner drink? Or we could show you around Brooklyn," Alphonsine interrupted, hoping to derail the topic.

"Great idea," David said. "We can go in five minutes." He signaled the waiter for more coffee. "What were you saying, Dashiell?"

"It's funny you mentioned Callas," he said, turning toward her, "This one actually got me to go to an opera."

"Really, are you a big fan, Camille?" David asked, staring at her intently.

She'd heard him pause briefly before he said her name. Whatever was happening was not her imagination.

"My boss always gets tickets for clients," she said.

"How European." He turned to his son, "What did you see?"

"*La Traviata*," Dashiell said.

She was desperate to stop the conversation, but every means she thought of seemed so obvious, and a strange sort of mental paralysis had set in.

"*La Tra –vi –ata,*" David repeated, nodding, looking down. She noticed his lips curl just slightly into a smile, but by the time he looked up it was gone.

"You want to know who she really looks like?" Dashiell asked.

"Dashiell, David, I wish you guys would talk about something else besides women I resemble. It may be less complimentary than you think."

"I'm sorry if we're making you uncomfortable. Of course, we should change the subject, but I think I know where my son was going with this. As soon as he told me your name, and showed me a photo, I made the connection, maybe because you're French. Has anyone commented on your resemblance to Marie Duplessis?"

She had killed men for less.

"But you actually *remind* me of a woman I only saw once," he continued.

"That sounds intriguing," Dashiell said.

"I mentioned Callas before. " David took a sip of coffee and leaned back in his chair. "I met her. Maybe that's an exaggeration. It was summer, 1966. I was traveling, part of my writer's education. Young, unattached. A proto-backpacker, drifting through Europe on a few dollars I'd earned, a meager advance on my first book. On Mikados, I'd met a young German, equally adrift between university and further studies. Bright guy. Funny as fuck, for a German. Excuse my Fren uh language. He was torn between medical school and pure sciences. Three generations of doctors, so there was some family pressure, and there was a girl waiting for him he wasn't quite sure he wanted to marry."

"You remember a lot about him," Dashiell said.

"It's stayed on my mind." He breathed in deeply. "We somehow wrangled our way into a party on a yacht. I'm a little fuzzy how, but it involved some girls we'd met on a beach. She was there, Maria Callas."

Alphonsine had an idea how the story might end. She was trying as hard as she could to get into his brain, project a thought, give him a headache, or something, anything to distract him, but she felt blocked.

"She was surrounded by her own clique most of the time. There was this one young woman. I thought at first she might be related to *La Divina*, as they called her. They had similar features. She looked very much like you, Camille. Very much."

"They say everyone has a double somewhere in the world," Dashiell said.

"I got close enough to hear part of their conversation. They were speaking French, and mine wasn't great. She even sounded like you," he said looking at her, and then quickly turning his eyes to his son, pausing like he was trying to remember something. "Callas was saying how she wished they'd met when she was younger. Her new friend seemed to her a perfect model for Violetta Valéry. *'Violetta, c'est toi.'* I remember her saying that. Something about the way she moved, and smiled, an inner light she had, and how she so casually broke hearts."

"And that's one way we differ," Alphonsine said. She looked over at Dashiell. "My heartbreaking days are over."

"Tristan, that was my friend's name. Tristan Schiller, he somehow caught the young lady's eye. He was a handsome guy. Not as good looking as this one I'm sitting across, but a similar type."

"I'm sure you were quite the lady's man as well, David."

"Maybe," he said, "I recall leaving with a red-head."

"And your friend with the brunette?" Dashiell asked. He turned to Alphonsine and said playfully, "Good thing I don't get jealous."

"I saw them having what looked like an intense conversation. I can't be sure they left together. I just have a hunch."

"A hunch?" Alphonsine asked. "I guess he wasn't the type to kiss and tell."

"He disappeared."

"Disappeared?" Dashiell asked.

"We were staying in a hostel, dorm style. I didn't make the curfew. But in the morning I went back to get my things. He wasn't there. We had tickets for a ten a.m. ferry to Cyprus. I thought about taking his stuff in case he was running late."

"He didn't make the boat?" Dashiell asked.

"No, he didn't."

"Maybe he got *very* lucky," Alphonsine said looking at Dashiell. "Maybe they ran off together and had lots of babies."

"I don't think so," said David, "although I was pretty sure it was something like that at the time. I thought we might catch each other later, at the next port of call. We'd discussed some possible itineraries. Nothing was settled."

"But you didn't see him again?" Dashiell asked seriously,

following something in his father's tone.

"No, no I didn't." He looked like he might go on with his story, but then he said, "Let's get out of here. Go somewhere we can drink."

They stopped at an old writer's bar in the West Village, then went on to another couple of places. They ran into a few people David knew but hadn't seen in years, as well as strangers who recognized him and wanted to buy a famous writer a drink. The old man introduced his son and "the lovely" Mademoiselle Camille St. Valois. There was little real conversation. Mostly, Alphonsine and Dashiell listened to his stories, none of which had anything to do with his offspring. They might as well have been fans on whom he was bestowing the gift of his presence, yet Alphonsine was certain he loved Dashiell in his way. What else could explain that underlying anxiety? Which she now understood came from his suspicion of her.

What he thought and what he could prove were different things entirely. Creative minds were capable of great intuitive leaps, but what could he know of her true nature? If he went to Dashiell what would he say?

"Have you ever seen your girlfriend in daylight?"

The answer would be yes.

"Have you seen her eat food?"

Again, yes.

"Has she entered a residence without being invited?"

Well, that would just be rude wouldn't it?

The myths kept her safe. Yet, he might need to be dealt with, which wasn't something she wanted to do. Dashiell seemed so happy to be with his father. She knew what it was like to have neglectful parents. One loved them no less. And when they reached out even a little, as David was doing, the grudges melted away.

If something needed to be done, she would ask Pierre to help. Of course he'd chide her, remind her this is what comes from getting too close to mortals, from living too much in the spotlight. But he'd come through and make sure the old man's end was quick and painless, and then she'd do what she could to comfort her lover.

By the end of the evening, David was slurred and sloppy, so they rode with him back to his hotel. Dashiell escorted his father into the lobby and let a bellhop take it from there while she waited in the taxi. They were quiet most of the ride back to Brooklyn.

"A kiss for your thoughts," he said leaning over and pecking her cheek.

"I was just thinking how cute you must have been as a boy," she answered.

ॐ ⊕ ॐ

She woke up alone the following evening. Rosa had left the tub filled for her. Sinking beneath the bubbles, she found herself analyzing her dream. *She and Dashiell were having a candlelight dinner, celebrating an anniversary.* Within the dream she wondered if they were mortal or her kind. She didn't find it strange she couldn't remember. There wasn't much more to it, only that they were together and they were happy. It put her in a good mood.

He had left a series of texts explaining he'd run into one of his band mates. He'd quit when all the California business came up, but the new vocalist wasn't ready and they had an important gig. He felt he couldn't let them down, so he'd agreed to go on with them that night. Showtime was around eleven, at The South, a new place on the south side of Williamsburg. He'd invited his father, who'd meet them there.

"Sounds fun," she texted back. "Stop by here before?"

"Can't. Rehearsing."

She checked her e-mail and was reading the news and enjoying her coffee when the doorbell rang. There'd been no announcement on her intercom. She made sure her robe was tied, thinking it must be something building related, but when she looked out the peephole, she saw David Alexander on the other side.

"Come in," she said. "I thought you were going to meet us at the bar."

"I thought we were going to go together." He was lying. She stuck her cheek out instinctively. He didn't kiss it, just walked in. He was carrying a brown paper bag.

"They let you come right up? No one rang."

"Your concierge is a fan. I told him I wanted to surprise you."

"Well, take a seat. We have plenty of time. It's only a few blocks away. I'm not near ready, but maybe we can order in or go out first? Can I get you something?"

He sat down on the white leather sofa, taking in the view. "A couple of glasses might be nice," he said, removing a bottle of Black Label Scotch from the bag. "Join me? *Si'il vous plais?*"

251

"*Bien sûr.*"

"Is that music Liszt?" He asked.

"Yes. *La Camponela*," she said. She could feel his eyes on her back as she reached up to the high cabinet to grab two shot glasses. Her robe stopped mid-thigh. She had on nothing underneath. "Are you a music lover?" She asked turning around.

"Not really."

She sat down on the chair across from him, landing carefully, in a way that gave him a nice view of her bare leg, but not of anything more.

She took the whiskey he'd poured, and raised her glass. "What shall we drink to?"

"My son," he suggested. "May he find success and lead a *long* and happy life."

They drank quickly, and were both silent for a moment.

"I really should get dressed," she said pulling down her robe just slightly, and shaking her still damp hair.

She watched as his eyes moved briefly to her thigh. He was trying to see what he could, which was less than he thought.

"We have time," he said. "Let's talk."

"All right."

It was a strange feeling, like an awkward date. She thought of the men who'd bought her favors, old ones like him. They often wanted to talk first, but then there wasn't much more they could do, at least not back in those days.

"What's funny?"

"Huh? Was I smiling?"

"A Mona Lisa smile."

"Don't tell me I look like *her* too."

"You're not what I expected," he said. "I mean from Google."

It had been a very long time since the father of a lover had come to see her. Would he try to seduce her, or would he offer her a cash payout to leave his innocent child alone? She was afraid it was neither. He knew something, which was unfortunate. It was her job to find out what he knew, and what he'd told others.

"I'm not?" She asked, sounding slightly astonished.

"No, you're … You seem like a nice girl."

Seem. From the same root as similar, simulation.

It was better to let him talk. The quieter she was, the more he would reveal. He continued, "So, you went to the Sorbonne?"

252

"Only for a short while."

"Before you got the position at Dumont's."

"Yes."

"That was very lucky."

"It was."

"Your parents, your mother was American. Dashiell told me they both died."

"I'm afraid so."

"Didn't leave you much?"

"Like you said, I was lucky when the job came along."

"You know I had lunch with our mutual friend today."

She pretended not to know whom he meant.

"Sam Piccolini. He does remember you by the way. Spoke very highly of you in fact."

"How sweet. Would you like anything else? I think there are some peanuts."

"No thank you. Do you mind if I pour myself another?"

"It's your bottle."

He poured one for her as well. They both drank quickly.

"I didn't finish telling my story last night."

"You told so many. Which one?"

"Tristan. I was talking about Tristan Schiller."

She waited a beat as though thinking. "Your friend who went off with my double?"

"Yes, with your *double*." There was no mistaking the emphasis.

He leaned back in his chair and began, "Like I said, he didn't make the boat, and I didn't run into him again. But I didn't think much about it. Came back to the States. Got married. Wrote another couple of books. Sold one to the movies. Got divorced. Wound up back in Europe, on a book tour."

"No more hostels," she said, raising her glass to him.

"First class all the way, baby. I thought I'd look him up, my old friend. They didn't have the Internet. They had phone books." He stretched out his hands to indicate. "There weren't too many Schiller's in his town and only one doctor, TM Schiller. Figured if it wasn't him it would be a relative. I didn't call. Wanted it to be a surprise. Bought a fine bottle of scotch – like this one.

"Turned out it was his father's office – on the side of the house he'd grown up in. It was closed that day, so I went to the front door. His mother answered. When I said his name, I watched her face, and

I knew. Instantly. She practically pulled me into the house. Told me he'd never come home from his trip. By the time they realized he was missing, it wasn't clear exactly where or when he disappeared. They'd checked with all the embassies. She treated me like … like I could lead them to him. Bring him back. Her husband came home. They couldn't get enough details from me. They brought out an old calendar, so we could try and figure out the date of the party. They asked if I had the ticket stub from the boat – the one he'd missed. His mother got out photo-albums. Do kids even know what a photo-album is? Each postcard he'd sent – Paris, London, Istanbul all lovingly preserved. He was *missed*."

David paused, and poured himself another shot.

She felt sad for the parents. They were most likely dead now too. Human life was so horribly short.

"How many years had it been since he …?" She asked.

"Eight."

"And still they mourned."

David looked at her strangely. "Yes," he said, "A parent never recovers from the loss of a child."

"Of course," she said. Their son had been so sweet and strong. Not the most experienced lover, but young and energetic. Eager to please her. She'd taken him just before dawn, enjoying his tender embraces until the last second. She could still remember the feeling of his body on top of her, the sweat from his chest. His heartbeat slowing as every bit of sweet red juice flowed into her mouth, warming her throat, revitalizing her entire being, His blood had been intoxicating, among the best she'd ever tasted.

"The Schillers invited me to stay for dinner. They wanted to hear about every moment we'd spent together. As long as I kept talking, for them it was like he was alive again. I had to go. There was a reading scheduled. His mother made me promise I'd return. On the train back to Hamburg, I kept thinking of being on that boat – hung over and annoyed. But I should have known, gone back, looked."

"You can't blame yourself," she said.

"Oh, I don't blame myself. I don't think it would have made a damn bit of difference.

"What did the family think happened?"

"The sea got him. But it wasn't like him to go off swimming in the ocean by himself. There were no ferry crashes or anything around the time he went missing."

254

"What do you think this has to do with …?"

"The last postcard he sent was from Mikados. With the words, *Boat to Cyprus tomorrow.'* When I got back to the States, I talked to a private investigator. I'd used him for some research. Ex-cop. He happened to be Greek, which made things easy. We flew to the island, tried to retrace Tristan's steps. I figured if nothing else, it might be a magazine article."

"Did you find anything?"

"Not much after all that time. There was a pattern that summer, up and down the Mediterranean. Greece, Lebanon, Italy – people going missing, more than would be expected. Mostly young, but others too. And there were stories about attractive strangers. Some said they had a yacht. People had different ideas about what country or countries they might have been from, how many were on the boat. The descriptions didn't match. I had a sketch done of the dark haired woman, by a police artist. How I remembered her, anyway. Some said she looked familiar. Others didn't recognize her at all. But in every town where somebody was gone, there were stories of the beautiful people on the boat."

He poured more whiskey and took a breath.

Alphonsine seized the opportunity to speak. "These were tourist towns, weren't they? Ports of call for what they used to call the jet set? Just because they were there, I don't know how you or your investigator connect them to these …"

"I tried to get in touch with Maria Callas, herself," David said. "See what she remembered. Finally, got a letter to her through her agent. And she sent me one back. Still have it somewhere in my files."

"Go on."

"When she read my letter she thought I was crazy. She didn't remember ever meeting a woman she thought would be *'the perfect Violetta,'* and she wrote she certainly would've recalled that. But then within a few days, it came to her. There was a couple at the party. She couldn't think of where or how she met them, why they were there. And she couldn't picture their faces. Her vision wasn't very good, but it bothered her. She'd stood close enough. Her memory for everything was normally sharp. She thought it was a result of having to learn so much repertoire."

That had been Pierre's work. There had been no nip, just a suggestion she'd had too much to drink and some things would be fuzzy the next day. Pierre had gotten them the invitation, though he did so mostly for Alphonsine's benefit. It had given her great joy. Years before she'd dream-walked Callas, but had never dared meet her in a waking state. She'd seen her in *La Traviata* more than once, and felt except possibly for Garbo, the singer had come closest to capturing her essence.

Alphonsine stretched her arms and put one of her legs out, curling her toes. She watched David's eyes traveling to see if the new angle would provide him with a glimpse of her snatch. *Control the gaze, control the man.* That wasn't something the *divos* had needed to teach her.

"It's an interesting story," she said. "The mysterious dark lady you think looks like me."

"She could be your twin," he said.

"Twins aren't born so far apart," she said lightly.

"Not usually. But it's a strange world isn't it? With more things in heaven and earth than we've ever dreamed of. And believe me, I've made a living dreaming of some pretty outrageous things."

"So is this how your mind works, how you think of ideas for your books? It sounds like a fine line between imagination and lunacy."

"Sometimes," he said.

If only it had just been some silly idea in his head.

"So tell me then, how might I be connected to her? Is she my grandmother?"

"I suppose you could be her clone. Or maybe she's immortal."

"Immortal?" Among her collection of expressions, she used the one for astonishment at the moment of clarity. "Are you saying you believe I am she?"

He said nothing.

"You think I'm some kind of immortal being that ... that lures men to their doom?" She was laughing now.

After a moment he was laughing too. "Had you going there? Didn't I?"

She stood up. "I should probably get dressed."

He grabbed her hand, "You mean you're not going like that? You look so ... fetching."

"Let me throw something on. I'll just be a minute." She pulled her hand away, went into her room, and changed quickly, trying to think how she might play this. If he really knew anything, she reasoned, he wouldn't have come. He'd have seen the danger. Then again, after years of pursuit, he might be impatient, and careless, and drunk.

When she returned to the living room, he was examining some figurines. He didn't touch them but indicated one with his eyes. "It's very old, isn't it?"

"It was a gift." One of her brethren had procured it during *La Belle Époque*. It came up at auction and was said to have once belonged to the notorious Marie Duplessis, given to her by the Count de Guiche. She didn't mention that to David.

"So tell me," she said as she went over to her refrigerator and brought out some vegan dip and crackers, purposefully putting a cracker in her mouth before continuing, "How would you work these ideas into a novel?"

"It would be easy. A group of wealthy glamorous blood suckers who …"

"Vampires?" she said making a face. "Hasn't that been done to death?"

"Actually, I was thinking of non-fiction. I've met some people with strange tales to tell."

"But you don't believe in them, right? I mean even people who believe in vampires don't really believe in vampires."

She took the tray, still in her arms, over to the coffee table, and sat down on the sofa.

He moved to sit next to her, inches away. He took a cracker. "I'll keep my beliefs to myself, for now."

He really deserves to die, she thought. *Coming here, at night no less, with this.*

"Maybe, in my book, I'll claim most of what we think we know about them, the usual tropes, are crap," he continued.

"Hasn't that been done too? Sparkly emo vamps who survive on cow's blood? Enchanted sunshine immunity rings, so you can work on your tan?"

What are your sources, old man? Cite your sources.

"I talked to a priest once. Well, a former priest. Somewhere along the line he'd lost his faith – in the church, not in God, he said. He had a PhD in history, a Jesuit. Brilliant man. For a few years he worked at the Vatican. He'd seen papers, archives indicating they knew about supernatural beings, *revenants*, I think was the word they used."

"The Vatican? Is it going to be a *Da Vinci Code* kind of thriller?"

"I don't think there's any papal cover-up or conspiracy. It was just something in a file. A mad priest in the early seventeen hundreds claimed to have lived among vampires. But he didn't want to betray them. The church used some persuasive methods."

"They tortured a lunatic you're saying? Sounds like a reliable source. Did they get anything out of him?"

"Anyone can be broken," he said, and then he recited, as if from memory, "They choose to take the young and beautiful as their kind, but they'll feed on whatever prey is easiest. They have no kings or popes. Their senses are sharper than ours and they enjoy sin of all types. They generally avoid us except to feed." He paused to pour himself more scotch. "Realize at the time it was written, the legends had them looking like corpses. It wasn't till years later that Polidori wrote *The Vampyre*, the first book in which they could pass easily for human."

"I was raised Catholic," she said, "but I doubt the archives lend credibility to your story. They burnt women for witchcraft, blamed Jews for poisoning the wells. Is it so odd they investigated the undead?"

"It wasn't just the Jesuit. I talked to people who thought they'd had encounters."

"Really?" She was smiling to show him she wasn't taking this seriously, but also in relief. That a priest had seen the archives and told him about them was disturbing, but how convinced was David? He might be at least partly putting her on. Even if he did recognize her, it would be easy to convince him his memory was unreliable.

"Were these the same people who'd been abducted by aliens? Maybe they were vampires from outer space?"

"Most of them *were* kind of nutty," he admitted.

She looked at him skeptically, and waited.

"You win. Nothing panned out. There was never any proof. Just anecdotes. A thin slip of a girl easily overpowering a group of men. A man and woman emerging from a burning wreck – uninjured. A mysterious neighbor who was never seen in daylight. The occasional homicide in which the victim bled out, but there's no blood at the scene."

"You mean when the body is moved after death?"

"I mean, when it's unlikely the body was moved."

"Were there fang mark's on these victims' necks?

He shook his head. "I'm not the only one looking into this. There are other people, credible people doing research as well. And we've all reached the same conclusion."

"Which is?"

"If you'll pardon the pun, it's the twilight of the vampires. They're doomed."

"Doomed?"

"From the moment, your countryman, Niépce, created the photograph."

"How so? I thought you couldn't capture their image on film."

"Another myth. Probably one they've been spreading themselves. An image is a record. Even more reputable than a portrait."

"The camera doesn't always tell the truth."

"Maybe. But soon we'll have technology that'll allow anyone to take an image of a face, and search the entire world wide fucking web for the same face."

"Maybe they're camera shy."

"Some of them probably are. Others may have a hard time staying out of the limelight. Is something wrong?"

"Huh? No."

"Just for a second you looked … Never mind. I tried to track down photos of that party – on the yacht. Maybe something in the local news, given *La Divina's* presence. Nothing. But I kept thinking about the woman, how in her element she was. That's when I started looking at pictures of various hot spots going back to the beginning of the century and even before."

"You expected her to emerge Zelig-like from the shadows?" She asked refilling both shot glasses. She clapped her hands. "How clever."

"It didn't happen. It was 1974 when I went back to Greece, and started on this journey. By 1984, I'd given up. I felt I'd gone as far as I could with all of it. Maybe he had simply drowned, but then something happened."

"I'm dying to know what."

"I had it in my head to do a thriller set in Hollywood in the nineteen-twenties. I was going to base a character on Louise Brooks. I was researching. There was this one photograph in this one book, taken in a Berlin nightclub. Her and another young woman, unidentified. My dark lady."

"Who you think looks exactly like me? Even after the conversation we had last night, in which as it turns out, I bare an uncanny resemblance to every brunette who's ever lived."

"Marie Duplessis."

"Her too."

"I meant the dark haired lady, *is* Marie Duplessis."

She laughed again, meaning to convey, '*What an imagination you have, Mr. Alexander.*' "How did you deduce that?"

"As soon as I got back to the States, after that visit to Germany, I kept replaying everything I could remember about the party, in case there was something I should have told the Schillers. Wrote it all down. Even with the world's greatest opera star there, she dominated the room. And then there were Callas' words, '*the perfect Violetta.*' So I looked up the opera in ye olde Encyclopedia Britannica. I checked the entry for Marie Duplessis."

"Who died at twenty-three, with half of Paris at her funeral – an open casket and ..."

"They might appear to be dead for a time."

"You do know that her lover had her dug up? Just like in that ... novel." She'd caught herself in time. She'd almost said dreadful novel.

"They're clever enough to have pulled it off, if they wanted her."

"Why? Why her?"

"She's a honey-trap," he said looking straight at her. "Every man's fantasy. She can be anything a man wants. She can bring them, her kind, whatever they need. And you, *madame* are she."

She smiled at him with exaggerated indulgence, and rolled her eyes. "You think I'm a ..." she stopped, putting down her glass, laughing. "Have you discussed this with your son?"

"No, not with him. And I have no intention of telling you with whom I have discussed this. I understand that would be their death warrant. I've already signed mine. But I should warn you, before you carry out my sentence, my files are on several computers and flash drives. If anything were to happen ..."

She sensed he was lying about that, but she'd need to find out for certain.

"And when did you concoct this theory that I was ... one of them. Her, specifically?"

"When Dashiell and I were sharing a cab from the airport. He took out his phone and showed me your pictures. The moment I saw your face, I started asking him questions. Then I googled you. It all made sense. And your boss, Dumont, he fit the description of one of the others people saw that summer."

"David, are you on some sort of ... medication? You don't seriously believe ...? I mean what could I do to prove to you this is a ... a ... delusion? Would you like me to cut myself so you can watch me bleed? Or shall we meet at high noon tomorrow, in the sunlight? I could eat a clove of garlic, I suppose."

"I don't doubt you could do all of those things. It won't change my mind."

"Why confront me with this? Why not just go to ..."

"The authorities? I'm not *that* crazy. No one would take it seriously. Even if I decide to publish my research, if I can dig up more evidence, what does it matter? Like I said, your kind has reached its end. Maybe you and Dumont are the only ones left. Photos last and people take them all the time. We live in an age of transparency. Sunlight might not kill you, but selfies could."

She'd met other mortals who suspected before, but only one who'd come anywhere near as close. He was also old. He thought he could blackmail and bribe his way into immortality. He'd been wrong. This was different. David was not trying to get in. He knew there was no future in it.

"I understand you're telling me if anything were to happen to you, all this goes out on the web, but if you actually believe what you're saying, you must know the chances of your leaving this apartment alive are very slim. Why on earth would you be sitting here, at night, telling me you suspect I'm a ruthless killer who lives off of mortal blood?"

"I don't think your kind kills indiscriminately or indiscreetly. There'd be questions."

"Why take the chance?"

"I love my son."

"Do you? You have a strange way of showing it. When was the last time you saw him? "

"I haven't been a perfect father. That doesn't mean I wouldn't do anything in the world to protect him."

"I'd never hurt him. I love him too."

"In your way, maybe."

"In every way. We love each other in every way possible. Didn't he tell you that? We want to spend the rest of our lives together."

"Marie," he said, staring straight at her. She'd carried that name many times through the years, yet it sounded so odd to hear it from his lips. "He's not like you. He could never live the way you do."

If it had been daylight, her head would have been spinning. It was a scene straight out of a melodrama – a very specific melodrama – the one in which the devoted father explains to his son's whore-girlfriend she must break it off before she ruins his life.

"And if I were to give him up?"

"You'd need to leave town."

"If I were to leave forever and break it off, preferably in some way guaranteed to wound his pride, then ... "

"I'd never tell him what you are. I'd never discuss the topic again – with anyone. There wouldn't be a book, or an article, or even a whisper – at least not from me or through me."

"You'd have no problem then with *my kind*," she said using air quotes and rolling her eyes, "continuing their reign of discreet mayhem? That wouldn't weigh too heavily on your conscience?"

"Like I said, telling the truth isn't going to accomplish much. But I think I could make it impossible for you to continue with Dashiell. Even if I couldn't convince him, there'd be a seed of doubt."

Her phone buzzed.

"Are you going to answer it?" He asked.

"We're having a conversation. That would be rude."

His phone rang.

"Don't," she started to say.

But he did. It was his son. "As a matter of fact, I'm in Brooklyn already. I stopped by Camille's house ... Yeah, you heard me ... I'm here now ... Just killing time ... Yes, she's being very gracious."

He looked at her, "Would you like to talk to him?"

"Tell him we'll see him in a few minutes."

"Yeah, we should be leaving soon. Okay, yeah, bye."

He had barely clicked off when she came up behind him and nipped his neck. His head dropped. She placed her hands on his shoulders.

"Relax, old man," she said. "I won't hurt your boy. I want you to remember that. Now pick your head up and look straight ahead. We need to talk."

The first thing she asked about were his files. There *was* a decaying photocopy taken from a book – her and Louise Brooks, along with some notes in a file cabinet for the abandoned thriller. The sketch by the police artist had crumpled to dust years before. No copies existed. There was another handwritten file called "vamps." It included an old cassette tape of an interview with his defrocked priest. There were additional notes and a few typed pages, but everything read as fiction, or a put on. The story about his visit to Germany and later investigation in Mikados had all been true. He theorized there might have been some weird cult practicing human sacrifice. Even after he heard the priest's tale, he wasn't convinced of a supernatural explanation, but that picture with Brooks had shaken him. He'd started writing a story, *She Who Was Marie Duplessis,* but had abandoned it.

"Why didn't you write more explicitly about your suspicions?"

"Not suspicions. Crazy ideas for a book. I didn't believe it. It couldn't be. When I saw photos of you on Dashiell's phone, I started asking him questions. I spent the afternoon reading about you on line. It was a game in my head. I didn't really think ... but when you walked into the restaurant, everything about you, your scent ..."

"My scent?"

"Fragrance. It brought it back to me. I knew then."

If he had only been a harmless crank, but fame and money were power, and he had both. Even if she was prepared to give up Dashiell, which she wasn't, he was a danger to all of them, a danger which she knew she must eradicate.

"After last night, did you write anything on your computer? Any e-mails? Or anything on a flash drive?"

"No."

Just to be certain, she made him account for all his time since the previous evening. As for his lunch with Piccolini, the mayor's wife had been there, and her name was barely mentioned.

It was ten forty-five. Dashiell would expect her to be late. That was good.

If she enlisted Pierre, they might be able to make it look like a robbery, but she didn't need another encounter with the police, and there was too much that could go wrong. Besides, it was her mess, and it was best to clean it up herself.

She knew several ways to make a bloodless death look natural. One method involved the use of a certain poison, but she didn't have any on hand. The other she'd only put into practice once, and that was at the abbey. Pierre had demonstrated it first. Then under his and

Ana's tutelage, she tried it on an old vagabond who'd had the bad luck to wonder onto the estate and take a couple of days work on the grounds. She'd been so young and naïve in those days that she hadn't been able to fathom a reason they'd ever need to kill a mortal other than for feasting.

She shook her hands out for a moment as though readying herself to play a piece. Then she placed her left hand on David's left shoulder, and her right wrist against his cheek. "Do you feel the beating of my pulse?"

"Yes."

"We're singing together, with our blood. Match your beat to mine. Slower. Slower. That's good. You're a very good singer. Let's pick up the tempo. Nice. Faster. Keep up." She passed two hundred beats per minute, and then kept going. He was huffing and red faced.

"That's it. We're almost at the end. A little faster."

He made a sound, an involuntary grunt. His eyes rolled up, and then his head dropped. He slumped in his chair. His last breaths sounded like snoring. When she was sure it was over, she ran back to the bathroom, threw off her clothes and jumped into the shower. A few seconds later, she dried herself off and put on a bathrobe – Dashiell's which was terrycloth and covered her like a burka. She wrapped a towel around her head, went back to the living room, and called 911.

Showtime.

≈ ⊛ ≈

In the days that followed, there was some unfortunate gossip.

Alphonsine stuck to her story. She was taking a quick shower while David relaxed on her couch. She opened her bedroom door and started talking to him as she was drying her hair. He didn't respond. She came out and found him, too late.

While he'd had episodes of increased heart rate before, according to the medical experts relied upon by the tabloid presses, it was unusual he was not exerting himself when the fatal episode occurred. There was no official inquiry, but the medical examiner's office had gotten in touch to ask a few questions.

"Are you certain he wasn't doing anything strenuous?"

"I don't know what he was doing. *I* was taking a shower."

When she finally sat down with Anton and Pierre to go over all of it in detail, Anton again stated it might be time for Camille St. Valois to go on a very long vacation. "You know what they're saying?" He asked.

"Dashiell has no doubts. That's all I care about. And the notoriety probably only brings more business to the gallery. I think we're an official stop on the Big Apple tour bus."

"She made the only choice she could under the circumstances," Pierre told Anton.

"The circumstances are what I'm concerned about." Anton turned to Alphonsine, "If you hadn't been such a Callas *fangirl*, you never would have been at that party, and even now you're running around with a man who not only has or had a famous father, but is probably on the verge of being a movie star." He looked at Pierre, "And you. You should know better. You indulge her. What do they call it here? You're an enabler."

"I'm not her keeper."

"Maybe she needs one."

She walked away from the conversation, turning around only to shout at Anton that he needed to stay out of her brain.

"I'm not in your brain. It's so tiny I couldn't even find it."

When Chi-chi Chavez, the *New York Eye's* gossip columnist called her, he asked point blank if the old man had died *in flagrante*.

"Honestly darling, you've seen him. You've seen his son. Which one would you be fucking? And don't tell me you have a fetish for old bears." She gave him a juicy blind item regarding the Hollywood/rock star spawn whose work the gallery had featured. In return, he promised to do his best to quash the rumors.

The body was cremated and there was no funeral, per David's instructions. The ashes were delivered to the estranged final wife. David's agent had assured Dashiell a memorial ceremony of some kind was in the works, and would be scheduled shortly before the release of what would now be his final book. The proofs were almost done, and the agent gave Dashiell a sneak peek, and an offer (refused) for the son to continue the series.

There might be two ceremonies – an East Coast and a West Coast, or maybe they'd happen simultaneously with a video hook-up between the two. The agent added enthusiastically, "David would have loved that."

Dashiell, two older-half sisters he barely knew, and a respectable conservation organization were the only beneficiaries. There were other claims, and things might be tied up for a while, but in the end young Mr. Alexander would be very rich. The media spotlight had helped green light his film deal. He'd not only get the screenplay credit, but would be starring as well. The director was an up and comer, but already hailed as the next Scorsese.

While Alphonsine knew things had worked out for the best, she was surprised by how hard David's death hit her lover. For a week or so, Dashiell had been very quiet and sad. They hardly spoke of it. Then in the early hours of the morning, after they had made love, as his head lay upon her chest, and she stroked his hair, he said, "I miss him. It's weird. He was hardly in my life. But I miss him now. When we started talking on the plane, I felt we were finally connecting. I'd never had that with him before. All of a sudden, he was so interested in my life. In *us*. You wouldn't believe how many questions he asked. He cancelled something so we could get together. He really wanted to meet you."

"My poor baby," she said. "I'm so sorry."

"Did he say why he decided to stop by your apartment?"

"No. I thought maybe you'd suggested it. He brought a bottle. He was drinking a lot. Maybe he was lonely and wanted to talk. Or he thought getting to know me he'd get to know you. When he was going on and on with his stories in the bar that night, I had the feeling it was his way of saying 'love me, love me' to *you*. I think that's all he wanted. Maybe he sensed he didn't have long."

"He didn't try to ..."

"No. Or if he did, I missed it. He was a gentleman."

"What was he talking about exactly?"

"It doesn't seem important, does it? He asked if I'd heard the band before. He said any musical gifts must have come from your mother. Honestly, I wasn't paying a lot of attention."

Dashiell left her before dawn. He said he was restless, thought he might stop by his gym, then do some work. California had been demanding changes. There were two veteran screenwriters involved as well, and hours of conferencing daily. They were already putting together a film crew, scouting locations, casting minor parts. He'd be going back soon.

As she sat by her piano, trying to do something constructive before the day broke, she wondered what an extended separation would mean for them. Did he still take their "pre-engagement" seriously? Was his passion fading? Hers wasn't, but how long could their relationship sustain? If she went with him, he'd probably want her on the set. She'd become an old hag, completely useless in no time.

Anton had a point. It was a dangerous game she was playing. Yet, what would it be like to give him up? She thought more and more of how hard it would be to watch him on a movie screen growing older, to read about his latest divorce. Long ago, she and Pierre were in Argentina when she happened across an item about Liszt. He was ailing. Pierre had to stop her, physically stop her, from returning to Europe to see him one last time.

She couldn't go through it again.

Yesterday she wouldn't have considered hurting him, but now the idea of tasting his sweet elixir, allowing him the privilege of dying in her embrace – while he was still young and beautiful – had a certain appeal. Death would freeze him in time. He would be with her, in a way, forever. It would be a memory she could cherish in the long sleepy days of summer. Finality might come to him softly, in a dream, or perhaps in the midst of an orgasm.

But even if she could bring herself to do it, it would be horrid to deprive him of his success, of the only kind of immortality besides her own. It would be selfish. *Selfish.* Her kind never thought of selfishness when it came to mortals. One might show them mercy, let this or that one go because of children or some great work, especially if one wasn't too famished, and another was available, but the idea that there was anything *selfish* in denying an individual his life didn't enter the equation. You could be kind to a dog or any lesser being. However, selfishness or selflessness implied you were on an equal footing, and that was blasphemous.

She'd been spending too much time around mortals. It wasn't just Dashiell either. She'd come to care about Cara, and even some of the young people, the hangers-on at the gallery, and of course there was that child at the orphanage. She hadn't even told anyone about that. She was becoming attached to humanity in a way that couldn't possibly end well.

She stood and walked the glass perimeter of her apartment. The sky over Manhattan was becoming lighter every second.

In the first few years of her elevation, she missed the daylight, but that passed. She had gained much more than she had lost, yet looking out the window, watching the traffic build on the East River Drive, the city coming alive, as she fought the familiar fatigue, she was aware of the old feelings. Daytime was a world unavailable to her. Each morning, Dashiell went out into that world where she dared not follow. She went into her bedroom and pulled the curtains to shut out the light.

Chapter 15

Pierre had discovered a small encampment of homeless living near the Harlem River in upper Manhattan. As Anton would soon be leaving New York, and it was time for she and Pierre to feed, it seemed a good opportunity for the three of them to hunt together. While going out of town would have been safer, they knew they could take what they needed quickly and cleanly. Between the three they had five, sharing the last two, and tossing the bodies into the water after weighing them down. Then they walked stealthily to the Upper Eastside, stopped for a drink at a wine-bar, and found a taxi.

It had been almost too easy, lacking the intrigue and glamour of past times. Still, even if a bit shoddy, it satisfied. She sat in the backseat of the cab between the men, one hand on Pierre's lap and the other on Anton's, while each of them had a hand working on her.

"Where does your friend think you are tonight?" Anton asked.

"Strategic meeting. I told him I wouldn't be too late." She couldn't quite believe it was Anton's long fingers bringing her off, yet it felt so right.

She was tempted to demand the driver stop at a hotel so the three of them could get a room, spend a few hours working off all the energy that came from live blood, and then collapse in each other's arms when day broke.

Anton read her thoughts. "Pull over," he told the driver as they were approaching the Sherry-Netherland.

"No, I can't," she said.

"Then don't," he said curtly.

It was rude to hunt and then leave. She thought of when she had accompanied Jane. She'd only assisted, had not partaken, yet it was still exciting, and afterwards whatever silly competitive feelings she held onto dissipated, and were replaced by love. *They were all supposed to love each other.* She knew she should drop the negativity she was holding onto, share the night with her companions – love them both with a vigor no mortal woman could match. Watch them with no jealousy as they took turns with each other.

If Dashiell knew it would ...

"Screw him," Anton said aloud catching her thought.

She let forth a string of mental profanity as he and Pierre exited the cab at the hotel. The driver was confused.

"I'm still going to Brooklyn," she told him.

She answered Dashiell's text. He thought she was at the gallery, wanted to know if he should walk over and meet her. She wrote back there'd been a change of plan. Some work Pierre needed her eyes on. She was on her way home. He suggested a restaurant where they might meet – a new place.

She went straight there, catching him at the bar talking to an attractive redhead he'd run into. Her name was Leila, and he knew her from an acting class.

"Nice to meet you," Alphonsine said, taking the girl in. Her hair was worn up in a beehive like something out of a nineteen-sixties science fiction television show. The futuristic but retro look was enhanced by the exaggerated make up, including false eyelashes and white lipstick. She wore a silvery glittery sheath of a dress, very short, accentuating long, strong legs. There were boots with high stiletto heels. Another woman dressed that way might have looked like a drag queen, but the delicacy of her features left no doubt of her gender – though whether she had been born that way or surgically enhanced, who could say?

"Oh my God, I'm like your fan," Leila answered.

They asked if she wanted to join them for dinner, but she explained she was waiting for someone.

When they were seated, Alphonsine remarked, "She's a very pretty girl."

"Yeah," he said, glancing briefly back at the bar.

She turned as well, noticing Leila furiously texting.

"You look terrific by the way," he continued, "Am I seeing something different? Haircut? New make-up?"

"I don't think so," she said.

"No? Well, you're glowing. Your lips are so red. But you look like a cat burglar."

She laughed. She hadn't stopped to change and they'd all worn dark clothes on the hunt. Their table was in the center of the room, so any displays would be quite public, but she could hardly contain herself. She glanced over a couple of times at the girl.

She went to use the ladies' room, careful to walk by Leila who soon followed her.

Inside the bathroom, they both primped before mirrors. There was one person in the stalls. When she left and they were alone, the two women looked at each other. Leila giggled uncertainly. Alphonsine leaned against the door, and waved her fingers in a come-to-me gesture. The two hugged, and then began to explore each other's mouths with their tongues. Alphonsine fingered the girl's wet pussy, but after a few seconds, Leila pulled away.

"I don't usually ... I must be drunk," she said.

"It's all right. I like you," Alphonsine said, touching Leila's face with her damp hand. "Do you like boys?"

"Yes. Mostly, yes."

"Dashiell's been in kind of the dumps. Since his dad." She hadn't wanted to share him before, but the feeding had brought something out. Even he wasn't going to be enough for her. Besides, he really needed cheering up.

"How could someone stand you up? You're so beautiful," she continued. "You want to come home with me, don't you? With us? You like Dashiell?"

"He's so ..."

"This isn't going to be a thing, but just for tonight ..."

"Oh yes, please," the girl said falling to her knees. She pulled down Alphonsine's pants and started to probe with her tongue. Someone was knocking on the door. Alphonsine gently pushed her away.

"Just a sec. It's stuck," Alphonsine called out, and then she whispered to Leila. "Come to the table in two minutes. Then you propose it. I want it to come from you."

Leila returned to the bar, where Alphonsine watched her down another drink. "You're friend is coming over," she told Dashiell.

It was he who invited her to sit. They began talking about the acting class. The waiter came by and asked if they wanted coffee.

"Excuse me a moment," Alphonsine said, "That's one of our artists. I just want to say hello."

When she came back, Dashiell was sitting alone.

"Where'd our friend go?" She asked.

"I told her to give us a minute."

"Why?"

"She made a proposal."

"Oh did she?"

"She'd like to spend the night with *us*."

"And you didn't say no."

"Should I have? I should have. Right? I mean I didn't know what ..."

"If it pleases you, it might be interesting."

"You don't mind?"

"Not at all."

It turned out to be the most fun she'd ever had with two mortals that didn't involve killing them. It was rare for Dashiell to take anything, but he and Leila did some ecstasy, which Alphonsine cheeked, as it was not a good drug for her kind. She liked watching its effect on him. As for the girl, she was in wonderful shape. Supple and strong. Eager to please. As she rode on top of Dashiell, Alphonsine was behind her, rubbing against her back and holding her shapely, firm breasts. Alphonsine was watching Dashiell whose eyes went from one to the other. At some point when Leila had gone to pee, Dashiell said, "You have no idea how much I love you."

"Of course I do," she said, "because it's how I feel about you."

They didn't stop until sunrise, having gone through as many possible combinations as they could. At one point, as both she and Dashiell were exploring various parts of the very willing girl's anatomy, her longing for him to be as she was became almost overwhelming. It was all so *near* perfect. Perfect would have ended with the two of them sharing Leila's blood, and then pushing her lifeless body off the bed for a final fuck before settling down to sleep.

At dusk, her lover woke her. He'd brought in a breakfast tray with fresh coffee and croissants. Their friend was gone.

"Good morning," she said.

"Good evening," he said kissing her. "Why is it you never have morning breath?"

"Because I'm an angel?"

"Probably."

She rose and walked the tray over to her dresser." Let's have this later," she said, returning to bed.

"Last night wasn't enough for you?" he asked.

She shook her head. "Just once, please."

It seemed to have been enough for him, as he did no more than please her orally. She felt the same restless energy as usual the night following a feast. As wonderful as the ménage had been, it hadn't quite rid her of all her desires.

Later, when they were having coffee, he asked, "Can we talk about it?"

"About what?" She asked biting into her pastry.

"Last night. The … Leila."

"Didn't you have a good time?"

He squeezed her hand. "I'm just wondering. Obviously, you enjoyed being with another woman and …"

"I enjoyed your enjoying my being with another woman. I loved seeing how happy you were. Do you remember what you said to me when we kissed after I went down on her?"

Dashiell blushed. She couldn't recall seeing him do that before, and felt a need to tease him with details. "You said my mouth never tasted so good as when it was full of her cunt juice."

"I was *high*," he answered, shaking his head. "It was fantastic. Seeing how happy you were. But I didn't *need* it. I want you to know that. I'm not bored with *just* you."

"I know." she said, "But I love hearing you say it."

"Is it enough for *you*? I mean we never talked seriously about … other people. I didn't want to get hung up on stuff, like exclusivity. I don't now. But sometimes you seem so, so voracious, I wonder if any one person can be enough for you."

"You are," she said quietly. "Last night was great because we were sharing something, not because I had a chance to eat pussy. I know you're an attractive man and women throw themselves at you. I don't mind if you give in sometimes, as long as I know you love me."

"Intellectually, I feel the same way, but I'm not sure that …"

"If you want me to be exclusive it's not a problem. I am. I have been."

"Really?" He asked.

"Really," she said. She did not consider this a lie. She was being *emotionally* honest with him.

"I want you to know when I was in LA, I never …"

She put a hand on his mouth. "You don't have to say it. It doesn't matter."

They stayed in that night, watching old films, eating popcorn, and making love. It was nearly the next dawn when he told her. "They want me on the coast next week. I need you with me,

Camille."

"We've talked about this before. I can't give up my job, everything here."

"We have money."

"*You* have money. I don't want to be a hanger on, the movie star's girlfriend. What will I do all day?"

"Sleep?" he asked playfully. "I could get you work. Publicity or something. I could probably get you a part."

"And everyone would know how I got it. Darling, you'll come back to me, won't you? And while you're away we'll talk and see each other every day."

"It's not the same."

"I know."

"Marry me," he said. "That's not how I meant to ask, but I was planning to."

"Marriage?"

"I'm never going to have a better girlfriend, a better lover, a better partner. I want to be with you always. We're already pre-engaged."

"I want to be with you *always*," she answered.

"Then why do you look sad?"

"I wish I could tell you." He would never accept her offer of immortality, never be willing to prey on mortals, and if she dared ask him and he refused, he'd have to die. She felt truly damned.

"If it feels too soon, too sudden, I'll wait, but I can't be without you. You have to come with me."

"I want to," she said hugging him. "I want to, so much."

"You're crying," he said. "What is it?"

"It's … Of course I'll marry you. I'll marry you, and I'll stick so close you won't be able to lose me no matter how much you want to."

"I'd never want to."

"I'll do my best to make sure of that."

ॐ ⊕ ॐ

He left before she woke, and wouldn't be returning till late in the evening. There was going to be another conference call about the screenplay that might go on for hours. She sent out some texts. Pierre was at the gallery while Anton was in the apartment he kept in her building. She invited them both over and told them her plan.

Pierre's expression conveyed more sadness than shock. As for his thoughts, he was consciously keeping them from her.

Anton held back nothing. "You've known the boy for what? A few months? Have you lost your mind?"

"We don't prohibit each other's desires."

"No we don't. But you're talking about suicide. You were minutes from death. We didn't even know if you'd rise. You do recall the illness will return?"

"In those days one could die of a cold. There are pills now for what I had. It's curable."

"You can't *know* that. You've never studied medicine. Besides, look at what happened when we tried it before."

"I have. A woman walked in daylight and bore a child."

"It killed her."

"That used to happen a lot too."

Pierre jumped in. "I know you've thought about this. Everyone knows it's our end times, but even if they're hunting us in fifty years, we'll still be young. Beautiful. Strong. If you do this thing then in ten, fifteen you'll be …"

"I have to believe I am more than my face, that when Dashiell sees me he …"

"To believe that a man is in love with you for …" Anton shook his head. "You *have* lost your mind."

"I am not so stupid to imagine he fell in love with me for my brain, *mon cher*. But I'm certain he'll always see me exactly as I look now."

"You of all women should know how fickle men are. Couldn't you simply marry him, try to stay out of the sun, and see how you feel in a few months? I'm sure by then you'd be bored and could take him one way or another, making your family very rich and happy."

"I would never harm him."

"Then you could simply leave."

"I won't do that either."

"Since your mind is made up why even bother to tell us? Ana is the only one who can help you. You didn't expect to get my blessing. Did you?"

"I don't need that, Anton. I need a way of contacting her. The only thing I know about the new abbey is that it's in South America. An email address or a phone number would be useful."

"She doesn't use the Internet to socialize," he said. "But I'll get in touch with her. That doesn't mean I support this insanity."

🙚 ⊛ 🙘

Dashiell came back that evening bearing a new ring.

"How did you get it sized so quickly?"

"I wasn't lying when I said I was planning it."

The stone was huge, the size and style like something Dick might have given Liz. "It's absolutely vulgar," she said, admiring it on her finger.

She caught the anxious look on his face.

"I meant that as a good thing. I love it."

They were sitting on her couch. Her back was against his chest, his arms surrounding her. He started to kiss her neck, talking between smooches.

"We could go to City Hall tomorrow," he said.

"No, that's not going to work."

"I didn't think you'd want a big wedding. Do you? We could wait till California. I'll invite my mom. You haven't even met her."

She pulled away and turned to face him. "Do you trust me?"

"Completely."

"I'm going to test that. There's a condition."

"Anything. Whatever you want."

"You have no idea how completely I want to be yours. What I would do. What wouldn't I do? But there's something I have to take care of before we can be married, and I can't give you any details, and you can't ask me about it. Ever."

"That sounds pretty bizarre, but I'm listening."

"I have to go away. Maybe three weeks. Possibly longer. It's a kind of a retreat, but that's all I can say."

"Are you in some kind of cult?"

"No, it's nothing like that."

"Is there a first mister St. Valois I need to …"

She kissed him. "Only you. It's always been only you. Let's not play twenty questions, please. When I said you'd have to trust me, I meant it. Can you?"

"Is what you're doing dangerous?"

"Neither dangerous nor illegal. But no more, please. Yes or no?"

"Yes, of course, yes," he said, and then he began to kiss her all over.

276

She was wearing her bathrobe with nothing underneath. He untied the belt, and she moved her shoulders allowing it to slip down. She loved when he took her with his clothes on. Although she could kill him barely lifting a finger, she liked to pretend he was capable of overpowering her. Closing her eyes, she let him lick and lap her like a hungry kitten. When she was with him, she never fantasized about being with another, but sometimes she felt as though he carried within him the souls of others whom she had loved – that she was eighteen again in the country house with Adet, or that she was twenty-one sneaking away from her own party to be with Franz. She hadn't loved like this since her first life. Perhaps there was something to the myths about her kind. To live without the intensity of love was not to live at all. In that sense, they really were *undead*. Yet, with him, she felt spectacularly alive, and she longed to feel that way always. She *would* feel that way every day once she was mortal again. She swore it to herself.

She thought of the story Dashiell told her about the monk and the strawberry. Each moment of her new life would be like that – beautiful and delicious – made even more so by its fleeting nature.

She let out a moan, pushing his head away as it was too much. He moved to kiss her lips as she fumbled with his zipper. He slipped his cock inside her, even as she continued to writhe with pleasure.

"You're killing me," she said. Her nails dug deep into his back, ripping through his shirt. She could smell his blood. They flipped around, slipping from the couch onto the floor, with her on top.

"I may need a minute," he said.

"Get on your belly," she commanded.

"What do you have in mind?" he asked, a bit uncertain.

"Not *that*," she said, "At least not at the moment. Just, please."

He did as he was told. She pulled up his tee-shirt and saw eight lines, scratches seeping blood. *How could he not have noticed?* She licked his wounds. Her saliva caused the marks to close, but her desire for more of his blood was strong. Her fangs descended. She wasn't planning to bite; she wasn't planning anything. But what did it matter? He'd hardly feel it. She wouldn't go too far she promised herself, before giving in to her urge.

"That feels weird," he said.

She froze. "I guess I got carried away," she said. "I really scratched you. Let me get a wet cloth and clean it up."

She ran to the bathroom and splashed her face with cold water.

It was a tiny nip, and she had stopped the second he said something. But it was a warning. For too long, she'd pretended she was incapable of hurting him. She could see that wasn't true. If she remained as she was, she would kill him.

She was making the right decision, the only decision she could if they were going to stay together.

๛ ⊛ ๖

In the final nights before Dashiell's trip they hardly left the apartment. It was just the two of them, except for a return visit by Leila. She'd brought another friend, Jasmine, a remarkably tall Japanese girl, who joked that her childhood nickname had been Spider for her long skinny legs. It was a slow seductive evening. Drinks, chat, dancing, pot, and ecstasy. Dashiell serenaded them with his guitar as they sat in the darkened living room watching the lights of the city reflecting on the river. Leila's head was in Alphonsine's lap. She was absentmindedly stroking the girl's hair while listening to Dashiell's soft tenor. She wondered how this might have played out if the girls had been Ana and Jane, and Dashiell some mortal they'd chosen for entertainment or sustenance. They were all so young and beautiful. It was easy for her to imagine gorging on each of them, waking the next evening surrounded by three cold bloodless bodies.

Once she got the thing done, she reminded herself, she would never have to hold back her passion. The urge to kill would be gone.

The tension continued to build gradually through dancing and conversation, but once they started, there was the added energy that came from knowing she and Dashiell would soon be separated. They often caught themselves looking at each other even when entangled with one or both of the others. She had never felt so connected to him. She loved the look of pure joy in his eyes, how contented he seemed, how awed he was that she felt only love for him and never jealousy even as she watched Jasmine sitting on his face, as Leila slowly and rhythmically rode him. She was sitting behind him, her legs wide apart, her cunt against the top of his head, caressing his ears and telling him how much he meant to her.

Later, he watched resting, as she was sandwiched between the two women, Jasmine's delicate finger playing in her butt-hole, as Leila expertly pushed the most exquisite dildo in and out of Alphonsine's twat. Her orgasms seemed to go on and on. She was looking straight into his eyes. She was certain he could feel at that moment what she was feeling, and it wasn't through the magic of the *divos*. It was love, and it would be like this even when she was mortal. It didn't matter how long they'd have together, as long as they had each other.

After the women left, after she had shut the curtains to darken the room, a "habit" he still found eccentric and charming, they lay together spooning. He said, "That was fun, but I don't think I want us to do that after we're married."

"Hmm," she said, noncommittally.

"I mean they aren't even our friends."

"If they were, it would be complicated," she replied.

"I know. It just seems *indulgent*."

"Well, that's true. But we're all consenting adults. You seemed to enjoy *indulging* yourself."

"Yeah," he said, "But I don't think I could keep doing that without its getting messy. Besides, I'm not sure I'm crazy about the parents of my children participating in orgies."

She laughed. "It's not important to me. I want whatever you want."

"Maybe every fifth anniversary," he said kissing the back of her neck. "Make that every third, second. Oh my God, I just love you so much."

That final evening in the backseat of the car on the way to the airport, they made out like teenagers. "You still smell like pussy," she whispered in his ear.

"I've had so much. You've stained me like ink."

"I'm going to miss you so."

"You can still come with me. Just get on the plane."

"No, I can't. But when I do come, you'll never be rid of me."

When they got to Kennedy, she stayed in the car. The chauffeur helped unload his bags. She watched him as he pushed through the glass doors to the counters. Heading back to Brooklyn, she felt his absence sharply.

The night before her own trip began, Pierre showed up at her door, bearing a dozen red camellias, and two bottles of champagne. "I would have brought a couple of beautiful young people as well, but I wasn't sure if you'd taken some sort of pledge."

"He's becoming more broad-minded," she said. "But I'm glad it's only you."

They both understood that once she was transformed there

would be no more nights together or even casual visits. There hadn't been enough conversions to have developed protocols, but direct contact would be kept at a minimum for all their sakes. She would no longer be in the community though they might be monitoring her in some way, and could become powerful enemies.

That evening they talked and drank, but mostly they danced in the various styles of epochs they'd spent together. When they sensed the coming dawn, they gently undressed each other and went to bed. They didn't make love, but slept in each other's arms.

As they drifted off, she said, "I'll miss all this so much, and I'll miss you."

"You don't have to do it."

"I want to," she said. "I want to make this sacrifice for him, even though he'll never know, but I feel like a child leaving home."

"A child can come back and visit. It'll never be the same between us."

"I know," she said, squeezing his hand.

Act IV – Metamorphosis

Chapter 1

The community plane was not available, or so she'd been told. The journey was harrowing – commercial flights, layovers, connections in the middle of the day. She arrived in Bogota before midnight. She understood the trip to Ana's would take several hours, and the roads would not be safe after dark, and so it was on to an airport hotel. Behind the reception desk was a glass wall, and beyond it a bar, which was neither empty nor crowded. There were several hookers surrounding businessmen. It was difficult to say who were the predators and who the prey. All the women had long hair only in different colors, and each in her way was beautiful. She found herself focusing on the muscular neck of one dark-suited man, and the meaty thighs of the woman with whom he was negotiating. *Never to taste blood again.* She almost heard the thought and wondered if Anton was sending it out to bait her. *Could his mind reach into hers from so far?* She could never be sure. Nor was she positive she'd be free of him once she was mortal again.

What a perfect abattoir this entire country was – a dangerous place where kidnappings and murder were common. Even with her poor telepathic skills, she could read the thoughts of the couple in the bar, sense their desires. She wasn't in need of a feast, but it would be a long night and this might be a final opportunity. The man she would take by that thick neck, the woman by the femoral artery. *What would Dashiell think?* He'd think nothing; he'd never know. And yet, she sensed the woman had a family she supported. The man wore a wedding ring, was on a business trip, like her own fiancé. *How was this man's life less important than Dashiell's?*

It was impossible to support this type of thinking. She knew the answers. She'd learned them long ago. Death and suffering came to all mortals. The *divos* took only a tiny fraction of their allotted time, prevented their inevitable decline and decay. Besides, it was all predetermined by fate, and to die at the height of one's powers was a privilege, not a tragedy. To die in the arms of a god was an honor.

"Would you like anything else?" the clerk behind the desk asked, his American accent as flawless as her own.

"*Si, por favor,*" she answered. "I'd like a bottle of champagne sent to my room."

She walked away from the desk, still unsure if she would enter the bar or not. Going in for a drink did not mean she was hunting, and taking someone to bed did not mean she would feed. Yet, not going into the bar meant she would neither kill anyone nor fuck anyone. It made sense to her to begin her mortal life that very evening, to behave in the manner in which she would live from this point forward, to go straight to her room.

The generic chamber had an odor of disinfectant hiding mold. She tried to make herself comfortable, turned on her music, and downloaded some new books, but found it difficult to focus. She kept staring out the window. Up close she could see into the blackness, hear the insects chirping beyond the walls. In a few days or perhaps weeks, she would no longer own the night. It would not sing to her, or rather it would, but only in the old way – the puny human way she could barely remember. It would be like going back to poverty after living so long with great wealth.

Nevertheless, she had no doubts. She loved Dashiell. Fifty years with him, twenty, five, would be better than hundreds without him. Everyone dies, she reminded herself. Even for her kind the inevitable was inevitable though it might be put off indefinitely.

In the morning, Ana's van arrived. The driver showed her how the backseat could be laid flat if she wished to sleep. There were shades on all the windows and a privacy partition. For added measure, there was a large black blanket she could wrap herself in. The drugs she'd taken that morning to stay awake soon wore off, and she fell into a deep sleep.

She dreamed of her father. *He was trying to sell her to the gypsies, telling them how nimble her fingers were, what a good pickpocket she would make with proper training.* This had happened, but in life they told him they didn't buy children. *In her dream, they said she was defiled. He insisted her hymen was intact, another of his lies. The old gypsy woman corrected him. It wasn't her lack of virginity that corrupted her. She was a soulless thing that could bring only death.*

She felt herself waking. Dusk had come and the night was alive. In the darkness of the car, below the blanket, her eyes still shut, she sensed creatures around her – hunters large and small. She felt part of that great chain. She might run alongside the jaguar this night as she used to sometimes at the *estancia* they'd owned so long ago. She smelled Ana nearby, and realized the car engine was on, though the vehicle wasn't moving. There was a light tap on the door. She opened it, and there stood her friend.

"Welcome," Ana said. "Welcome home."

"How long have I been here?"

"You arrived hours ago. I'd told the driver to let you sleep, to leave the engine running and the air-conditioner on. I hope you were comfortable."

"That was kind of you."

It was just past sunset, but already quite dark. Something ran quickly by in the bushes to her left. No mortal would have caught it. But she had seen it – an ocelot chasing a hare. Somewhere close by she smelled freshly dug graves.

"It sings," she said, "the night sings." She breathed in deeply taking in more. Strong floral scents – hibiscus, bougainvillea, papaya, and others new to her.

Ana smiled, and took her hand. "But I understand it's your wish to be cut off from the song."

"Tonight I only want to savor it," she said. "You were there for me the first night I awoke to this life. I can't imagine anyone better to …"

She sensed Ana telling her to speak no more of it. She wanted to reach out and kiss her, but felt uncertain.

"You stayed away so long," Ana said, releasing her grip.

"I meant to visit."

"The contemplative life has never been for you. Come, let me show you around."

There were buildings and structures similar in type to those at the old complex – gardens, greenhouses, barns, and fields. Ana suggested Alphonsine might wish to freshen up after so long a journey. They came to a small stone building, which she described as her bathhouse. They stepped into a warm room, which smelled strongly of fresh herbs, lemongrass in particular. Ana began to disrobe and Alphonsine followed her lead. While Ana seemed placid, Alphonsine could sense within her questions, and many feelings.

"I told myself I wouldn't try to talk you out of it," Ana said aloud, "but I can't help but wonder if you really understand what it is you are doing."

Alphonsine did not answer her with words. She followed Ana
through a door into a sauna. The heat was mild. If not for the
skylight, it would have made a fine sleeping chamber. In the center
was a pool, perhaps six by nine feet, the water covered with rose
petals.

"I rarely use this," Ana said, "but I thought you might enjoy it."

They each stepped in from opposite sides. Alphonsine's desire
to be again in her friend's arms was strong, made more so by what
she felt was Ana's coolness. Ana's body was unchanged. If anything,
she seemed more luminous. Alphonsine's memories of her days
under Ana's tutelage returned to her vividly. She physically ached.
Her womb felt hot, and for just a moment she doubted the course
she had set for herself.

She could not resist the urge to go toward Ana, to embrace her
warm wet body, to sink to her knees and rest her mouth on Ana's
labia, sucking on salty skin, holding onto the outside of Ana's thighs
and bringing Ana down underneath the water with her. Ana sat on
the bottom of the pool, her legs spread, her long hair shooting up
vertically, as she allowed Alphonsine to service her.

She could hear Ana's thoughts as though they were spoken –
*How can you betray us? How can you allow yourself to be brought down this
way?*

She projected back that it was not a betrayal, that she would
always be loyal.

Ana slid below Alphonsine. The two kissed, and with lips locked
together, turned till Ana was on top. Freed from the constraints of
gravity or the need to breathe, they rolled, fingers thrusting, mouths
moving until both surfaced together satisfied, and then wordlessly
they retreated to opposite corners.

Ana clapped her hands. A young woman appeared. She had
honey-colored skin though her hair was streaked blonde. She was
dressed in a costume such as one might see in a silent movie
depicting ancient Egypt – a shimmering gold plated bikini top barely
covering her ample breasts, and loose harem pants made of gauzy
transparent fabric. Her green eyes had the dead look of one
consistently injected with the venom.

"Get your sister," Ana ordered. "Hurry."

The girl ran out.

"You keep servants here?"

"Yes. As we needed to in the old abbey. But our method of procurement is rather different."

"That uniform seems a bit theatrical."

"Anton's idea," Ana said. "He brought lots of costumes last time he was here. I thought it might appeal to you."

"Then you don't hate me."

"You know I don't."

The girl entered again, this time with another who looked a bit like her. Ana and Alphonsine now each had an attendant helping them wash."

"How do you come by them?" Alphonsine asked.

"The local drug lords and their hired killers believe I'm harvesting and selling organs. They bring me people – informers, competitors, witnesses, ex-girlfriends, and other unfortunate beings they've marked for death. Sometimes they take entire families to avoid vendettas. I try to make them comfortable and keep their stays mercifully short. My thinking hasn't changed. It's wrong to enslave humans, but sometimes it's necessary. When I'm done, I see to it they are put to rest with dignity, except I'm often required to return their heads as proof of death."

"Entire families," Alphonsine repeated, as the girl massaged shampoo into her hair. "They are so heartless."

"Worse than beasts," Ana replied. "And yet you wish to … I'm sorry. I promised myself I would not judge. You've made up your mind, and we all have a right to choose our destiny."

"The one I love is gentle. He won't even kill an insect. He harbors ill will toward no one. He's never been cruel."

"Does he have any idea what you're sacrificing for him?"

Alphonsine wondered whether they suspected her of revealing their secrets, and found herself consciously trying to block her thoughts. "How could he? I've told him nothing."

"And if he knew?"

"What I am? He'd hate me. I'm sure of that."

"Yet, you're willing to give all this up."

"I love him."

"And you don't love … us?"

"It's not the same. If they came for you, if they came for your beautiful head, I would offer mine. But if *he* came for *me*, if he were of our kind and I were mortal, if he wanted to take me as prey, I would submit myself to him with no need for venom. I could think of no better way to die than in his arms, at his pleasure."

"But you'd deny him that same pleasure?"

"I wouldn't wish to go on without him."

"I will try to be happy for you," Ana said with resignation.

"I'll miss our honesty with each other. A mortal might have said, 'Then, I *am* happy for you,' but we don't lie to our own."

"No, we don't."

The servants helped dry them off. As the slave wrapped a towel around her, Alphonsine felt aware of the girl's body brushing against hers. She turned and grabbed her, hugging and kissing, probing with her tongue deeply into her mouth. The towel fell to the floor.

"You're welcome to feed, if you'd like," said Ana. "But it might slow things down if we are to begin the process."

"In that case, I shan't," Alphonsine said. "But would you mind if I took a little nip?" She asked lightly touching the girl's neck. "It sounds like it might be my last, and she smells divine."

"Of course. This is the abbey. It's still a place where we share all that we have. I'd planned something else for myself, but I could take her now, and allow you a small portion."

"What do you call her?"

"Rosa."

Alphonsine thought for a moment, but only a moment, of the hardworking woman who came five days a week to clean her apartment and shared the name. She was loyal and kind and had a family.

Alphonsine kissed the girl again, taking in the sweetness of her scent. She helped take off her garments, and instructed her to lie down. Then she sat on her knees beside her. She began to lick the body, listening to the beat of the heart and the singing of the blood. Ana came over, seating herself behind the slave's head. She clasped her under the shoulders, but gently, pulling her up until her head rested on her chest. Alphonsine was sucking on the moist fatty flesh of Rosa's thighs, without breaking the skin. She moved up to the girl's *chatte*, and began to lick. Even in her narcotized state, Rosa found the sensation pleasurable. Then moving back down onto the thigh, she searched for a good spot. Alphonsine felt her fangs descend, and she bit in, careful not to nick the artery, which might have led her to bleed too quickly. She had to suck hard to pull out more than a trickle. She looked up to see Ana stroking Rosa's hair with one hand, another on a large round breast, whispering softly into her ear. Then Ana tilted her head and bit. As Alphonsine slowly filled her mouth, rolling the sweet liquid around her tongue, she could feel the flow of the blood racing toward the wound in the neck, and through it into Ana's mouth. She could see herself through Ana's eyes. Never had she had this intense a sharing. Although the girl, with such a high load of venom, was barely conscious, it was as though the three of them were intimately connected, perfectly united. She and Ana shared their thoughts as Rosa became physically weaker. Her memories, her very essence came to Alphonsine, flooding her with emotions. She could see the boyfriend, how he rescued her from a rough life, showering her with clothing, jewels, a beautiful apartment, but then she was raped by his partner who insisted she'd seduced him. Her lover sided with his friend and hired a killer who'd been instructed to take her sister as well, and the sister's child. Alphonsine felt the familiar rush that came as the heart slowed to its final beats. She pulled her fangs from the skin, allowing Ana to enjoy the finish. Here was life in its most vital form.

She watched the eyes, the change that came. Death could be so peaceful and beautiful, yet she would never kill again.

"*Never is a long time,*" Ana's thought entered her mind. Ana pushed the body to a corner and went back into the tub. Alphonsine did as well. She took another look at Rosa. She marveled at the stillness. She wondered what her own body had looked like as it lay in a coffin before she rose. It was too late to give the girl the gift of immortality, and there was no reason to think she would have been worthy of it. It was a gift she had never bestowed, and now she would never have the chance.

"*You are a gentle and beautiful creature.*" It was Ana again in her head. They had drunk from the same blood and the bond between them would be strong for days.

They stayed a while longer in the pool, slowly working off the excess energy that came with every fresh injection of life. When they were ready, Ana again clapped her hands. Rosa's sister, who had been standing passively in the corner awaiting new orders, came forward, and helped each dry off and put on fresh robes.

"There's a dead cat over there," Ana told her pointing to the lifeless body. You see a dead cat."

"Yes, señora."

"In the morning, you will tell the gardener that he must bury the cat in the usual place. But your son must not see. It will upset the boy.

289

Do you understand?"

"Yes."

Ana and Alphonsine walked to the main house. It was a simple adobe structure, no larger than a suburban home, but it felt familiar, like the old abbey. She'd only been back there once after her training, just before the incident that caused them to abandon it. *Could it really have been over a century since they'd seen each other?*

There were no servants about. Ana fetched a bottle of wine and poured two glasses.

"To love," she toasted, smiling benevolently.

"To love," Alphonsine answered. "In all its forms."

They spoke for a while of the old days. Ana rarely used the Web, and mostly to follow scientific research in fields that interested her, but she had from time to time looked at the gallery website, and had some questions about contemporary mores. They discussed Dashiell's father, and what his knowledge meant, or did not mean, for the future of the community.

"We're fortunate, I suppose," Ana said, "that with so much nonsense out there it's just more noise. Still, it might be time for us to take better control of the narrative."

"What are you suggesting?" Alphonsine asked.

"We might influence the creation of new myths designed to confuse and …"

"Disinformation?"

"What?"

"It's a bit like false-propaganda. Something their politicians and governments do to control the populace."

"The vicious leading the blind and stupid," Ana said, shaking her head. She asked after Pierre, mentioned Jane had written about running into her in Miami.

When they sensed the approach of dawn, they shared a bed. In response to Alphonsine's question, Ana confirmed that "the boy" she'd spoken of in the bathhouse, was Rosa's nephew, and Ana was caring for him in one of the small cabins.

"I'm glad we took her tonight instead of Pepito. He's very bright. I'd like to keep him another month."

"If you really enjoy him, why not allow him to grow up? There's a place, an orphanage in Sainte Trinité we support."

"What crazy thoughts you're having," Ana said, hugging Alphonsine, whose back rested against her breasts. "There was a contract. The boy was dead when he arrived."

"But if you got him out of the country, no one would know."

"Could you imagine the logistics involved in such a thing? Smuggling a child? We've survived here because we keep a low profile, and because the dead stay dead."

"I suppose," she said softly. "Ana, I know we said we wouldn't speak of it tonight, but can you tell me about the transformation?"

"It won't be easy. Your theory, that we should be able to cure your consumption is logical, but untested. There's no reason why it *shouldn't* work. I've gotten hold of some powerful medications. I want you to start taking them tomorrow evening. They'll probably be ineffective until your body changes, but they can't harm you."

"How long will it take?"

"As little as five nights, as much as three weeks. That's only based on the others. There were a couple I never told you about. They gave up."

"Why?"

"You'll see soon enough. Let's not ruin the evening. It might affect your sleep, and you'll need all your strength. We'll begin next dark. If I think it's going to kill you, I will stop."

"Will I be dead? I mean, like before, when we first appear to be without life?"

"No. You won't lose consciousness, but you may well wish you could."

☙ ✦ ❧

Despite the closed shutters, she stirred often throughout the day, falling in and out of unsettling dreams. Dashiell appeared in several. Each time he kept insisting he didn't know her. When she woke, Ana was already gone from her bed although it was barely dusk. The slave from the bath was by her bedside, the sister of the girl they'd taken, the mother of the child. Alphonsine wondered if Ana might take her next, and save the boy for later. Ana was attached to him, but it was hard to get good help.

The slave was dressed in a maid's uniform – the skirt rather short, and the heels a bit high. The stockings were silk and made her strong, shapely legs glisten. Alphonsine was sure the costume was more of Anton's work, and wondered if his tastes were really so pedestrian, or if he were trying to be ironic.

"Come here," she demanded.

The girl approached. Alphonsine fiddled with hooks and zippers until she was undressed. She looked very much like her sister except her breasts were larger – surgically enhanced, and her ass as well had a firmness and perfection that could only have been achieved under the knife. Still, she'd do. "On the bed. No, there."

She placed the girl's head between her legs and gave her further instructions. She was more than competent. Despite the weirdness of the porno breasts, if she were Ana, she'd be tempted to keep this one around. Alphonsine closed her eyes. Her thoughts did not distract her from her pleasure. This was a luxury she didn't have at home, mortals available to meet every need. Like any modern woman, she now relied on appliances for jobs people used to do.

Later, as the girl helped her dress, Alphonsine asked, "What is your name?"

"The lady calls me Carmencita."

"What was your name before?"

"I cannot remember."

"What was your life like before you were here?"

"I do not know. La Señora told me it was better to forget."

Ana was right. Her kind were not the monsters. All the people here had been marked for death, and Ana did the best she could for them, even for the children.

She found her mentor downstairs in the kitchen.

"When do we begin?" Alphonsine asked.

"We can start now."

They went into a small room. There was a single bed and a table on which some medical instruments were laid out. The only narrow window had bars. Ana picked up a syringe and a tube. "I'm going to take some blood," she announced.

"Wouldn't it be more fun to just drink it from me?"

"It's better this way. From this point on you must think of me as your doctor. It's best we not be too intimate."

"But it's good blood."

"I'll find some use for it."

Ana explained her body would create more blood to replace whatever was taken, but this would stimulate her appetite. She was then left to rest a few minutes though she was not in the least tired. Ana returned holding a closed flask and a small metal basin.

"Are you feeling light-headed?" Ana asked.

"No, just hungry," Alphonsine replied, adding in jest, "Can I take Carmencita?"

"Only if you plan on forgetting this madness and making it a social visit. I've brought something for you to drink. Take the whole thing. Try not to taste or smell it."

Ana placed the flask and the basin on a table and left the room.

The second Alphonsine loosened the cap, the odor hit her. She felt dizzy and nauseous. "Are you trying to kill me?" She shouted.

Ana's voice came through a speaker. "You need to have all of it."

She managed to get about half down, but it came up again so quickly she barely had time to grab the basin. The stench of the vomit was unbearable. Red-faced, with tears, she asked, "Is that the plan? To poison me?"

"This is the way back you seek," said Ana's disembodied voice.

"It wasn't simply stale," Alphonsine said, thinking aloud. "It was dead blood, from a ... a corpse."

Carmencita, dressed in a nurse's uniform, including the cap, came in to replace the basin with a clean one. She didn't take the flask, but made sure the lid was tightly closed, and then sprayed some kind of heavily scented disinfectant. Ana entered.

"At this moment we are the only two beings alive who know the means to transform a *diva* into a mortal. That was only the beginning," Ana said. "You're going to have to drink much more."

"How much more?"

"A half-liter every hour this night. A different dose tomorrow. We'll see. I can't tell you for how many days or weeks."

"Is there no way to dilute it?"

"None."

Ana handed her the closed flask. Alphonsine opened it. Ana held onto her hand as she gulped down the rest. She could tell nothing of the blood's source. The sweetness, the flavor, the *life*, were all gone. What was left was metallic, bitter, putrid. Worse than the taste was the smell. She had always trusted the others, but suddenly she wondered if this was all a lie, a scheme to dissuade her. She could imagine Anton behind such a trick.

Ana replied out loud. "I assure you this is the only way. A great deal of trouble has been taken."

"I'm sorry," Alphonsine said, "It was only a thought that popped into my head."

The servant returned through the night with more for her. She kept down very little. As daylight arrived she had a throbbing headache, an upset stomach and a burning need for fresh blood. Even in her mortal days, near death, she had never felt so miserable.

She no sooner fell into the day sleep, then she was awakened by Ana, who announced she needed to take her vital signs while the sun was up.

Alphonsine groaned.

"I told you it wouldn't be easy."

"I'm so very tired and my head is pounding. Could you at least give me some morphine?"

"I dare not," Ana said firmly.

The next evening her hunger was overwhelming. When Carmencita entered with the first flask, Alphonsine grabbed the girl before she was even out of bed, pulling her over her body. Some small part of her knew it would undo the work, but she couldn't help herself. The smell of the fresh blood underneath the woman's skin caused her to salivate to the point of drooling. She was about to sink her fangs into that sweet neck, could taste her already when Ana entered and pulled Carmencita away.

Alphonsine reacted as any predator would. She attacked Ana, who by that point was much stronger and subdued her easily.

Holding her down, Ana asked, "Do you still wish to go through with it?"

Her resolve returned. "Yes."

"Are you certain? You can take her if you'd like."

"I won't harm her," Alphonsine replied with determination.

It was decided she'd be locked in her room at night. Escape through the window would not have been impossible, and she could probably knock down the door, but those impediments would at least keep her from acting so impulsively.

"It will be a strange sort of prison as you'll always have the option to leave, but if you do, this will all be over," Ana warned.

From that point on Carmencita would be kept from the house at night. Ana brought in the flasks though she would leave before Alphonsine could open them. Sometimes Ana would take her for a supervised walk or a visit to the bathhouse, but she felt weak, and there was a strain between them. Once the sun was up and she couldn't feed, Carmencita would come to record her blood pressure and pulse rate.

Her day sleep was constantly interrupted, not only by the servant, but by minor noises that wouldn't normally disturb her, and physical symptoms unlike any she had experienced since her first life – fever and chills, pain in her bones, but worst of all the combination of unrelenting nausea and unquenchable thirst. In the midst of all that were her doubts and internal arguments. When night came, she felt only slightly better.

After a week or so, the hunger didn't bother her as much. Her body had become used to it as it had when she was a child and never had quite enough to eat.

Just before dusk one evening, she was hiding under her covers, sensing the approach of night. She heard a click at her door and assumed she was being locked in, but then she felt someone coming toward her – a mortal.

She pushed down the blankets and saw him – a handsome man with dark wavy hair. His sharp nose and almond shaped eyes hinted at mixed ancestry. He was holding the familiar silver tray with the flask and a clean basin. He wore no special uniform – just jeans that fit him well, and a white tee-shirt. He had on a pair of boots that looked worn but well cared for. She could smell the leather polish, and his fresh, pulsing blood. What she did not smell was venom or fear. He seemed fully sentient – a mortal who knew what she was and was not afraid.

"What's your name?"

"Roberto," he answered.

"What are you?" She asked appraising him. "Some kind of cowboy?"

He said nothing, but his pouty lips curled up just slightly. He appeared no older than she did.

She took in his beauty, the flawlessness of his skin, that perfectly natural blush of youth, and she wondered if he'd been sent to test her. She sensed he was deliberately blocking her from his mind – a skill that someone would have taught him. She could read nothing.

"Thank you, Roberto, for delivering my medication. Would you mind feeling my head? I think I may have a fever."

Her appetite was awakened. She wanted him, knew if she took him her strength would return to her.

He placed his palm against her forehead. She looked up at his wrist and grabbed it, almost biting into him, but instead she let him

295

bring his hand over her mouth, and she kissed it. He took off his shirt, pulled down her covers, and climbed on the bed.

"*Dona* Ana said I should serve you," he said in Portuguese. His accent, Brazilian, was as mellifluous as a samba. "She said you must do with me as you please."

He leaned over and began with her breasts then worked his way down to her poor neglected pussy.

"I think we're doing what you please," she said, offering no resistance.

She'd barely thought of sex since she'd started on her dreaded medication. His licking reminded her of what it felt like to be well. She thought of Anton, of how she had once welcomed his ministrations. She closed her eyes and allowed him to continue, summoning Dashiell's image, fantasizing it was Dashiell sucking on her clitoris, bathing her labia. She would see him soon, and she would be his completely. Mortal. She would follow mortal rules. She would be a good wife and someday a mother.

Roberto seemed to anticipate her. Moments before she would have come, he moved up and over her. She felt his chest next to hers, his steady human heart beating against her own. His hands reached back and under, grabbing her ass. He slid his tongue into her mouth while expertly slipping his cock inside her. She was very wet, very aware of his hard smooth member as it thrust against her clit. As the heat built up inside of her, so did her hunger.

Who was this mortal who dared to come to her? She still could not read him. Was that Ana's teaching or had her faculties already diminished?

She was on the verge of exploding. Her hands grasped his sweaty back. She licked his cheek, tasting the saltiness of his skin. She knew if she bit, she would lose Dashiell and go back to being what she was. Yet, he had offered himself to her for her pleasure. *He wanted this.* She felt a vibration from his cock, and then as he started to come, she did as well. Her fangs went forcefully into his neck. She hadn't planned it, but the desire to feel well again, to feel alive and strong, overcame her.

Just a taste, she told herself. Maybe it would only delay her transformation a few days. She took a larger gulp than she'd meant to. She felt his blood warming her body. His mind was open to her now. He had come to Ana to become one of them. He would complete any tasks she asked him to. He wasn't afraid, not even of death.

She moved a hand to the back of his head. Felt his soft hair. How easy it would be to slip back. She took more, could feel his blood flooding her, warming her, healing her.

And then she thought again of Dashiell, could see flashes of the life they could have together, could hear his tender words. With all the will she could muster, she disengaged her fangs and pushed him away. He landed in a corner of the room with a thud and a bewildered expression. She watched his cock become flaccid.

Ana walked in. "Go now," she told him.

"Why did you send him?" Alphonsine asked after he'd left.

"You stopped." Ana said with a slight tone of surprise."

"And if I hadn't?"

"We would have known where we stood."

"Who is he?"

"An acolyte, or a treat. I haven't quite decided. He came to me. It's not good when they come to us, but our numbers are dwindling, and …"

"I wanted him. I wanted him so much," Alphonsine confessed.

"Don't think it was willpower alone that held you back," Ana said. "You've passed some point." She handed Alphonsine the flask.

"I can't," she said. "I can't stand it anymore."

"I'll leave it here then, but if you don't, we'll have to wait until daylight and force it down your throat."

"Or what? What if I just stopped now?"

"If that's what you want, I can send him back in. You could close your eyes and imagine he's your lovely Dashiell as you bleed him."

Alphonsine noticed something in Ana's face she had never seen before – a slight cruel curl of the lip. *Had Ana's features change, or was it her own perception that had?*

They stopped locking the door at night. She began to wake earlier. Ana told her it would not be dangerous to go out into the sunlight.

"Won't it age me?"

"No faster than it will any mortal."

One day she woke in the middle of the afternoon. She felt queasy, with a strange sensation in her stomach. She wandered into the kitchen where Carmencita served her coffee.

"Did Doña Ana leave any medication for me?"

"No, señora. She said you might be hungry. Would you like me

297

to prepare something?"

Hunger. That was what she felt, but it was a different type than any she'd experienced over the past one hundred sixty-five years. She wanted food, and not merely to experience the flavor on her tongue. She desired all that went with eating. She wanted to chew. She wanted to swallow and feel it go down her throat. She longed for a full belly.

At her request, Carmencita made her an omelet with bacon, which she enjoyed as much as any blood meal. She'd forgotten the saltiness of pork, the texture of the fat, the way one could taste the slightly crusty edges. How would she explain her newfound meat cravings to Dashiell? He claimed to be able to smell carnivores. She'd have to give it up again, for him.

Roberto walked into the kitchen. He poured himself a cup of coffee and sat down across from her.

"What's your story, cowboy?" She asked.

"You mean you don't know? You can't *read* me?"

"You're making it difficult."

He smiled, took a sip from his mug, and asked, "Why would you give it up?"

"You do understand the price we pay?"

He shrugged. She knew then that killing was not new to him.

"You remind me of someone," she said.

"Oh?"

"One of our kind. One of my favorites."

"I thought *we* didn't have favorites?"

She smiled.

"It's a shame," he said, looking at her, taking in her face and her body.

"What is?"

"That you're going to get old." He reached out and squeezed her tits. "That these are going to shrivel up, and you're going to die."

"There are worse things than death," she said hearing an echo in her words. *Who had told her that?* Had it been the priest? He'd tried to warn her. But it was too late to warn this one.

"Are you aware what will happen if she decides not to ..."

"Of course, but she won't."

"And when you came to me, you weren't afraid?"

"She told me she would let you feed, but stop it in time to change me."

Carmencita refilled Alphonsine's coffee cup. Alphonsine

thanked her automatically, forgetting for a moment that the servant was no longer a fully conscious being. She turned again to Roberto. "You don't mind giving up your family, your friends, your ..."

"To be a god?" He asked.

She felt a sudden pang.

"What's wrong?"

"Nothing," she said, "I think I ..." She excused herself quickly and went to use the toilet. Normally, what little food she ate would simply be absorbed by her body, but suddenly her kidneys and bowels were working again. It was a sensation she hardly remembered, yet she did not find it unpleasant. Hours later, when Ana was examining her, she surprised both of them with a loud fart. She laughed, but caught the look of disgust and sadness that crossed her mentor's face.

"You may not need more of the blood."

"Then am I ...?"

"We'll see," Ana said. "You could still revert and require another course of treatment." She leaned her head against Alphonsine's chest and listened. "Any coughing?"

"No."

"Good. I'll give you another injection of the antibiotic for the tuberculosis, but I want you to start these." She handed Alphonsine a bottle of pills – the same kind she had delivered to the orphanage.

"The disease is within you and it's important you see a doctor when you return to the world," Ana added.

Over the next week, she became less nocturnal. Her appetite for food increased, while the acuity of her senses diminished. Examining her, Ana asked her to speed up her heart. She found she could not do it, or could not do it by will alone – only by running around the room, and that made her feel faint and sweaty. Her emotional state too was changed. She felt more pity for the servants. She had seen a young boy she assumed was Carmencita's son. She couldn't bear to speak to him, knowing his fate.

One evening, when Ana examined her, she suggested they do a test to see if her *diva* nature could still be brought out.

"What kind of test?"

Ana pulled out a small knife and cut herself. Before the wound had time to cauterize, she ran her wrist over Alphonsine's teeth. Her fangs did not descend.

"That's interesting," Ana said. "Did you feel anything? A

tingle?"

"Nothing."

"Good. Still we can't be sure. I'd like to try something else."

Ana left the room, returning moments later with Roberto.

"Does this one's blood sing to you?" She asked.

"No," Alphonsine said, then lightly added, "I'm deaf to all his charms."

Ana caressed Roberto's neck with her fingers, leaning in and sniffing. "But you remember the taste of him? So young. Strangely innocent despite his many, many transgressions. That's the beauty I suppose of mortal blood. Constant renewal." She turned to Roberto and told him it was time for his elevation. She would take him in front of Alphonsine to test whether or not watching would awaken any latent signs.

Alphonsine sensed something new, the slightest hesitation in Roberto's voice, as he started to ask, "What will ...?"

"I'll bite your neck. You'll hardly feel it. The area will become warm and numb. You'll be aware of the blood leaving your body. As you know from your experience with our patient, it's a peculiar sensation, but not a painful one. Your heart will slow down. You may lose consciousness, but you don't need to be afraid. When you are on the brink of death, I'll feed you and you'll sleep, but you'll wake again. I tell you now so you won't feel any panic or discomfort."

"I am so honored, Dona Ana."

Alphonsine watched them staring into each other's eyes. She saw how compassionately Ana was looking at him, as though he were one of her children, and how worshipfully he looked back at her. They moved into an embrace. He bent his neck slightly, and she bit into the flesh that was offered. Her arms were around him, and as he weakened, her grip became stronger. Roberto's eyes rolled slightly, and his head began to fall back. Ana, without loosening her fangs, must have felt his movement. One hand moved up to support his head, and then a few seconds later, she let go, and he dropped to the floor.

Alphonsine saw the wound was not closing, as it would have if he'd been alive. Nor was Ana racing to cut herself and feed him. Instead, she pulled out a handkerchief and wiped the blood from her lip.

Alphonsine let out a brief involuntary scream, which Ana ignored as she turned toward her, and came forward to look into her mouth.

She ran a finger across Alphonsine's teeth. "Nothing?"

Alphonsine shook her head.

Ana stepped away. "The others didn't approve," she explained. "They were right, of course. He was a very impulsive boy. Still, I was fond of him."

Alphonsine said nothing, and hoped her thoughts would not betray her.

"You look a bit pale. Would you like some coffee?"

"No, I ..."

"I didn't mean to frighten you. I only deceived him out of pity. We would never harm *you*. We trust you to keep our secrets."

She nodded. She felt tears coming down. Her body was shaking. Ana wrapped her cold arms around her. Alphonsine remembered something from her childhood — an old man who'd bought her favors from her father, an undertaker, who smelled of death.

"You will always be our sister," Ana continued. "We haven't lied to you. We would welcome you back to us."

She turned her head away before Ana's lips could reach hers.

"Do I really seem so monstrous to you?"

Alphonsine replied, "No, of course not. It just seems so ..."

"Would you like to leave this place tomorrow?"

"Yes."

"I'll leave the door to the attic unlocked. There's a computer you may use. We don't have wireless and the service is slow, but you should be able to make your arrangements."

"Thank you, Ana," she said, willing herself to reach her arms out to her friend.

Ana smiled slightly, but did not approach her.

"Good-bye, my sweet girl."

"Good-bye," Alphonsine said weakly.

Ana lifted Roberto's body and flung it over her shoulders as though it weighed no more than a blanket. She left the room, closing the door behind her. Alphonsine collapsed on her bed, hugging herself and crying.

Chapter 2

She expected to feel physically week, to be confused by the sudden muting of all sensation, but was surprised most by the dullness of her desires. She still longed for Dashiell, wanted to feel him inside her, to the point where on the flight to New York she caught her hands under the blanket absently touching her crotch. She went into the bathroom and tried splashing cold water on her face. When that didn't work she brought herself to climax as quickly as she could. Yet, she felt less desire for others. It wasn't that she didn't notice attractive men and beautiful women, but she was not able to sense how receptive they would be. She couldn't smell their blood, or hear its delicious song as it raced through their veins. Choosing one and pulling him or her into the restroom for a little bit of fun, might have been possible – but there could be consequences that hadn't existed before. *Complications.* She wasn't sure if her new awareness was a bad thing or a good thing. Certainly it would make her remaining faithful to Dashiell much easier.

Changing planes in Miami, she nearly bought a ticket for Los Angeles, but stopped herself. She would rest first, and see a doctor. She would take care of her health. Not like last time.

Between flights, she read and reread texts and emails from Dashiell. She was reasonably sure he'd been faithful. If not physically, at least in his heart, which was all that mattered.

As she waited to board, she caught a text from Pierre. Anton had told him she'd be returning. She wondered who had told Anton, or if he had some kind of link to her mind that knew no boundaries. More likely a connection to Ana, probably the ordinary electronic kind.

Pierre was going to throw a party in her honor. She was popular with the artists, as well as clients, and he wanted to make sure no one thought she'd been fired or mistreated. Normally, she would have made the arrangements for such an event, but he'd gotten someone else to do it, some boring "ordinary" girl. He made it clear that other than at the celebration, he had no desire to see her because as he wrote, "It will break my cold dead heart."

When she arrived home in the late afternoon, the concierge helped her with her luggage, and for once she felt she really needed his assistance. He inquired if she was well.

"I'm fine. Why do you ask?"

"You just look a little tired. But I suppose it's jet lag."

"I'm sure that's all it is."

She had texted her maid with a shopping list. The place was not only spotless as usual, but the potato chips she had requested were in the cupboard. She savored each one. The salt, the fat, the crunch. She remembered the bacon she'd had only days ago. She would need to avoid meat for Dashiell's sake. She couldn't imagine how she might explain she'd gone back to it. Besides she'd read it was terrible for the heart.

But what if her constitution now required animal protein? Would he still love her? She resolved to continue being a vegan, but thought she might start the next day. She'd never had an American hamburger, and knew a restaurant that specialized in them. They only used the meat of cows fed on organic grass in pastures, and they delivered. She ordered two deluxe, as well as a large chocolate milkshake, and a double order of "french" fries.

As she was waiting, she turned on the television. She watched without paying much attention as she surfed the net, googling Dashiell Alexander to see if there was any new gossip. She came across something about casting. An actress she had never heard of would be playing his love interest. She knew how passionate relationships could be on a set. The sooner she could get out to the coast the better. Still, she had faith in him, and though much of her arsenal had now been disabled, she could fight for him if she needed to. The tack she would take would be disinterest. If he wished to have an affair with the sweet young thing, she'd give her permission. He'd come back to her. How could he not?

She sensed something was missing. All her figurines and books were in place, even the three antique volumes that had once been in her Paris apartment, including the very copy of *Manon Lescouts* that Adet had given her and later referenced in his dreadful novel. Anton had found it at an auction in the eighteen-nineties, and had one of her kind bring it to her in Rio. She'd sent him a rather formal thank you letter, noting she was not sentimental about mere things.

Camellias. The flowers, which Anton had been sending daily, were not in the vase on the counter. He must have stopped his order. She wondered if he was still in Brooklyn. He'd spoken of leaving since the day he'd arrived. She almost texted Pierre to ask, but stopped. What did it matter? She'd never see him again.

When the food came, she ate heartily, grateful that aromas and body odors could not yet be transmitted via the Internet. When she had cleared away all traces, she skyped Dashiell, using her large flat-screen as a monitor.

"Hello darling," she said.

"Hello wife-to-be," he paused, a moment staring at something on his screen. "Where are your rings?"

"I left them when I went away. It wouldn't have been safe to take them."

"You haven't been wearing your engagement ring?"

"I'm sorry. But I've been a very good girl."

"Well go, put them on now."

She ran to her bedroom and found both the rings he'd given her. Each was slightly tight. She wondered if she might have gained weight.

"Here," she said showing off her hand, and then she belched.

He laughed. "I've never heard you do that before. What did you eat?"

"A burger. A garden burger. I must have eaten too fast. I just got home." She couldn't believe she'd already lied to him. She told herself she'd try harder, do better.

She had to remind him twice she wouldn't talk about her trip. He was more forthcoming about the film. They hadn't started shooting yet. He couldn't understand why it would take her another week to join him.

"I have to stay for my own party," she said.

He looked different to her. It wasn't simply that he was tanner, or that he had shaved the stubble. She felt like she was seeing him through new eyes, or perhaps very old ones. It was as though her time with the *divos* had been a dream, that yesterday she was Marie Duplessis, dying in her Paris flat, and today she was here in the twenty-first century – and somehow he had always been by her side. Was he a totally new being, she wondered, or could he indeed be the reincarnation of one of her lovers? If creatures such as she had been

304

could exist, then how could the transmigration of souls be ruled out? But if he were Adet reincarnated, would he too desert her? *No*, she told herself. *Fate would not be so cruel.* Besides, the social barriers that had driven Adet away were gone, and his compassion and ability to forgive would have grown. Wasn't that how karma worked?

"Promise me we'll always be together," she demanded as she slowly removed her blouse.

"Always," he said as he matched her striptease. While it might have amused her to make him dance and perform, she understood it was her role as a woman to visually stimulate *him*. With an old Smokey Robinson tune playing, she slowly disrobed and sat on the ottoman, spreading her legs in the air, exposing herself for his inspection, telling him how much she wanted him, how wet and open she was.

"You're still a tease," he said.

She opened her mouth and licked her lips, no longer afraid of errant fangs. "I can taste you," she said, "I can taste your hot hard cock in my mouth. I'm tasting you now. Can you feel it?"

After they were both as satisfied as they could be without actually being in the same room, they talked more. He in bed in his hotel. She on her couch. Both naked. She yawned.

"You're sleepy?"

"It's two in the morning in New York," she said, continuing the conversation on her laptop as she walked into the bedroom.

"I've never seen you actually sleep before dawn."

"I've had a long day with the flight."

"It's weird. I don't think I've ever even seen you yawn before."

"Well, I fart too. Please don't be too freaked out," she said getting into bed.

"You're not perfect?"

She shook her head.

"I'm still going to marry you," he said closing his eyes.

She placed the laptop on the pillow beside her, and drifted off to sleep with Damon's soft snore her lullaby.

ॐ ⊕ ॐ

That night she dreamed she was at the Opéra Comique in Paris. Anton was sitting next to her. But she turned around and it wasn't him. It was Franz Liszt, and she was shaking because she couldn't believe he'd come back to her. Then she looked again, and it was Adet. Then Dashiell. The music stopped, and the manager came out to tell everyone to leave because there was a fire, but it wasn't a fire. It was a river of blood flooding the theater, and Dashiell grabbed her hand and they ran. Out on the streets, blood spewed from fountains and came up sewer grates. It rained from the sky. She lost her companion and found herself in the cemetery, where she was surrounded by women in rags. She recognized them at once – her prey. They did not look decayed, but dirty as though they had risen from the earth. They pointed at her accusingly. They came toward her with nails as sharp as tiger claws and began to attack. Strips of skin peeled away. She was being devoured. She tried to scream, but no sound came. Someone was calling her name.

"*¡Doña Camilia! ¡Doña Camilia!*"

Her eyes opened, and it took her a moment to realize where she was. "*Rosa, gracias. Tuve una pesadilla. ¿Cómo has entrado?*"

"I hear you. You no lock the bedroom. I'm sorry. It sound like someone is killing you."

"No, just a bad dream. *Nada mas.* I'm fine now. Please." She gave Rosa a smile, and indicated the door with her eyes. Rosa left the room quietly shutting the door behind her.

It was gray outside, but the light and the daytime view startled her. She hadn't closed the curtains. She sat up trying to convince herself she was awake, and the dead did not rise – usually. It was strange to imagine those on whom she fed as "victims" who would seek revenge. The venom made them so pliable. When she would remember particular feasts it was as though they had been willing participants. Now it seemed different. Horrible.

Was this what killed them or drove them mad – the others who had come back?

She wondered if they would haunt her the rest of her days, if she would cringe whenever Dashiell spoke of his father. In her first life, after she came to Paris, she learned to put the past behind her. Marie Duplessis existed only in the present. There was always a way to push back what she didn't wish to think about. She would practice that habit again; only she'd be pushing back nearly two centuries.

She thought of a coffee table book Pierre had given her. It was on the great beauties of history, *From Nefertiti to Monroe*. There were a few lines about a certain French courtesan. The author had written, "*While both Rose Alphonsine Plessis and Norma Jean Baker were masters of reinvention, Marilyn never really left her old self behind. In the end it killed her. Marie died of consumption – not personal demons."*

She would stop these thoughts and images in their tracks. She had not been responsible for acts committed when she was an unnatural being. She was someone else now. She was Camille St. Valois. Who was to say she had not always been Camille St. Valois?

She placed a hand on her belly. It felt swollen and sore. She thought it might have been the pills Ana had given her. Then she noticed blood on the sheets.

She put her head down and smelled it, lingering for a moment. Her blood, her very normal menstrual blood. She had stopped having periods a year before her natural death. The doctors said it was the illness, but she thought it might have been due to the herbs she'd sometimes take to induce miscarriage. Whatever the problem had been, now she was cured. Surely, it was a sign she had been forgiven for past sins.

She dressed simply and after a light breakfast went for a walk although the day was overcast and cool. She made her way across McCarren Park into Greenpoint and stopped at a Catholic church. She hadn't seen the inside of a church in many years. It wasn't that her kind couldn't enter one. Most services occurred during daylight hours, and there was a tradition of not harming priests. The institutional power of Rome was not to be trifled with.

She thought of Pascal's wager, and decided confession might do her good. Ever discreet, she included no murders although she did say she'd "hurt" people, also fornicated, prostituted herself, and lied. Her penitence was perfunctory. She wasn't sure what she was hoping for, or if priests flogged sinners on request. Perhaps one went somewhere else for that kind of thing. Afterwards she took communion, and lit a candle in memory of her mother, her sister, and her son. When she stepped outside, the weather had cleared, and the sky was a lighter blue then her lover's eyes.

She had barely walked down the steps when she heard someone call, "Camille." It was Cara who came up and hugged her. Alphonsine wondered how much of the dream-walk had worn off, whether it had magically dissipated once she'd been transformed. Was Cara trying to charm her to remain close to Dashiell? Or did she just like her? It was hard to tell, but Alphonsine was aware of a need for friends, and Cara would serve that purpose. The detective had a "comp" day, whatever that was. She was running some errands and visiting a dentist later.

"I spoke to Dashiell, yesterday," Cara said. "He told me you were back."

She wondered how often Cara spoke to him, but reminded herself the cop was no threat to her.

They stopped at a cafe, taking an outside table. There was only a small wind, and Alphonsine felt no sting against her skin. When the coffee came, she took a minute to enjoy the aroma. She was sure her ability to taste the elixir, to savor the subtlety of flavors had been sharper when she was a *diva*, but she hadn't appreciated it as much. They talked about nothing of consequence, but Alphonsine was enjoying herself – enjoying just being alive – and somehow she felt, despite the diminishment of her powers, that she was truly alive in a way she hadn't been for a long time. It was a new beginning. How wonderful it was to live liberated from the social restrictions that had plagued her first life, and now she was free of so much else. She invited Cara to her farewell party at Dumont's. "You can bring someone if you'd like."

Cara confessed she and Justin had finally admitted their feelings for each other and were now dating.

"How's that working?" Alphonsine asked, surprised she was actually interested in the doings of two ordinary mortals.

"Actually pretty good," Cara said smiling. "But what do I wear to something like that? I don't have a ball gown."

"Believe me, you could wear anything. I'd give you something of mine, but I'm a stick compared to you."

"That's one way of putting it," Cara said.

"Come on. You really don't know how men see you? You have a gorgeous body. Don't tell me you've never used your sexuality during an interrogation."

Cara blushed slightly. "Maybe. But I'm not nearly as good at it as you."

"That may be true," Alphonsine answered, "but I envy your independence. Your competence. You contribute to the world. The best I've ever been able to manage is to inspire."

"That must be something. To have someone dedicate a song to you."

"My kind is on the way out," she said sipping her coffee. She wished she could talk openly to Cara, to anyone for that matter. There was a brief silence before she continued. "What *will* you wear?

I'm sure we could find something cheap and chic at one of the thrift stores. I'd love to dress you."

"I hate to shop."

"I get that. I'll make it painless."

They started walking, and hit a couple of the better local consignment stores, managing to find a spectacular vintage nineteen-eighties dress by a designer who'd never quite made it to the big leagues. Cara complained it was tight at the waist, but Alphonsine thought it was just the thing to accentuate the cop's curves. She insisted on paying for it, mentioning she was "flush" and joking about marrying a movie star.

They separated when Cara left to go to her dentist. Walking home in the daylight, Alphonsine felt both exhausted and happy. She couldn't remember having so much fun with a mortal woman that didn't involve either sex or death. *Friendship.* Pierre had been her partner, her accomplice, her incestuous brother at times. But were they friends? There hadn't been a *woman*, a *confidante*, since Paris, and even then they always wanted something.

It was three o'clock when she got home. With a bit of trepidation, she called the doctor, wishing she'd been able to take care of it online, or have someone else do it. The receptionist asked stupid questions about insurance, and said there was nothing open for several weeks.

She told her she was certain Dr. Rand would have something sooner for Camille St. Valois. The woman said she'd check and call her back. The doctor's husband was a financier and collector, a friend of the gallery. The call was returned quickly. There was an opening at four-thirty. If she hopped in a cab she could just about make it.

She could see Dr. Rand's concern when she showed her the pills Ana had given her, and explained she got them from a clinic near an orphanage where a friend was volunteering in Colombia.

"You say you've never been diagnosed with TB before?"

"Never to my knowledge. I was sick a lot as a child. I remember having coughs, asthma, being on medication. It's possible my parents never told me."

"Could you ask them?"

"They both passed away."

"Oh? I'm sorry. What about your medical records?"

"We moved around so much. I wouldn't know where to start looking."

Blood was drawn. An X-ray was taken. Skin was pricked. She was told to come back the next day, not to worry if welts formed signaling a positive reaction.

While she knew it could be cured completely, she was surprised by the way the doctor had looked at her, and all the questions. She had never been a pessimist, yet she began to imagine the disease might present an obstacle to her dreams. She'd be taking pills for several months. She wondered if she should tell Dashiell. Better to keep it from him. It wasn't a lie, simply an act of omission. The doctor had assured her that once past the active stage, she would not be contagious.

The following day there were additional tests, including one that involved stepping into a coffin-like device that emitted a deafening noise. They took more samples of her newly mortal blood. Then came a conversation she had not expected.

Chapter 3

Cancer. It was separate and apart from the tuberculosis which was already under control. The tumors on her lungs would spread. Surgery would not help her.

"Incurable but not untreatable," said the specialist.

What it came down to, once she cut through the euphemisms, was simple. Her particular disease was rare. There was medication that "worked" for most. There would be side effects including hair loss and nausea. Everyone grew resistant, usually within a year, but it might buy her time until there was another drug or a clinical trial.

"And if it's untreated?"

"You'll be dead within months."

"What about remission?"

"With the drugs it's likely for a time. You might have a good year or even two. Without them, we really can't say."

"I see. Thank you. You've given me a lot to think about."

She went home and cried. By evening she was together enough to return Dashiell's call.

Stroking his cock as he watched her play with her toys, he asked, "Can't you just fly out tomorrow and go back for that stupid party?"

"Just a week more, darling," she said trying to hold back her tears, "Then we'll be together, always."

She wasn't certain what she would do, but telling him the truth was not an option. He would quit the film, delaying and possibly destroying his career. He'd insist she take the medication, so they could have more time, and he'd want to care for her. It would be worse than dying. It would be as though they were both dying, and in the end he wouldn't love her. He'd pity her and feel trapped. *That* would be unbearable.

She played the scenarios in her head. She might arrange for him to catch her in the act with someone else. Would Pierre be willing to go along now that she was what she was? But she couldn't hurt

311

Dashiell that way, and besides she was not afraid of death. The only thing she feared was not dying in his arms.

She resolved to go ahead as if the disease didn't exist. She wasn't ruling out the drugs entirely. She could make that decision after she got to the Coast. If the effects weren't so bad, she could hide the illness altogether for a while. If they were, she'd stop taking them. The important thing was not how much time they'd have, it was that she'd be there for his work, and if her luck held out, she would make it through the filming. The doctors told her she might not have many symptoms until near the end. He would come home to her – too tired after a long day to notice her fatigue. He wouldn't know until she was too weak to hide the truth, and then it would be quick.

Or maybe they'd take her back.

How could she even think such a thing? She had spent years angry with Anton, insisting she never would have chosen to live off the blood of others. Since her return to mortality, she couldn't stand thinking of all the wrongs she'd committed. The blood on her hands would never be washed away. They tried to take those who would not be missed, but everyone was missed by someone – that much was clear to her now.

Their monstrosity seemed so obvious it amazed her more mortals didn't sense it. She was sure if she were to come across a member of the community unknown to her, she would understand his true nature immediately. But beyond all that, beyond the repulsiveness, if she returned to being what she was, if such a thing were even possible, it would mean giving up Dashiell, and it was easier to accept death, than life without him. He'd changed her. It was he who saved her, saved her soul, though he'd never know it, he that brought her back to humanity. What would be the point of going on if she couldn't be with him?

What she was planning was the opposite of selfishness. She would make no demands on her lover. She would begrudge him nothing. Why not give him a few months of perfect happiness? Besides, what if the doctors were wrong? How many times back in Paris had the quacks told her she would not live through a season? Yet, she'd managed for years to handle the grim reaper as deftly as she'd handled the bill collectors.

The evening of the party she wore a pink dress – a sheath that exposed one shoulder. It was locally designed but meant as an homage to Givenchy and *Breakfast at Tiffany's*. To enhance the look, she added long white gloves, and put her hair up in a French twist. Studying the mirror, she realized she did not look like a dying girl, but she wondered if Pierre would sense it. She was certain Anton would have, but he had gone back to Europe, and for that at least, she was grateful. She put her illness out of her mind. She would just be a girl that night. Not a sick girl.

She found some amphetamines, the kind she sometimes took to day-walk, and was careful to take only a human-sized dose to help her maintain her energy.

She hadn't stepped into the gallery since her return, and when she spotted Pierre and they met and hugged, they were both unsure how to react to each other. She thought of all the hunts they shared. She couldn't see him as a monster, yet he was no longer her brother. She noticed his companion Mika was not there, and asked about him.

"He's gone," Pierre said.

A sound came from her throat before she could stop it. "I'm sorry," she said.

She hadn't really known the boy beyond Pierre's assessment of his lack of intelligence, of talent or potential. She couldn't judge for herself because Pierre kept him narcotized with the venom. She was certain he'd feasted on him. Strange how weeks before, she might have shared in the carnage, or comforted him afterward in some kind of duel or multi-party fuckfest. Now the idea of Mika's death made her feel sad, even a little sick. But there was no chance to linger over it. Artists, clients and various hangers-on and courtiers made their way to her. There was a jazz quartet in white dinner jackets. Pierre took her hand and led her to the dance space. Her humanity did not cause her to lose a step.

He whispered to her, "Your blood smells so sweet and young."

She smiled at him and hoped he couldn't read her thoughts. While she truly loved him, she never wished to see him again or hear from him or know anything about his activities.

As she came up from a dip, he told her, "You never need to be scared of me. Of any of us."

She remembered how Ana had reassured Roberto before she slaughtered him. *They didn't lie to their own kind, but she was no longer one of them.*

Others joined them dancing, while some of the hipsters stood on the sidelines, bopping their heads to the beat. Why did they insist on lacing every movement with irony rather than joy? She was glad

Dashiell wasn't like that. There was something timeless about him.

His honor and the missus arrived, and took to the dance floor. The wife, a stately blonde, stood several inches taller than her husband, even in flats.

Alphonsine thought of what the mayor had told her about women changing. Mrs. Piccolini still had a regality about her. She looked as good as a woman her age could. Alphonsine had been sure Dashiell would still love her once her beauty had faded, but now she realized she'd be unlikely to ever find out.

She caught a look from Pierre and felt herself flush. She couldn't be sure, but guessed he'd sensed or smelled something.

"I should dance with our first lady. You know they bought a number of our paintings." He winked at her, and tapped the mayor's shoulder. He and Piccolini traded places.

"You dance so well," his honor said, "but then you have so many talents."

"I'm glad you came, Sam. That we have a chance to say goodbye to each other."

"Any possibility of our finding a quiet place for a real goodbye?" He asked.

She smiled and said nothing though she knew he wasn't joking. She displayed her left hand, showing off her engagement ring. He whispered obscenities in her ear.

She waved to Cara and Justin, gesturing for them to join her on the dance floor. Cara shook her head. The band stopped to take a break at the end of the number. She was clapping when she felt a hand tapping her shoulder. She turned around and there was Dashiell.

Before they could even say a word, her lips were on his.

"I had no idea. I'm so happy," she said.

He was wearing a tux. She didn't know he even had one. She'd never seen him looking so good.

"I couldn't miss this," he told her. Reaching into a pocket, he pulled out a fresh camellia for her hair. As the music started again, he explained he had three free days and then she was going back with him. "Whatever you have to do, get it done," he ordered.

They could hardly keep their hands off of each other. After staying long enough to not seem rude, they went straight home. In the elevator, he laughed trying to pull up her gown, but it was too tight. Instead, they rubbed their clothed bodies against each other. In her apartment, fiddling with hooks and zippers, they joked about cummerbunds and gloves. He still had his pants on when he carried her into the bedroom, but she was naked, and felt more vulnerable than she'd ever been.

"He could kill me," she realized. It wasn't that he would, but the idea of his strength, his power over her physically, was exciting. She had often fantasized drinking his blood, feeling his life recede, but now she imagined as he was fucking her, that he would surprise her when she began to come. *He* would bite into *her* and drain her until her frail human heart would beat no more.

She climaxed before he did. Her orgasm intense and lasting. After he caught up, they took what they knew would only be a short break. She brought out a bottle of champagne, and from her bed they drank, watching the night from her windows.

"You're real," he said. "I can't believe you're real."

"Wasn't I real before?"

"You were ... I don't know. I guess it's not seeing you for so long."

"You're just how I remembered you. Do I seem different?"

"I'm not sure what it is. You're softer somehow, more relaxed maybe."

"Relaxed?"

"You always seemed like you were wired differently. Incredible energy, but almost frantic. Now it feels like you're at peace."

From the moment she saw him, until he uttered that word, she had almost forgotten the doctors' verdict. Now all she could think of was the peace of the grave.

She buried her head in his chest.

"You're crying," he said. "I don't think I've ever seen you cry."

"I must look a mess."

"No, never."

"I just want to be with you so much."

"Me too. Why don't we get married?"

"Isn't that the plan?"

"Why don't we just do it tomorrow? City Hall?"

"Yes," she said. "Yes, yes, yes."

The night went quickly. Their backdrop, the lights across the river. The soundtrack slow and romantic – jazz, bossa nova.

He woke her with espresso and pastries in bed. It was almost noon.

315

He was already dressed and ready to go. She showered, but as she was deciding what to wear, he approached her from behind. She fell onto the bed and got on her hands and knees for him.

Afterward they both agreed that while they could easily spend the rest of the day making love, they should get to the clerk's office. They took a cab downtown and were surprised to learn there was a twenty-four hour waiting period.

"Maybe you can ask your friend," Dashiell joked, "the mayor."

It was the clerk who told them even his honor was not above New York state law.

"That's it then," Dashiell said, "Two o'clock tomorrow, we're back."

They stayed to fill out paperwork. He noticed she was giving up her name. They hadn't discussed it beforehand.

"It seems so old-fashioned," he said.

"When you get right down to it, I'm an old-fashioned girl."

They debated holing up in a downtown hotel, surviving on love and room service until they could get the deed done. Instead, they spent the day walking, checking out galleries and shops. Alphonsine felt so energetic, so alive, she was almost convinced the doctors had made a mistake. Dashiell talked of their future. She knew her death would hurt him terribly. He'd grieve, but she didn't see an alternative. Why steal his happiness before it was necessary?

They took the ferry out to Staten Island and back, only because neither of them had done it before. Then they walked over the Brooklyn Bridge, and found themselves on Montague Street, dining at a vegetarian version of a French bistro.

"Do you ever think of eating meat again?" She asked him.

"Not seriously. Do you?"

"I'm tempted sometimes."

"I couldn't go back. It's murder. They're sentient," he said.

"It's that easy for you?"

"What are you getting at?"

"Even chimpanzees will kill for meat. It's our nature."

"The same could be said of war and slavery. We're more than prisoners of our nature. Our lives are about something else. Something bigger. Aren't they? If you're asking me whether or not I could forgive you if you ate a steak every now and then, I wouldn't be thrilled," he said grabbing her hand and kissing it, "but I'd forgive."

316

"I know you would," she said. "But I wouldn't test you that way. I love you because you make me want to be better."

"Wait a sec," he said putting down his fork, "Meat cravings? You aren't …"

"Not yet," she said.

"Good," he said, "That wasn't what I meant. God knows I want you to have my babies, but I think we should take a year at least. It's not like we're in our thirties."

She felt exhausted though they were home by nine. She hadn't even packed. The furniture would stay. It came from community funds, even if she had earned them. There were a few things – her old volumes and a couple of figurines that had all belonged to her long ago. *What did it matter?* They were part of the past. Pierre could dispose of them as he saw fit. Auction them off. Put them on eBay.

There were some photos she liked – black and whites from an exhibition she'd gone to with Dashiell. Billie Holiday with a flower in her hair – he'd asked if that was where she'd gotten the idea. Maria Callas in a black ball gown as Violetta – he'd said La Divina looked like she could have been her older sister. Those she would take with her.

They made love only once that night and rested in each other's arms. He told her he'd never been so happy. "Me too," she said. Despite her illness it was true. She'd wake up the next day and get married, not for money or a title, not to make another man jealous. *For love.* Finally, a man she loved who loved her enough to want to be with her always.

She might not have long, but she could not remember a time she felt so content, so *sated,* and complete. If time could be broken down into nanoseconds, there was an infinity of joy ahead.

"Remember what you said about not wanting any more three ways?" She asked.

"Yeah," he said.

"You're right. I don't want to either. I don't want to share you with anyone."

☙ ✦ ❧

When morning came, she felt for him beside her, but he wasn't there. She took off the sleep mask she needed to keep the light from waking her. It was after ten. In less than four hours it would be twenty-four since they'd gotten the marriage license, and they'd be able to marry. With her right hand, she felt for the two rings on her left hand – the pre-engagement ring, and the official one.

It would be bad luck if she lost them. She felt happy and she felt well. She had adjusted to her mortal body. Waking in daylight was beginning to feel natural, and though she couldn't inhale as deeply as she would have liked, she had all but put aside the doctors' pronouncements. She knew what it felt like to be deathly ill, and that was not how she felt. The sky was clear, the sun bright. *How could a long life not be ahead of her?* When she got to California, she'd find a specialist, and he'd explain the error or at least offer her another treatment option or surgery. She told herself she would think no more about it – not on her wedding day.

Dashiell, she imagined, was sitting by the kitchen counter, drinking coffee, or perhaps he'd run out to the bakery. There'd still be time to make love. She went into the bathroom, not bothering to shower. She liked smelling him on her body, liked the feeling of the wetness of his cum inside her. They could bath together before they left, or maybe they wouldn't even bother. Maybe they'd get married marked with each other's scents.

She came out into the living room wearing only her silk robe, expecting to see him in one of the counter-level chairs sipping an espresso, but then she noticed the back of his head popping up over the sofa.

"Good morning," she said approaching.

He said nothing. Something was wrong. It was as though cold were emanating off his body.

"What is it?" She asked sitting down beside him.

His iPad was in his lap. He handed it over. Without looking at her, he rose and went toward the window. She watched the clip. *Twenty-three blurry seconds. Her face was never visible. The mayor's was. He was supine, enjoying the young woman writhing on top of him. His stubby paw reaching out and gripping her perfect ass. Her high-pitched breathy moans could be heard. She arched her back and placed both her hands on the back of her head with her elbows out as she bounced with exaggerated delight. It was one of her signature moves.* There was a date and time stamp.

"It's not me," she said instinctively before she even read the article.

He said nothing.

She came toward him. "Look at me," she said.

He wouldn't. He said very softly, "Watch the rest and we'll talk."

The rest was a press conference and interview featuring Natalie – Piccolini's ex-mistress, along with her lawyer. She had taped them. Alphonsine could usually hear the high frequency of a cell phone, but even a *diva's* powers of perception could be thrown by mind-altering substances and plain carelessness.

Natalie had been set aside and fired weeks ago. She claimed the mayor tried to pay her off, but she'd decided to go public, alleging sexual harassment, that he'd pressured her to participate in orgies, including with prostitutes, and to use cocaine.

She didn't name the brunette, but she might as well have. In answer to a question about the woman's identity she replied, "My impression was she was there as kickback for a deal he made. It was a personal investment, not city business."

A reporter asked whether the *other* other woman was Camille St. Valois, to which Natalie replied with a smirk, "No comment." Her attorney announced, "No more questions."

Alphonsine said, "This is crazy. Dashiell, please, talk to me."

"I can't if you're going to tell me lies," he said. He wasn't yelling. That was the worst of it. Yelling would have been better. It would have implied passion. There was ice in his voice, and in his eyes.

"Dashiell, please. It's not …"

"Do you think I'd need to see your face? I know every inch of your body, Camille. I know how you move, and how you fuck. For God's sake, you can even see the birthmark on your ass. You must think I'm the stupidest man in the world. All of New York does."

"I'm sure no one does."

He went over to the counter and threw his iPhone toward her. She didn't catch it.

"Forty messages, and sixty texts," he told her, "seeking my comment, wanting to know if the wedding is still on. I was going to leave, but I didn't feel ready to deal with the paparazzi. You can see them from the window."

"It, it didn't mean anything," she blurted.

He looked right through her. She realized she'd made a tremendous error. If she'd held fast in her denials, maybe she could have convinced him, maybe not, but he hadn't wanted the truth.

As he approached, she thought for a moment he might strike her, but instead he sank to his knees, resting his head on her thighs. He was crying, and she reached out to touch him.

319

He looked up at her. "Why? Why would you?"

She moved off the couch, onto the floor beside him. She wanted them to be on the same level, eye to eye. It wasn't that she thought she might get him to stay, only that she needed to put off his leaving. She knew once he left it would be forever. She thought of Alexandre. She'd played this scene with him, not nearly so dramatically. They were French after all, and he'd known exactly what she was.

Dashiell continued, "You lied to me. You told me there was no one else."

"But there wasn't," she said, reaching out to touch his cheek. He turned his head away.

"There are dates, Camille. We were already together."

"I didn't feel anything for him. I ..."

"You didn't *feel* anything? That's supposed to make it okay? Finding out my fiancée's a ... My God, you fucked him for money."

"Independence," she said. "I don't expect you to understand. How could you? You have a mother who loves you, and a rich father. I had nothing. I needed a ... a safety net."

"Are you fucking kidding me?" Dashiell yelled, looking around the apartment.

"The gallery pays for this," she said. "I never had anything. I was poor, Dashiell. You've never been poor."

"You went to the Sorbonne. You ..."

"No," she said quietly. "I didn't. I was an ignorant country girl who came to Paris with nothing. I was fourteen, and men were kind to me. I should have told you everything. I'm sorry."

He started to laugh manically. "Do you hear yourself? You can do better. You sound like an old movie."

"I do?" She asked. "And you the enraged fiancé? You're fine having another woman with us. Two. You act like you're oh so open-minded, and now ..."

"Don't throw that at me," he said. "You lied to me. I don't know you. I don't know who you are."

She thought for a moment of all the likely ways this was going to end, and saw this was probably the one that would give him the least pain.

"I didn't mean to lie. It's just my nature." She pulled off her rings. "I suppose you'll want these," she said, offering them.

His voice cracked, "Keep them."

She wondered for a moment if she should continue to fight, to plead her case. She had already sacrificed so much for him.

"I don't understand one thing," he continued, "When we started, you didn't know who my father was. I didn't have any money. What were you after?"

"I liked you."

"But not enough to turn down a good offer."

She didn't say anything.

"I can't say it wasn't fun," he said bitterly. "Maybe when I'm over the complete feeling of humiliation, we can even get together again. Physically, I mean, not this romance shit."

She looked at him, feeling a glimmer of hope that ended when he added, "I mean those rings should be like some kind of down payment at least."

She shut her eyes and looked down. She couldn't bear to see him walk out of her life. The sound of the door shutting behind him hit her like a bullet.

Chapter 4

Pierre called her after sundown. Despite his misgivings regarding interfering in mortal folly, he offered to have Natalie killed.

"Unnecessary," Alphonsine told him. "I'm sure the mayor will take care of her in his own way, and the whole thing will blow over."

"And your boyfriend?"

"Gone back to La-la Land to lick his wounds."

"And you?"

"I've survived the end of love affairs before."

"I meant …"

"I'm fine."

"As you are?"

"Enough is still enough, Pierre. I've made peace with it."

"If you need to stay on at the gallery or the apartment …"

"I have plenty of money," she said. "I'll be out of here as soon as I find a place."

"It won't last forever, one million."

"It should last long enough."

She wondered if he knew about her illness. Best not to see him. She didn't want his pity or his pleading. The idea of an afterlife was a gamble, but she'd always loved games of chance, and though she almost always lost, she enjoyed the moments when winning was possible. Consciousness would stop forever, or she might be reborn. Maybe there was a heaven, or time to avoid hell. She might try to make it mean something – even if "it" was only a matter of months. To regress again, to awaken the beast, this was not an option. Those she had killed weighed upon her now, visiting her dreams. She would not add to their number.

That night she packed a suitcase and made a plan. By the following afternoon she was on her way to Sainte Trinité, arriving at the orphanage before dark. She did whatever tasks Melanie assigned her, including working in the laundry. They used machines for the wash, but hung out clothes to dry.

In her earliest days, when she had first come to Paris, she had worked at a laundry – twelve hours a day, half a day off on Sundays. It hadn't taken her long to realize there were easier ways for a pretty girl to get by. Yet, now she found the tasks comforting, almost meditative. She enjoyed the warm sunlight on her back as she hung the sheets and towels with wooden pins. She tried not to dwell too much on the past.

She took her pills for the tuberculosis. For the other, she took only something to help her sleep, to suppress the cough, which mostly came upon her at night. After about two and half months, Melanie finally commented on her weight loss and fatigue. Alphonsine admitted nothing to her, but could no longer deny the facts to herself. The orphanage might be as good a place to die as any, but Melanie had enough responsibilities with the children, and they had seen too much death already. It was time to say good-bye.

The day she left, Marie-Thérèse hugged her tightly, and asked why she could not go with her.

"I told you, *princesse*. Your government isn't releasing orphans, but you'll always have a home here. Mademoiselle Melanie takes good care of you, no?"

"*Oui*, but who is going to take care of *you?*"

She hugged the child tightly, wondering whether it was Dashiell who had changed her, or whether it was this girl, this special one she had decided to save. Ana had talked of fate, but there was luck too in the world, and even miracles. This living, happy creature was proof of that.

Her new apartment was waiting for her. All arrangements had been made online. The building was located on a dreary treeless street in less fashionable Greenpoint. She had an open kitchen and a living room about a third the size of those in the old place. The bedroom was smaller as well. No wall to ceiling windows, but there was at least a tiny balcony, which offered a partial view of the city. It was only a few blocks west of Cara's place. They had been e-mailing, though she hadn't told the cop about her illness. Her friend had been pestering her about getting together, and so they had set a date for lunch.

They met at a combination Italian-Polish restaurant that was trying too hard. They shared a bottle of red wine and a brick oven pizza. She didn't need telepathy to know what Cara was thinking.

"I look like shit."

"You've lost weight," her friend said.

"I'm dying." She hadn't meant to say it. She'd meant to say she was dying of thirst, or make some joke, but the words stopped in her throat. In the old days, in Paris, everyone had known of her fatal illness, and there was nothing to do but laugh about it. Dying was common then.

Of course, once said, it couldn't be unsaid. She and Cara spent the rest of the evening discussing her prognosis. Alphonsine expected young mortals of the twenty-first century to be ignorant of death, to shy away from it, but Cara was familiar with the course of her disease and what needed to be done.

"Have you told Dashiell?"

"We're not in touch. He's busy with the film."

"Busy," Cara said absently.

"Do *you* still speak to him?"

"Not lately. I wasn't crazy about how he treated you."

"Let's not …"

"When you love someone there should be room for …"

"I am not going to judge him. Neither should you."

"Understood. I haven't heard from him in weeks. He travels in higher circles these days."

"Please don't tell him," Alphonsine said. "I couldn't stand it."

Cara nodded.

"Besides, it's better, don't you think, that he hates me?"

⁊⊛⦊

Le scandale was old news. The notorious video had been scrubbed from the Internet. Natalie had withdrawn her suit. Her whereabouts were unknown. The mayor refused to answer questions about it, not that reporters were impolite enough to ask, and his wife was traveling.

Camille St. Valois, the "art vixen" was no longer either a headline or a punch line. Although Alphonsine lived barely a mile from her old apartment, she never seemed to run into people she knew or who recognized her. She'd cut her hair in Sainte Trinité. She'd lost weight. She dressed more simply. But she didn't think that was it. It was exactly as it had been in her first life. People saw death when they saw her, and they looked away.

Once she could no longer walk unsupported, she made the decision not to leave her apartment. It wasn't vanity, as it had been in Paris. She didn't want to chance being seen by one of Dashiell's friends. She was afraid if he found out, he would come to her. She could live with his hating her, but not with his pity. Besides, as much as she wanted to see him, to hold his hand and look into his eyes, to see forgiveness if not love, she couldn't bear the thought of taking him from his work. She still reached out for him when she woke. She cried, not just missing him, but mourning the life she imagined they would have had together. But then she reminded herself she had never been fated to have that life. She hadn't deserved it, and God hadn't willed it. Freedom was the one gift she could offer him. She wondered what might happen after her death. Would he write a novel about her? A screenplay would be more likely. A story that made her seem nobler than she could ever hope to be. The thought amused her. It was all an endless cycle. She was sure of that now.

Rosa had given up her other jobs to care for her, and even arranged for her cousin and ex-sister-in-law to be there when she couldn't. Cara dropped by often. There were no other visitors.

When she was up to it, she read. Sometimes she browsed the web, though worldly things interested her less and less. Still it stung her one morning when she came across the news that Dashiell Alexander had married his co-star, Anissa Dailey, a promising young actress. The bride, a petite, blonde cross between Kate Winslet and Kiera Knightley, was already rumored to be sporting a baby bump. Alphonsine told herself this was the best she could wish for him, but the tears ran down her cheeks.

Her phone buzzed. It was Cara.

"You heard?" her friend asked.

"You got that from hello?"

"I'm so sorry."

"For what? Were you supposed to warn me?"

"I just saw it on twitter. It's trending. He's a star."

"Yes. He belongs to the world now."

"I'll come over after work. Can I bring anything?"

"Ice-cream would be nice. And not that tofu shit either. I'm not feeling so much sympathy for the cows these days."

She was reading that evening when she heard the buzzer. Rosa and the others worked out their shifts. It was probably just the changing of the guard.

Then there was a knock on her bedroom door.

"*Entrez*," she said instinctively in French.

It was Pierre. He had come bearing a box of Parisian chocolates. "I knew I shouldn't have come," he said. "I just felt I needed to."

"It's delightful to see you, *mon ami*," she said grasping his arm. It felt so strong. So full of life. She could see in his face a fullness, a sign he'd recently fed.

"Is there anything I can do?"

She understood the parameters of his question.

"Everybody dies," she said. "Like you, I'll die young, but make perhaps not so beautiful a corpse."

"I'm truly sorry," he said.

"As sorry as you can feel for a lesser being. Who told you?"

"I ran into your policewoman, but I sensed something the night of the party. I wasn't sure if I should talk to you about it. Then the next day ..."

"*Le scandale.*"

"It affected the gallery as well."

"You're still here."

"We've, I've sold it. I'll be leaving Brooklyn soon."

"As will I. Do you know where you'll go next?"

"I'm entitled to a few years liberty. I might visit Ana."

"Ah good. You can tell her the result of her experiment."

He kissed her hand. "You are certain then?"

"I shall miss you," she said, her voice hardly more than a whisper.

"And I you."

After all their time together neither had more to say to the other. It was hard for her, even in mortal form to grasp the idea of eternity. *They would never see each other for eternity.* How much harder must it be for him? A being for whom time stood still?

"*A la prochaine,*" he said as he walked out the door.

Cara brought her ice cream. Rosa put the Breyer's vanilla fudge into bowls, topping each off with a fresh strawberry. Alphonsine took hers on a bed-tray, while Cara sat on a chair beside her.

Alphonsine ate her strawberry first. "It was delicious," she said and she began to laugh.

"What's funny?" Cara asked.

"Just something Dashiell once told me. It's too silly."

Cara looked at her strangely.

"I'm sorry," Alphonsine said composing herself. "I guess you had to be there." After a moment she asked, "So tell me whom you brought to justice today? How did you make the world a better place?"

This had become their routine. Cara would bring her something – ice cream, a candy bar or some other culinary treat and they would talk about Cara's day.

"The feds officially took the case from us."

"The Russians?"

"Yes."

"I'm so sorry."

The story was in the papers – two murdered prostitutes, pieces of whom were found in several midtown dumpsters. The suspects were a pair of brothers, based for a time in Brooklyn, bigwigs apparently in the world of international sex trafficking. One of the girls had been killed with the jagged edge of a broken beer bottle, found shoved up her vagina. Cara was certain the brutality was meant as a warning to others.

"We were at a dead end. I mean we figured out who did it, but it's bigger than us. The perps are gone. The women's families are missing – in the Ukraine."

"*Mon Dieu.*"

"There's no record how the brothers got out. They might have gone through Canada."

"How awful."

"It's horrendous how much evil there is in the world."

"Yes, but you're there to fight it. That's something."

Cara wasn't so sure. She complained that most of her cases, most homicides, were bar fights gone wrong or bungled robberies committed by people who were stupid and desperate, yet when something like this happened, something truly monstrous, the criminals often got away.

Justin, whom she was still seeing, had gotten a job as a federal prosecutor and was moving to Baltimore. "He'll get to go after some of the big boys, maybe," Cara said.

"And you? Have you made a decision?"

Cara shook her head.

Alphonsine understood her friend was at a crossroads. Justin wanted her to move with him. There was a possibility she might go to law school, or maybe apply to the FBI. Both choices seemed amazing to Alphonsine, not only that women could pursue such work, but that anyone not born of wealth would have these options. *What a world it was.* She was sorry to be leaving it.

"I hope I'm not holding you back."

"No," Cara said.

Something hung in the air – the knowledge they both had that she would not be holding anyone back much longer.

Someone was at the door. Rosa had gone out for groceries, so Cara answered. It was a delivery.

There were three white camellias. The card was blank.

"Do you know who sent them?" Cara asked.

"I have an idea," Alphonsine answered.

ঌ❀ঌ

Her condition worsened. The nurse who visited every couple of weeks had arranged for a morphine drip to help with the pain, and tubes went into her nostrils delivering oxygen from a tank. This was described as comfort care. It was pointless, but she felt too fatigued to object. Sometimes she'd think of Pierre, wonder if she could summon him, mentally or the conventional way – tell him to put her out of her misery. It would satisfy his bloodlust, and keep him from choosing a less willing victim, but it would be awful to ask him to end the life of a friend. He had taken dozens of his mortal lovers. Yet, these were men and occasionally women whom he cultivated with his appetite in mind. In the weeks before he feasted, he would watch every morsel they'd consume, encourage them to try certain herbs and spices that would flavor their blood. She would not be his prized pig.

Besides, when it came to the abyss, she was in no rush.

The flowers arrived every day. There was never a note.

"Do you think they're from Dashiell?" Cara asked, serving her an ice-cream float.

Alphonsine was aware Cara knew that was unlikely. Dashiell was still working on his movie when he wasn't telling *People Magazine* how deliriously happy he was. She doubted he knew she was ill, or would have cared if he did.

"You're interrogating me," she teased.

"I'm not."

"It's all right. I think it's charming."

"No, I'm just making conversation."

"Ha." She reached over, and with what little strength she had, grabbed her friend's hand. She wanted to kiss her and wondered if that would be weird. "Talk to me about your day. What news of the Russians?"

"The feds aren't exactly keeping me updated."

"But you're the one who cracked the case? Yes? Originally."

Cara smiled. "We put it together."

"The girls, why were they killed?"

"Yuri, that's the older brother would have someone pretend to be an undercover cop to test their loyalties."

"And they didn't pass the test?"

"Apparently not."

"And the younger brother?"

"Dmitri? He was more the scout. He'd find the women and bring them to the locations."

"Why weren't they loyal?"

"They were brought here under false pretenses. They were forced. Beaten. Blackmailed. Their families were under threat."

Alphonsine and Cara had never talked about the video with the mayor, or the rumors of her activities, or even the investigation that brought them together. Alphonsine was not unaware of the care Cara took as she continued. "There's usually coercion, of one kind or another."

"But ultimately don't you think people, adults have the right to have arrangements?"

"This has nothing to do with that. Maybe there are women making good money in porn who don't find it degrading, or wanna-be-models who realize they can make more in an hour than in a night of waitressing. But these are mobsters – rapists, kidnapers, murderers – and wherever you've got the sex trade, you've got their kind."

"You wouldn't if it were legal."

"I'm not so sure, and I have to deal with the world as it is."

Alphonsine nodded. She sipped her drink with a straw. She could still taste sweet, but got full quickly and pushed the glass away. Rosa and Cara helped walk her to the toilet. She noticed a look pass between the two.

"I'm not dead yet," she reminded them.

She was determined not to wet her bed although they had gone to rubber sheets just in case.

Rosa had to leave, and her cousin was going to be late. Cara insisted on staying during the interim. Alphonsine was sleepy but restless. She was running a fever and foggy from painkillers, afraid of what she might say. She thought *they* might be listening to her thoughts.

She wanted to confess, she wanted to talk about all of it, admit her sins. She asked Cara to find her a priest.

"Tonight?" Her friend asked.

"Yes, tonight. Right now."

"It's late. You don't need to take confession this moment. I'll find someone tomorrow. I promise."

"You must talk to Dashiell for me – after. Please, Cara."

"Yes, anything."

"Tell him not to hate me," she said. Then she began to babble.

When she woke up the next day, she couldn't remember what she'd said. *Could she have let something slip that placed Cara in danger?* Rosa handed her an awful "nutrition" drink mixed with ice cream and watched her till she'd gotten down half of it. Then Alphonsine called her friend.

"What did I tell you last night?"

"Tell me? You just went on about Dashiell. How sorry you were."

"And that's all? I've been having crazy dreams. I didn't tell you about them, did I?

"No. I'm not sure. You started speaking in French. I couldn't make it out."

"Forget whatever I said. I don't want you to talk to Dashiell about me, ever."

"I won't."

She felt relieved, but at the same time prayed the end would come soon. She was afraid of revealing something. *But what would it have mattered? Who would have believed her?* She drifted in and out of sleep. She still dreamed of her prey, mostly the women she took, the ones like her who drifted into cities and into sin, the expendables.

They would follow her and circle her, not speaking. They no longer attacked, but seemed to be waiting.

Cara brought her a French-speaking priest, his parish filled with refugees from Sainte Trinité and francophone Africans. When she saw him, she was convinced she'd gone mad. Either that or God or the devil were playing with her. He was young, a Quebecois with the same wide nose and freckled country face as the Norman who'd given her final unction in Paris.

She hadn't killed anyone since her last confession, so her list of sins was not so long. She told the priest there had been horrible transgressions in her past – years and years of them, and she did not feel she'd done sufficient penitence. He assured her God was loving and forgiving.

She told him more than anything she regretted the meaninglessness of her life.

He said it was his understanding she was leaving everything she had to an orphanage, and surely that would be pleasing to God.

"Are his favors bought so cheaply then?" She asked.

After he left, she pulled the morphine drip out of her arm. These were her final days, and she had decided to stay awake for them.

Her mind felt clearer, though she wasn't sure it actually was. She thought more and more about what was to come. She wondered whether the conventional wisdom was correct. Had she lost her soul when she gained her immortality? Had it been returned to her? At what precise moment? And, if it existed, where would it ultimately reside?

She remembered the early days at the abbey – Ana's lessons. She'd learned that long ago, even after they gave up eating the flesh of the living, her kind remained brutish and arrogant. They tried to rule over humanity, and humanity rebelled. They became the hunted, and then they changed again. Ana taught them to be discreet, to select those who would not be missed, to use stealth and hide among mortals, sometimes even in plain sight. *But could they learn more?* She wondered. Could they learn *not* to kill?

She imagined Ana was with her, that they were arguing, but they were hardly speaking the same language. "Being good" as a *diva*, meant fealty to one's community, not to humanity. You couldn't spare human life when your own life depended on taking it. There was no other blood that would satisfy, and no craving as strong as the desire not only to feed, but to hunt. To hear the night sing, to be one with it, *meant* predation.

Over the next days, the conversation in her mind grew more intense even as her body became more feeble. She felt herself on the edge of a great truth, but wasn't sure she'd live to realize it. The *divos*

331

existed for pleasure and beauty. They put themselves above humanity, bestowing the mercy of a painless death. They never thought of bettering mankind. Their lives had no greater purpose. They were not gods, no matter what they called themselves. Gods *created*. They only destroyed. But what if they used their destructive power to obliterate evil? *Could they learn to adhere to an even stricter code?*

She dreamed of her prey, all in a circle as before, but this time they opened their mouths and spoke to her, begging her to avenge them.

"But how shall I?" She asked. "I brought you death."

"No," she was told by a young woman she recognized, her first solo kill, the night of the Great Feast at the abbey – the one they had let go so that she might catch her – the stupid child who thought she'd be her savior. "You can bring us justice."

"I killed you. I did it so softly you didn't know," Alphonsine explained.

"It wasn't your fault. My master sent me there. You only gave me release."

They circled her but did not attack, continuing to shout, "Avenge us! Avenge us!"

Then she saw him – Anton. She understood she had been dreaming, but couldn't be sure she still was. He was laughing at her. "It's not our job to save mankind," he said.

"What about just the women then?" She asked. "Or perhaps the children?"

"We try to take the ones who won't be missed."

"What if we committed only to take those the world would be better off without? There are enough of them to feed multitudes."

"And why would we bother? What do we owe these creatures?" He asked.

"We owe them nothing, but we are no different than they."

"It's our nature to hunt, not to judge."

"Nature is not destiny to a god."

"We're free to do as we please. No one would stop you, dear Alphonsine, if you wished only to dine on popes and kings."

She awoke from her slumber. The red illuminated numbers showed it was past four in the morning. Rosa was asleep in the chair beside the bed, her short legs resting on an ottoman. The curtains were open, allowing in some light from the street. As Alphonsine's eyes adjusted, she made out a figure by the door. It began to move.

She blinked a few times, not sure whether it was a vision. It was Anton.

Silently he unbuttoned his shirt and threw it on the floor. She watched him put his hand on Rosa's shoulders. He bit into the servant's neck without taking any blood and whispered into her ear.

"Anton, I don't ..." Alphonsine said.

"You summoned me."

"Did I?" She knew the truth of it. "Anton, I want it to be different this time. I want ..."

"I know what you want."

"Then you would take me back?"

"We don't have much time, and I won't go through this dance with you for the next century, *mademoiselle la comptesse*. I must hear you tell me with no equivocation that this is your choice."

"It is."

"Tell me," he said. He was sitting next to her on the bed.

She looked at a framed photo hanging on the wall, one of the ones she'd picked up with Dashiell – Maria Callas, looking so lovely and noble as Violetta.

"I'll never be that girl," she said, thinking of the opera's final act.

"No," Anton replied, "You're so much more."

"Please, make me as I was."

"You won't claim later like some blushing virgin I took you against your will?"

"I know my will. I've always known my will. I wanted it before. I convinced myself I didn't, but I did."

"You won't leave us again?"

"That appears to be impossible. But I won't live as I did, only for pleasure. There's more to being alive than that. We can't change what we are, but we can change what we do."

He began to unbutton her nightgown and started to caress her neck. His very touch made her feel stronger. The pain was lessening.

If this was a dying dream, she thought, then God was truly great.

"Why there?" She asked as he nuzzled her shoulder. With her eyes, she signaled for him to move his head lower. "A girl likes a little foreplay."

"We must hurry, but I promise to make it up to you," he murmured, remaining where he was.

This time she would remember it – the sting that lasted only a moment as his fangs went in, and then the numbness, but just where he'd bit, not in her body. She coaxed him on top of her, and managed even in her weakened state to spread her legs and wrap them around his hard torso. She started to work his zipper, but felt his hand pull hers away. Mentally, he told her he didn't need the distraction. Weak as she was, she pressed on, and he gave in. Her pussy pulsed in response to the gentle pressure of his cock. The pleasure did not detract from her awareness of her blood being drained, of her dying. The possibility that it might not work, might even be a trick or a fantasy, only enhanced the sensation. With her last bit of strength, she started to sway rhythmically with him. He didn't take his mouth from her throat, but still she heard his deep voice in her head, calling her an insatiable wench.

His thrusts became quicker than her slowing heartbeat. She felt as though the universe itself was dissolving, and she along with it, fading into a giant ball of pure light.

Even if it didn't work, if she didn't rise, she could think of no better death. She grabbed him as hard as she was able, hugged him as close to her as she could, and sensed he could feel all of her love, all of her passion.

"Anton, Anton," she whispered. She couldn't continue, but she knew he understood.

As she came, she felt as though she were falling, being pulled away by some great force, and then she felt his hand on the back of her neck breaking that fall. Her eyes were shut, and she had not the energy to open them. Her mouth was open, and she could taste his blood trickling down her throat. She swallowed instinctively like a baby bird. *Fledgling. That was why they'd called her a fledgling.*

"You will sleep now," he said gently.

She wanted to say something, tell him she didn't think it had worked. She was sure she was truly dead, but she couldn't speak, and then it all went black.

Epilogue

Amsterdam wasn't the worst place in which to find oneself stranded. Beer, pot, and pussy, but you couldn't make a living.

Moscow was still hot. All of Russia and the Ukraine were, and America was out of the question. That bitch-cop in New York had been smarter than they'd thought, and now the whole world was on their tail. But just a matter of time till things cooled. They had their connections, and could at least find girls and sell them, even if running them was too risky. Plus, Yuri's son was a computer genius. There was a lot they could do online. That was the way to go. Live action cams. There was a market now for novelty, the stranger and sicker the better – women with dogs, with horses. Some old slag put gerbils in her cunt. Men would pay a lot to watch a live rape, which was easy enough to arrange, but you had to be careful how you marketed it or it could be more trouble than it was worth. He and Yuri had been tossing around ideas. The one with the biggest payout would be an on-demand snuff film. Millions could be made in a single night with a select group of men paying a premium price. Like with a closed circuit fight. They could be watching from anywhere. Live so the viewers could suggest things – interactive. Make it last hours, maybe even days – a beautiful woman begging for her life as she was fucked and tortured. Cut her up afterwards and sell the pieces like relics.

He just had to find his star.

It was a Monday night and the bar was not in the busiest part of town. He'd only come in because it was cold and rainy. A voice in his head reminded him he could use a drink. He caught the girl's American accent when she asked for a beer. She wasn't bad. Thin. Tight jeans. Not much on top, but they could enhance surgically. Short blond hair, reminded him of a girl on a movie poster he'd seen – an American girl in some old French film. But men didn't like short hair. They could grow it out or give her extensions, a wig maybe. The glasses would have to go too. Still a lot of potential there – creamy skin, long legs. But what was he thinking? *What could he offer an American?* She wouldn't need a green card. It would be difficult to get to her family. Then again, no one was more naïve than an American. She might be easy, more than willing. She might think working for him, getting a new pair of tits and being in the movies, would be a great adventure.

The first thing would be to get her into bed. Make sure the body was acceptable. See if she had any talents or special abilities. If they were going with his multi-million dollar idea, they might not do it at once. They could put her in some films. Get her trust. She could even do a little tour and meet her clients. They'd have a chance to see how real she was, knowing the whole time how the story would end. She'd just think it was a personal appearance.

He dug into his pocket. He had a roofy, but he might not need it. He went up to the bar, took the stool next to hers, and ordered a beer.

She looked up for a second. He noticed her book. "Tourist guide?" he asked.

"Huh? Oh no, actually it's for a test. My folks are pressuring me to go back to college."

"Tough life." Up close, she was prettier than he thought. Something girlish, an innocence, and that whispery soft voice. Not the usual American twang.

"You're not Dutch," she said. She took off her glasses fidgeting with them. The tip of the arm kept going into her mouth. "Your English is really good. Where are you from?"

"Why don't you guess?" He asked. Her eyes were an intense shade of green. He'd have assumed they were contacts if it hadn't been for the glasses.

"Oh I'm terrible with accents."

He offered her a cigarette, but she shook her head. He couldn't tell if she was flirting with him. That was a good sign. He could see her being very photogenic. Images of her naked in certain situations were already popping in his mind. Even if she wasn't the snuff girl, she would be a moneymaker – the old-fashioned way on her back.

"I'm Russian," he told her.

"You don't say! That's one place I haven't been yet. Where'd you learn to talk like that? You almost sound American."

"I lived in Brooklyn for a few years. Brighton Beach." She was really sexy he thought. *But what was it about her?* Nothing obvious.

"Brooklyn, huh? I'm from LA. So, what's Brooklyn like?"

"You'd fit right in," he said.

He didn't have to ask her more questions about herself. She was a talker. She said she'd had a year of university in Paris and then dropped out. Had he ever been to France? She wanted to know. He had, but hardly had a chance to tell her about it.

"My great-great-grandfather came from some shit-hole in Normandy, Nonant Le-Pin? Turned out to be pig farms. I could see why he left," she told him.

Her teeth were perfect. The Americans were good at teeth. Her features reminded him of a figurine he'd once lifted back in his burglary days. He'd gotten a few rubles for it, but then read in the paper how it had been a family heirloom and was worth a lot more. He sensed she'd be worth a lot, if he could get her to shut up. She was classy, and she even smelled good.

He told her he spoke some French, so they tried to speak it together. Her accent was typical American. She'd been traveling around Europe but now her parents had cut her off. Money was "super tight." When she said the words "super tight" an image suddenly popped into his mind of doing her against a wall, and her pussy being super tight. He was pretty much high on weed all the time, but still it was weirdly vivid.

He wasn't following every twist and turn of the convoluted tale she was telling him.

"So to make a long story short. I'm broke. Busted. If my friend doesn't show up with my money, I can't even afford to stay in the hostel tonight. But there's no way I'm going home. Somebody's got to have a job for me. Right?"

He suggested she could stay with him. It would be fine, he promised. She could sleep on the couch. He told her he wasn't expecting anything.

"That's a little sudden. I don't know. Do you live alone?"

"With my brother, but he's never home. Working all the time. Married man very much loves his wife."

"I'm not sure."

"Look, it's early," he said. "Maybe we go to coffee shop, get a little hash, whatever you want."

She laughed. He liked the laugh. He couldn't stand how the pictures were popping now. All kinds of scenes. It was distracting, almost like she was doing something to put them there. He had the feeling this one could be a really big earner.

"I don't even know your name," she said.

He put out his hand for her to shake. "Sergei," Dmitri said. "Sergei Andropov."

"An-dro-pov," she said carefully. "Hello, Sergei, I'm Marguerite, like in *Faust*? You know, the opera? But everybody calls me Maggie. Maggie Gautier. It's French."

Afterward by the Author

This story was originally conceived of as a "stand alone." You may feel satisfied with the ending or you might hate it, but it is an ending. The possibility of revisiting Alphonsine in the future exists, but it would be hubris to plan a sequel without knowing whether or not the original will succeed. If there is a demand for Alphonsine's services, she may make an encore.

If you'd like to see that happen, tell your friends about this book. Write a review and place it somewhere others will see it. Join the conversation at twitter and facebook. You can find links at the author's blog: http://www.blooddiva.com. Be the buzz.

ॐ ❀ ॐ

For readers who came to this story with no prior knowledge of Marie Duplessis, I hope I have not confused you terribly. Below is a brief overview of her life:

Rose Alphonsine Plessis was born in Normandy, France in 1824. She came to Paris as a teenager and soon became Marie Duplessis – a courtesan, known for her wit and delicate beauty. She died at age twenty-three of tuberculosis. Shortly after her death, Alexandre Dumas *fils* wrote a novel, *The Lady of the Camellias*, based on their love affair. A few years later, he wrote a version for the stage, which became immensely popular. In his novel and play, the Marie character was called Marguerite Gautier. Later, Giuseppe Verdi wrote the opera, *La Traviata*, based on the play. In the opera, the character was renamed, Violetta Valéry. In the play, novel and opera (but not in life) Marguerite/Violetta made a great sacrifice for love. There are several film versions of the story, including *Camille* with Greta Garbo, in which the heroine is known by the name of her favorite flower. Readers may recognize the story as the basis for the film, *Moulin Rouge*.

Out of respect for Mademoiselle Duplessis, let me reiterate that my protagonist, (referred to on these pages as Marie, Alphonsine *and* Camille) is a fictional creation. Her musings on life, love, and men, as well as her thoughts and mannerisms, are all made up. She is a character in a book. The real Marie (Alphonsine) died in 1847. You can visit her grave on your next trip to Paris. While tuberculosis and vampirism have sometimes been linked in the popular imagination, it is highly unlikely she lived on as an immortal who survived on the blood of innocents.

About the Author

VM Gautier is a pen name the author has chosen for this book. The author has other published titles in different genres and will likely "merge" identities at some point in the future. Readers wishing to know more can visit the book's website: http://www.blooddiva.com.

Made in the USA
Charleston, SC
13 September 2014